NOTHING IN HER WAY

When Michael Belen runs into the cherubic con man named
Wolford Charles in New Orleans, he has no idea he has just
opened the door to his ex-wife Cathy. She and Charles and
Judd Bolton are working a con on a man named Goodwin, who
had been a partner with a contractor named Lachlan down in
South America. Lachlan had worked a swindle which had
wiped out Cathy and Michael's parents, and now as far as
Cathy is concerned, it's payback time. From Goodwin to
Lachlan, Belen commits himself to Cathy and her scheme.
When a drug-addled gangster named Donnelly starts
threatening her, Belen takes care of him. When C̶h̶a̶r̶l̶e̶s̶ and
Bolton try to work a double-cross, Cathy matches them with a
cross of her own. They a̶_____go up
against Lachlan—and the̶

RIVER GIRL

All deputy sheriff Jack Marshall wants to do is escape his
troubles when he heads upriver for a little fishing. What he
finds instead is Doris, who lives in a shack on a small island
with her sullen husband, Roger Shevlin. Back in town,
Marshall can't stop thinking about Doris, and keeps coming
back to her shack while Shevlin is away, always looking for an
excuse to visit. But Shevlin grows wise to his visits, and
Marshall is forced to make a decision—to take Doris away or
fight for her. Marshall's decision is complicated by the fact that
Sheriff Buford and his office are coming under close scrutiny for
graft. Somebody needs to disappear before it all blows up, and
Marshall begins to hatch a scheme. If he can pull it off, he can
escape with Doris and they can both have their freedom. But
things are never as easy as they seem....

CHARLES WILLIAMS BIBLIOGRAPHY (1909-1975)

NOVELS

Hill Girl (1951)

Big City Girl (1951)

River Girl (1951; reprinted as The Catfish Tangle, UK, 1963)

Hell Hath No Fury (1953; reprinted as The Hot Spot, UK, 1965)

Nothing in Her Way (1953)

A Touch of Death (1954; reprinted as Mix Yourself a Redhead, UK, 1965)

Go Home, Stranger (1954)

Scorpion Reef (1955; reprinted as Gulf Coast Girl, 1956)

The Big Bite (1956)

The Diamond Bikini (1956)

Girl Out Back (1958; reprinted as Operator, UK, 1958)

Man on the Run (1958; reprinted as Man in Motion, UK, 1959)

Talk of the Town (1958; reprinted as Stain of Suspicion, 1973)

All the Way (1958; reprinted as The Concrete Flamingo, UK, 1960)

Uncle Sagamore and His Girls (1959)

Aground (1960)

The Sailcloth Shroud (1960)

The Long Saturday Night (1962; reprinted as Finally Sunday!, UK; and Confidentially Yours, both 1983)

Dead Calm (1963)

The Wrong Venus (1966; reprinted as Don't Just Stand There, UK, 1967)

And the Deep Blue Sea (1971)

Man on a Leash (1973)

STORIES

The Strike (Cosmopolitan, 1954)

And Share Alike (Manhunt, 1954; condensed Touch of Death)

Flight to Nowhere (Manhunt, 1955)

The Big Bite (Manhunt, 1956; condensed version)

Hell Hath No Fury (Nugget, 1957, abridged)

Operation (Cosmopolitan, 1957; condensed Girl Out Back)

Stain of Suspicion (Cosmopolitan, 1958; condensed Talk of the Town)

The Sailcloth Shroud (Cosmopolitan, 1959; condensed version)

Aground (Cosmopolitan, 1960; condensed version)

The Long Saturday Night (Cosmopolitan, 1961; condensed version)

Pacific Honeymoon (Cosmopolitan, 1963; condensed Dead Calm)

The Wrong Venus (Cosmopolitan, 1966; condensed version)

NOTHING
IN HER WAY
- - - - - - -
RIVER GIRL

by Charles Williams
Introduction by Rick Ollerman

1909 - 1975

STARK HOUSE

Stark House Press • Eureka California

NOTHING IN HER WAY / RIVER GIRL

Published by Stark House Press
1315 H Street
Eureka, CA 95501
griffinskye3@sbcglobal.net
www.starkhousepress.com

ISBN: 1-933586-63-X
ISBN-13: 978-1-933586-63-2

Cover design and layout by Mark Shepard, www.SHEPGRAPHICS.COM
Proofreading by Rick Ollerman

PUBLISHER'S NOTE

First Stark House Press Edition: January 2014

0 9 8 7 6 5 4 3 2 1

Contents

Contents

Charles Williams:
The Best Known Unknown
Paperback Original

by Rick Ollerman

Is there anyone out there as justly famous yet frustratingly unavailable as Charles Williams? He wrote 22 books, worked on numerous screenplays and short stories, had most of his books translated into languages such as French, Italian, German and Spanish, and is in the top ten list of sales of all Gold Medal writers, ahead of the likes of "The King of Paperbacks" Harry Whittington and Gil Brewer. There has been only one book written *about* him, a Spanish biography called *La tormenta y la calma (The Torment and the Calm)* by Hernán Migoya (Glénat, 2001), but even that has been out of print for years.

Williams' long-time agent and friend, Don Congdon, who also represented writers like Ray Bradbury, Jack Finney and William Styron, described him as "a hard luck kind of guy. He was much better than many writers who really made it. Not that he'd ever tell you, of course. He was genuinely modest, maybe a little down on what he wrote. You could never be sure if he thought what he did was quite respectable. He was, after all, writing paperback originals, and this was still in the 1950s."

John D. MacDonald, number one on the Gold Medal sales list, said that Williams just never got that break he needed and was perhaps better than all of them, meaning the paperback original thriller writers. When sales of paperbacks began to flag at the end of the sixties, it was suggested to Williams that he write about a series character, but he thought that would be boring for him. He did give two pairs of sequels, the first narrated by a seven year old boy and was comprised of *The Diamond Bikini* and *Uncle Sagamore and His Girls*. The second, a seagoing pair written in the third person made up of *Aground*, and one of his most popular novels, *Dead Calm*, later filmed twice but only once released, with yet another version on the way.

Between 1951 and 1960, he published seventeen of his twenty two novels, three more during the rest of the sixties, and his final two in the early seventies. Then, tragically, he took his own life.

Searching for the facts of this particular Charles Williams' life is a very difficult thing to do. First, there was an earlier writer with the same name

(British, born 1886, died 1945) who was a member of J. R. R. Tolkien's and C. S. Lewis's Inklings, their Oxford-based literary discussion group. This Charles Williams wrote many things, but is perhaps best known for his books of supernatural thrillers, which is a way of saying he wrote theological novels with popular themes. And some of his titles, like perhaps his best known *Descent Into Hell* (1937), would sound perfectly at home in a stack of Gold Medal or Dell paperback originals.

Some bibliographies mistakenly list some of this Charles Williams' books as the one we're interested in here. Others list a book by "our" Williams published by Avon in 1961 called *Nude on Thin Ice*. However, Williams' friend Gil Brewer published a rather well-known book with Avon in 1960 with that same unusual title. Why some attach Williams name to the Brewer book is a small mystery; perhaps there's a hidden ghostwriting story in there. It is known that Brewer once finished a novel by his friend Day Keene—could Williams have had a hand in helping the self-destructive Brewer with his book? Or did someone just make an Internet mistake that been too often repeated? In any case, Williams had two books published in 1960, which means they'd already been written by then, or at least earlier in the year, and nothing published in 1961, so it's possible that something like this could have occurred but there is no evidence to support it.

Another book, *Fires of Youth*, written by "Charles Williams," was really authored by a man named James Lincoln Collier. Some have claimed that the style of the book is similar enough to that of "our" Charles Williams that there was some doubt until the author's real name was finally revealed by researcher George Tuttle and that question put to rest.

This leaves us with twenty-two novels by Charles Williams and not the twenty-three or twenty-four we sometimes see attached to his bibliography.

We do know that Charles K. Williams was born on August 13th in the west central Texas town of San Angelo in 1909. It's just about in the middle of the state, not particularly near the sea that would inform a large part of Williams' writing, but he seems to have moved to Brownsville at some point in his early life, which is right at the southern tip of the state. Here, of course, water would be all around him. His parents were Orris Lloyd Williams from Pottsboro, Texas, and Maude Williams (née Tennery), born in Indian Territory in Oklahoma. Charles was one of six children and named after his paternal grandfather.

He left Brownsville High School after the tenth grade and we know he joined the Merchant Marine in 1929 and served as a radio operator. Marine radio technology would play a role in his 1971 Edgar-nominated book *And the Deep Blue Sea*.

1939 was a significant year for Williams. Not only did he change jobs to become a radio inspector for the Radiomarine Corporation in Galveston, site of so many vacation and honeymoon getaways in his books, but he married Lasca C. Foster in San Antonio and they give birth to one child, daughter Alison. The family stayed in Galveston until 1942 when Williams became an electronics inspector at the Puget Sound Navy Yard in Bremerton, Washington. In 1944 his father passed away and in 1946, Williams moved again, this time to San Francisco where Williams became a radio inspector for the Mackay Company.

This was to be Williams' last full time job before he quit in 1950 to write full time, just prior to the release of his 1951 debut, *Hill Girl*. The book had been making the rounds for several years but wasn't considered worthy of a hardcover publication. Finally it was suggested he send it to Fawcett for consideration for their new line of Gold Medal paperback original novels, and a solid fit was born. *Hill Girl* sold well over a million copies and in that same year, Gold Medal put out the rest of his initial *Girl* trilogy: *Big City Girl*, and *River Girl*.

As with many writers, Charles Williams' books contained elements adapted from his real life. This explains the common settings of his land-based books that take place among the places he lived, especially East Texas, along the Gulf Coast from Texas to Florida, and San Francisco. He also enjoyed fishing, and bird hunting, which also have roles in various books.

When he started writing, especially with his first two *Girl* books, Williams clearly seemed to be writing in the Erskine Caldwell rural tradition vein. Caldwell was at one time one of the world's bestselling authors with books like *Tobacco Road* and *God's Little Acre*. Williams tended to be a bit prolix in these early books, and became less so later on, though the tendency never altogether left him.

In one example from his first book *Hill Girl*, Williams describes the unhappy yet gorgeous eighteen-year old daughter of the main character's neighbor:

> Angelina was sitting at the kitchen table cutting a big sheet of newspaper with a pair of scissors. She had on a heavy blue woolen dress with long sleeves, and it was bigger than that thing she'd had on before, and looser, so she didn't seem about to burst out of it in so many places. But even as loose as it was and as poorly as it fitted, it couldn't disguise that figure. Her hair was down over her shoulders in two blonde braids, tied at the bottom with little wisps of pink ribbon. She didn't look quite so much like a sex crime looking for somebody to happen to, but her eyes were still the same. They regarded me sullenly and she didn't say anything.

It's fair to say that after a few books, Williams would have written the same passage much more concisely, perhaps once he got the idea of the sort of books Gold Medal was looking to publish:

Angelina was sitting at the kitchen table cutting a big sheet of news-paper [...]. She had on a heavy blue woolen dress with long sleeves, [...] so she didn't seem about to burst out of it in so many places. But even as loose as it was and as poorly as it fitted, it couldn't disguise that figure. [...]. She didn't look quite so much like a sex crime look-ing for somebody to happen to, but her eyes were still the same. They regarded me sullenly and she didn't say anything.

As the first of the *Girl* books, and his first novel of any sort, Williams tells the story of the return home of the long-gone second son of a man known as the Major. Bob's older brother Lee still lives in town with his wife, Mary, but all Bob wants to do is settle into the land that was once his grandfather's and begin his life as a farmer.

During the years Bob had been away at college, Lee's drinking and carous-ing had grown increasingly worse. Lee talks to his brother about the irre-sistible Angelina, the neighbor's daughter, and contrives to meet her at every opportunity. At first Bob and the girl don't care for each other, and it soon becomes clear that she's not all that interested in resisting brother Lee's lady-killing charms.

Lee rushes headlong into trouble with Angelina's father and when Bob steps in to release the tension, he ends up getting a lot closer to Angelina than he bargained for. Lee has other ideas, though, and the stage is set for a scene of bloody disaster.

Willams' second novel, *Big City Girl*, features an ensemble cast and could very well take place on a farm just down the road from the one in *Hill Girl*. This book centers around a disintegrating family trying to save a cotton crop in a bad weather year in order to keep a toehold on their continually crum-bling way of life. It's difficult when Cass, the clan patriarch, has been slowly losing his marbles and for the past few years selling off almost everything the family had possessed, including their actual farmland. Now, forced to become tenant farmers on land they once owned, they're accommodating Joy, wife of brother Sewell, who left the life long ago for another one in the city.

Sewell's chosen path took him even further than that, though, as he traded plowing and picking for violence and killing. He'd met Joy when she thought he was a high-stakes gambler and not just hired muscle for thugs. Though an attractive girl, Joy was a wild one. With son Mitch trying to keep Cass from doing more damage to the family's slim holdings while trying to shield little sister Jessie from the influence of their wily house guest, Sewell ends up fight-ing for his life, at least long enough to wreak revenge on the one person he hates most.

Like *Hill Girl* this is not a straight crime novel. Williams is still in Erskine

Caldwell/John Faulkner mode but the level of suspense that builds throughout the story is intense, and though he still tends toward prolixity in spots, the sense of place and time, the poverty and the despair, and the complex interpersonal interactions make for an absorbing book. Joy hates Mitch for not being as susceptible to her physical charms as she thinks he ought to be, so she manufactures and colors events so as to turn Jessie against him. Cass is lost in his own world, begging out of the farm work while losing himself in the radio news, thinking whatever's being reported is happening to Sewell in real time.

It's an intoxicating mix and as in the best crime novels, we're not sure where Williams is going until he gets us there, which isn't until all the way at the very end.

River Girl is Williams' transitional novel from the rural East Texas farming country to the dark and different kinds of sins that happen in civilization. We still have the obsession, the story of a man who meets a woman and despite all circumstances cannot keep away, similar in that regard to *Hill Girl*. Both of them are married (married yet available women being a constant we see in Williams' work), and both of them have things to hide. But most importantly, they cannot keep away from each other.

Williams is still a bit wordy in spots, and the book is sometimes slowed by its self-analysis and internal monologue. It's written in the first person, like *Hill Girl*, but it's worthwhile to point out that whether Williams wrote in either the first or third person, he always—except for one notable exception—wrote from the perspective of a single character. All but one of his books could have as easily been written in either first or third person, the choice made by the author as opposed to being dictated by the demands of the story.

Williams' male characters are frequently former football players. Since he only attended school through the tenth grade, he probably hadn't been very accomplished as a player himself, if he even played, though he was clearly a fan. In one case he has a character who is an ex-baseball player, but shortly after we meet him, we get another ex-footballer. The men are rugged individuals, often loners and even when they're married they are prone to keeping secrets. Whatever the reasons, ex-jocks seem to personify the personal traits Williams likes in his main characters. Their opponents often seem to be just a little more ruthless, a little bit tougher, and either a little more immoral or amoral. Perhaps they're the dirty football players, the ones who go after opponents' knees from the blind side.

The women are frequently drop dead gorgeous but troubled, often with moral issues of their own. They're always smart, usually at least as smart as their male counterparts, and sometimes even a good deal more. In the end, though, it's the man who usually goes down for the woman, a kind of twisted nobility that's a Williams trademark.

In *River Girl* (originally *The Catfish Tangle*), Jack Marshall is a bent cop in a small town, unhappily married and wanting a change. When he stumbles upon a fugitive living in a cabin high up on the lake, and more importantly, his irresistible wife, Jack hatches a plan to get out from under a pending grand jury inquiry as well as his own troubled marriage.

Jack over-plans but also overlooks a couple of small points. It's precisely those points that catch up to him and when offered help by yet another gor-geous woman who happens to fall in love with him after only a few minutes' acquaintance, Jack turns it down. He continues clutching at ever-shrinking straws all the way to the tragic end.

This is Williams' first real "crime" novel, and it retains its rural elements but moves the thrust of the action into an actual city. His archetypical male and female characters are present, as well as the PBO trope of love at first sight, but another Williams technique continues to emerge here: the perfect crime that turns out to be not quite so perfect. Oh, it seems so for much of the book but then someone yanks on a thread, and almost before the reader is aware of it, the thread begins to unravel the bigger, complicated tapestry that makes up what just a short while ago seemed like a genuinely foolproof scheme.

If this is Williams' Caldwell-to-crime transition novel, it is a bit rough. Wordy passages, lost plot lines, etc., all make for a book that is a bit long-winded in places, overly complicated in others, and consequently probably goes on too long. We have constant ruminations on Jack Marshall's feelings (by Jack Marshall) and not enough groundwork on the other characters to re-ally show why women who meet him would fall in love with him so damn quickly. Again, a trick not unique to Williams, but one whose absence is wel-come in some of his later books.

River Girl is important in that we see further development of some of the Williams traits that we will see over and over again in later books. With his first three novels, the *Girl* books, Williams features women in critical roles but none in the primary one. While the books could certainly have been written from their point of view, and possibly been better for it, they also serve to get Williams moving his next three books from the rural to the small town to the city, all in various mixes. All of these are quite different from the *Girl* books: we have a classic man-eating femme fatale noir (*Hell Hath No Fury*); a ruthless con novel (*Nothing in Her Way*), again with a plot driven by a woman but told from a man's point of view; and a nail-biting mystery in *Stranger, Go Home.*

In 1953, we get what many consider to be the ultimate Charles Williams book: *Hell Hath No Fury*, re-titled *The Hot Spot* in Great Britain and filmed under that name by Dennis Hopper in a fine neo-noir film starring Don Johnson, Virginia Madsen and Jennifer Connelly.

In keeping with the last book, the perfect crime is exactly that, at least for a while. Williams does a wonderful job of painting a thoroughly thought out and executed crime, all from the perpetrator's point of view, only to have a few threads gradually picked away until the entire scheme begins to unravel. Just as he does new things with each book, he carries some elements along that he's used before.

Harry Madox, as amoral as any of Williams' male leads, has placed his neck in an irresistible noose. When he finally finds someone who makes him want to be a better man, so to speak, he's already in too deep with his perfect crime. It comes undone much like Jack Marshall's scheme in *River Girl* only this time it's helped along by that classic noir element: the femme fatale, the woman he can't leave alone and whose pride won't allow it. Once she's had him he belongs to her and she'd rather lose everything than be given up by her man. Pride overrides sin.

Madox is an aimless, casual troublemaker type on the run for some minor offenses in Houston. When he meets a man in a restaurant who says he needs a salesman, Harry claims to be one and gets the job. His entire life consists of taking whatever shortcuts he can find, legal or not, and usually with whatever woman will have him at the time. This is not a long range career path for him.

A fire in town changes everything. Harry conceives of a plan, foolproof of course, that will net him a lot of money and set him up for his next move, whatever that may be. But what he thinks is a casual dalliance with a (married) woman turns into something that he can't run away from; she simply won't let him. Harry brushes it off and goes on planning his perfect crime.

There are two things he doesn't see coming, though: he meets another woman, someone he can actually fall in love with, someone he can see himself marry and make a life with. The second thing is the focus of the other woman's obsession.

The crime comes off, though, almost without a hitch, but there's more afoot and as Harry finally gets to the bottom of it, he sees that what he's done is bound up with the fortunes of his new love. To help her he can't afford to get himself caught. Unfortunately for them, together they're firmly clutched in the grip of Harry's femme fatale, and when she enlists the help of a local grifter, Harry and his girl have nowhere to run, and no way to get out from under unless it means going to prison for them both. Harry's short term gain turns into a long term prison sentence of its own, a private hell that he can't get away from.

Hell Hath No Fury completes Williams' transition from his Caldwell-esque origins to full on hard-boiled crime writer. The lengthy passages aren't so lengthy and they're much more germane to the setup of Harry's schemes and his efforts to try to repair the damage he's caused.

While *Hell Hath No Fury* may be as good a hard-boiled noir as was ever written for Gold Medal, it may owe too much to those who came before (e.g. James M. Cain) and not be uniquely enough Williams to be called *his* best book. If the best Charles Williams book would be one that *only* Charles Williams could write, this wouldn't be it, if only because we've seen this structure before. The writing, pacing, suspense and surprises are all very well done, nearly flawless, but even taking Williams' character types and seemingly perfect crimes into account, we may not know *how* the femme fatale will win out, but we know that she *will*. That was the formula he was writing against.

To quote Anthony Boucher from a review in *The New York Times*: "The striking suspense technique may remind of Woolrich; the basic story, with its bitter blend of sex and criminality, may recall James M. Cain. But Mr. Williams is individually himself." The book shows Williams' considerable talents, but it still has to be compared with those that came before: it just isn't original *enough*.

In contrast, in 1953 Williams gives us another of a type of book that he would return to several times: the con-man novel. With *Nothing In Her Way* he gives us a wonderful example of an under-represented sub-genre of the crime novel: bunco noir, or the story of a con game. The story is told from the point of view of Mike Belen, a man with a past that not only includes his family's ruin, but his relationship with his childhood sweetheart, Cathy. Some time after their divorce, they run into each other again, this time in a many layered, multi-step game of revenge enacted by swindle.

Mike isn't a criminal out of vocation or even temperament, but he is willing to go along with Cathy and her cohorts as they try to right a wrong done to their families many years ago. As the plot goes on, Mike grows concerned for Cathy's safety, especially after the appearance of new, gun-wielding strangers on the scene. Mike has a growing sense of never being quite sure exactly what's going on and doubts as to whether their group, led by Cathy, can actually get away with it.

What makes the book so special are the interactions between the different con men (and women)–nothing is quite what it seems. Mike always seems to be the last one to know, all the way to the end. The final question turns out to be whether the game itself and the desire for revenge, have so corrupted Cathy that she is longer be the woman Mike thought he knew and loved.

This is another Williams book that, while far from the tenant farms of his first books, takes place half in a very rural area and half in a big city. Remarkably, none of the flavor of the story or the sharp characters suffer for their change in locales. Williams is clearly in control of his story and the constant traps and turns keep readers turning the pages as quickly as they can.

Nothing In Her Way shows one of Williams' greatest strengths to a degree that even his earlier books don't quite make clear: his ability to plot. A con-man novel that fools the reader as well as the characters is perhaps the most difficult sort of crime novel to write, and Williams is almost pyrotechnic with his ability to so deftly structure this book.

Another thing he does here is combine the smart female protagonist with the amoral nature of so many of his main characters while still keeping intact the fact of her nearly irresistible charms. The male lead, Mike, is not a weak man, just not quite as strong/tough/clever/immoral as his opponents, or for that matter even his ex, Cathy. This is classic Williams that shows many of his strengths as a writer in this, his fifth book. Compared to a book like *Hell Hath No Fury*, this is uniquely Williams, a book one can't imagine having been written by anyone else.

1954 was another big year for Charles Williams, with two novels published, as well as two short stories: the uncollected "And Share Alike" from the August, 1954 *Manhunt*, actually a condensed version of the novel *A Touch of Death;* and from the January issue of *Cosmopolitan*, Williams' favorite non-novel outlet, comes a story called "The Shrike," the only one of his stories not to be expanded into a novel or condensed from a longer piece.

The first book we get is *Go Home, Stranger* which is interesting on a number of levels. First, it's a mystery novel, told at a breakneck thriller pace. Second, it's told entirely from the viewpoint of the protagonist, Pete Reno, but written in the third person. This could have easily been written in the first person and is similar to how Williams handled the story in *River Girl*. Lastly, he advances firmly into Day Keene territory where the set up is that a woman—in this case Pete Reno's sister, Vicki—is literally caught in a locked room with the murdered body of her husband, Reno's best friend.

This happens before the book opens and the motivation for Pete to seek out the answer to the mystery is saving Vicki from the electric chair. The driving factor, as in many Keene novels, is that physical circumstantiality is enough to fear the electric chair. Motive and reasonable doubt play only minor roles, if any consideration is given to them at all, and fail to carry the sort of weight we've come to expect in more contemporary fiction.

For all that, *Stranger* is interesting in that much of it takes place in the bayous of Louisiana, involving boats and ships and has even more of a water setting than Williams used in *River Girl*. Williams has already had a character come out of the Naval reserve, as he himself did in his own life, and having water be central to at least some of the action foreshadows its prominence in some of his later works.

Ultimately, *Stranger* consists of a rather convoluted plot, where the character of Reno shares his questions and doubts constantly throughout. The ending is an action piece following the actual solving of the mystery, but it is difficult to follow exactly as Reno has to use a knife of some sort to cut some kind of strip out of a watermelon-like lead container, all of which is very hard to picture in your mind as you read it. If this had been a pulp novel one could easily see how a Virgil Finlay illustration would have aided the story immensely.

Despite Williams' considerable talent, this bit of looseness concerning the climax of the book weakens the ending. It does, however, foreshadow the use of another element he uses in his very last book, 1973's *Man on a Leash*, where a character is compelled to act against his will with a mechanical aid being crucial to the plot.

The second book from 1954 is *A Touch of Death* and represents a return to the sort of territory covered in *Hell Hath No Fury*. *A Touch of Death* shows Williams' evolving style, not only in his continued movement to a more terse writing style, but takes the femme fatale to a new and ultimate place. The book combines the noirish aspects of *Hell Hath No Fury* with the twists and turns of the confidence schemes from *Nothing in Her Way*, and produces the story of a man ripe for the picking by the wrong sort of woman. It's also another portrayal of a character who was once known for playing football.

Lee Scarborough is a bit down on his luck when he meets a woman who proposes a crooked scheme, the kind where no one gets hurt, and there's only the righting of a wrong and the making of a profit. Or so he lets himself believe. The chances of his getting caught are small, he thinks. But Diana James isn't exactly looking out for his best interests and while she herself is eminently qualified to bear the femme fatale label, she's a Girl Scout compared to the woman she's aiming Scarborough at, a Mrs. Madelon Butler.

Madelon is a drunk but she's smarter by far than everyone else in the book, and twice as ruthless. Everyone who tries to get the better of her winds up in far worse shape than if they'd had the good sense to just stay away. But there's money at stake, and the obsessive lure of beautiful women, and that combination has always been a deadly one, especially in a Charles Williams novel. Note again that we have a tough guy football player, not stupid by any means, but dominated and outwitted by the female characters.

Williams breaks new ground with this noir-as-a-con-man mash-up as he shows a mastery of tension in this superbly crafted novel, with strands of Madelon's web seemingly coming together inexorably into a pattern that neither poor Scarborough nor the edge-of-his-seat reader sees until the very end. Williams growth as a writer, directly influenced by his earlier books, shows he is now clearly focused on writing the kinds of books he knows he can write well. That confidence is shown in the strong writing suffusing each page.

Up to this point in Williams' career we've seen an evolution from an Erskine Caldwell, with maybe some John Faulkner influence, to the embrace of the full-on crime novel with some direct influence from the James M. Cain-esque mold. We've seen repeated elements in the characteristics, moral fiber and backgrounds of his male characters; the gorgeous yet often smarter-than-the-male portrayals of the women in the books, and a sort of common landscape that seems to follow the Gulf Coast seascape from Galveston, his chosen garden spot for honeymoons and weekend getaways, to the big city of Shreveport, Louisiana, to a fictional place that seems in most respects to be a stand-in for Shreveport that he calls Sanport. As his novels progress, Williams tends to move eastward along the coast, moving through Louisiana and into central Florida and its west coast. In other words, we're moving closer to the sea, where we arrive firmly in 1955 with another uncollected short story, "Flight to Nowhere," which appeared in the September, 1955 issue of *Manhunt*, and the first of his seagoing thrillers, a book called *Scorpion Reef*, which was also his first hardcover.

Water is never far from any of Williams' books. He gives us action in swamps, rivers, lakes, sloughs, the Gulf of Mexico, but this is the first of five books where much of the plot takes place on board a ship. All five of his seagoing thrillers–*Scorpion Reef* (1955), *The Sailcloth Shroud* (1960), *Aground* (1960), *Dead Calm* (1963) and *And the Deep Blue Sea* (1971)–are uniquely Williams and he is justly known as dominating this sub-genre.

Scorpion Reef opens with the framing device of the discovery of a ghost ship, its tiller lashed and the ship making way but with no one on board. The captain of the discovering ship notices two things, however: the coffee pot is still warm, indicating that *someone* at least had been on board not less than an hour before; and the second thing is a journal.

The bulk of the book then relates the ostensible contents of the journal, and tells the story in the first person of a marine salvage diver caught up in a web of murder, the Mob, a missing thief, and of course, the classic Williams stunningly beautiful woman.

The book is another example of what happens when a man, be he a good one or bad, gets caught in the gravity well of an irresistible beauty. In a Williams book she could be either good or bad, and in this case there's a certain amount of back and forth before our hero, Manning, finally makes up his mind. Or better said that they make their minds up about each other.

It's also yet another example of that tired PBO trope that if the police have a strong circumstantial case against you, the appearance of such will not only certainly doom you at trial, but make it so that you believe it's pointless to even consider trying to explain your side–it simply wouldn't do any good, and a life on the run is better than no life at all. It's a pity Williams felt like he had to resort to this sort of set-up again and again.

Was this an accurate description of our criminal justice system in 1955, the time of this book's writing? That a criminal can leave a body in your house, kidnap you and abandon your car at the airport, and the only plausible explanation the police will consider is that you, the home owner, *must* be guilty? That the idea of a third party leaving your car at the airport to make it *seem* as though you took to running wouldn't be enough to even raise the question? Let's not overlook the fact that we're given no discernible motive.

In any case, Manning and the irresistible woman end up trapped on a boat along with two armed men, forced to try to locate a downed aircraft somewhere out in the Gulf of Mexico. Manning knows the task is virtually impossible but how can he make the others see this and not face instant execution? Perhaps more importantly, how can he and the girl stay alive long enough to find a way out of this lethal situation for good?

The captain of the finding ship who has taken the abandoned ship in tow, eventually finishes the journal that tells this story of abduction, fear and tragedy. With the captain and Manning both being nautical men, the captain spots room for either subtle mistakes or clever misdirection. The captain comes to his own conclusion and the book ends with a certain degree of ambiguity to it, and is the better for it.

It is significant to note the manner of death of one of the characters as depicted in the ghost ship's journal. Suicide by drowning. The character goes overboard and swims down and down and down, knowing that once past a certain point, they'll never come up. Williams will use this element again, and it will mean something to his life in more than one way.

In 1956 Williams' mother, Maude, dies. We don't know what effect this has on him, but he publishes perhaps his most pedestrian crime thriller of all, *The Big Bite* in this year.

Football players (again), con games (again), drop dead gorgeous dames (again), and of course a spot here and there of murder come together in *The Big Bite*, which is not a bad novel but curiously blends quite a lot of elements that Williams has used before in a style that almost parodies the genre. Has he grown weary after so many books in so few years?

Written in the first person, it's the story of an amateur criminal crossing paths and matching wits not only with crooks who happen to be more experienced than he but who are also much smarter.

It's also a book where Williams takes his prose to a different, almost over the top, Michael Avallone-like level, especially in the first part of the book, with pithy phrases and euphemisms tossed off left and right, using a patois he'd always avoided before:

...she drank like somebody trying to finish a highball while a cab was waiting outside with the meter running.

His clothes looked as if he dressed by jumping into them from the top of a stepladder.

"It's just the breaks, Brown Eyes. Some days you can't murder a soul without getting caught at it."

His mouth twitched, he hadn't shaved for two or three days, and his eyes had the wild, staring look of a man who was going to swing at the next cockroach who laughed at him.

Another theme we've seen before is that of watching the perfect crime un-ravel, thread by thread, until it not only disappears, and we wonder why we ever bought into its infallibility in the first place. Put this together with the reversals from Williams' con-man book *Nothing in Her Way*, and add a twist worthy of Cornell Woolrich, not to mention a dash of despair, and you have a more or less standard crime novel that manages to achieve something a bit more at its conclusion. The book doesn't end per se, as events will go on af-ter the book itself is ended, and the emotional impact we're left with has an effect. But in the early going, one almost wonders if Williams had run of steam, at least for the time being.

In addition, Williams has completed the first set of books that appear to form a loose sort of cycle, which includes the backwoods noirs, the hard-boiled noirs, a con-game book or two, and some seagoing thrillers. Moving into a sec-ond cycle that has much in common with his first books, and beginning with *The Diamond Bikini*, Williams shows he can bring back the originality and give us something different with his backwoods novels: humor. Not to mention sequels.

As in *Hill Girl* and *Big City Girl* a crime is not at the center of the story. While there is crime, the violent stuff occurs off screen and the rest of it is mostly a collection of rural cons, swindles and moonshining.

Narrated by seven-year-old Billy Noonan, who travels with his father, Sam, and has never known anything outside the life of his father's career as an itinerant racetrack tout, the pair end up visiting Sam's brother, Billy's Un-cle Sagamore. Sagamore Noonan is a genius at not only coming up with a va-riety of schemes that invariably turn him an unlikely profit, but his ability to frustrate and embarrass the county sheriff and his deputies is legendary among the townfolk.

We know Williams can construct a hard-boiled noir as well as anyone. We've seen him write rural crime novels with healthy doses of Erskine Caldwell and John Faulkner. What we see now is a good-sized dollop of the droll chicanery often found in the works of someone like James B. Hendryx.

Billy is a reliable if naive narrator and part of the humor comes from seeing the ways his father and uncle explain the world to him. Billy lives where cities don't go by their real names and identifies them by their nearby race tracks. Thus Billy thinks he's never been to New York but he's quite familiar with Aqueduct. He doesn't know Los Angeles but he knows Hollywood Park and Santa Anita, as well as other "cities" like Pimlico and Gulfstream Park. Billy has trouble reading regular books with all those extra letters in the words, but he can decipher the many abbreviations and notations in a racing form like a pro. Which, in a way, he is.

The clever thing about The Diamond Bikini is how Williams inverts his normal unraveling of a crime and instead builds it up a layer at a time. Like the characters in the book, you know many of the things that are going on, and there are quite a lot of them, but you're never quite sure how the prodigious genius Uncle Sagamore is pulling them off.

A Broadway production of The Diamond Bikini was rumored to be in the works in the 1960's, and in 1971 a French movie with the title Fantasia chez les ploucs (Fantasia Among the Squares) was made by director Gérard Pirés.

1958 was another prolific year for Charles Williams. We get the novels Girl Out Back (originally appearing as a shorter piece in Cosmopolitan and published in Great Britain as Operator), Man on the Run (Man in Motion in Great Britain), Talk of the Town (Stain of Suspicion in GB) and All the Way (The Concrete Flamingo in GB).

Continuing Williams' second cycle of novels, where he loosely follows the pattern of the type of books he wrote up through The Big Bite, Girl Out Back is a slow burn of a story. It has the rural elements of the original trio of Girl books (the word "girl" in the title sticks out) but this one features the owner of a sporting goods store who lights out for the backwood areas to go fishing as often as he can.

One day at the store a customer pays him with some uncirculated twenty dollar bills. This is followed up shortly by a visit from the FBI. Barney Godwin, the store owner, gradually works out where the money must have come from—and how much more of it must still be out there.

The book moves slowly as Godwin has no real way to get at the money, merely an almost irrational desire to obtain it. The plot has a lot to do with Godwin planning on making a plan to get the money, while not knowing exactly where it is or how he can find it. We get writing where things move slowly, with passages that don't have a lot to say, like:

> *People were still up in several near-by houses. I drove on into the garage and closed the overhead door. There was a smaller side door that faced the kitchen porch. I went around to the front of the house and let myself in. I turned on a light in the kitchen, drew the curtains, and brought the suit-case and bundle of clothes in through the back.*

Simple declarative sentences like these take up much of the space on the pages. It's not until the last fifth of the book where a Williams-like plot finally begins to shape up, and the oft-used Williams' technique of having the pro-tagonist's foolproof considered plan that begins to fall apart, little by little, catching him unawares and leaving him ultimately empty-handed comes into play.

Girl Out Back may have all the characters of a noir novel, the rural and wa-tery settings of a Charles Williams book, but the sum is not as great as the parts in this case. While the kind of targeted but unspecified planning of Bar-ney Godwin may more accurately resemble the organic nature of what would happen in real life if an ordinary, law abiding citizen were to suddenly en-tertain the same sort of criminal ambitions as Godwin, it leaves the reader of the novel with a slower than average paced book for a thriller. Perhaps this was why the book was published by Dell and not Gold Medal?

Sanport is used again as the big city in the book and given the rest of the locations used, Shreveport again seems like the model. In any case, as a Charles Williams novel, this one lacks the tightness of his better work. Per-haps its shorter version in *Cosmopolitan* reads better.

The second cycle continues but there are some differences. In *Talk of the Town*, ex-cop Bill Chatham is held up in another small Williams Gulf Coast town after a car accident. His witness to the event is the beautiful but tor-mented widow Georgia Langston.

But in *Talk of the Town* there is no prominent femme fatale, no one to bring the hero down but himself, and this he does by taking pity on the widow Langston after she's offered herself as a witness against the other driver. It turns out her husband has been murdered months before and virtually the en-tire town suspects her of complicity in the deed, yet the cops don't have enough evidence to actually charge her. Enter Chatham, her white knight in waiting, who lays his bankroll, his experience as an ex-cop, and his life on the line to try to help her and her business.

This is more of a potboiler for Williams, with the constant ratcheting of ten-sion between Chatham and the police, the townsfolk and Georgia Langston, and Chatham's stubborn refusal to leave town (and Georgia Langston) in the face of attempted murder, vandalism, and other trumped up charges against himself.

The pages fly by as Chatham falls into a trap and is forced to make a run for his life to the only place he can go. Not only does he hope to save his own skin, but he has one last shot at solving the mystery of the murder once and for all.

Again, though, in many ways Williams seems to have continued this second cycle of novels by using a major element from Hell Hath No Fury as a minor element in a flashback here: the use of arson to distract attention from other crimes.

Many of the recurring elements of the Williams novel are here again: for-mer football players, beautiful yet available women, the Gulf Coast setting, the brutality of men in power. Notably, the conniving woman is moved to the background here, almost invisible, and there is no big money motive. Talk of the Town is probably most remarkable for its pace and potboiler nature, es-pecially after Williams' previous book, Girl Out Back. It's much truer to the Williams form.

And then, just when you thought it was safe to go back in the water....

The Florida Keys, Louisiana, Houston: these elements are all present in All the Way (also reprinted as The Concrete Flamingo). There's no football player as a character but one is mentioned. What we have here is a real departure for Williams and is a heavy and somber noirish masterpiece.

Williams wrote so many "perfect crime" books that ended up being not quite so perfect, but not here. Not with the crime Marian Forsyth presents to Jerry Forbes, who just happens to have a voice very similar to a man named Har-rison Chapman, a man she wants above all else to destroy.

The plan is intricate but put forth as foolproof. Much of it depends on how well Forbes can pull off his impersonation of Chapman, and the biggest weakness of the book comes from how well he really does it; it's far too easy for him. Chapman's intimates question none of Forbes' actions, no matter how out of character, apparently because he can speak exactly like Chapman. Re-gardless, the real dirty work, the deadly stuff, is handled by Marian. The prob-lem, though, is the plan doesn't unravel–Marian does.

After the caper itself is an unqualified success, Forbes has to face up to his weakness: he's fallen in love with Marian. Rather than share the money and run off together as promised, Marian simply runs away from Forbes, al-though he catches up to her eventually. That's when Williams hits us with the real tragedy of the story: can you truly destroy another human being with-out destroying part of yourself? Marian has her own answer and she can't es-cape it.

Later, after time seems to move Forbes past that period of his life, he real-izes he can't escape the ghosts of the past, the what-ifs, the if-onlys, the what might have happened had he handled things differently.

So he takes a chance, and does something he knows he shouldn't. Slowly he's drawn deeper and deeper into his own sense of darkness, possessed by his own demons and while his gut tells him he's making a mistake, his heart, or his guilt, won't let him stop. All the way to the second and perhaps largest tragedy of the novel.

This is an intricately planned crime story featuring an impossible love and the absolute ruination of people who probably ultimately don't deserve it. It is a noir novel in its sense of doom, in the presence of the character of Marian, and of the inexorable downfall of the would-be lovers. This is noir with another dimension, and while it doesn't follow the classic Cain sort of mold like *Hell Hath No Fury*, it is heartrending noir nonetheless.

If you've read Williams' previous books, part of you is expecting the crime to start breaking down, and in an odd way that only adds to the tension. If this is your only Williams novel, then the ending is even that much more of a twisting though downbeat delight. Filmed as *The 3rd Voice* in 1960 and directed by Hubert Cornfield, starring Edmond O'Brien and Julie London, it is the first of Williams' books to be made into a movie.

It may not be as flashy as some of his land-based stories, but it showcases all of Williams' considerable strengths. This one should be considered among his very best books.

Man on the Run is a bit unusual for Williams. It has the familiar elements of football players, ships and sailors, and the fictional town of Sanport, but otherwise it is a much less complicated novel than any of his others.

The title tells you the plot of the book, where Ray Foley, through unfortunate circumstances, finds himself on the run from not only one murder, but two. He's innocent, of course, but the eyewitnesses that put him on the scene and no alternative explanation, Foley runs. This is Charles Williams so the police could never be credited with interpreting circumstances as anything but indicative of clear guilt, and Foley runs with desperation, somehow keeping half a step ahead of the law.

He ends up with help from an unlikely source, a stunningly beautiful women who, again, is also *available*. There is a lot of action in the book though almost all of it comes from Foley's continuous running, Williams' precursor of Roy Huggins' *Fugitive* character.

Beyond that, there's not much here. It reads more like a longish pulp novel from twenty-five years earlier than what you would normally expect from Williams. If there's anything complex here, it's the backstory that doesn't take place in the book. If there's any character development, you'd be reaching to say that his aider and abettor experienced a transformation at the end.

Man on the Run is fast, exciting, not hard on the intellect, and reminds one of nothing more than a throwback from an earlier era. It's a departure for

Williams, but a regressive one, nowhere near as sophisticated as the previous *All the Way/The Concrete Flamingo*. No brain cells will be harmed by the reading of this novel but your eyes will be flying across the pages just the same.

In 1959 we return to the backwoods setting of *The Diamond Bikini* with its sequel, *Uncle Sagamore and His Girls*. As fun and as clever as the first book was, this sequel is just more of the same, which is both its biggest strength and its greatest weakness. In order to shortcut the backstory of the inept sheriff's deputies on the lookout for the telltale smoke from Sagamore Noonan's rumored stills, there's an overlong scene in the beginning that comes off as a rather silly outtake from *The Dukes of Hazzard* television show. Williams gave us the same scene in *The Diamond Bikini*, and it was shorter, fresher, and did a better job of showing us the inferior intellects Sagamore is up against.

As a sequel the book does its job of giving us more of what we expect after reading *The Diamond Bikini* but now that we've become so familiar with Uncle Sagamore, it's not terribly difficult to figure out not only that he's conning the sheriff and the good people of Blossom County, but this time how he's doing it.

Well, maybe not exactly how he's doing it: Sagamore Noonan is brilliant when it comes to manipulating the law and events to his own advantage, including orchestrating his own arrest. Williams still gives us a fun romp through the Noonan farm in Blossom County and if we suspend our belief just a bit more than usual we can still sit back and enjoy the ride. *The Diamond Bikini* should probably be read first to get the most out of this one. In some ways the plot is less believable than in this sequel, but it gives a better introduction to Sagamore and his brother Sam than we get here.

The significant thing about these two books is that we get another glance at Williams' extraordinary versatility. He can be as noirish as anyone or almost slapstick-funny like Craig Rice. His rural novels can be serious, ruminative affairs on the complex interactions between different kinds of men and women, city folk and farm folk, the criminal and the law-abiding, but in these two books he combines elements of most of those things in truly humorous and interesting ways.

Williams wrote his twenty-two novels in two basic cycles, with the last of his books (*And the Deep Blue Sea*, 1971, and *Man on a Leash*, 1973) coming after a half-decade interval and seeming to approach a more mainstream, Alistair MacLean-type audience. But if you look at the first cycle, from *Hill Girl* through the pulpish *The Big Bite*, *The Diamond Bikini* through 1966's *The Wrong Venus* roughly match the rural to seagoing to comedy pattern seen in that first group. A far more common way to view Williams' work is to separate his land-based books from his seagoing ones.

While water has never been far from almost any of his books, *Scorpion Reef* was the first where most of the action takes place aboard a ship. And that is just the beginning.

1960's *The Sailcloth Shroud* is filled with sailing jargon but none of the action takes place while actually at sea. In fact, apart from the nautical language, unnecessary really to the plot, this book is more like *Talk of the Town*, a page-turning thriller with an ordinary man caught up in something larger than himself. At the end, refreshingly, the man isn't necessarily changed by the ordeal. In today's literary landscape, one hears too often of the mythic hero "rule" saying that the protagonist must always be changed by the events that happen to him.

Other than sustaining broken ribs and a swollen face, Williams throws that convention out the window as charter captain Stuart Rogers can go right on being charter captain Stuart Rogers at the end of the book. The just warming-up female encounter doesn't even end in a happy romance. In a way this book could be called Williams' anti-thriller.

Before the action begins in the book, Rogers buys a ketch in Panama and signs on two crew members to help him sail it back to the states. They're bound for a town called Southport, which sounds an awful lot like the oft-used Sanport but is definitely situated on the Gulf coast of Texas. An accident occurs which results in a burial at sea, and the book opens with the ship already in port in America. One of the crewmen has been found murdered and he's got a lot of money on him that no one can account for.

This leads to a load of trouble for Rogers, the only one of the three sailors still alive. If the cops aren't certain whether to believe his story or not, the crooks that come after him certainly don't. The water turns from warm to hot to boiling as Rogers takes off across the Gulf to find out what really happened to his third crewman, the one that didn't survive long enough to make it to port. Not only that, but Rogers needs to find out who the man really was, why people were after him, and why no one seems willing to believe the truth.

While it's yet another variation of Williams' "man on the run" theme, it's a good, solid thriller and the sailing jargon certainly adds to the verisimilitude of the Captain Rogers character as well as demonstrates Williams' own passion and expertise where boats and the sea are concerned.

If *Scorpion Reef* cast a line for the seagoing thriller, *The Sailcloth Shroud* set the hook, because next we get *Aground*, also published in 1960, and while it starts on land, the setting quickly moves to a vessel caught on a shoal, and again pits a tough man against a tougher man. It also pairs him with another beautiful and available woman. The woman, who likely as not turns out to be the case in a Williams novel, turns out to be the cleverest person in the story.

This is Williams at his slow burning, tension-building best. As opposed to *The Sailcloth Shroud*, this book very quickly gets the action onto the water and once there, it never gets off. Also filled with sailing jargon, it suffuses the story with atmosphere as we really believe John Ingram is the superb sailor he's supposed to be.

After raising the boom with the topping lift until it was well clear of the gallows, he secured it, and hauled on the halyard until–as well as he could tell in the dark by feel–the strain was evenly divided between the two.

The book is written in the third person, but takes place entirely from Ingram's point of view, so it could just as easily have been in the first person, much like *The Sailcloth Shroud*. This way, though, the technical language can be stated neutrally, without the device of having Ingram having to explain it to someone else, or worse, saying it out loud or to himself when it's clear he knows it so well he wouldn't have to.

The plot centers around a missing boat, one that Ingram had been engaged to look over a few days before it disappeared. The police pull him in and while they think his actions probably helped the unknown thieves steal the boat, they don't believe he actively had any intention to aid them, or indeed, have knowledge that a crime was even being planned.

Into the mix comes the volatile owner of the boat, a divorcee from Texas, and the two set out on the longshot of finding the stolen *Dragoon*. A bit of luck and a lot of Ingram's expertise lets them locate the boat from the air, and when they get dropped off and make their way on to the presumably abandoned ship, they're quickly overwhelmed by what awaits them.

There's murder, treachery, and above all, the feeling of overwhelming doom as both Ingram and the woman Rae Osborne are in a no hope situation. Or are they? Can Ingram find a way to get the boat unshoaled and away, and to protect both himself and the woman he's beginning to fall hopelessly in love with?

Williams' next book, in 1962, was originally titled *The Long Saturday Night* but was also reprinted under the name *Finally, Sunday!* Its best-known title now, though, may actually be *Confidentially Yours*, a direct translation from the French *Vivement dimanche!*, the name given to the adaptation by Francois Truffaut for what turned out to be his final film. Truffaut had already made movies based on books by other PBO luminaries such as David

Goodis and Cornell Woolrich, and in 1983 made this film starring Fanny Ardant, his one-time companion and mother of his child Josephine, as well as an actor named Jean-Louis Trintignant.

Williams goes back to the more traditional thriller here. In a welcome refinement to the innocent man, who when faced with circumstantial evidence against him must run because no one could possibly believe his innocence, John Warren is well and truly framed, more hopelessly than in any other of the books where Williams uses this device. And of course Warren has no idea why this is happening to him.

When it's clear to Warren he needs to run, he does it with a plan, and buys himself just enough time to hire some detectives, each of whom comes up with a tiny piece of the larger puzzle. With the help of an unexpected ally, he eventually turns himself in and, unbeknownst to him, the local police, once thinking him a confirmed homicidal maniac, had laid just enough of a trap to capture the real killer.

Again, there's a beautiful and available woman involved, and she's the smartest person in the book. Without her brains and willingness to help, Warren wouldn't have had a chance.

The book has a happy ending, and all the people who were killed ended up being somewhat "deserving" of it, so it's not a book that fits easily under the noir label. But it is another nail-biting suspense novel, with Williams showing one of his specialties: the seemingly iron-clad plan/trap/scheme and how the tiniest thread can unravel everything. This time, though, the plan is not that of the main character.

The best part of the book is when Warren seems completely hemmed in and appears to have nowhere to go. The happy, good-guys-win ending may seem a bit of a letdown after simmering through all those early trials, but it's a very entertaining mystery.

Interestingly, in Truffaut's version, which is fairly true to the book, the brainy woman, the savior of the Warren character, is repeatedly physically slapped, sometimes to the floor. She's belittled and called things like "ninny," all while risking herself to try to save him. At the same time the pair are busy falling in love. Perhaps this, along with some of the sharp cuts of the movie, are part of French cinematic tradition of the time, but it certainly seems jarring to watch it today. 1983 wasn't that long ago, at least not in the United States, and possibly there was an anti-feminism or some sort of need to keep the strong female character in check, even though it is precisely those traits that are required to make the story work.

It is important to note that even though Williams is fond of repeating himself in his books, he often changes the details in small ways. Sometimes that's enough to make the book seem fresh, as it does here, but that's not always so.

From 1963 to 1968 Williams did screenplay or dialogue work for Hollywood, but he found the job disappointing. In 1963 he worked on the screenplay for the French *Banana Peel* directed by Marcel Ophuls, starring Jeanne Moreau and Jean-Paul Belmondo. The movie was based on Williams' fifth book, *Nothing in Her Way*, but most critics seem to think that all of the double-crossing among the various con-men (and women) was too confusing as shown on screen. He also worked on an adaptation of Day Keene's *Joy House*, released in 1964, another French film, this time directed by René Clément and starring Alain Delon and Jane Fonda which appeared under the title *Les félins*.

More importantly, though, is the release in 1963 of what is perhaps Williams' best known work, a seagoing thriller that's a sequel to 1960's *Aground*. This book is called *Dead Calm* and starts out with the main characters in *Aground* safe and sound and following through with the dreams they had laid out in their first adventure. It doesn't take long for things to go terribly wrong.

Dead Calm is a wonderful book of suspense and for the first time, Williams writes a story in the third person that actually requires it. The ability to move back and forth between different settings lets the reader know what's going on in several locations, although the characters themselves can only guess. When John and Rae Ingram improbably come across a psychopath rowing a raft toward their ship, his story about his old ship just doesn't ring true.

With Ingram's gut telling him to find more answers, the newly rescued visitor slugs Rae and starts the Ingrams' *Saracen*, leaving Ingram aboard their visitor's ship, the *Orpheus*. Instead of finding what their guest said was on board, Ingram discovers something quite different.

Williams takes us back and forth between the two ships as Rae tries to handle the disturbed young man, knowing that one way or the other if she doesn't regain control of the *Saracen*, Ingram and the *Orpheus* are going to sink. And she only has a matter of hours, not only to re-take the *Saracen* but to find her way back.

On the *Orpheus*, Ingram begins to figure out what has really been going on but it's taking everything he's got just to keep the ship afloat as long as he can. It's a losing battle though, time's running out, and it's clear at some point the *Orpheus* won't last the night.

What cuts down on the suspense, though, are the two times the back story is introduced. Rae basically recounts the events of *Aground* to her captor under the guise of gaining his trust and attempting a sense of empathy. Williams does this in one long chunk and it comes off as a device to make *Dead Calm* able to exist as a standalone book. Since it can be read on its own anyway, and with the long monologue coming more than halfway into the book, it seems pointless, or at the very least overdone.

This is followed not too much later by another expository section on what had gone on aboard the other ship. Much more necessary to the plot, it isn't out of place but its proximity to the prior recapping slows the story down even more, which is a shame for this otherwise fine novel.

These are perhaps the only problems, though. Williams does use a method of death he's used before, and it stands out if you've read the other book and because it's unusual. No one would notice if the bad guy was shot down by police at the end of a few books but what Williams chooses is a method uncommon enough to stick in your mind. This has an ominous resonance to events still to come in Williams' own life.

One of the reasons his seagoing books are so popular has to be the strong sense of place he gives us. It's not a wide open setting in the sense of a large city like Los Angeles, but Williams with a very real understanding of being becalmed and stranded in the equatorial Pacific, with its constant heat, lack of wind, the need to conserve fresh water, daily swims in the ocean, and not least of all, the many specific concerns involved with staying alive on a wooden platform hundreds and hundreds of miles from any possible sort of help.

A movie of *Dead Calm* was made in 1989 starring Nicole Kidman, Sam Neill and newcomer, Billy Zane, directed by Phillip Noyce. The back story's changed, and the setting is near Australia, but the source of the movie's tension is the same as in the original book.

Perhaps a more interesting story is that of Orson Welles' interest in the novel. At a time when Welles' personal reputation had been sustaining hit after hit for not being able to finish a project and actually deliver a completed film to the big screen, Welles had planned for his adaptation, which he called *The Deep*, to bring him to the masses once again. With a screenplay by Welles, and starring himself alongside Jeanne Moreau and Laurence Harvey (of *The Manchurian Candidate* fame), the film looked to be an even truer version of Williams' book. Peter O'Toole, once approached to appear in the film, read the script and said it was "beautiful." Welles began the movie around 1967 and worked on it while also pursuing other projects. As was typical with Welles, financing was always a problem. To save money, Welles did his shooting in the Adriatic Sea, rather than the Pacific.

Alas, the movie was never finished. A few scenes remained to shoot, the film needed to be scored, but the death of star Laurence Harvey from stomach cancer at age 45 ended all hope. Today the negative has disappeared, but both a color as well as a black and white print remain. An earlier version of the script had the movie titled *Dead Reckoning* and at some point it seems Welles offered the film to television, who declined because of the lack of sex and overt violence. Some footage of *The Deep* can be seen in the documentary *Orson Welles: One-Man Band*, a history of Welles' unfinished projects that is currently included in the Criterion Collection DVD release of Welles' *F for Fake*.

More recently, Paramount has announced plans for a science fiction movie called *Equinox*, to be based on *Dead Calm*. The loneliness and emptiness of the open sea transported to the even lonelier and emptier openness of deep space seems a natural fit for today's special effects-happy world.

In 1964, another French film was made from a Williams book, *Le gros coup*, adapted from his *The Big Bite*, followed by yet another in 1965, *L'arme a gauche*, an adaptation of *Aground*, with Williams himself credited with working on the script as well as the dialogue. In 1968 we get an American film directed by Ron Winston and starring Robert Wagner and Mary Tyler Moore, called *Don't Just Stand There*. The screenplay was written by Williams from his 1966 novel, *The Wrong Venus*. This same year Charles' brother Carol died in Kirbyville, Texas.

The Wrong Venus is an interesting book. It's a comedy, like *The Diamond Bikini*, only it has more of a crime element. It is a sophisticated story, where a very smart man meets an equally smart woman, and they find themselves becoming more and more attracted to each other while trying to save a friend while banking some money at the same time. The casting of both male and female leads as intellectual equals is a Williams refinement to one of his own characterizations that really pays off here.

Fans of Williams' hard-boiled, noir and seagoing thrillers can justifiably scratch their heads and wonder exactly what kind of book they're reading. If features tight plotting by Williams, and many comic moments, but its flaw is that it simply introduces too many characters throughout.

Above all else, this is a smartly written, clear and crisp novel filled with humor, near-slapstick situations, and enough consecutive crises to fill many another book. The beginning of the story puts the main male character and the main female character seated next to each other on a plane. From there, one situation after another develops as these two sharp-as-razor people somehow handle everything Williams can throw at them.

Starting with the kidnapping of a missing novelist's ghostwriter and leading to attempted murder, the story moves on to a false murder, a missed deadline for an important book, France's most notorious killer stalking his only living witness, and so on. This is a very busy book.

Technically, it's a brilliant achievement but Williams keeps more balls in the air than you'd find at a convention of juggling clowns. There's suspense, but it's more comic than sinister. It's Craig Rice meets Nick and Nora Charles. It's the interplay between a man, Colby, and his female match, Martine, and how they take turns plugging each hole in the dike as the cracks continuously appear, one after the other.

This is a fun, smart book that needs to be read in as few sittings as possible. There are so many characters that come in and out of the book—a key ingredient of its madcap, non-stop craziness—that it can be difficult to match the names with the characters. If there's a flaw with the book, it's this. Sometimes a character is introduced as such-and-such once, but then reappears later without the identifying context. Sometimes a character is referenced by his last name for a while and then his first name and then again by his last name. It leads to a bit of head-spinning that's unnecessary given that the plot of the novel has plenty of that already. In spades.

Williams certainly needs to be recognized for stepping outside the typical crime fiction boundaries periodically. He's very good at it and though he never tried a truly mainstream novel, there doesn't seem to be much doubt that he could have been successful outside the genre. Indeed, some of his novels came out of long stories he'd already published in the slicks, *Cosmopolitan* in particular, back before they replaced fiction with articles on 21 new positions to drive your man crazy.

The Wrong Venus ends what is roughly the second cycle of Williams' writing. He went from backwoods noir starting with *Hill Girl* in 1951, to hard-boiled noir to a seagoing book to a con-man story in his first nine published novels. Starting in 1956, with *The Diamond Bikini*, he repeated a similar cycle with his next eleven novels, that included backwoods stories (that now included humor), more hard-boiled books like *All the Way* and *Man on the Run*, to more seagoing thrillers. He ends this period with his most urbane and sophisticated book yet, *The Wrong Venus*. That's twenty books he published in a fifteen year period, with several of those years seeing the release of multiple titles, as well as having worked on multiple screenplays.

Most of his books have been made into either French or American films, and have been translated into editions across Europe. Williams was active in Hollywood, but like many authors didn't care for it much, though he worked on over a dozen movies. In 1968 he wrote the screenplay for Delbert Mann's *The Pink Jungle*, starring James Garner, Eva Renzi, and included a scene-stealing performance from George Kennedy. Williams apparently didn't like what was done to his screenplay, and this was the last script, along with his own *Don't Just Stand There* (based on *The Wrong Venus*), that he was credited with working on. *The Pink Jungle* was based on a book by Alan Williams (called *Snake Water*), but he was no relation to Charles.

He'd written a lot in those fifteen plus years, and had paperback success as well as later hardcover success from publishers like Macmillan, Viking and Putnam. In any case, Williams reportedly said, "Sometimes I wouldn't mind just giving it all up and being a beach bum."

We don't get a new book from Williams in the years following *The Wrong Venus* all the way until 1971.

Charles Williams earned his only Mystery Writers of America Edgar nomination in the category of "Best Paperback Original" with his penultimate novel, *And the Deep Blue Sea*, released by Signet in 1971. It lost in its award year to Frank McAuliffe's third book in his "Commissions of Augustus Mandrell" series, *For Murder I Charge More*. Ironically, this book seems to be even harder to obtain than the Williams book.

Not only is this the last of his seagoing thrillers, it is also far and away the most sophisticated writing we see from Williams. Told in the third person but from the perspective of the main character, Harry Goddard, there are a number of asides where Goddard, an ex-Hollywood producer, relates things in his mind in the form of make-believe dialogue between anonymous studio executives, perhaps mirroring Williams' own frustration with Hollywood. It's a bit odd, and maybe even overdone, but it adds an almost experimental element to the writing itself. There's little warning or explanation of these transitions and they can be jarring to the reader when they jump in out of nowhere.

Goddard is the victim of personal tragedy, leading him to ditch all and sail the Pacific by himself. A middle of the night disaster strikes and he finds himself stranded at sea, miraculously crossing paths with another ship three days later. We've seen this device before in *Dead Calm*, but there aren't a whole lot of options when you have two ships on a vast ocean that need to intersect for the book to form.

The new ship, the *Leander*, has problems of its own. Not all the passengers are who they say they are, and neither are the crew. Goddard is soon caught up in murder and attempted murder, an amorous female passenger, the affairs of another, and a mutinous plot that had been in place long before Goddard was ever brought aboard.

And the Deep Blue Sea is a lively sea thriller and is cinematic in its scope, drama, and use of last minute coincidence. It features again the tough guy hero, though he's not always the toughest guy in the room; this time there's no connection made to football. But Goddard makes up for not being the best in a fight, or even the smartest, with his intuition, supported by his viewing the situation as an unbelievable Hollywood script. These give him the tools to overcome the schemes of the murderous fugitives onboard. He's also the oldest of all of Williams' heroes, and perhaps that's on purpose, as it takes away the physical superiority often required of William's male protagonists.

This is also the most direct of Williams' books in terms of sexuality. There is no ambiguity in the desires and lusts of one of the female passengers, and Williams plays it out with a certain amount of emphasis and explicitness. While not necessarily all that important to the plot, certain things could have been made clear without the sexual aspects written out. It may indicate that Williams was reaching for perhaps a broader audience beyond his typical genre books. This one could easily be shelved among the bestsellers of the day rather than in the mystery/crime section, and this is depicted on the original cover of the Signet paperback, which shows a ship in the distance with smoke billowing from an unseen fire.

While it may not be remembered as a classic noir novel like *Hell Hath No Fury*, it follows an entirely different path, has much smarter writing, and a broader appeal to a wider audience. Williams was writing a book to sell, it seems, and the ending is as Hollywood as its main character would have made it in one of his own movies.

On October 1st, 1972, Charles Williams was faced with the greatest tragedy of his life. Lasca, his wife of more than 32 years, passed away from cancer in San Diego.

After her death, Williams moved to the border area of California and Oregon and lived in a trailer with thoughts of developing some land. When that fell through, he moved back to the Los Angeles area at his agent's urging.

In 1973, Williams' last book was released by Putnam and ironically for an author remembered as a PBO writer, never saw a paperback release. The book is *Man on a Leash* and reads like another attempt, after *And the Deep Blue Sea*, to reach a broader audience. However, the book is an almost poetic wrapup of his previous 21 novels, with many of William's standard elements in play.

The main character, Eric Romstead, wasn't a football player–he played baseball player–but there are other characters that are ex-football jocks. It's not a seagoing book, but those elements comprise the back story of the novel. There's a beautiful older woman, and a beautiful younger woman. There are remote control explosive devices. The southern geography is represented by Texas, and we see Williams' version of San Francisco again. The main character hires private detectives on his own dime, as in *The Long Saturday Night*. The police don't believe what Romstead knows to be the truth, as in many of his books.

But more like the previous one, sex is still more explicitly present than in his first twenty novels, and the writing is more cool and detached. *Man on a Leash* is something of a mystery/adventure novel, again seeming to aim for more of the bestseller market than his earlier books.

At the story's beginning, Romstead's father has been murdered, execution-style, by a method that paints him as a heroin dealer. But to Romstead, as well as to everyone else who knew his father, this was difficult to believe, despite the evidence police have to the contrary. So Romstead begins digging, going beyond the effort the local cops are willing to put into it. With the help of one of his father's girlfriends, he uncovers a few small details missed by the cops. Unaware of the technological sophistication of the crooks, however, his actions don't go unnoticed.

After a few more deaths, all adding to the mystery, the murderers' next target, or targets, becomes clear. And by that time, it's too late for Romstead. The only question is whether or not he can stop it in time.

The use of technology in this book is also new for Williams. It shows Williams' background in electronics dating back to his profession in the forties. The story itself is an eerie foreshadowing of the 2003 death of Brian Wells, a pizza delivery man who robbed a bank wearing a bomb collar around his neck while claiming he had to get back to the people who put it there before it exploded. Unfortunately for Wells, the bomb detonated while he was sitting handcuffed on the ground in front of a police car.

If Williams wrote in two cycles, with an odd variation thrown in here and there, the last two books represent a distinct change in direction, one that seems geared to broaden his audience. Whereas at the start of his career, the influence of others seems to be clearly present in the backwoods settings, and again in the femme fatale noir tales he wrote so well, he took his writing to his love of the sea and made that sub-genre his own with books like *Scorpion Reef*, *The Sailcloth Shroud*, *Aground*, *Dead Calm* and *And the Deep Blue Sea*. His screwball books, *The Diamond Bikini* and its sequel, *Uncle Sagamore and His Girls*, and the later, more sophisticated *The Wrong Venus*, show his humor and wit, though these touches are present in all his books. He wrote complicated con-man/woman books like *Nothing In Her Way* and *The Big Bite*.

In the end, Williams proved himself an extremely competent writer, often excellent as when he took the backwoods tramp story and made it a thriller, or the James M. Cain type story (e.g. *Hell Hath No Fury*) and took it to a more intricate level. His humor was especially evident in his bunco books, and the seagoing stories showed his ability to write technical details into the genre without slowing the action. If his best writing, though, were saved for the last two books, they were also perhaps the most broad in reach as well as the least defining of his career, which is a bit ironic since *And the Deep Blue Sea* garnered his only Edgar nod.

The final mystery for Charles Williams comes at the very end of his years. Whether, as his agent believed, he was depressed after losing his wife a few years before, or for other reasons, Charles Williams took his own life sometime in the spring in 1975, at age 65.

Some state the actual date is April 5th, others say April 7th. One story is that Williams died in France. Other rumors say that he killed himself by one of two very different means.

According to an essay by author Ed Gorman, Williams' long-time agent Don Congdon told Gorman about a letter or telegram he received from Williams that contained an ominous message:

"It was very strange. So cold and purposeful. One morning I'm sitting in my office and I get a letter from Charlie and it says that by the time I read this, he'll have killed himself, which is exactly what he did.

"I couldn't tell you why, not for sure, and I would rather not speculate on it.

"Charlie was a smooth and polished writer, and he worked so hard on his books. He deserved more attention to his work in the United States, particularly in the film studios. He had the misfortune of writing suspense novels when the public didn't seem to have as much interest in the genre."

–from "Fifteen Impressions of Charles Williams"
by Ed Gorman, *Murder Off the Rack*, Scarecrow Press,
ed. Jon L. Breen and Martin Harry Greenberg, 1989

A dozen or so years later, Gorman says, "There really isn't any mystery to how Williams died. [...] Congdon said that he'd been begging Willims to come back to the small town where he'd been living. Congdon, as I recall, said that Williams hadn't been writing and was deeply depressed following the death of his wife from cancer. He stayed on his boat alone after his wife passed. So, after sending the telegram to Congdon, he went over the side of the boat and drowned. [...] No real mystery that I'm aware of." (This from a post on the rara-avis discussion group that can be found at www.miskatonic.org/rara-avis.)

If Williams had gone over the side one has to wonder if life imitated art, in this case, his own life imitating his own art. In one of his books Williams has an increasingly depressed woman go diving at night, then swimming down further and further, until she can no longer come back up, swallowed by the crushing pressures of the deepening water. In another, he has two characters fighting each other for their lives, choosing to sink ever downward rather than to break their grips and save themselves by trying to reach the surface.

The truth seems somewhat more prosaic. According to his death certificate, Charles Williams was found in his Van Nuys, California apartment on April 5th, 1975, the victim of a "gunshot wound through head." No screens for any drugs or alcohol were run, and the body was later cremated. His middle initial, "K.", which had fallen away sometime in the distant past, was left a blank spot on the paper.

It is often said that Charles Williams never wrote a bad book. Taste is a relative thing, so that could certainly be true. Clearly, however, some of his books are better than others. *The Big Bite* reads like something he started to quickly knock out. *The Diamond Bikini* is genuinely funny but the main plot is more of an excuse for the rest of the story, and he repeated himself in its sequel, *Uncle Sagamore and His Girls*. Many people point to *Hell Hath No Fury* as his true classic but it may read too much like a James M. Cain book to be considered groundbreaking. *A Touch of Death* is solid, hard-boiled noir, but it shares the same basic plot of *The Big Bite*, although better executed.

In the end, it may just be that Williams produced too many books in too short a time to let more of his originality meld better with his unique talents. His characters were often too similar, he did the perfect crime (that ended up being not quite so perfect) too many times, many of his characters were interchangeable, and he reused too many of the same situations too often. For all that, a Charles Williams book is always a good, solid read, often well representing the genre even if not quite able to fully break away or rise above it. His first book, *Hill Girl*, is perhaps his most original novel, and its main weakness is merely the tendency to overlong descriptive passages.

Some people seem to be put off by the sailing jargon used in his five seagoing novels, but it never gets in the way and adds verisimilitude to the stories. These books are where Williams is at his most original, and his most filmed book, *Dead Calm*, is perhaps the real quintessential Williams book.

Charles Williams broke into publishing writing paperback originals, and that's what he was himself: a paperback original. He was able to understand the genre he was working in and took a number of chances to distinguish his books from other copies on the racks. Perhaps more time between releases could have afforded him the opportunity to avoid some of his own pitfalls.

Not much is known of Williams' private life and only a few scattered details are available to find here and there. How Williams felt about things like the deaths of his family members is not recorded in an easily accessible source, if indeed anywhere at all.

On the other hand, Williams clearly wasn't interested in depicting the plight of society's downtrodden or mean streets and back alleys. He was interested in writing about certain types of men, one good and one bad, but neither that far apart from the other. And he was interested in certain types of women, also good and bad, or shades thereof, with often only a thin line telling the difference.

But most of his books evoke truly original concepts, and although mixed with the recycled ones, these are not necessarily fatal flaws. At best, it may explain why Williams never reached the heights of popularity that some of his lesser-talented contemporaries achieved. At worst, each individual book will take fans of solid, exciting, suspenseful writing and give them what they have every right to expect: one hell of a good read. In the end, that's what Charles Williams always delivers.

—October 2013
Littleton, NH

NOTHING
IN HER WAY
by Charles Williams

Chapter One

He looked as if he'd got lost from a conducted tour of something.

I didn't pay much attention to him when he came in, except in the general way you notice there's somebody standing next to you in a bar. Unless it develops he's dead, or he has fingers growing on his ears, or he tips your drink over, you probably never see him. He did it that way, in a manner of speaking. I tipped *his* drink over.

I wasn't in any mood for an opening bid about the weather. The track had gone from sloppy to heavy during the afternoon and outside the rain was still crying into the neon glow of Royal Street. It'd be soup tomorrow, and unless you tabbed something going to the post with an outboard motor you'd do just as well sticking a pin in the program or betting horses with pretty names. I'd dropped two hundred in the eighth race when Berber Prince, a beautiful overlay at four to one, just failed to last by a nose. I was feeling low.

It was one of those dim places, with a black mirror behind the bar, and while it was doing a good business, I hadn't known it was *that* crowded. I'd just put my drink down and was reaching for a cigarette when I felt my elbow bump gently against something, and then I heard the glass break as it went over the bar. I looked down at the spreading Daiquiri, and then at him. It was odd. There'd been plenty of room there a minute ago.

"I'm sorry," I said. "It didn't spill on you, did it?"

"No. It's all right." He smiled. "No harm done."

"Here," I said. "Let me get you another one." I caught the bartender's eye and gestured.

"No," he protested. "I wish you wouldn't. It was just an accident. Happen to anybody."

"Not at all," I said. "I knocked it over. I'll get you another one." The barman came up. "Give this gentleman another Daiquiri. And charge me with a glass."

The barman mopped up and brought the drink. I paid for it. He picked it up and said, "Thanks. Thanks a lot. But don't forget the next one's on me."

He looked like a cherub, or an overgrown cupid. He had on a blue serge suit too tight under the arms, a white shirt too tight in the collar, and a cheap hand-painted tie with a can-can dancer on it. You knew he'd been saving the tie for New Orleans. There wasn't any convention badge, but maybe he'd been left over, or he'd lost it.

"My name's Ackerman," he said. "Homer Ackerman. I'm from Albuquerque."

"Belen," I said. He pumped my hand. Well, I thought, I can always make it to another bar, even in the rain.

"Belen?" he asked happily. "Why, that's the name of a little town right near Albuquerque."

"Yes, I know," I said. "I've never been there, though."

He was disappointed. It was obvious he was hoping I knew old Ben Um-laut who had the tractor agency, or maybe the Frammis boys. I wished he'd go ahead and ask me where a fella could find some—uh—girls, and then beat it, but you couldn't just brush him off. Not with that face. It'd be like kick-ing a baby.

"Say, this New Orleens is some place, ain't it?" he said. "To visit, I mean. Sure wouldn't want to live here, though."

He went on talking. I only half listened to him, and looked at a girl who was sitting on a stool at the other end of the bar. She had red hair, but it wasn't quite the same shade of red.... It never is. I wondered if I'd ever break myself of it. After all, it'd been two years.

"Gee, my feet are killing me," Ackerman was saying. "I must have walked a hundred miles around this place. And then standing around out there at the race track—" He broke off and turned that cherubic smile on me again. "You prolly won't believe this, but I won over ninety dollars out there. There was this horse running named Dinah Might, and it was raining, and I used to know an old boy named Raines who was a powder monkey—get it? Powder monkey, dynamite? And I'll be dad-burned if he didn't—"

I didn't say anything. Dinah Might was the cheap plater who'd beaten out Berber Prince by the nose at something like forty to one. Maybe he'd go away.

"Say," he said suddenly, "there's an empty booth over there. Le's sit down."

I looked at my watch. "I'd like to, but I've got to run. Man I was supposed to meet—"

His face fell in on itself. "Oh, shoot. You've got time for just one, haven't you?" he asked earnestly. "You can't go off without me buying you that drink, after you bought me one."

It was something about those open blue eyes, I guess. You just couldn't de-stroy his faith in the people he picked up in bars. "O.K.," I said. "Just a quick one."

We carried our drinks over and sat down. The seats were leather-uphol-stered, with high backs. He started to light a cigarette, and then said, "Ex-cuse me."

"How's that?" I asked.

"Oh." He looked at me blankly. "I thought I kicked your foot." He leaned down sideways a little and peered under the edge of the table. "I see what it was, I think. Looks like there's something lying there on the floor."

"There is?" I asked, without much interest.

"Uh-huh. Wait a minute. Maybe I can reach it." He leaned down farther and grunted. "Nope. Can't quite make it. I tell you. Push your right foot a little, straight ahead."

I shoved the foot, and then he grunted again. "Now I got it." He straightened up, his face red. "Le's see what it is." He stopped, and his mouth dropped open. "Say, Belen, look at this!"

It was a wallet, an expensive-looking job, and from the thick bulge of it there was plenty in it. But by now I wasn't looking at the wallet. I was looking at him, and remembering the way that glass had happened to get in the way of my elbow. No, I thought. Nobody could dream up a character like this.

His voice had dropped to an awe-struck whisper. "Holy smoke, Belen! Twenties, fifties.... Boy, there's a wad in this!" Almost unconsciously, he had hitched his shoulder around so the wallet was hidden from the rest of the bar.

"Any name in it?" I asked.

"That's a good idea," he said excitedly. "Maybe we can find the guy and give it back to him. Le's see." He nodded. "Here it is. J. B. Brown, Springfield. Can't make out the name of the state."

"That ought to be a cinch," I said. "Just try Illinois, Ohio, and Massachusetts, and then work your way down to the others."

He looked at me with innocent helplessness. "That many Springfields? What you think we ought to do?"

"I don't know," I said. I was still just waiting. "You have any ideas?"

"No-o," he answered. "Except that we ought to try to return it. Wouldn't be honest to—well, just keep it, would it?"

"No," I said. "Of course not. Unless you just couldn't find anybody named Brown living in Springfield."

"Maybe you're right. If we kept it for—say a reasonable length of time, and he didn't come forward to claim it, I'd say it would be perfectly honest for us to divide it up."

Well, I thought, I'll be a sad son. There wasn't any doubt of it now. I began to burn a little. Was he stupid, or new at it, or what? I knew I didn't look like somebody who'd go for it.

Maybe the thing to do was ride along with him just for the laughs. "What do you mean, divide it up?" I said. "You found it. I didn't."

He shook his head. "No, by golly. You were right here with me, and you pushed it over where I could reach it. We both share in it. That is," he added hastily, "if Brown doesn't show up to claim it. Say, I think I've figured out a way we can handle it. There's an old boy over at this little hotel where I'm staying, he works in a bank and he's as honest as the day is long. We'll let him hold it for us. And then, if nobody claims it, we'll split it right down the middle. How's that?"

"Sounds fine to me," I said.

"Good." He nodded, and then paused, a little uncertainly. "But there's one thing."

"What's that?" I asked, knowing very well what it was.

"Well, it's just in case Brown should show up *later*. I mean, to sort of prove good faith, and financial responsibility, in case we did have to give it back later on, I think each of us ought to be able to show cash of his own equal to his part of it."

"Yeah," I said. "I see what you mean. Something like a bond, to prove we *could* pay it back if we had to. We give it to your friend to hold, along with the wallet."

He nodded. "That's it, exactly."

"All right," I said. "Down, boy. You can put it back in your pocket and fade."

"How's that?" he asked, the guileless blue eyes growing wide.

"Look. It was old when the pharaohs were in the construction business. If you have to work the pigeon drop, why don't you try the neighborhood bars?"

The smooth, pink face split open then, and he laughed. "Nice work, Mike."

"Mike?" I asked. "You know me?"

He looked pained. "Really, Belen. You don't think I'm that stupid in casing a mark? And I haven't pulled anything as crude as a pigeon drop in twenty years."

I was still a little angry. "Well, what's the gag?"

"Don't you know me?"

I shook my head.

"Charles," he said. "Wolford Charles."

It rang then. I'd heard of Wolford Charles—or Prince Charlie, as he was known to half the bunco squads in the country. But as far as I knew, I'd never seen him.

He must have been reading my mind. "You have an atrocious memory for faces, Mike. Don't you remember that crap game in my hotel room in Miami last fall? You took four hundred dollars off me."

I thought for a minute. "Sure. I remember that. But the only man I recall who looked anything like you was some gold-plated Bourbon from Philadelphia, by the name of—" I stopped.

He smiled reminiscently. "Precisely. Er—Shumway, as I recall. Eccentric chap. Cursed with an absolutely unshakable belief that he could make a six the hard way. A touching bit of faith in these days of spiritual bankruptcy, but mathematically unsound."

I leaned back in the booth and lit a cigarette. "All right, but I still don't make it. You didn't think you were going to get your four hundred back that way."

"One moment, Mike, please." He shoved the Daiquiri away and asked the girl for Scotch without ice. "The late Mr. Ackerman's feeling for drinks was almost on a par with his taste in cravats." He looked down at the can-can girl and winced. "But to get back to your question. Call it an intelligence test."

"Why?"

"I was curious as to your reaction."

"And so I spotted it," I said impatiently. "What do I get? A merit badge?"

"I was thinking of something a little more substantial. To be exact, a piece of a small business venture I have under advisement at the present time."

"I just got off," I said. "It was nice meeting you, Charlie."

"But Mike, old boy, you haven't even heard it."

"And I don't need to. I already own an Arkansas diamond mine."

He shook his head. "You misunderstand me. You put up no capital at all. It's really in the nature of a job, with a nice slice of the bood—er, profits. Say ten per cent."

"Nothing doing," I said.

"But why?"

"I'm a gambler, not a con man."

He gestured impatiently. "There is nothing whatever illegal about this. It's just a simple matter of—ah—enhancing the value of a piece of real estate. But let me tell you about it, and about Miss Holman."

"You're wasting your breath," I said.

"Miss Elaine Holman, a very charming and lovely young lady I met in New York. She's connected with the theatre. Her mother and father are both dead, and she comes originally from a small town in the West. She was reared by an uncle who must be, from all accounts, one of the greatest scoundrels out-side the pages of Dickens. You see, Mike, through a small irregularity in her mother's will, this girl has been cheated of an inheritance of nearly seventy thousand dollars. All quite legally, of course, and there's nothing the courts can do for her."

"Yeah, I know," I said. "And the uncle is in a Mexican prison, and the sev-enty thousand dollars is in the false bottom of a trunk being held by customs in Laredo. Cut it out, Charlie. Everybody's heard of that one."

He was hurt. "Please, Mike. I'm trying to tell you this is strictly on the level. All I'm trying to do is help this girl get back what is rightfully hers. For a slight—ah—commission, of course. After all, I'm not a philanthropic insti-tution, and the idea I have in mind will entail some expense."

"Roughly, around sixty-eight thousand, if I'm any judge," I said. "Provided, of course, the whole thing's not a pipe dream. But why are you telling me?"

"Because I want your help. I'm offering you a job."

"But I've already turned it down. Remember?"

He sighed. "I wish there was some way I could convince you this is strictly legitimate." He looked up then, past my shoulder, and brightened. "But per-haps Miss Holman can. Here she comes now."

I looked around, and then stood up, trying to keep my face still and stiffen the weak feeling in my knees. She was wearing a clear plastic raincoat with a hood, and her hair was the color of a bottle of burgundy held up to the light. As he had said, Miss Holman was a very lovely girl.

The only catch was that her name wasn't Miss Holman. I was reasonably sure of that. I'd known her for twenty-three years, and I'd been married to her for two.

Chapter Two

It was insane.

There wasn't a quiver of an eyelash as Charlie introduced us. She'd never seen me before. She looked at me and said coolly and quite pleasantly, "How do you do, Mr. Belen?"

I could hear Charlie still talking. "Mike is an old, old friend, my dear. I am trying to persuade him to join us."

I took it from her and played it deadpan. There didn't seem to be anything else to do, and I was too dumfounded to think. God alone knew what she was up to, and there wasn't any use even trying to guess. Was Charlie lying to me, or was she lying to Charlie? Since there was no known record of Charlie's ever having told the truth about anything, the answer would seem to be obvious, but I wasn't too sure. Dullness had never been one of her faults.

We sat down again, and she ordered a Ramos fizz. She was on Charlie's side of the table, directly across from me, and when the drink came she leaned forward a little and said, wide-eyed, "I do hope you'll help us, Mr. Belen."

She could open a safe that way. In Salem, they'd have burned her—or they would have if there'd been enough women on the jury. Nothing had changed in two years. The dark red hair was short-cropped and as carelessly tousled as a child's. Her face just missed being heart-shaped and petite, but there was nothing of the expressionless doll about it. It was mobile and almost flamboyantly alive, with only a subtle hint of the temperament you knew damned well was there if you'd ever been married to her. She had a little dusting of freckles across the bridge of her nose, and her eyes were dark brown and a little long for her face. Right, now there was a blue silk scarf knotted about her chin, the big bow coming up beside her cheek and giving her a deceptively little-girl look. She was a little girl, all right—the same loaded little girl with a short fuse.

We were divorced two years ago, and the only thing I'd heard of her in all that time was that she'd married some New York bookie named Lane. I thought of the last time I'd seen her. It was raining that night, too, and I remembered how black and shiny the streets were as we walked down the hill from the hotel in San Francisco. We said good-by quite calmly at the airline office on Union Square, and then I'd gone on to the men's bar in the St. Francis and ordered a drink, suddenly conscious of how peaceful everything seemed—and how empty.

I snapped out of it and came back to the present, realizing I'd been staring at her. Charlie's proposition had been nothing but a bore, but now it had exploded right in my face. There was a horrible fascination about it, and it boiled down to that same question: Just who was bamboozling whom? Was Charlie trying to sell me the sad story of Elaine Holman, or was she selling him?

But that was unbelievable. Charlie was a pro; he'd dealt in flimflam all his life; he had a mind like a steel trap; and he'd been around so long he wouldn't bet you even money you didn't have three hands on your left arm unless you'd let him take it home first and look at it. She couldn't have the colossal nerve to try to pull something on him. Oh, couldn't she? I thought.

I lit her a cigarette, and then one for myself. She gave me a smile that would warm a duck blind, and turned to Charlie. "I do hope Mr. Belen will join us. He's perfect for the job, and you just know *instinctively* that you can trust him."

I loved that. Maybe, I thought, in this idea they're cooking up, they have to leave somebody alone for a few minutes with a red-hot stove.

"Charlie," I said, "I still don't get what you want me for, but would you mind telling me a little more what this is all about? Just how are you going to get Miss Holman's money back for her?"

He took a sip of his drink and looked at me with a benign smile. "The *modus operandi* is somewhat involved, Mike. And we'd only bore Miss Holman, since she's already familiar with all its ramifications. Suffice it to say that its axis, or focal point, is a real estate transaction of a rather novel sort."

"Who owns the real estate?" I asked.

"Miss Holman's uncle."

"And who's going to buy it?"

He raised his eyebrows in gentle surprise. "Why, Miss Holman's uncle, naturally."

"Oh, I see," I said. "That was stupid of me. But what are you going to do if the uncle's guardian catches you at it? I take it they must have him put away somewhere where he can't hurt himself."

"Miss Holman's uncle is a banker, Mike," he said, a little pained, "and a very astute businessman. As I remarked, the deal is a bit complicated, and, as any masterpiece, it suffers in condensation."

I could see very well he wasn't going to tell me anything unless I came in. Charlie was no fool. And I didn't want to get mixed up in their shenanigan, whatever it was. What I wanted to do more than anything in the world was to get her alone for a few minutes, before this thing had me wondering who *I* was, and see if I couldn't shake a little truth out of her. I'd never realized before just what a beautiful thing a simple, unvarnished fact could be—if I ever ran into one again.

Just then she looked at her watch and said, "I'm going to have to run. I'm expecting a telephone call at the hotel." She stood up. "I'm very glad I met you, Mr.—ah—Belen."

Charlie let me beat him to it, a little too obviously. You could see his angle. Let *her* work on me. "I'll walk around with you," I said. "Or get you a cab."

"I wouldn't like to trouble you," she said.

"No trouble at all," I replied. "It'll be a pleasure."

The rain had slowed to a fine drizzle. Instead of turning toward Canal as we came out, she went the other way, toward the French Quarter. I fell in beside her and took her arm. We walked in complete silence for a block and then turned off into a side street and went another block. I looked back. Charlie hadn't followed us. We stopped under an awning, out of the misty rain that swirled beyond us under the cone of light from a street lamp. She looked up at me, big-eyed, her face still.

"All right, Miss Holman," I said. "Make me cry."

"Mike, please," she said. "I didn't know it was you. He said he had somebody in mind—to help us, I mean. A friend of his. But I had no idea who it was."

"Never mind who I am," I said. "I can still guess that—I think. What I want to know is which one of you erratic geniuses is the mother of Elaine Holman, and why?"

"Well," she said hesitantly, "I am."

So my hunch had been right. She *was* trying to sell Charlie a gabardine mink. I wondered if she had any idea of the probable odds on that. But it could wait. "Well, look," I said. "I suppose you can explain it. Let's give it a try. I mean, why you're mixed up in something with Wolford Charles, and what the hell you're trying to do."

She hadn't changed expression. She was still watching me quietly with those big brown eyes.

"Isn't there anything you wanted to tell me first, Mike?" she asked softly.

"Such as?" I asked, trying to sound tough about it.

"Well, I'm glad to see you."

"I'm always glad to see you, Mrs. Lane."

"I'm not married any more, Mike."

"Off again, on again, Flanagan."

"Jeff was killed. Eight months ago, by a holdup man."

"Oh." I wanted to crawl down a sewer. "I'm sorry, Cathy. I'm sorry as hell."

"It's all right. You were right, anyway. We were about to separate."

"It's too bad."

"I've missed you, Mike."

"And I've missed—" I stopped. What was the use in digging that up again? I'd always feel empty when she was somewhere else, and we'd always fight when we were together. You couldn't win. "But let's get back to this Holman pitch," I said briskly. "Start talking, Cathy."

"Well, there is an Elaine Holman," she said.

"I thought there might be. But where is she?"

"In New York. I met her last year. And she *does* have an uncle who's a banker in a small town named Wyecross near the Mexican border."

"But what are you up to?"

"All right, I'll tell you," she said quietly. "I've found Martin Lachlan."

"You've what?" I grabbed both her arms.

"That's right."

"When?" I demanded. "And why didn't you write me?"

"I didn't know how to reach you."

"Wait a minute," I broke in. "This man in Wyecross—this banker—he's Lachlan. Is that it?"

She shook her head. "Lachlan's in Mexico."

"Where in Mexico?"

"If I tell you, will you help me?"

"Look," I said. "I've been waiting to catch up with Lachlan as long as you have."

"All right. He's in Lower California—fishing, at La Paz. But he has an apartment in San Francisco, among other places, and that's where we'll find him when we're ready."

"Ready, hell. We're ready now."

"No, we're not," she said. Then she looked up at me. "Unless— How much money do you have?"

"Thousand—eleven hundred dollars. About that."

"Then we're not ready. It'll take a lot more than that, even with what I have."

I began to catch on. "Then you dreamed up this Holman thing to raise the money? You sold Charlie on it, and he's going to split with you?"

"Yes," she said simply.

"I see. The end justifies the means." It always did with her. "Even if it means helping Wolford Charles swindle some man who never heard of Lachlan?"

"That isn't quite the case. You haven't asked me yet who this Wyecross man is."

"Who is he?"

"His name is Goodwin."

"What? Not that one!"

"Yes. Howard C. Goodwin."

"You sure it's the same one?"

"Mike, darling, I spent a week in Wyecross, doing a survey for—for— I've forgotten the name of the agency I said. I know everything there is to know about everybody."

As I said, dullness wasn't one of her faults.

I was still holding her arms. For some reason I'd forgotten to turn them loose. "Mike," she whispered, "you'll help us, won't you? I need—I mean, we need you."

There's always a warning, if you'll listen to it. It buzzes when you're playing cards with strangers and get an almost perfect hand, and it's always smart to listen. I could hear it now, but very faintly, as I thought of the law and of Wolford Charles and of the mess we could get into. But I was touching her and she was looking at me, and Lachlan was somewhere at the end of it. I couldn't hear it very well.

"Yes," I said. "I'm with you. Let's get started."

I should have turned up my hearing aid.

We flagged a cab and went around to her hotel. We'd go out somewhere for dinner, she said, and she wanted me to meet Judd Bolton, a friend of hers from New York. He was in the deal.

"Does he know who you are?" I asked. "I mean, what name do you use around him?"

She laughed. "I've known him a long time, and he knew Jeff. I asked him to help me, and he was the one who suggested getting Charlie. Charlie's the only one who thinks I'm Elaine Holman."

"If *he* does," I said.

I was itching to find out what else she had learned about Martin Lachlan, and to get a line on this thing they had rigged for Goodwin, in Wyecross, but there wasn't time to get much information out of her. She said Charlie'd brief me on the Wyecross deal in the morning.

"They don't know anything about Lachlan," she said. "We do that alone."

"That's right," I said. "Lachlan's ours."

He'd been ours for a long time. Except for the slight matter of finding him.

At the hotel she went up to the desk to call Bolton's room. I watched her across the lobby, conscious that she was still one of the most beautiful girls I'd ever seen and thinking it was a shame more of them didn't learn to walk. While she was talking, I drifted over to the newsstand to see if the Racing Form had come in. It hadn't, and it was while I was standing there looking idly around the lobby that I discovered I wasn't the only one watching her.

He was sitting like a limp doll in a big overstuffed chair near the doors with a paper in his hands, dark, thin-faced, a forgotten cigarette hanging out of the side of his mouth. The paper was lowered into his lap and he was watching her with the unwinking intensity of a hungry child. In a minute she turned away from the desk and he put the paper up again. I stood there a minute, wondering about it. It was probably nothing. Everybody looked at her. It was just 1926 again and he was asking her if she'd ever seen the view from his apartment window, before going back to tomorrow's selections at Hialeah.

Maybe, I thought uneasily. If that'd been spring in his face, they ought to get the women and children out before winter.

In a few minutes Bolton came down, and she introduced us. He was about thirty, big, expensive-looking, and tough in a civilized sort of way. Maybe it was the eyes. They were gray and they didn't say anything, but you got the impression they could be hard as well as urbane. We got off to a bad start.

She explained who I was and told him I was in the act. He smiled at me, with not quite enough nastiness to pin down.

"Horses a little off their form, eh?" he asked. It wasn't hard to translate. I was a broke horse player looking for a handout.

"Are they?" I said.

I could see dinner wasn't going to be much if we had to have him along, but I was ready to try. We were going to be in this thing together, and we might as well make some effort to hit it off.

We went over into the French Quarter and stopped in a little hole in the wall for a drink while we made up our minds where to eat. There were some Navy uniforms up front at the bar, and a row of empty booths, and in the back a jukebox with colored lights was sobbing its heart out over something. We walked back to one of the booths, while the uniforms looked her over for spavin and bowed tendons, and she and Bolton sat down on one side and I got in across from them with my back toward the door. She ordered a Martini, and Bolton and I settled for Scotch.

The drinks came. The uniforms drifted out and the place was empty except for us. The flood of tears from the jukebox shut off and it shifted over to something by Vaughn Monroe.

"*Salud y pesetas,*" I said to Cathy.

She started to raise the Martini and then stopped, as if she had run into an invisible glass wall. The door had opened and closed behind me, and now I heard footsteps coming along the row of booths, unhurried footsteps sounding like a sequence out of a B movie. Bolton looked up over my shoulder and I could see his face get dirty with fear. I turned my head to try to see what it was in the mirror behind the bar. It was the man from the hotel lobby.

He still looked like a corrupt and undernourished child, even in the baggy overcoat and with a gray snap-brim hat pushed back on his head. The dangling cigarette was gone now, but he carried the thin face tipped to one side as if the smoke still trailed up past the expressionless black eyes. As I watched him I was conscious of the odd impression that he looked like a gangster would who spent most of his time at crime movies studying the dress and mannerisms of hoodlums. He stopped and stood looking at us. Or rather, he was looking at Cathy. He gave me one negligent glance and forgot me, and appeared to have no interest in Bolton.

"I guess you forgot me," he said. "In such a hurry to leave, you forgot all about me."

"No," she said. She put down the drink at last. "I didn't forget."

"Then maybe you just didn't care."

She was watching him the way a tiger eyes the man with the chair and whip. It wasn't fear in her eyes, just watchfulness. "I think I told you once. I haven't got that much money."

"You can forget that dodge," he said. "I know all about the insurance he left."

Before she could say anything, Bolton spoke up. You could almost smell the fear in him. "I'm sure Mrs. Lane will pay you, Donnelly. It's just that it takes time to get that much money."

She gave him a quick, sidewise glance of contempt.

"How about it?" Donnelly asked, ignoring him.

"I told you—" she began.

He moved a leisurely step nearer the table, leaned over it past Bolton, and his arm swung. The whole thing was so unhurried and deliberate it caught me by surprise and I sat there like a fool. His opened hand cracked against the side of her face with a sharp column of sound above the honeyed crooning of the juke. The arm came back and I caught it and turned.

It was like twisting a pipe cleaner. There was no strength or resistance in it at all. He half turned, with his elbow on the table, and looked at me utterly without interest as if I were a roach that had just crawled out of the wood-work.

"Who's the strong boy?" he asked Cathy.

The barman was running up. I let the arm go and Donnelly straightened up. The side of Cathy's face was stinging red, but she made no move to put a hand to it.

"What's going on here?" the barman asked with a truculent glance at all of us.

Donnelly jerked a negligent thumb. "Beat it. We want anything, we'll call you."

"You want me to call the cops?"

"No," Cathy said. "We're all right."

He went back to the bar, but kept watching us. Donnelly leaned on the table. "You better think it over, sweetie," he said. "Don't make me look you up again. You wouldn't like it."

He turned and started to go out, and then looked back. He nodded at me without even looking at me. "And if Strong Boy here is a friend of yours, you ought to tell him about putting his fat hands on people. I don't like that rassling stuff."

I started to get up to follow him to the door, but she gave me an urgent glance and shook her head.

He was gone. She picked up her drink and took a sip of it, then turned and looked at Bolton.

"You can finish your little drink now, dear," she said. "I don't think he'll be back."

Chapter Three

I didn't get much sleep that night. There were too many questions going around in my mind trying to mate with answers that weren't there, and I was busy with twenty-three years' accumulation of Cathy Dunbar Belen Lane. That was a large order of just one girl, I thought. Wasn't it enough for one lifetime? Did we have to go around again?

If she was mixed up in something dangerous, was it any of my business any more? Who was this Donnelly, and what did he want? She'd only shrugged him off when I'd asked her. "A cheap hoodlum," she said indifferently. "He has some stupid idea I owe him money."

Then she turned and smiled charmingly in Bolton's direction. "I do think it's cute, though, the way he impresses Mr. Bolton." If she got the knife in you, don't think she wouldn't turn it. She despised people she could walk on.

His face was red with impotent fury. "I tell you, Cathy, the man's dangerous. He's as deadly as nitroglycerin. He's not all there."

"I agree with you, dear," she said sweetly. "If he thinks he's going to collect money from me, he's certainly not all there."

Bolton didn't add up at all. When you dipped into him, you came up with both hands full of nothing. It was easy enough to write him off as a coward, the way she did, but something said it wasn't that simple. Why? There wasn't anything you could put a finger on, for God knows his face and his voice had been rotten with that cringing before Donnelly. Maybe, I thought wearily, as I gave it up, he's read Donnelly's clippings and I haven't.

It was strange, the way you couldn't escape from the past. Or was it the past? Maybe she was the thing I could never get away from. I lit another cigarette and tried to think objectively about it. Of course I hated Lachlan; but why was it always intensified when I was with her? Just how had I thought about him during the past two years?

No, I thought, that's not right. I'm just trying to blame her for something I've got the same way she has. It's all tied up with both of us and we're all tied up with it and with each other, and we always have been.

When she was four and I was six it was a white-nosed bear with a terrible voice and flashlights for eyes that made her tell stories and get into trouble. I believed it about the bear. She convinced me. It wasn't that I lacked sophistication in the matter of bears, for I had seen them, in the Sierra Madre, with my father and hers; it was just that her bear was very real. You could almost see it yourself when she told you about it, and if it had flashlights for eyes—well, stranger things had happened. Stranger things had happened to her, anyway.

It was a long way back to those days when we were a couple of imaginative and bilingual kids playing with real Indians and imaginary bears, when the construction firm of Dunbar & Belen had built a lot of bridges and dams in the republics south of the Rio Bravo. That was before the firm had become Dunbar, Belen & Lachlan, and then had become nothing at all with the dev-astating suddenness of a dam going out. That was what it had been, a dam. And when it collapsed, it took Dunbar and Belen. It didn't take Lachlan.

It was a long time before the whole story was pieced together, and when it was, it didn't matter very much. Dunbar was dead—he died two years af-ter they were released from prison—and while my father was still alive, he never seemed to take much interest in the fact. It wasn't that there had been any loss of life in the disaster; as they said afterward, that was their only piece of luck. It hadn't killed anybody. It had just cost them their company and their good reputations and two years of their lives.

Lachlan was the junior member of the firm, both in years and in seniority. He had been in residence on that job in Central America, in charge, with a second in command by the name of Goodwin. Of course, Dunbar and my fa-ther had been there a dozen times or more, but you can't see everything, es-pecially when you trust the man who's doing the job. And when the dam folded up like water-soaked cardboard, they flew in in a chartered plane. Po-lice were waiting for them at the airport.

Lachlan hadn't sold any of the reinforcing steel. That would have been too easy to spot. But with Goodwin in charge of the concrete work, government inspectors for sale, and native labor who didn't know a mix specification from the second chorus of "The Peanut Vendor," it was just stealing candy to di-vert around a hundred thousand dollars' worth of the cement into his own channels. Most of the proceeds had gone into the campaign fund of another eager beaver on the make—an army colonel who had his eye on the presidency. The two of them pulled it off. About a week before the dam folded, the colonel had taken over the government in a palace revolution. How could Lachlan lose? He didn't. Dunbar and Belen went to jail, while Lachlan and the colonel took over what was left of the firm and only God knows how much of the damages collected by the government. You'll never go broke taking it out of one pocket and putting it in another.

That was in 1936. I said I'd kill Lachlan when I grew up. Cathy said I'd have to get there first, because she was going to kill him. She was ten years old.

We grew up that way, the two of us with that shared obsession for revenge. After a while, of course, we gave up the childish and impractical idea of killing him, since that wouldn't prove anything at all and would probably land us in the electric chair besides. What we were going to do was more poetic. We were going to take him the way he had taken our fathers. It was a large project for a couple of kids.

I ground out the cigarette and lay looking up at the dark. We knew where he was at last. But could we do it? How could we do it? Lachlan would be nearly fifty now; he'd been everywhere and done everything; and he was a swindler himself and knew all the angles. It was still a large project, and I didn't know.

And then it occurred to me that I didn't even know yet what this plan was they had cooked up for Goodwin.

I found out in the morning. Charlie told me. And it was sweet.

He was staying at the Roosevelt. When I got over to his room around eleven A.M. Cathy and Bolton were already there. Charlie was still in a silk dressing gown, the plump, angelic face pink from fresh barbering, and was just finishing a breakfast consisting of a Persian melon and a large pot of *café créole* in the living room of his suite. He lighted one of his precious Havana cigars with slow, loving care and leaned back to smile benignly at me.

"Ah, come in, Mike," he said. "I see that Miss Holman's powers of persuasion are somewhat better than my feeble efforts."

Did he really think she was Elaine Holman? I wondered. But we had to keep up the act. I looked across at her. She was very lovely and chic in a brown suit with a fur piece dangling in casual elegance from her shoulder.

"If that puzzles you, Charlie," I said, "take a look at yourself and then at Miss Holman."

She smiled at me and said, "Thank you, Mr. Belen."

I still wondered about it. Nobody had kidded Charlie about anything since he was five. But, actually, what difference did it make whether he thought she was Elaine Holman or Florence Nightingale? He could still run out with all the money either way.

Bolton and I nodded curtly to each other to get it over with for the day. I thought about last night, and wondered if she still had the harpoon in him. She seemed to despise him—but why was she mixed up with him?

Maybe it was an act for my benefit, I thought suddenly. Maybe there was more to their "business" relationship than met the eye. I stopped, silently cursing myself. What was I getting jealous for? We weren't married any more, were we? What did she mean to me? Nothing at all, I told myself. Nothing.

"Well, I'm here, Charlie," I said. "I take it I'd only be wasting time trying to get you to raise your offer of fifteen per cent."

"A very sound hypothesis, Mike," he agreed, "if a little weak in the statistical department. The figure was ten per cent."

I shrugged resignedly. I'd known it was ten, of course, but to make it look good I had to haggle a little.

"All right," I said. "Just when and how do we sandbag Miss Holman's uncle?"

He winced. "Mike!"

"O.K. But how? Remember, I know nothing at all about it. What do I do?"

He removed the cigar and looked at it thoughtfully. "Ah, I intended to ask you last night, Mike. Did you ever study chemistry?"

"In high school," I said, puzzled. "By the time I got to college I knew bet-ter. Why?"

"It isn't important. You're a chemical engineer in this little venture we have in mind, and a slight knowledge of chemistry would, of course, be no great liability."

"I'm glad you told me," I said. "I used to know that salt was sodium some-thing. Remind me to look it up sometime."

He smiled soothingly. "As I say, it doesn't matter. The secret of a thing of this kind, Mike, is never to talk shop with people who do know. And, since you are to conceal the fact that you're a chemical engineer, you should en-counter no difficulty."

"Then there's nothing to it," I said. "It's easy. I'm not a chemical engineer, but I'm pretending to be one, so I can pretend I'm not one. Is the rest of the scheme that simple?"

Bolton was boredly reading a copy of *Fortune*. Cathy was listening and watching us, but without much interest. They both knew the whole thing by heart, of course.

Charlie delicately tapped the long ash from his cigar. "A quite—ah—un-derstandable bewilderment, Mike. At first glance it might seem a little in-volved, but there is a very good reason behind it. Now, to begin with, you go to Wyecross alone. The entire first act—aside from what has already been done—is yours, and I need not add, of course, that the success of the whole venture depends upon you. Miss Holman is driving to San Antonio to-morrow to visit friends, and no doubt she would be glad to have your com-pany for that part of the journey. Beyond San Antonio, I suggest you travel by bus. Mr. Bolton and I shall be in Houston until later developments neces-sitate our appearing on the scene. You will, of course, have our address.

"Now, to get to the core of the matter. Mr. Goodwin, who is a man of about forty, is cashier of the Stockmen's Bank, the only bank in Wyecross. From his father he inherited a large block of the bank's stock, in addition to some fif-teen thousand acres of land lying just east of Wyecross. Practically all this land is utterly unfit for anything, being nothing but a sort of Sahara in miniature, an endless waste of sand dunes. I have observed it from the club car of the train, Mike, and a more utterly desolate landscape I never hope to see. My only hope is that, since you will be there some time, you don't go stark mad."

"Never mind the description," I broke in. "What's all this got to do with it?"

He raised his eyebrows. "Everything, my boy. Now, upon your arrival in

Wyecross, you will go to Frankie and Johnnie's Kottage Kamp." He closed his eyes and shuddered slightly, and then went on. "You will go to this revolting caravansary and engage a room, or a court, as I believe it is called."

He went on talking, and he told it well. After a while I began to see the basic pattern of it, and had an idea of what he was aiming for, and it was a sweet piece of work. There was one hitch to it, however, and that was I couldn't make out where the money came in. The way it was set up, it didn't make sense. I broke in and asked him, and when he told me, I saw the poisonous beauty of it all at once like a light coming on. It was really rigged.

It wasn't just a simple matter of having it explained to me once. I had to be coached in it. We went over it for hours. We adjourned for lunch, and then came back and went at it again. I went out in the afternoon and visited the bank, and bought the few props I'd need, and returned to my hotel to pack.

Bolton disappeared somewhere. Charlie and I took Cathy out to dinner, and I stayed with her until she was back in her hotel. I was still thinking of Donnelly. We didn't see anything of him.

We left early in the morning. She was driving a '51 Cadillac, and she rode it hard. We talked very little. She was concentrating on the driving, and I was trying to stay off the "do-you-remembers."

Once she said, "You're not sorry, are you, Mike?"

"About what?" I asked.

"That you came in with us?"

"No. Of course not. I want Lachlan as badly as you do. And Goodwin too, for that matter."

"That's the only reason, then?"

I turned and looked at her. "I don't know," I said.

"We had a lot of fun, didn't we, Mike?"

"And a lot of fights."

"Do you know why I'm going to San Antonio?" she asked.

"Why?"

"We might get to see each other once in a while. It's not too far to Wyecross. And, of course, I couldn't stay in Wyecross with you, because Charlie thinks I'm Goodwin's niece."

"You hope."

We got into San Antonio around eight P.M. She went to a hotel, while I took my bags around to the bus station and checked them. The next bus going west was at ten-forty-five. I met her in the lobby and we went out for dinner, both of us a little quiet.

Afterward we climbed down the steps at the end of one of the bridges and walked along beside the river. It ran through the middle of the city in a series of little pools and falls, with stone walks and benches along the banks. The night was brilliantly clear and a little frosty, and straight up beyond the glow of the city you could see the cold shine of desert stars.

She was wearing a gray fur coat with the collar turned up against her cheek, and a crazy little hat was perched on one side of the tousled red hair with a sort of schoolgirl carelessness. She was very lovely.

We stopped and watched the shine of lights on the water.

"Mike, do you remember—" she began.

"No," I said. "I have a poor memory."

"Why?"

"It broke down. Overload, I think."

"It's too bad."

"Isn't it?"

According to the best scientific theories, a girl has no glamour, enchantment, mystery, or attraction for the man who has known her since she was three years old and who has fought with her and played cowboys with her and swum off sand bars with her under the blazing sun on tropical rivers the color of coffee and who has been married to her and has fought with her again and who has been divorced from her and has forgotten her entirely in two years. It's very scientific. I made myself watch the lights.

"What time does your bus leave, Mike?"

"In about an hour."

"Do you have to go tonight?"

There wasn't anybody else around. I turned away from the lights on the water and they were shining in her eyes until she closed them, and the lashes were very long like shadows on her face when I raised my head after a while and looked at her.

"No," I said.

Chapter Four

When I began to see the sand I knew I was almost there. Beyond the rusty strands of barbed wire it stretched away toward the horizon on both sides of the highway in desolate and wind-ruffled dunes, with only a tumbleweed or gaunt mesquite here and there to break the monotony of it. Then I could see the water tank up ahead.

Wyecross was a bleak little town lost in the desert like a handful of children's toys dropped and scattered along the highway. It was afternoon now under a sky like a blue glass bowl, and the three blocks of the business district were half asleep in the glare of the sun. I climbed down at the bus station and stood on the high sidewalk while the driver dug the two bags out of the luggage rack. A gust of wind slammed up the street like a balled fist, pushing at me, and I could taste the grit.

I took the bags and went into the restaurant that was also the bus station. The coffee was bitter with alkali. There was a jukebox at the other end of the counter and it was crying the same dirge the other one had, in that bar in New Orleans. I thought of Donnelly. He couldn't find her in San Antonio. Couldn't he? He'd found her in New Orleans, hadn't he? The coffee didn't warm the cold ball of uneasiness in my stomach.

I turned and looked out the big flyspecked window in front, past the shoddy Christmas decorations that had never been taken down, and the cardboard signs propped against the glass. They were blank on this side, but you knew they advertised Coca-Cola and some brand of cigarettes and maybe what was playing Sun., Mon., Tues. at the only movie in town.

I saw it then. It was diagonally across the street, on the corner. It was like a thousand others between Chesapeake Bay and Puget Sound, with two marble or imitation marble columns in front and the name and assets written on the window in gold leaf. Stockmen's Bank, it said. The door was closed now, because it was a little after three, and a small blind was pulled down in back of the glass. They'd still be at work, though, and I thought of him inside there, not knowing that after sixteen years I was right across the street from him.

Lachlan had always been the one, because he was the top boy, the brain, the one who'd engineered it. I hadn't thought of Goodwin for a long time, and in fact had even forgotten his first name was Howard. But now that I was so near and had actually caught up with him, I began to feel that same old hatred for him that I'd felt so long for Lachlan. He was just as guilty. I wanted to cross the street and see him, just look at him, but I didn't. That wasn't the way to do it. I'd meet him when the time came, but it had to be done according to plan.

I picked up the bags and walked back along the sidewalk the way we had come in. It was only two blocks to the edge of town. The sidewalk ended abruptly, as if it had got scared and quit when it saw the desert. There was a gas station on the left, and just beyond it, on the right, was the motel. It was about a dozen frame cabins painted a scabrous brown and grouped in a hollow square with the open end facing the highway. The sign on the arch over the driveway said, "Frankie & Johnnie's Kottage Kamp—Vacancy." The first cabin on the left was the office. I walked across the gravel and rang the bell.

Frankie or Johnnie was a fat man somewhere around forty who hadn't shaved for two or three days. He had on cowboy boots, and his paunch hung out over the top of a pair of skin-tight Levis apparently held up by the friction on his legs and backside. The eyes were muddy brown and questioning. "Yessir?" he said.

"Vacancy?" I asked.

"Sure thing." The eyes went beyond me, sweeping the driveway, and then looked down at the suitcases. "You got a car?"

"I came on the bus," I said.

"Oh." He considered this. Apparently nobody had ever stopped here before without a car. "Sure. We can fix you up. Just for tonight, huh?"

I shook my head. "I'll probably be here for some time. I'd like to have it by the week, or month, if I could get a rate."

We arrived at a deal after a few minutes' haggling, and I paid him a month in advance and signed the register as Julius Reichert of New Orleans. I could see the curiosity working on him. He got a key and we walked up the gravel drive.

It was a small cubbyhole as bleak as a Grosz drawing. The front of it was furnished with an iron bedstead and a shaky night table and an old rocker, while at the rear there was a sink and a two-burner gas stove on a table. He bent down and stuck a match to the open gas heater, which had flakes of asbestos up the back behind the flame. The asbestos turned red in the heat.

"Don't go to sleep with it burning and all the doors and windows closed," he said. "It'll suffocate you."

"All right," I said. I put the bags down.

He paused on his way out, with his hand on the door. "Salesman, I guess, huh?"

"No," I said. "I don't sell anything."

"Oh." He went out.

I sat down on the bed and lit a cigarette. The gas heater burned with a slight hiss, and outside I could hear the wind searching restlessly around the cabins. I tried to think about it. It had gone all right. In less than a week the whole town would be as curious as he was right now. Why would a man—and an obvious Easterner, at that—come to a whistle stop like this in the middle of nowhere, take a cabin by the month, and just stay here, doing nothing at all? And if they thought that was odd, they would have their hands full when they began to get the rest of the act.

Then I wasn't thinking about it. I was thinking about her. I could see her. I could almost feel her there in the cabin. The hell, I thought; it wasn't this bad before, when we split up. I'd missed her, but not like this. It was just the bleak loneliness of this God-forsaken outpost at the end of nowhere. That had to be it. Before, there had been the gambling, and big cities, and other girls, and always the horses running. Sure, that was all it was, just the loneliness.

I could see I didn't want much of this—this sitting around here thinking how it had been in San Antonio and listening to the wind. I wondered how long it would take. A month? But we couldn't rush it. That would be fatal. He had to come to me. All I could do was set out the bait and wait for him. But she was going to drive up Saturday night, a week from tomorrow. It was only eight days.

I went into the cold bathroom and shaved. I looked strange with the crew haircut and the steel-rimmed glasses. Dr. Julius Reichert, I thought, the dedicated chemist who doesn't know a compound from a mixture. We were taking long chances. Would Goodwin go for it?

After I changed clothes I walked back to town and sat around the drugstore, reading magazines. Around six I picked out the most likely-looking of the town's three restaurants and ate dinner—pork chops and applesauce—thinking of the bisque d'écrevisses at Antoine's. Since it was Friday night, the movie was a Western. I walked back to Frankie and Johnnie's in the windy dark and thought of Sunday and shuddered.

The bank was open a half day Saturday, but I didn't go near it. I'd do that Monday. I read the rest of the magazines and listened to the coveys of jail bait chatter around the drugstore. The waitresses in the restaurant were beginning to recognize me. I didn't talk to them except to agree to whatever they said about the weather.

I awoke at dawn on Sunday, and could hear the coyotes somewhere out on the prairie. It was funny, I thought, remembering, how only two or three could sound like thirty. After I'd eaten breakfast I put on the boots I'd bought, dressed in khaki trousers and a flannel shirt, and went for a long walk, taking a couple of the little cardboard boxes in my coat pocket. A half mile east of town I left the highway where the dunes began and went out across country, skirting the edge of the sand. It was clear, with a cold wind blowing and making a lonely sound in the telephone lines. I thought of what Charlie had said. He hoped I didn't go mad.

There was no danger of getting lost, with the highway always to the north and the haze-blue shadows of the mountains far off in Mexico as a landmark to the south. The highway was out of sight, but I could still see the telephone lines after I'd gone a mile. I sat down in the sun on the south side of a dune, out of the wind, and smoked a cigarette. It was lonely and wild and desolate, but it was better than the cabin or the town.

Before I went back I filled the two boxes with sand and stowed them in my coat pocket. They were about the size of the boxes kitchen matches come in, but stronger, and I had three dozen of them and some about twice as large in one of the bags in the cabin. When I got back I wrapped them in brown paper for mailing and wrote on them the address Charlie had given me. It was an actual address, some friend of his who knew about the deal.

Early Monday morning I took them down to the post office and mailed them. Neither the clerk nor the usual post office loiterers paid much attention to me. As soon as it was ten o'clock I went around to the bank. I had a cashier's check for six hundred dollars made out to Julius Reichert, which I'd bought in New Orleans.

There were two desks in the railed-in area up front, before you got to the tellers' cages. They were both empty. I cursed myself for coming too early. I'd wanted to get a look at him, at least. Well, it didn't matter too much. I'd be in and out often enough. As I went past, toward the tellers' cages, I sneaked a look at the names on the desks. The rear one was his. H. C. Goodwin, it said.

I deposited the check and made out a signature card to open an account. The teller gave me a checkbook. As I started to turn away, he asked, "Are you new here in town, Mr. Reichert?"

"Yes," I said shortly.

"Going to make Wyecross your home?"

"I don't know," I said.

As I moved away from the window I saw a man entering the gate in the railing up front. I slowed, waiting to see which desk he went to. He hung up the Western-style hat on a rack and sat down at Goodwin's desk, the rear one. I turned, very casually, and looked at him, feeling the hard beat of the pulse in my throat. This was one of them, at least. Not the big one, but one of them. There was nothing about him that I remembered at all, but then I had seen him only two or three times, sixteen years ago. He had a square, tanned face with sun wrinkles at the corners of the eyes. The eyes themselves were brown and alert behind gold-rimmed glasses, and his hair, which was also brown, was thinning out high on his temples. It wasn't a hard or unpleasant face any way you looked at it. Well, I thought, Charlie looks like a well-fed angel or an archbishop, when he hasn't got his hand in your pocket.

It was a little hard to connect the bank cashier and big landowner with the bull-o'-the-woods job on a construction in an O. Henry banana republic of sixteen years ago, but as Charlie had said, he came here originally and had more or less inherited the bank job along with the bank stock and land when his father died.

I went on out. The next stop was a hardware store in the next block. It had a small sporting goods department in the rear. I walked back and stared owlishly at the half-dozen rifles and shotguns standing on a shelf behind the counter. In a minute a clerk came over.

"Yes, sir?" he said. "What can I do for you?"

"Oh," I said, "I was just wondering. When can you shoot jack rabbits?"

He smiled, a little pityingly. "Any time you see one, and got a gun."

"Then they don't have any closed season on them?"

"Nope. On cottontails, yes; but not on jacks." You could see him thinking: Dumb dude.

"I see," I said. "Well, I'd like to buy a gun. A twenty-two."

"Sure." He reached back on the shelf and picked up a little slide-action pump. "This is a nice job." Then he stopped and looked at me with inspiration. "You really want to blow up some jacks? Let me show you something."

He put the .22 down on the counter and reached back again. This one was a bigger rifle with a long telescope sight. "Look," he said. "Here's a job. It'll explode a jack at two hundred yards like a bowl of Jello. It's a two-twenty Swift, a custom deal with a ten-power scope. Man it was ordered for never did come back. I'd buy it myself if I had the money."

"How much is it?" I asked innocently.

"Let you have it for three hundred. It costs more."

I winced and shook my head. "I'll take the little one."

"Sure thing," he said, a little disappointed. "I guess you're right. This other one's too much gun unless you really got the fever."

I bought a box of .22 rifle ammunition, and as I started to leave, he said, "You can tell a jack from a cottontail, can't you? I mean, you got to have a license to hunt cottontails."

"Oh, certainly," I said. "I can distinguish them. Jack rabbits have longer ears."

When I was out on the sidewalk I shot a quick glance through the window. He was talking to another clerk and laughing.

I went out that afternoon with the rifle. Not too far from the highway I set up a rusty can for a target and shot at it for a while. Then I went for a walk, circling toward the dunes. When I came in I had two more boxes of sand in my coat pocket. I wrapped and addressed them in the cabin, exactly as I had before, and took them down to the post office the next morning.

I kept it up all the rest of the week. I spent most of every day wandering around in the dunes, carrying the gun and a little canteen of water, and when I came in I'd have the boxes of sand in the pocket of my coat. The next morning I'd mail them. On Thursday I deliberately skipped going to the post office, and on Friday I mailed five.

The rifle and jack rabbit idea was a good one. They couldn't help wondering what kind of screwball it was who didn't have anything better to do than hunt jack rabbits. And from there it was only one jump to wondering what kind of *stupid* screwball it was who'd hunt for them in the only place in the county where there weren't any. There was no life of any kind in the sand dunes.

And there was one other angle to it. Goodwin belonged to a rifle club.

I had already located the rifle range. It was about a mile south of town, on a dirt road going toward the border. I went by it a couple of afternoons during my walks, but there was nobody shooting. I had an idea, though, there would be on Saturday or Sunday.

By the time Saturday came I was so full of the fact that I was going to see her that night that I had a hard time concentrating on anything. I went to the post office and mailed the two boxes. This time the clerk stared at me curiously, and when I went out two of the loafers who had been talking near the door broke off abruptly and fell into an awkward silence as I walked past. Somebody had begun to wonder if I was sending my laundry home a sock at a time.

After lunch I took the gun and started east of town on the highway, swung off it before I got to the dunes, and circled toward the rifle range. Before I got there I could hear the big rifles. It was in an open flat with a low ridge about four hundred yards behind it to stop the lead. As I came across the road I could see there were four of them taking turns on the firing line, shooting at a two-hundred-yard target. They had a spotting scope set up to check the shots.

When I got near enough to see them, I knew I was in luck. One of them was Goodwin. Another was the clerk from the hardware store. I didn't know the other two. I sat down on the ground well back out of the way and just watched, smoking a cigarette.

The clerk looked back after a while, and when he recognized me he grinned. "Got any jacks yet?" he asked.

"Not a one," I said. "Can't seem to hit them."

"They're tricky."

He came over in a few minutes and asked for a light. "Your name's Reichert, isn't it?"

"That's right," I said.

"Mine's Carson."

I got up and we shook hands. He called to Goodwin, who wasn't shooting at the moment. "Hey, Howard, why don't you let Reichert here shoot that bull gun once? I'm trying to sell him a rifle."

Goodwin came over and I shook hands with him, keeping my face still. It wasn't easy. There's a lot of Spanish blood in the family.

He was very pleasant, and there was a quiet sort of self-possession about him. "Here," he said. He slid a cartridge into the chamber of the gun and handed it to me. "Try it."

"You don't mind?"

He shook his head and smiled. "If I did, I wouldn't have asked you."

I walked over and lay prone on the sand, sliding my arm into the sling.

"You've shot them before?" It was more of a statement than a question.

"Only in the Army," I said.

"Hold right on," he said. "It's sighted for two hundred."

I didn't ask him about the trigger pull. It was lighter than I'd expected, and I missed the bull. It didn't matter. I didn't want to look like a sharpshooter. I worked the bolt, throwing the empty shell out on the sand, and watched to see if he picked it up. He did.

"Oh, you save those?" I asked innocently.

He grinned. "Sure. I reload them."

"You do?" I did a big take on it, as if I'd never heard of it.

"Yes. It's cheaper. And you can put up just the load you want."

"I never thought of that," I said. "It sounds interesting."

He agreed politely that it was, and I let it drop. To hurry now would be stupid and dangerous. But I had found the opening I was looking for.

Chapter Five

The night was still and cold, and the sand looked like snow in the moon-light. I flicked the cigarette lighter and looked at my watch. It was seven-ten.

I was standing near the highway about two miles east of town, where a dirt road turned off and ran south through the dunes. I was supposed to meet her here at seven. Having her come into town would be too risky, since she had spent a week there talking to practically everyone in that phony survey of hers. We couldn't be seen together.

A few cars went past, going very fast. I waited. In about five minutes I saw one coming more slowly. I watched eagerly. It might be Cathy, looking for the turnoff. It was. I was on the inside of the turn so the lights wouldn't swing across me, just in case it was somebody else. The car pulled off and stopped twenty or thirty yards from the highway. I could see the Cadillac fish-tails and the New York license plates. I jumped into the ruts and started trot-ting toward her.

The second pair of lights almost hit me. Out of the corner of my eye I saw them swinging as the other car made the turn, faster than she had, and I dived for the brush. I made it off the left side of the road just as they straightened out and spattered against the rear of the Cadillac. And then the car was be-yond me and sliding to a stop almost bumper to bumper with hers.

I came to my feet and onto the road, running toward them. There had been no time to think. It might be Charlie or Bolton, or both—but why another car? They'd have been with her. I couldn't even make myself say the other name. I was still eight or ten yards away, running desperately and silently on the sand, when the car door opened and a man got out. He was a small black figure in the moonlight and he was carrying something in his hand.

"All right, sweetie," he said. "Pile out."

I heard the low-throated rumble of power as she gunned the Cadillac. The rear wheels spun for an instant and sand flew up like spray. He shouted some-thing, and was bringing up the thing he held in his hand. Moonlight glinted on it. It was too big to be a revolver, and now he had both hands on it. I was still a long leap from him when I saw what it was. The car was moving now, at last, as he swung it, and then I fell on him.

I fell on him all over at once. It was like tackling an empty overcoat. He was just a bagful of light bones inside and he folded like a swatted spider. One bar-rel of the sawed-off shotgun went off with a roar as we crashed down, and then it was either under us or loose somewhere in the sand. I got to one knee, grabbed him by the shoulder, flipped him onto his back, and swung. He jerked and straightened out. It was Donnelly. In the moonlight he looked like a child who'd been starved to death.

I was raging, throwing my hands in every direction, trying to find the gun. It was right in front of me, oily-shining and black and deadly against the white gleam of the sand. I'd been too wild to see it. I grabbed it up and rammed the sawed-off barrels into his face. I heard a tooth let go so I shoved it, hard, and groped for the triggers. Then I thought a mountain lion had jumped on me.

My face was full of fur. I seemed to be wrapped in it. It was in my eyes and mouth, cool and suffocating and smelling faintly of perfume, and a voice was screaming in my ear. "Mike! No! Stop it, Mike!"

I had forgotten about her. She had her shoulder against my face and was trying to push me back while we grappled for the gun. I had sense enough left to throw it before we fell on it. Then I grabbed her.

"He tried to kill you!" I raged.

"You hot-headed Spanish idiot!"

"Are you hurt? Cathy, are you hurt?"

"No, I'm not hurt!"

"Well, stand back. Look the other way if you want to."

"Mike, stop it! Oh, my God, can't you see—"

"See what? He tried to kill you, didn't he?"

She straightened up, trying to get her breath. Her hair was wildly tousled and the big eyes were flashing angrily. "Listen, for the love of heaven, Mike. We've got more important things on our minds than that stupid hoodlum. Do you want to ruin everything?"

"You want to let him keep on till he gets lucky someday and hits you?" I asked furiously.

"He probably wasn't trying to shoot me. He was trying to scare me. That's how stupid he is."

The anger was turning against her now. At bottom, of course, it wasn't anger at all; it was fear. I'd been so scared when I saw him swinging that shotgun after her I was sick at my stomach now. "Well, do you mind," I asked coldly, "if I unload his gun before I give it back to him? I mean, if I'm very careful not to scratch it?"

She was suddenly contrite. "I'm sorry, Mike," she whispered. "Forgive me for screaming at you like that. But I didn't want you to kill him. I was scared."

I grabbed her. "*You* were scared?" That was as far as I got.

It was a few minutes before I thought of him. I looked down. "What are we going to do with this?" I said, and then suddenly became conscious of something I'd been hearing for the past minute or two. It was a freight train, laboring across the desert to the north of us. I heard it whistle for the yards at Wyecross. It was westbound, and it would probably stop there for water.

"Wait here," I said to Cathy, and stooped down for him.

She put a hand on my arm. I turned, and I could see her eyes go wide in the moonlight. "What are you going to do? Mike, you're not—"

"No," I said. "You're right. I'm just going to put him in the mail. It'll only take a few minutes."

I pulled his big overcoat together in front for a handle and picked him up like a bundle of old rags. He probably didn't weigh over a hundred pounds. The door of the car was still open. I heaved him in and pushed him over, away from the wheel. He sagged, and I leaned him against the other door.

"Be careful, Mike," she said anxiously.

The road was too narrow to turn around in, but there was enough moonlight to see my way out, backing. There were no cars in sight. I rammed out onto the highway, stopped, and shot ahead toward Wyecross. Just before I got into town I turned off to the right and went north toward the tracks. I could see the train and hear the brake shoes squealing as it slowed.

There wasn't anything out here except an abandoned work train on a siding. The water tank and station were several hundred yards to my left. I cut the lights and stopped. The freight was passing the other side of the cars on the siding, but I could hear it bumping and shuddering to a stop.

It won't be good, I thought, if I get caught loading something like this on a train. I got out of the car and looked carefully around. I could see the running lights of the caboose about a hundred yards away to my right, and a swinging lantern going up the other side of the train as a brakeman headed for the front end. He'd be past in a minute.

I opened the door and dragged Donnelly out. He was so limp he was hard to handle. I got him across my shoulder and hurried toward the work train. If I went around I'd pass too near the caboose, so the only thing to do was go under. I was panting now, and sweat was breaking out on my forehead. It was hard getting him up onto the roadbed with the ballast turning under my shoes.

I set him down at the end of one of the work cars. We were in shadow now, and I looked around again to be sure no one had seen me. The moonlit plain was empty except for Donnelly's car. As I bent down to roll him under the coupling between two cars he groaned and tried to sit up.

"What the hell?" he mumbled. Then he looked up. "Hey, you—"

"Remember me?" I asked, and swung. He didn't see the hand.

I massaged my hand and felt it for broken bones, then got down and rolled him between the rails. I crawled over the coupling and dragged him out on the other side. We were between the trains now, in deep shadow. Remembering the brakie, I squatted down on the ballast and looked for the lantern. It was far up near the front end.

I left him lying there and moved along the cars, looking for an empty. The third boxcar had a door open. I walked back and got him, letting his feet drag. The floor of the car was chest high, and I was getting tired now. I finally got him high enough and rolled him in. I took a long breath and leaned against the door for a moment, completely winded.

It took only a minute to slide the door in place, but I had to tug and push to get it positioned correctly so I could fasten the latch. Then I thought about the other one. It had been closed, but it might not be fastened. I ran to the end of the car and climbed through, across the coupling. The lantern was still far up at the other end of the train. I fastened the door and came back again.

Next stop, California, I thought, and then went back under the work train.

I ditched the car beside the highway near the dirt road, left the keys in it, and walked back to where she was. She was sitting in the Cadillac smoking a cigarette, and when she saw me coming she got out.

"Darling, is everything all right?"

"He's on his way to Los Angeles in his private car," I said. I walked over and picked up the gun and broke it to take out the two shells. Before I threw the unfired one into the brush, I looked at it, and it made me a little sick. It was a ten-gauge Magnum, with Number 2 shot. Anything hit at close range with that would look like a dish of raw hamburger. I buried the gun in the sand.

I walked back and stood looking at her. "Start giving," I said. "I want to know about Donnelly."

"Darling," she said innocently, "I've already told you. He's just a stupid thug who thinks he can scare money out of me."

I caught the fur coat with both hands and pulled her toward me. "Don't try any innocent double talk on me, you redheaded little hellcat. Maybe he can't scare you, but he can scare me. I want to know who he is and why he's following you, so we can do something about it. I saw him swinging that shotgun on you, and I don't intend to go through that again. Not twice in one lifetime."

"Mike," she said softly, "you *do* still like me, don't you?"

"Shut up," I said.

"I've missed you so terribly."

I shook her. "*Who is Donnelly?*"

"Mike, darling, it isn't anything, really. He just claims Jeff owed him some money before he was killed, when those men held him up. He hasn't got any proof of it, and I won't pay it."

It sounded fishy, and still it didn't. At least one part of it rang true—that about not paying it. Anybody who tried to fast-talk her out of a buck was odds-on to kill himself before he got through if he really took it seriously. And then, somewhere in all the anger and the fear for her going around in my mind, I was conscious of that same old crazy question: How could you be this much in love with a girl you fought with all the time and who kept the world in perpetual uproar? But I was. God help me.

It must have made me angrier. "All right," I said. "But how in hell does he manage to find you everywhere you go? He located you in New Orleans, and now out here in the middle of nowhere in this sand pile. How does he do it?

Do you write to him or something?"

She gestured impatiently. "Who cares, Mike? I tell you, he's just a cheap chiseler. Quit worrying about him. As for his finding me here, he probably just followed me from San Antonio."

"Well, you've got to get out of San Antonio before he can get back there."

"Oh, for heaven's sake, Mike," she flared up, "quit being such an old woman. We've got a job to do."

Here we go, I thought.

"Look, Cathy," I said. "For the love of Pete, let's quit knocking ourselves out, just for an hour or two, shall we? God knows why, but I've looked forward all week to seeing you. Maybe I'm just stupid that way. And in five minutes we're going at each other like a couple of punch drunk pugs. I'm sorry I lost my temper. It just scared me. Donnelly, I mean. Let's try to forget the whole damn thing for a little while."

"All right, Mike," she said contritely. "I'm sorry too."

We got back in the car and drove on down the road about a mile until we were out of sight of the highway and lost in the rolling white immensity of the sand. I saw the dry remains of an old mesquite, and broke off enough limbs to build a fire behind one of the dunes. There was a robe in the back of the car, and I spread it on the sand, up against the slope before the fire. It was beautiful and incredibly still in the wintry moonlight. It was wonderful. She had a bottle of champagne and a couple of glasses in the car. I opened it and we drank some of it, watching the fire and talking. Firelight was shining in her eyes, and she was still the most beautiful girl I had ever seen. It occurred to me that this was corny, that girls were always having firelight shine in their eyes while they turned beautiful, but when I tried to look at it objectively, nothing changed. She was still beautiful, and I was in love with her.

"How did we ever manage to make such a mess of things, Cathy?" I asked after a while. "Let's go to El Paso for the weekend. Look, we could be married again."

"That would be wonderful, Mike," she said. "But not until after we get through here. You can't leave now. This is too important to take any chances."

That about sums it up, I thought, trying to suppress the anger and not start another battle. Trifling incidentals like being blasted at with a ten-gauge shotgun, or brushing off a package-deal proposition and proposal, are entirely beside the point and can't be allowed to interfere with the main objective. Nothing mattered except sandbagging Goodwin and then ganging up on Lachlan.

No, that wasn't quite fair, I reminded myself. The thought of the two of them getting away with what they had done haunted me too, and if it didn't ride me all the time the way it did her, it was probably because I was lazy and inclined to take the easy way. Maybe if I'd quit trying to pick her to pieces and take a good look at myself.... Maybe I was the one who wasn't so hot. I always let things slide.

"You see, don't you, Mike?" she said. "I mean, that we've got to do this first?"

"All right," I said wearily. "I just forgot for the moment that you're the girl of destiny. I'll take it up through channels."

"You're a lamb," she said, making a face at me. "And I do love you. Why do you think I'm staying in San Antonio so I can be near you?"

"Well, don't crowd me out of my side of the bed," I said.

"Stop grumbling, darling. Now, tell me about Goodwin. I mean, could you detect any curiosity at all when you met him out there at the rifle range? And don't forget, never hurry him. You have to play it hard to get all the way."

Progress report and pep talk in the moonlight, I thought bitterly as I lay in bed in the bleak cabin afterward. Vice-president making a swing through the territory to keep the district managers on their toes. Damn her. But what about San Antonio that night? She *could* relax and be human when she wanted to.

I cursed myself. That was nice. So I was finding out all over again all the things I'd learned in two years of being married to her and a lifetime of knowing her, and now they were big revelations. We were just going around again. She was a whirlpool I was trapped in. I ground the cigarette savagely against the ash tray and tried to get back to Goodwin.

It began to break faster than I had expected. Little things tip you off. You turn your head suddenly while walking along the street and find the two people you have just passed are staring after you and talking. You come in the door and a sudden hush falls over a group of three or four men enjoying some joke along the counter in the restaurant. You get a lot of innocent sounding and thinly disguised questions along with simple transactions like buying a pack of cigarettes or picking up your laundry. Are you going to work here? How do you like our town? Good, healthy climate, isn't it?

People were beginning to wonder what I was doing here. And what in the name of God was in those boxes I mailed every day?

On Tuesday I mailed four of them. The clerk at the window smiled. "You're our best customer," he said, with a lame attempt at joking. "We ought to give you a rate."

"Oh?" I said coldly.

During the week I dropped into the bank a couple of times to cash small checks, and both times Goodwin looked up from his paper work to nod and smile. And then, on Saturday, I got another break. Taking a chance he'd be out at the rifle range, I put two of the larger boxes in my coat pocket before I took off on my daily walk east of town. Filled with sand, they weighed over five pounds each.

Late in the afternoon I circled around to the rifle range. I was in luck. Goodwin was there, with two other men. I leaned my .22 against a mesquite and sat down to watch them. After a while Goodwin asked me if I'd like to try the gun again. Before I shot, I took off the coat with its bulging pockets and left it by the .22.

When the session broke up he offered me a lift back to town, as I had hoped. I put the rifle and coat on the back seat and got in up front with him.

"Well, how do you like our town?" he asked, as we wound through the mesquite on the little dirt road.

"Just fine," I said. "It's just what I was looking for."

He didn't ask me what it was I was looking for. I didn't think he would. He was by nature rather reserved himself, apparently well educated, and had better manners than the town loafers and most of the other natives. He might be curious, but he wouldn't pry.

"We're trying to build up our rifle club," he said. "How'd you like to join?"

I hesitated a little. "Thanks," I said. "It sounds fine, but I'll be frank with you. Those guns are a little steep for me right now."

He nodded. "Yes, they are pretty expensive. But it's a fine hobby, and keeps you out in the open." He stopped suddenly, as if he'd said more than he intended.

I knew then it was beginning to work. He'd thought about me. And he'd decided it was health that brought me here, or rather the lack of it. The next thing, of course, was to make him wonder if that *was* it.

"Well, anyway," he said, "come on out on Saturday afternoons and take a few shots with this gun of mine."

We were in town now, but he ran on out to the end of the street and dropped me off in front of the motel. I thanked him and got out, purposely not looking toward the back seat where I'd left the rifle and coat.

He started to drive off. "Oh," I called out, waving my arm and running toward the car. "I forgot my stuff."

"Sure thing," he said. He turned around in the seat and reached for the coat, to pass it out the front window.

"No, that's all right, I'll get it," I said hurriedly. I reached for the handle of the rear door, but let him beat me to it. He picked up the coat, and I saw his arm sag at the unexpected weight of it. Almost involuntarily his eyes swept down toward it, but there was nothing to see except the square outlines of the boxes in the pockets.

Chapter Six

In a couple of days he invited me out to the house. For dinner, he said, and he'd show me his workshop, where he did his reloading.

He had a nice place, a big two-story house out on the edge of town about three blocks off the main drag. I met his wife. She was a young blonde who wasn't as young or as blonde as she had been, but she was nice, and a wonderful cook. She did water colors, and she was a bullfight fan. I admired the landscapes she had done, and we had a good session with the *corridas*. I told her I'd lived in Mexico a couple of years, working for some company I never quite mentioned.

They had swallowed the idea by this time that I had come out here because my health had gone back on me, though we very pointedly never talked about it. I think they felt sorry for me. I knew, of course, that he'd also heard about the strange boxes I was always mailing, because everybody knows everything in a town of that size, but he didn't mention them.

I let it ride along about a week, going out in the dunes every day with the little gun, and continuing to mail the boxes. They had me out to the house again on Saturday night for dinner, and to return the compliment I took them to the restaurant and to the movies. We were getting quite chummy. They liked me, and, oddly enough, I liked them when I wasn't thinking about the thing he had done.

Cathy met me twice that week, but it was just the same old pep talk. She was wild to know how it was coming along, and full of suggestions as to what to do next.

It was near the end of the following week that I knew the time had come to let him have the stinger. I'd walked into the restaurant late one evening, and two men who were playing the pin-ball machine near the door didn't see me come in. I passed close behind them and as I went past I heard one of them say, "It's rabbit feet, I tell you. Don't he spend all his time huntin' jack rabbits? He's got a friend in New York sells 'em for him." I heard them laugh as I went over and sat down at the counter.

All right, boys, I thought, I'll clear it up for you. After I'd eaten I went back to the motel and started getting it ready. I got out the bottle of sulphuric acid I'd brought from New Orleans and mixed a little with some water in a glass jar to the approximate strength of battery solution. Then, taking out a cardboard box—one of the larger ones—I wet it along the corners and seams with the solution and let it dry. Filling it with sand I'd brought in during the afternoon, I wrapped it with paper, tied the parcel with white string, and addressed it, just as I had done with all the others. To finish it off, I put a drop of the acid solution on the string in three or four different places, let it set for a minute or two, and wiped it off. It was ready.

In the morning I waited until after eleven before I started downtown with it, to be sure he'd be in the bank. I had to handle it carefully. He was at his desk, and he looked up and waved as I walked in. I set it down on the edge of the glass-topped stand, got out my checkbook, and started to write a check, keeping my left elbow near the parcel and taking a long time to make it out. It'd be a lot more effective if he came over, though it would work whether he did or not. I was in luck. He did.

I heard the gate in the railing open and close, and then his footsteps coming up behind me. I tore the check out, paying no attention.

"Say, Reichert, Mrs. Goodwin told me to ask you out tonight for some *frijoles* and *cabrito*," he said behind me as he came up.

I swung around. "Thanks. That sounds—" I began, just as my elbow hit the box and knocked it off. "Damn!" I said explosively, and lunged for it. It was too late. It hit the tile floor, and the acid-weakened box came apart across one side like a dropped squash. Sand spilled out onto the floor.

He looked down, and wasn't able to control the amazement on his face. Then he looked at me. I flushed and stammered something, and then bent down hurriedly and began trying to scoop the sand back into the box, as if trying to cover up while I thought of something.

"I'm sorry about the mess," I said uncomfortably, when I stood up. "It's— well, you see, my niece, back in New York, she's bedridden. I was sending her this box of sand to—well, she colors it, you see, and uses it in a sort of Navajo sand-painting idea."

"Oh, I see," he said in a tone that meant he didn't see at all. "Well, don't bother with it. The janitor'll clean it up. It's too bad it broke, though." He paused, then tried an embarrassed joke. "One thing about it, you can find plenty more around here."

I managed a hollow grin. "Yes, that's right, isn't it?"

I went back to the motel with the remains of the box. It had gone off beautifully. He knew I was lying, of course. That was the most obvious part of it. And then, after an hour or so, he'd probably decide I wasn't crazy, in spite of the way it looked. It would really begin to get him about that time.

Try it, pal, I thought. It's not as direct as diluting a concrete mix, but it's interesting when you work on it—and tricky.

I called up and begged off on the dinner date. I said I had a bad headache. The next day was Friday. I didn't go out to the dunes at all, or mail anything at the post office. Saturday was the same. I sat around the drugstore most of the time, reading all the new magazines. I didn't even go out to the rifle range.

Sunday morning I decided I'd let him wait long enough, and I could try it. This time, instead of taking any boxes, I stuffed my pocket with about a dozen little cloth bags like tobacco sacks, a bunch of string, and some tags. I took the gun and walked east on the highway, the way I always did, left it before I hit the sand dunes, and circled to get into them some distance from the road.

This was a phase of it now that I didn't have much control over. If I'd played it right up to this point, I should have him now. He should be ready to go along with me. I was doing something crazy, something he couldn't figure out, and I was doing it on his land. The fact that it was his land and that I not only hadn't told him about it but had actually lied about it should be enough to overcome his natural reluctance toward spying on anybody. If I'd guessed it right, it would be Frankie or Johnnie who'd let him know when I went out there again.

As I wandered around I kept watching the highway. Time went by and I didn't see anything of him. After a while I began to worry. Had I bungled the whole thing? Hadn't I made him curious as to what I was up to? If he wasn't interested now, the whole thing was a fizzle.

In another quarter hour I was sure it had gone sour. And then I saw a car that could have been his coming down the highway. I watched it out of the corner of my eye. It went behind some scraggly mesquites growing along the fence, and it didn't come out. I felt a tingle of excitement. We were getting him.

In a moment I saw the glint of sunlight on something near the end of the mesquites. I knew what that was. He had the spotting scope with him. It was a twenty-power job, and with it he could see what I was doing as well as if he were sitting in my lap. I began pacing, taking long steps like a man measuring something. At the end of twenty strides I squatted down, scooped up some sand, put it in one of the bags, and tied it. Then I fastened on a tag and made a show of writing something on it. Of course, he couldn't see the tag, but it'd take him only a few minutes to figure it out.

I took twenty steps more and repeated the whole thing. I was going toward him all the time, but before I began to get near enough to scare him I turned ninety degrees and paced off the next twenty parallel to the highway. After tagging this bag and putting it into my pocket I made another right-angled turn, away from him.

He'd know now. Anybody with even normal intelligence could see what I was doing. I was laying out the whole area in an immense grid and picking up a sample of sand every twenty yards. It was completely systematic.

I went on two or three more laps and then sat down on a sand dune with my back to him to eat my sandwich and give him a chance to get away.

All right, pal, I thought, it's up to you now.

I didn't have long to wait. About four o'clock Monday afternoon Frankie or Johnnie came back to the cabin and said I was wanted on the telephone. I went up to the office. It was Goodwin, all right.

"Mrs. Goodwin and I wondered if you'd like to come out and try potluck with us this evening if you're free," he said.

"Oh," I said hesitantly. "Uh— Thank you very much."

"About seven, then."

"That would be nice."

I wondered how well I'd carry it off. This was tricky, and Goodwin was no fool. There was one thing in my favor, however, the same thing there had been all the time, and that was that there couldn't possibly be any reason for my trying to kid him. He owned the land, didn't he?

I dug the letter out of the bag, stuck it in my pocket, and walked over to Goodwin's. The moon wasn't up yet, and it was cold and dark and my heels rang on the sidewalk. Goodwin let me in, and we went into the living room. There was a nice blaze going in the fireplace. Mrs. Goodwin came in with some drinks on a tray and we all sat down.

I had to beat him to the punch, to make it look better, but I had to be sure he was ready, that he had figured it out. I was making a big show of being intensely preoccupied with something and under a bad strain. During the few minutes of small talk over the drinks I appeared not to hear half that was said to me and was always waking up with an "Oh? I'm sorry.... Beg pardon?" I had something on my mind, and I was burning. They could see it. Or I hoped they could; I wasn't too sure I'd ever win an Academy Award with it.

He waited until she left the room to see about dinner. The minute she was gone he put down his glass, lit a cigar, and looked across at me with a probing glance that meant business.

"There's something I want to talk to you about, Reichert," he said.

Well, here we go, I thought. I broke in on him. "There's something I've got to tell you, too. I've been trying to make up my mind about it all day. I suppose you'd call it a question of loyalty to the people you work for, and just how far that loyalty is supposed to stretch before it breaks."

"And who is it you work for?" he asked.

"Occidental Glass," I said.

He made an impatient gesture with his hand, and swore under his breath. "That was the thing I never could get," he said. "Glass. It was just so obvious, I guess, I couldn't see it."

I jerked my head up and looked at him. "Then you knew what I was doing?" I asked in surprise.

He smiled. "You're probably a good engineer, Reichert, but you'll never set the world on fire as an undercover investigator. You give yourself away everywhere you turn."

"Oh?" I said uncomfortably. "Well, what I wanted to tell you was that I'm not working for them any more. I've sent in my resignation."

"Why?" he asked.

"For two reasons. The first is that I couldn't tell you what I'm going to, as long as I'm drawing their pay. But the big one is that they've backed down on a promise they made me. If this thing proved up and we built a plant here, I was supposed to have a free hand with the whole design, and I was to have complete charge of production." I fished out the letter. Charlie had written it, and where he'd got the Occidental Glass Company letterhead only Charlie would know. "Apparently office politics got in the way."

I passed it over to him. "Take a look at that last paragraph. They're 'very sorry, but....'"

He read it, glanced again at the letterhead, and handed it back. "It's a rotten deal," he said. "And I'm sorry, Reichert."

I nodded, waiting. In about a minute he ought to get past my sob story to the real news. He did. His eyes jerked around to me again and he said, "But what about the plant? Are they going to put one up? Here?"

I stared at him, took a sip of my drink, and put it down, taking my time all the way. "If they don't," I said, "somebody else will. That's what I wanted to tell you. You've been a good friend since I've been here, and after the deal they've handed me I don't see that I owe them enough to help them hand you the same one."

"You mean—that exploration work you did, it proved up?"

I nodded. "You can just about name your own price for that sand deposit. Within reason, of course."

It's just as Charlie says. No matter who they are, the minute you dangle the big money in front of them they begin to get the fever. Anybody will go for it, if you make it look right.

"Are you sure?" he asked, trying to keep down the excitement in his voice. "I mean, it looks like any sand."

"They didn't want it back at the lab just to look at. If they wanted to look at sand they could go out to Coney Island."

"Then the lab reports were good? But why? I mean, what makes it valuable?"

"It's technical," I said. "But what it boils down to is a question of purity; that is, the ratio of silica to foreign matter and undesirable grit, dust, organic matter, and so on. They're working on a new line of high-silica glass—that's the stuff with the low coefficient of expansion—and this sand of yours out here is made to order for it. Of course, it isn't pure silica, because sand deposits like that don't exist, but it's so near it's unbelievable. They'll go plenty high to get it."

He was leaning forward, staring at me. "How high do you think they'll go?"

"They'll cry, but you can get a quarter of a million for it."

He whistled. "My God, Reichert." Then the businessman began to take hold again. "But why did you tell me? I mean, what's your deal?"

I shrugged. "No deal. I don't like what they did to me, and since I'm not working for them any more, I'd like to see you get what it's worth. Of course, I'm not implying they were going to steal it from you, or anything like that, but they probably won't offer over fifty thousand until you make them come across."

"Well, don't think I won't remember it. I mean, if it comes off and I get any-thing like that for it. But do you think they'll try to get in touch with me?"

"Of course," I said. "And it won't be long. I'll tell you why. My resigna-tion's already in the mail, and when they get that they'll be out here as if their clothes were on fire. You see what I'm driving at? There are several things I could do. I could buy an option on the land myself. Or, what's more likely, since I don't have that kind of money, go to work for some other glass com-pany, and let them in on it in return for the job Occidental was supposed to give me."

"By God, you're right," he said. "They couldn't take a chance, with what you know about it."

It was that easy.

Early the next morning I sent off the corny telegram to Charlie's address in Houston. "Congratulations to the lucky couple. May all your troubles be little ones." That was the code for him to call his friend in New York, who'd wire Goodwin from there that the head of the Occidental Glass Company's legal department, who was en route to the West Coast, would like to stop off in Wyecross and discuss a business matter.

It was like shooting quail on the ground. Wednesday night Goodwin called me, full of excitement and almost sputtering. He'd received the wire from New York, all right, and then another from the lawyer himself, from Hous-ton. He'd be in on the nine A.M. westbound the next day.

"All right," I said. "You're a businessman. You know what to do when you hold a hand like that."

"Yes," he said happily. "You bet I do."

I was looking out the window of the drugstore the next morning after the train came in and saw Goodwin go by with him. Bolton looked like the legal department of Fort Knox, in a camel's hair coat that probably cost as much as a small car.

He had to stay all day, since there wasn't another train until nine P.M. About nine-fifteen Goodwin called. He'd just got back from the station, see-ing him off. "I did it," he said, a little wildly.

"Good for you," I said.

"He knew you'd told me, but there wasn't anything he could do. He'd probably have killed you if he could have found you. I started him off at three hundred thousand, and he finally gave up at two-seventy-five."

"The deal already made?" I asked.

"Not yet. They have to have a meeting of the board. But he says it's almost certain to go through. They've got an option on it at that price, for ten days."

"Fine," I said. "That'll give you just about time enough to have your title searched. Then you're in."

I put that in to help him along. He still hadn't got it. He was going to, as soon as it soaked in, and as I said, it was poison. It could kill you if you had a bad heart. It wasn't until the next afternoon around three that it finally got to him. He called me at the motel.

"Reichert," he said wildly, "can you get over here right away? Something terrible's come up, and I've got to have some advice. I'm trying to get hold of my lawyer now, and maybe he'll be here by the time you are."

"Sure," I said. "I'll be right over."

He'd remembered it at last. The land was his, all right, and the title was clear, but about five months ago he'd sold the oil rights to a lease speculator by the name of Wallace Caffery.

The thing that made it bad was that the lease said "mineral rights." And Wallace Caffery, of course, was Wolford Charles.

Chapter Seven

It wasn't as dumb as it looked, and actually he probably hadn't forgotten it at all. It was just that it didn't matter. Land was often sold without the mineral rights, which around here meant simply oil, as that was the only mineral they had. Occidental Glass just wanted the sand. And sand wasn't a mineral. Was it? *Was it?*

The lawyer was already there by the time I made it. They had a copy of the contract out, and Goodwin was slowly going crazy. The lawyer explained it to me.

"I'd have to look it up before I could say definitely," he told Goodwin, "but just offhand I'd say you haven't got a chance." He turned to me again. "What is sand, Reichert? Technically, I mean. Rock, isn't it? Silicia—sil-something."

"Silicon," I said, praying Charlie's coaching wouldn't go back on me now. "Actually, it's the oxide. Silicon dioxide is the correct name for it. It's nonorganic, of course. Physically, it's nothing but small fragments of quartz."

The lawyer shook his head. "There goes your ball game. Quartz is mineral to anybody."

It was murder. Just a little matter of $275,000 thrown out the window for the miserable handful of chicken feed Caffery'd given him for the oil rights on land where there'd never been any oil and never would be any because there were two dry holes on it already. You could see it in his face. The eyes were beginning to look haunted. Pal, I thought, it took a long time, but how does it feel?

His only hope, of course, was to find Caffery and buy back the lease. And he had just ten days to do it. The only thing he knew was that Caffery was a small-time speculator and wildcatter who operated out of a hole-in-the-wall office in Houston when he wasn't operating out of his suitcase. He grabbed the next train east. He was gone two days, and when he came back his eyes were no longer haunted. They were wild. His face was haggard.

He'd found Caffery, all right. And Caffery had just laughed at him. So there'd been some big oil company geologists snooping around the land, and now he wanted to pull a fast one and get it back? Fat chance.

If I hadn't kept reminding myself of the thing he'd helped do to my father and Dunbar, I'd have felt sorry for him. He could lose his sanity. It was more wealth than he'd ever dreamed of, and it was lying just beyond his outstretched fingers in a nightmare where he couldn't move.

That was Monday. He kept calling Caffery and getting the brush-off every day until Thursday, when some girl who answered the phone said Caffery had gone out of town and she didn't know where he was or when he'd be back. You had to admit it; Charlie was a genius. It was magnificent. The final turn of the screw came within an hour or two after that last, useless telephone call. It was a telegram from El Paso, sent by Bolton, of course. He had received instructions from the president of Occidental Glass to take up the option, and would be in town on the nine-thirty eastbound Friday night with a certified check for $275,000. If you'd touched Goodwin he'd have twanged like a bowstring, or blown up before your eyes.

I was at his house when it came, and it was an awful thing to watch. He had to fight himself to keep from babbling and becoming incoherent when he talked. He was sweating as he called Houston again. He asked me to listen in on the extension, just in case Caffery was there, so I could see if I could detect any signs of weakening. The stupid girl popped chewing gum in his ear. Mr. Caffery? No, he was still out of town. But wait, come to think of it, he had called in from some little town just about an hour ago. She thought he was down there where he was drilling an oilcat well. No, she was trying to think of the name of the town, but she couldn't remember it. It sounded like Snookum. Was there a town that sounded like Snookum? It was on the coast somewhere, not too far from Houston—she thought. There was something familiar about her voice, even under the seven layers of stupidity.

I got off the extension and we both started tearing wildly through road maps, looking for it, while Goodwin kept the long distance line open. We couldn't locate anything that looked like it. Goodwin went back on the phone and pleaded with her. Couldn't she possibly think of it?

Oh, yes, she said; she'd just remembered. She had written it down and forgotten she had. And wasn't it funny, it didn't sound like Snookum at all. It sounded like Cuddly. The name of the town was Ludley. Mr. Caffery would be at the hotel there. There was only one hotel, she thought. Oh, you're welcome, she said sweetly, and popped her gum. God, I thought, Charlie must have hired Shirley Booth for the job. Then it rang on me at last. It was Cathy.

So she was in San Antonio, was she? So she could be near me? I tried to stifle the red blaze of anger.

Goodwin finally got through to the hotel at Ludley. Caffery was out. Then, the next time, his line was busy. I listened in on the extension when he got through to him at last.

It sounded as if a battle was going on in the hotel room, or they were having a stevedores' union meeting. If Charlie was making all the noise alone, he should have been a one-man band.

"Hello! Hello! Yes, Caffery speaking," he yelled. "Who is it? Who? Goodwin? What the hell do *you* want?... Wait a minute! Wait a minute!" His voice became muffled, as if he'd put a hand over the transmitter, but we could still hear him. "Pipe down! Give me a chance to answer the phone. You'll get your money."

Then he was back on the line. "Who is this now? Oh, Goodwin." He broke into a string of profanity. "How many times do I have to tell you? It's not for sale. I wouldn't take a hundred thousand. *What!*" This last was apparently for somebody in the room. We could hear his voice going on, muffled. "Look, this is none of your business. I told you I'd get it, and I'll do it. Go on out there and start fishing for that bit. I tell you my credit'll be good anywhere in the state the minute we bring it in."

He was yelling into the telephone again. "Look, Goodwin, where can I get hold of you if I have to? Will you be at home? All right! All right! But don't call me again. I'm busy." He hung up.

Goodwin was limp and ready to collapse over the table. "What do you think, Reichert?" was all he could say.

"I don't know," I said. "I think he's in a jam himself, from the way it sounds. Sweat it out. I've got a hunch he'll come to you." Some hunch, I thought. Charlie was due to make his appearance just after eight tomorrow morning, according to the schedule.

It was all over except tying up the loose ends and actually getting the money, and it was time to be getting ready to run. Bolton was already in the clear, of course, since he was in El Paso. As soon as Charlie got his hands on the cash, he'd head for El Paso, and Cathy was to come by from San Antonio at noon of the day we pulled it off and pick me up, and we'd meet them in El Paso at the hotel. We'd split up and be out of the state before Goodwin got wise, which would be when he met the train Friday at nine-thirty and there was nobody on it.

Mrs. Goodwin called me the next morning around seven-thirty. Would I come over and just talk to Goodwin? He'd been up all night, waiting for a call from Caffery, and there hadn't been any. Maybe I could help her calm him down before he collapsed.

I went over in a hurry, knowing Charlie'd be there at eight. Goodwin was on the telephone again, haggard and hollow-eyed. He had the hotel at Ludley, but Caffery had checked out. He put the phone back in its cradle, let out a long, hopeless sigh, and put his head down in his hands. He was whipped.

I was looking out the window when the mud-spattered car drove up in front of the house. I saw Charlie get out, and put my hand on Goodwin's shoulder. "Say, is this your man?" I nodded toward the street.

He came alive as if I'd prodded him with a high-voltage cable. "Hell, yes," he said excitedly, springing up. "But you'll have to get out of sight. We don't want to make him any more suspicious than he is now. I'll tell you. Go up there at the head of the stairs."

I made it just as the doorbell rang. By peeking around the corner of the landing, I could see them. Charlie was wearing khaki pants and boots and a leather jacket with mud on it, and he looked as if he hadn't shaved for three days or slept in a week. His eyes were red, and there were lines of weariness around his mouth. Charlie was a perfectionist.

He was magnificent. Watching him and listening, I was conscious of thinking what an actor the stage lost when Charlie became a crook. He was being crucified. Nobody kept faith with him. Goodwin was taking advantage of him. He'd bought the lease in good faith, and now Goodwin had found out some oil company wanted it, and his creditors were hounding him, and.... He could make you cry.

He said eighty thousand. Goodwin, recovering a little of his business sense now that there was hope, said thirty. They went at it again. Charlie came to a dead standstill at sixty-five thousand, and Goodwin finally had to meet it. Then Charlie said it had to be in cash, and he had to have it within an hour so he could get started back to the well. Goodwin agreed, but said it would take two hours. The bank wouldn't be open until ten.

Charlie nodded. "All right," he said wearily. Then he went on, with great bitterness. "Don't think I don't know what you're doing to me. Some big oil company wants to put down a well out there, don't they? Well, brother, you couldn't have beat me if we hadn't lost a bit in that hole last week."

To calm him, Mrs. Goodwin asked him to come out in the kitchen and have a cup of coffee. I sneaked down the stairs and left as soon as they were out of the room. When I was out in the street I let out a big sigh. I was weak myself.

Back at the motel I started throwing things in the two bags. She'd be here at twelve. I stopped, thinking how it would be now, with nothing to keep us apart. On our way to San Francisco, to hunt down Lachlan, we'd stop off in Reno as we'd planned. We would be married. I looked at my watch. It was only nine-fifteen. Keep your shirt on, I thought; Charlie hasn't even got the money yet.

At a quarter to eleven Goodwin called. He was almost hysterical with joy. "I'd ask you to come over, if it weren't that you're probably worn out too. I'd like for you to see this lease burning up in the fireplace."

"So it's all set?" I asked.

"He just left, five minutes ago. Boy, talk about your photo finishes! And, say, Reichert, don't think I'm going to forget you for all you've done."

No, you probably won't, pal, I thought, as I hung up—any more than I've forgotten you. It's going to be a little rugged around nine-thirty tonight when nobody gets off that train.

I was all packed. By eleven-thirty I was straining my ears for the sound of tires on the gravel outside. About ten minutes to twelve I heard a car come swinging in. I jumped up and threw the door open. It was somebody else. I sat down again, feeling the impatience mount.

By twelve-thirty I was chain-smoking cigarettes and wearing a path in the shabby rug. God knows she'd never been anywhere on time in her life, but she *couldn't* be late today. This was the day we'd been looking forward to for nearly a month. We had to get going.

She didn't come. It was two o'clock. It was three. I'd long since passed the stage where I could sit still at all. I felt as if all the nerves in my body had worked through and were on the outside of my skin. She was dead. She'd been killed in a wreck. I couldn't keep Donnelly out of my mind. She wouldn't listen to me, so he had gone back and found her. He'd killed her. I thought of that ten-gauge shotgun, and shuddered. He was capable of anything. Why hadn't I made her listen?

No, how did I know where she'd been? She'd said she was going to be in San Antonio, and still that was her voice over the phone from Houston.

How could I even find out what had happened? I had to get back there some way. It wasn't until then that the whole thing balled up and hit me. I sat down on the bed, feeling the weakness and the sick feeling come up through me. I'd been worried only about her, but what about myself, too? I couldn't go anywhere. I was trapped. She *might* be all right, but I was a sitting duck.

The bus had gone through twenty minutes ago, and there wouldn't be another one in either direction until eleven o'clock tonight. And by nine-thirty Goodwin would knew he had been taken.

It was about as near to complete panic as I'd ever been. For a few minutes I couldn't think at all. The only thing my mind could get hold of was that I was the sucker, the fall guy, the one they'd thrown to the wolves. They'd gone off and left me. No, I tried to tell myself, *she* wouldn't. She wouldn't have left me stranded like this.

But that meant, then, that something had happened to her.

I tried to calm down. I was in danger enough, without losing my head completely. There'd be the westbound train through at nine. But what good would that do me? Goodwin would probably already be at the station, waiting to meet the eastbound. Or if he wasn't, at least a dozen people would see me get on it. As soon as they told him, he'd know the truth, and police would be waiting for me at some station up the line before I got to El Paso. Even if there were a bus through, the same thing would happen.

Time went on in its slow crawl around the rim of my watch. There was no hope now that she was coming. It was four-fifteen. I watched the small oblong of yellow sunlight from the window creep up the wall as the sun went down. It was like sitting in a cell. I shuddered.

I couldn't just sit there and wait for them. I'd have to make a run for it some way. Maybe I could hitch a ride if I got out on the highway. Then I thought of it—that freight, the one I'd put Donnelly on. It would be along, westbound, a little after seven.

But I had to get away and get on it without being seen. The only way to do it was just to fade, and let them wonder afterward when I'd left and which way I'd gone. The only trouble, however, was that there was no way out of here except the drive and archway in front. The cabins and garages were joined in a solid wall all the way around. I'd have to leave the bags. No, there was a way to do it. The bathroom had a small window that looked out onto the open prairie to the east.

I sweated out another hour and a half until it was dark. I looked carefully around the harsh little cubicle to be sure I hadn't left anything that would identify me. The only things were the .22 rifle and the rest of the sand boxes. I put on the topcoat, carried the bags into the bathroom, and cut the lights.

I opened the window and then waited while my eyes became accustomed to the darkness. Two or three cabins up the line there was light pouring from a window, and I could hear a radio playing. When I could see a little in the faint light from the stars, I eased out the window feet first, and then lifted the bags out. I closed the window very gently and slipped away, angling a little to my right to stay clear of the highway.

It was slow going, dodging the clumps of mesquite and prickly pears, but I was in the clear and nobody had seen me leave. After about two hundred yards I swung toward the highway again. It was frosty and still, and in the cold starlight I could see the fog of my breath. I waited beside the road until no cars were in sight, then hurried across and into the desert on the other side.

It was about a half mile to the tracks. The suitcases were heavy, and I stopped once or twice to catch my breath. I tried not to think about Cathy. Every time I saw her I saw Donnelly swinging that murderous shotgun and I'd feel sick. I thought of Charlie and Bolton, safe in El Paso with $65,000 in their pockets, laughing probably, while I struggled through the cactus to catch a freight that might get me out of town before the whole thing caved in on me. Rage would come boiling up and take me by the throat. I'd done the job, and now they'd run out on me.

It didn't make sense. Sure, they didn't care what happened to me, but didn't they have brains enough to know I'd talk if the police caught me? *Talk?* I'd scream. I'd sing like a nightingale. But then, what difference would it make to them? They'd be gone, and you can do a lot of traveling with sixty-five thousand dollars.

I set the bags down for a minute and thought about it very coldly. If I didn't get caught, they were going to need a railroad ticket a lot longer than that.

When I hit the old work train, I swung around the end of it. I walked up it to about where I'd boosted Donnelly onto the freight, and ducked in between two cars. I set the bags down and flipped the cigarette lighter to look at my watch. It should be along in about a half hour.

Chapter Eight

It was a night that would never end. I sat on the suitcases in a dusty box-car that rattled through cold darkness and then jolted and screeched to in-terminable stops every thirty or forty miles. When I couldn't stand the cold any longer I'd get up and walk back and forth, swinging my arms and blow-ing on my hands. I ran out of cigarettes.

I tried to keep the worry about Cathy from driving me crazy. The terrible part of it was that maybe I'd never know what happened. I had to run, and I couldn't look back or wait.

I thought of Bolton. And I thought of Charlie.

Maybe it was the anger that kept me from freezing.

Just at dawn we slowed for the yards at El Paso. I tossed the two bags out and jumped. After I'd picked them up I hurried out of the yards. Nobody saw me. There was an all night café open on the second street. I went in, ordered some coffee, and bought a package of cigarettes. I called a cab.

"Bus station," I said when it came. The sun was coming up now. Maybe the bus and railroad stations were being watched, but I had to take a chance on it. There was no other way. I'd already thrown away the steel-rimmed glasses, which helped a little, and I was dressed differently than I had been in Wyecross. There weren't many people around this early in the morning. I shot a quick glance around, ready to ease out, but there wasn't anybody who looked like a plain-clothes cop. I checked the bags and went into the wash-room to clean up a little and beat some of the dust out of my topcoat. I counted the money I had left. It was less than two hundred dollars. I had to get to Reno. Manners would give me a job, dealing dice. And Reno would be far enough away.

There would be a westbound bus leaving in an hour and ten minutes. I'd better not hang around the bus station, though, in case they were shaking it down now and then. I went out in the street and thought of Bolton and Char-lie again and felt the rage take hold of me. There wouldn't be a chance they'd still be here, but I went into a drugstore telephone booth and started calling the hotels.

After I'd called three I gave up. Even if they were here they wouldn't be registered under their own names. The thing to do was forget them until I got out of this jam. I tried to. It wasn't much good.

It was too early to get a shave. I went into a hotel coffee shop to try to eat a little breakfast before bus time. I've got to quit looking behind me, I thought. The way I was acting was enough to make a cop suspicious even if he'd never heard of me.

The waitress at this end of the counter was slow getting to me because she was working on an order a bellboy was waiting for. I started to get up to go out to the newsstand for a paper while I was waiting. Maybe there'd be something about it in the papers. Then I looked back at the waitress for some reason I couldn't figure out. What was it? I saw it then. It was the order. It was the two halves of a Persian melon and a big silver pot of coffee.

What if the odds were a thousand to one against it? I didn't even stop to think. I followed the boy across the lobby and into the elevator. When he got out on the fourth floor I went in the other direction, pretending to be looking for a number, until he was halfway down the corridor. I turned then and watched him. He knocked at a door and in a minute it opened and he went in. I walked past it and looked at the number, and went on around the corner. When I heard him come out and get into the elevator again I went back.

It was dangerous. It was a stupid thing to do. We were all wanted by the police now, and the surest way in the world to bring them down on us was to start a brawl. But there wasn't room in my mind for thought. I knocked on the door.

"Who is it?" someone asked.

"Room Service," I said. "I forgot...." I let it trail off.

The door opened a crack. I saw the baby-blue eyes and the pink jowls, and I shoved, hard. Charlie was still off balance when I got in through the door and I put a hand in his face and pushed. He shot back into the table the boy had set up. The whole thing crashed down.

I kicked the door shut and swung at Bolton. He made an agonized sucking noise as the fist slammed into his stomach, but he was tougher than Charlie. He dropped the cup of coffee he was holding and belted me. I shook my head groggily as I slammed back into the door. Charlie was trying to get up, tangled in a white tablecloth with his hand in the melon. Bolton hit me again and I went down. He was a terrific right-handed puncher. I saw the foot coming for my face and grabbed at it. I got an arm around the other leg and heaved, straining with all the strength I had left. He came down on top of me.

Somewhere in all the wildness I could hear Charlie crying in an outraged and quivering voice. "Mike! What is the meaning of all this stupid violence?" I rolled and got Bolton off me, and when he started to get up I hit him. The shock numbed my hand. I hit him again. Blood trickled out of his mouth. He swayed dizzily and fell backward onto the floor. He wasn't knocked out, but all he could do was keep picking at the rug, trying to get a handhold on something to pull himself up. I was wild, and almost as groggy as he was. I stood up. Charlie was still trying to say something. I pushed him and he fell over Bolton.

I looked around. Their bags were all packed, standing by the door with their folded overcoats on them. In another few minutes they'd have been gone. Mexico City or Acapulco, I thought. I pulled a leg off the wreckage of the table and said, "All right, we're going to have a meeting. We're going to elect a new sucker."

I didn't get what it was at first. The next time around, I did. It was a knock at the door. I don't know why I opened it, unless I was still a little punchy. My head cleared then, very fast. It was Cathy. She was just standing there, white-faced, and when she looked at me she didn't say anything at all. She didn't have to. When I looked beyond her I knew I had waited too long.

There were two of them and they were wearing white frontier-style hats and gun holsters, and one of them was holding her by the arm.

They came on in, pushing her ahead of them. They looked around, and then at each other, and grinned. "Well, this is a cozy little group," the tall one with the pale eyes said. "Looks like His Royal Highness, Prince Charlie, and the one with the bent face must be Judd Bolton, alias Major Ballantine."

He swung his eyes around to me. "Drop it, friend." He meant the table leg. I dropped it. I couldn't say anything.

"All right, boys, on your feet," he said to Charlie and Bolton. "Shake 'em down, Jim."

The other cop came over behind us and patted us under the arms and down the sides. "They're clean, Shandy."

Charlie made a try at the outraged taxpayer. "I demand to know the meaning of this. And who is this young lady? I've never—"

Cathy turned on all of us, her eyes blazing with contempt. "You stupid, blundering idiots!"

Bolton lashed at her. "Why, you little fool! Why'd you bring 'em here?"

"All right, all right. Simmer down, boys and girls," the one called Shandy said. He was a great kidder, but none of it ever got as far as his eyes. "Keep an eye on 'em, Jim, while I go through the suitcases."

I collapsed into a chair and tried to light a cigarette. My hands were shaking. The whole thing was just a nightmare, and maybe I'd wake up in a minute.

Shandy had all the suitcases open and clothes scattered around on the floor. He grunted and came up with two big Manila envelopes. He took them over to the bed and emptied them. It was the money. There was a lot of it. "Let's see that list, Jim," he said.

The short cop passed it to him, and he sat down on the side of the bed with it. "If everybody was as sharp as that banker, we'd get these birds out of circulation," he said, more to himself than to anyone else. "Hmmm. Here we are." He lifted a bill out of the welter of currency and set it aside. There was terrible silence as he went on. "And here's another one. Numbers match, all right."

He looked across at Charlie and gave him that cold grin. "You should have stayed out of the sticks, Charlie, my boy. Looks like the wise guy slept in the hoosier's barn."

"I haven't the slightest idea what you're talking about," Charlie said.

"They never do," Shandy said. He turned to the other cop. "I better call in, Jim. Just keep 'em happy, and don't let 'em sell you anything."

He got up and walked over to the telephone on a table in the corner. He picked it up, with his back to us, and turned, watching over his shoulder. "Police Headquarters," he said. "Boy, what a bunch of sad looking wise guys!" Then he chuckled. "No, I wasn't talking to you, Operator. Extension Two-seven, please." He tapped a foot on the floor and whistled softly. "Hello, Sarge? Say, if you're interested in buying some stock in a sausage mine or a Pepsi-Cola well, I think we can fix it up for you.... What? Yeah.... Yeah. All four of 'em. It's Charlie, all right. And Ballantine. We even got the girl. She was asking for 'em at the desk. Yeah, the same one the motel man in Wyecross described. Redhead. The Caddy was parked right out in front of the hotel."

Well, if it meant anything now, I thought with weary bitterness, that explained how they'd got her. She'd come by for me, after all. Just about ten hours late—after the roof had fallen in.

This was the end of everything. They had us dead to rights. Goodwin could identify the three of us without any possibility of doubt, and they had the money with the serial numbers. We didn't have a prayer. Cathy was the only one who might beat it, with a good lawyer—if she kept her mouth shut.

And what would be the use in trying to explain who Goodwin was and what he'd done? The fact that he'd broken the law in some banana republic sixteen years ago wasn't going to cut any ice with a judge. It didn't excuse our taking the law into our own hands. That's fine, I thought bitterly. It's nice to think about now.

I looked up. Shandy had finished with the telephone and was talking to the other cop. He nodded toward Bolton.

"This guy's face is pretty banged up, Jim. Maybe you better take him on in so they can get a doctor or nurse to patch him up. I tell you. You take him and Prince Charlie and start booking 'em. Sergeant's sending over a couple of men, and they ought to be here by the time you get down front. One of 'em can go back with you, and the other one can come up here and help me finish checking this money and gathering up their stuff, and then we can bring in the girl and this other guy. How's that?"

"Oke," Jim said. "You want me to put the cuffs on 'em?"

Shandy shook his head. "Nah. These con men never get rough. Give the hotel a break. Looks like hell, guys going through the lobby in handcuffs."

"Yeah," Jim said. He jerked his head at Bolton and Charlie. "All right, boys. Let's go."

They went out. I lit another cigarette and walked over to the window to stare out because I couldn't look at her. I just couldn't. We'd been so near to making it. If it had broken the other way....

"Mike," she said behind me.

"I'm sorry, Cathy," I said. I didn't look around. Early morning sunlight was golden in the street. I saw the three of them come out onto the sidewalk below me. The other two policemen weren't anywhere in sight yet. The cop called Jim said something to Charlie and Bolton, and they walked over to a black Ford sedan parked at the curb. Bolton got in front, and Charlie got in the back seat. The cop went around and got in behind the wheel. I saw the exhaust fog in the chill air as the motor started.

And then the cop got out again. He came around the rear of the car and up on the sidewalk, apparently looking for the men from Headquarters. He must be stupid, I thought. It had become strangely silent behind me in the room now, but I still didn't look around. I was fascinated with the idea of his going off and leaving Bolton in the front seat of the car with the motor running. Then it happened so fast I could hardly follow it. There was a scream of rubber, and the Ford leaped ahead into the street. It must have been doing forty-five by the time it passed the corner. The short cop ran a few steps after it, waving his arms and yelling. He could have saved his breath.

I heard something behind me, and turned. Cathy was sitting on the bed with the pile of bills in her lap, laughing at me. The cop called Shandy was laughing too.

There had been too much. I couldn't absorb any more. I just stared at them as she counted out some bills and handed them to him. "Here's his, too," she said. "Five hundred each. And you can keep the guns."

I sat down weakly and watched them. It could have been a play I was seeing. I didn't seem to have any connection with it yet.

He quit laughing and was looking at the money a little hungrily. "That's a lot of dough, Red," he said. "Mebbe we ought to have a bigger slice."

She quit laughing too, and the brown eyes became very cold. "You know what you'll get a bigger slice of if you try to squeeze me," she said. "Impersonating an officer is a penitentiary offense."

"You wouldn't dare."

"Wouldn't I?"

He looked at her again, and must have seen the answer. "O.K., O.K. Don't strip your gears. I'll see you around."

He was out the door by the time I'd digested what she had said about impersonating an officer. But he had called the station! I'd seen him and heard him. It hit me then. How stupid could you get? He'd had his back to us, and it was the simplest thing in the world to hold the other hand on the hook.

I was beginning to get up to date at last. Charlie and Bolton hadn't double-crossed me at all. She just hadn't come by to pick me up because she had other things to do. She couldn't be bothered. She was too busy cooking up this act to double-cross them and take all the money. I could get out from under any way I could. I thought of the whole night in that boxcar sick with worry over what had happened to her.

She smiled. "I'm sorry I had to scare you like that, Mike, but...."

I got up off the chair and walked over to her. The whole room was going around in a dark whirlpool of rage. I reached down a hand and caught the front of her fur coat and yanked her up. I pulled her toward me and she looked at my face and tried to cry out. I opened my mouth, but there were no words. I threw her back across the bed with money scattering everywhere, and went out and slammed the door.

Twenty minutes later I was on the bus, going west. I didn't feel anything at all, and I didn't think about anything. I didn't want to.

Chapter Nine

It was snowing when I got off the bus in Reno, dry powder swirling down out of the Sierra and softening the harsh blaze of neon along streets plowed out and drifted again. I left the bags in the station and walked over to Calhoun's, feeling the wind search through my clothes. In the late afternoon the place was jammed with the crowd that seems to go on forever, and full of the whirring clatter of slot machines and the click of chips and a dice man chanting: "Here we are, folks. Get 'em down. New gunner coming out."

Wally Manners was in his office. He's tough, but a good friend, and he was glad to see me now. After we'd shaken hands and I refused one of his cigars, he said, "I got your wire. You still want to go to work?"

"Yes," I said.

"All right. Start tomorrow, after you've had some sleep. You look pretty beat."

"Two days on the bus," I said.

"How you fixed for money?"

"I'm all right."

"Fine. I'll see you tomorrow, then. And Belen. Stay out of here on your time off."

"O.K.," I said.

"We're not interested in winning back your wages. And if you get a hot streak, get it somewhere else."

I thanked him and walked back to the bus station. After calling half a dozen rooming houses I finally found a place to stay and walked across town carrying the bags. It was a shabby, two-story mansion a little down on its luck. I paid a week's rent, and after the landlady had brought me up to date on all the other tenants I managed to get away from her long enough to locate the bathroom. I took a shower and scraped off three days' growth of beard. The cut on my face where Bolton had hit me had healed pretty well, and most of the puffiness was gone from my hand.

It was a stage set for a boardinghouse room. I sat down on the slab of a bed and lit a cigarette and stared out the window. It was night now, but I could see snow eddying silently in the darkness beyond the glass and farther away the reflected neon bonfire of Virginia Street. I tried to remember if I'd eaten anything lately, but it didn't seem to make much difference. Nothing did. After a while I got into pajamas and turned out the light.

I'd been riding too long and the bed rocked the same way the bus had. I couldn't go to sleep. I was empty and washed out and beyond caring about anything, but I couldn't keep my eyes closed. They'd fly open and I'd be thinking about things, but the crazy part of it was that none of them seemed to make any difference. They didn't matter in the slightest. The police were looking for me. I was practically broke. I'd never find Lachlan now. Who cared? I was through with her at last, once and for all, wasn't I? After twenty-three years I'd got the last of her out of my system and she could go to hell, or Donnelly could use her for a clay pigeon, or she could find somebody else to double-cross.

So I'd been afraid Charlie would pull a fast one on her and take it all. I wanted to laugh, but there didn't seem to be any laughs in me either. I was going to protect her from Charlie, because Charlie was a crook. It was a shame about the laughs, because there might never be another masterpiece like that. It was a classic. Nobody would ever top it. Charlie, I suspect you of being dishonest, so unhand our little Nell. And tell her to give you back your arm.

I'll come by and pick you up at noon, dear, in my little Cadillac. But don't hold your breath.

I cursed and threw the blankets off and got up and dressed. The snow was slackening a little as I walked across town toward the lights. I remembered a little bar on a side street off Virginia and went in and sat down on a stool. A couple of shills nursed drinks at the blackjack table, the girl at the roulette wheel dribbled chips through her fingers, and a half-dozen people were shooting craps. Down at the other end of the bar four divorcees in slacks and fur coats were chattering over their drinks.

The barman remembered me, and nodded as he mopped the bar. "Haven't seen you in a long time."

"I've been away," I said.

He studied me. "Let's see. Bourbon, wasn't it?"

"Yeah," I said. "With plain water." I always drank Scotch, but it wasn't worth the effort.

He peered down the bar toward the covey of quail and shook his head. He hated women in bars. "One Planter's Punch, one Golden Fizz, one Orange Blossom, and one Alexander. And you know what?"

"No," I said. I knew what, because I'd heard it before, but maybe I'd get my drink sooner if I went along with him.

"Every damn one of 'em will pay for her own drink. With a fifty-dollar bill."

"It's tough," I said. I sat for a long time with the drink and then had another, but they seemed to have no effect on me at all. If anything, I felt worse. I got up and walked over to the table to watch the crapshooters. They were mostly women, making two or three passes in a row and betting fifty cents each time as if they were playing a slot machine. I waited until they came around to me, put five dollars on the line, and picked up the dice.

I had no business in a crap game now, and I knew it. I had about fifty dollars to eat on until payday, and I hadn't even started to work yet. If you have to win, don't gamble. That's not a sermon; it's a brutal piece of truth. It does-n't mean you're going to regret it if you lose; it simply means you probably *will* lose. Gamblers have another way of saying it, which implies the psycho-logical basis: A scared buck never wins. They call luck a lady, and gamblers found out a long time ago that scared indecision gets you about as far with one as with the other.

I tried to tell myself now to stay out of it because I needed the money if I was going to eat. The only trouble was that I didn't care whether I ate or not—or very much about anything else that I could think of. I shook the dice and threw.

They came up aces. Craps.

I put down another five dollars and bounced the dice against the end of the table. It was eleven this time. I let the ten lie on the line and rolled. I read four. Three rolls later two deuces came up and I shot the twenty. The stickman changed dice on me and I rolled two sevens in a row. I had eighty dollars on the line, got six for a point, and made it on the next throw. I was warming up, but when the stickman shoved them back he shook his head.

"You'll have to pull down sixty," he said. "Hundred-dollar limit."

I handed the chips over. "Cash me in. I'll come back and match pennies with you some other time."

You can feel it when it's like that. I don't know how to explain it except that there's an uncanny certainty about the whole thing. You couldn't lose if you tried. I felt that way now as I walked up the street through the snow, but it meant nothing at all. It just didn't matter.

This was a gambling house instead of a bar, and there was a table with a limit you could work with. When the dice came around to me I dropped forty dollars on two straight craps and then started throwing passes. I banged into the limit on the sixth one, pulled part of it down, and then threw two more before I lost the dice. When they came around again I racked up five passes, bumping the limit every time, before I fell off.

It was crazy. It was the wildest, most erratic streak of luck I'd ever run into in my life. They changed the dice on me until they got tired of it. I made wild bets—the field, on elevens, hard-way sixes and eights, and nothing made any difference. I won just the same. The crowd started to gather. I cashed in, went outside, took a cab to shake them, and moved on to another place.

I lost a thousand dollars there before I made a point; then I got hot and ran out a string of nine consecutive passes. My clothes, even the coat pockets, were full of money because I kept cashing in and moving around. The crowds made me angry. The word had spread now, and there was no getting away from them. Sometime around midnight I hit a run of bad luck and started los-ing heavily. I cut down the bets and zigzagged up and down for hours before it started running my way again. And it didn't seem to matter whether I was winning or losing. I felt just the same. It was just something I was doing to pass the time because I couldn't sleep. I couldn't remember when I'd slept.

It must have been around five in the morning. I was no longer conscious of anything but a blur of faces ringing the deep-walled pit of the dice table and of the dice themselves rolling out, bouncing, and spinning, and then being raked back. My eyes hurt. There was a tense quiet except for the stickman singing the point. I was trying to make a nine, and had five hundred dollars riding on it. Every number on the dice except nine and seven rolled up, over and over, until my arm grew numb. I wanted to take the dice and throw them against the wall or into the sea of blurred white faces staring at me. I had just picked them up and straightened a little to ease the kink in my back when I saw her. Her face swam slowly into focus, straight across the table from me. I was going crazy. She couldn't possibly be here.

I shook the dice and threw them. They bounced, and one caromed off another cushion and came to rest six up. The other was spinning on one corner. I watched it. It stopped. It was the three.

I pushed in the chips. Everybody wanted to talk at once, and they all wanted to talk to me. I stuffed the money in my pockets and shoved impatiently through the crowd. I wanted to get outside in the air and just walk through the snow.

"Mike, please!" She had hold of my arm. I turned. I wasn't going crazy. The collar of the gray coat was turned up against her cheek and her eyes were very big and pleading. And they were very tired. She must have been driving all the time I was riding the bus.

"I've got to talk to you," she said.

"Sure," I said. "Pick me up sometime. Bring your knife."

I turned away. She held onto my arm. "Mike, will you *listen?*" she pleaded desperately.

People were beginning to stare at us. And you never knew what she might do next. She was just as likely as not to start screaming and accuse me of wife-beating or poisoning her mother.

"Come on," I said, "I'll buy you a drink. You can tell me your little story, and then you can beat it. Or I will."

We went over to the bar, but people were still following me. She looked helplessly around at the sea of faces and begged, "Mike, can't we get out of here? What I've got to tell you is very important."

"All right," I said. Anything to get it over with. I'd had enough for one lifetime. I could get used to being dead if she'd just quit digging up the corpse.

We went out into the street. The snow had stopped, and beyond the glare of neon you could see stars like a million pin points of frost. A car went past with its tire chains slapping, and snow creaked under my shoes.

She slowed. "The car is right here."

We got in. There was just enough reflection from the neon signs for me to see her face very faintly. It was as lovely as ever, but it was awfully tired.

"All right, get on with it," I said. "It's cold out here."

"Couldn't you do anything about that?" she asked quietly.

"No," I said. "Let's have the sob story."

"You still think I double-crossed everybody, don't you?"

"Why, of course not," I said. "How could I ever think a thing like that?"

"Mike, darling," she said almost tearfully, "haven't you guessed yet what actually happened?"

"Sure. Everything just went black. And you only did it because you loved us."

"Mike! Please stop it. And listen to me. Don't you see yet? They double-crossed *us*. It was supposed to be *Saturday*."

"What?" I swung around and caught her by the arm. "No. Don't give me that. It was Friday. And you didn't come, so if it hadn't been for that freight train—"

"Mike, it was Saturday. Remember? Nine days after the beginning date of the option, which was Thursday."

She was right. They'd moved it up a day, knowing that if she didn't come by to pick me up they could ditch us both. I wanted to shout. I wanted to grab her and just yell. I wanted to—crawl under something out of sight, I thought.

"I'm sorry, Cathy," I said. "I'm sorry as hell."

"It's all right, Mike. You don't have to apologize." She smiled a little. "But it's still cold in here."

We found that together we could do something about it. Those two awful days ganged up on me all at once and I held her very tightly, trying not to think about it.

After a while she stirred a little and we got back to what had happened.

"It wasn't too hard to guess what they were up to," she said. "When I came back from Houston I had an idea they were speeding things up a little. I called the hotel at Ludley Friday morning, and then called Houston. And when Charlie wasn't at either place I knew our laughing boys had their shoes in their hands and were headed for the door. I tried to call you, but you were out. It was too late by then to pick you up, of course, but with luck I might get them before they could get away from El Paso. Of course, I could have just gone to them and demanded our share, but since they wanted to play winner-take-all—" She smiled coldly.

"Well, they asked for it," I said.

She turned to face me. "It's history now, Mike. We've got other things to think about."

She was always one jump ahead of me. "Such as?" I asked.

"Lachlan. The big one."

"Oh," I said. "But not right now."

"Why?"

"Right at the moment I'm too happy to hate even Lachlan. Wait here a minute." I got out of the car. In the bar that's never more than two doors from anywhere in Reno I bought a bottle of champagne and talked the barman out of two glasses. Somehow it seemed quite logical, just the thing you always did at six o'clock in the morning.

I slid in behind the wheel and drove, while she leaned against me with her head on my shoulder. We went out the Carson highway and turned off on the road to Mount Rose. It hadn't been plowed yet, but there were chains on the car and we made it as far as I wanted to go. It was a lookout point where you could pull off the road and look down across the valley. I got out and shoved the champagne and the two glasses into the waist-high barricade of snow left by the plows after an earlier snowfall.

When the champagne was cold it was growing light. I lifted her out of the car, because she couldn't walk in the snow in shoes that were only high heels and straps, and put her on the hood where she could see. It made her catch her breath. The valley was spread out below us, luminous and ghostly in the dawn, with nothing moving anywhere in all the white. I opened the champagne, the pop as the cork came out sounding strange and out of place in the frozen hush of early morning. We drank it all and then very gravely threw the glasses into the snowy pines below the road.

"Mike," she said suddenly, staring at me with a startled expression, "what makes your clothes so lumpy?"

"Oh." I'd forgotten all about the crap game. "Money."

She started laughing and slid down off the hood. I caught her and held her up. She was shrieking, and in a minute it struck me as funny and I began, too. We leaned on each other and howled.

Donnelly was very far away then—Donnelly and Bolton and Charlie. And even Lachlan. But it didn't last long.

She said a strange thing as we got into the elevator to go up to the room I'd got at the hotel. I only half noticed it at the time, but I remembered it later. We were standing in the rear of the car, and I wasn't paying any attention to anyone except her.

"Darling," she asked quietly, "will there be another one at Hialeah?"

I turned and stared at her. "Another what?"

She looked confused and changed suddenly to Spanish.

"I'm sorry," she said contritely. "I'm so sorry. I just forget."

We were on our way up to our room, and I didn't think any more about it then.

Who would?

Chapter Ten

We had fought a lot when we were married, and the thing we had fought about more than anything else was Lachlan. I could forget him once in a while, but she never could. She'd flare up and accuse me of being easygoing, lazy, and aimless. I wasn't dedicated.

I took the attitude that since we hadn't found him yet, there was no use staying in a perpetual uproar about him. He might even be dead, as far as we knew, and I didn't see any future in devoting our lives to anything as frustrating as trying to get even with a dead man. She couldn't see it that way, though. Weren't we still looking for him? We had to be ready to move in on him if we ever picked up his trail.

We watched the airline and steamship passenger lists in the New York, Miami, and New Orleans papers for all travel to and from Latin America. For a long time we had a detective agency working on it. We wrote endless letters to consuls in Central and South American cities. We picked up his trail in half a dozen cities, but it was always an old trail and he was gone. He'd disposed of his interest in the old firm of Dunbar & Belen long ago, and had moved out of the country when a new regime came into power. He'd been mixed up in oil in Venezuela, an airline in Colombia, and a land development swindle of some kind in Panama. He made a lot of money, one way or another. But so far as we could learn, he still hadn't come back to the States.

All this effort had been to find Lachlan himself. We'd never bothered much with Goodwin; that is, until Cathy had heard of him from her friend Elaine Holman. She said she'd learned from a few things the Holman girl had let drop that her uncle, whose name was Goodwin, had spent some time in Central America during his younger days. This and the name had started her wondering, so she had made a trip to Wyecross to find out. This had still been a more or less side-line issue, however; Lachlan was always the one we were after.

But it hadn't been the search that caused all the fights. The thing I could never go along with was her preoccupation with confidence games. She collected them. She studied them the way some people study chess, or Lee's campaigns in the Civil War. She read everything she could find about them, and devised endless ones of her own, and always she'd lose patience with me because I couldn't keep up any steady interest in them. It wasn't surprising that she knew people like Charlie and Bolton, because bunco artists had always fascinated her. It was part of getting ready to cut Lachlan down, because we were going to find him someday, weren't we?

And now we had. But I didn't know the half of it yet.

It was early afternoon. I lay on the bed and watched her. She was sitting at the writing desk, dressed in a blue robe and mules, and the red hair was all in a jumble from running her hand through it. She was chewing a pencil and writing something.

"This would be a fine day to be married," I said. "If you'd comb your hair."

She frowned at the paper. "You can make an honest woman of me sometime when we're not busy."

"Are we busy?"

"Well, I am," she said pointedly.

I lit a cigarette. "Well, let me know when you can work me into your schedule."

"You're already in it, *amigo*. Do you know how much money you won?"

"No," I said.

"Guess."

"Four pocketsful. Or is it pocketfuls?"

"Oh, for heaven's sake, Mike, you're hopeless. You won nine thousand, eight hundred and seventy dollars."

"Well, it's better than a kick in the backside with a frozen boot. What are you driving at? Besides going through my pockets while I'm asleep?"

"I'm adding up how much money we have altogether. With the sixty-five thousand—"

"You realize, of course," I said, "that you're going to get a bill from Charlie and Bolton for half of that, sooner or later." I was still kidding on the outside, but I was serious.

She smiled, a little coldly. "I have no objection to their trying, I'm sure. If they didn't learn last time—"

"Don't worry," I said. "They'll try. Incidentally, do you suppose they're wise to it yet?"

"Oh, certainly. They weren't fooled for any longer than it took them to discover that wasn't a police car. It was a U-Drive-It."

I don't know what made me think of it just then, but I suddenly remembered the strange thing she'd said in the elevator. I tried to remember it.

"Say, what was that crazy remark you made in the elevator?" I asked.

"When?"

"This morning. Something about Hialeah."

"Oh." She frowned and pushed her paper work aside and put a cigarette in her mouth. "That was it, darling. The opening gun of what we've waited sixteen years for."

"I'm listening," I said.

"Do you remember the man who was standing on your left? Big man with a deep tan?"

"Vaguely. Why?"

She struck a match and stared at me through cigarette smoke. "That," she said, "was Martin Lachlan."

"What!" I rolled over and sat up. I stared back at her.

"Mr. Martin Lachlan, swindler, oil man, playboy, big-game fisherman, lecher, and soon-to-be-sucker."

"Wait a minute. You knew he was in Reno?"

"Yes. Certainly."

"So that explains it. I see it now. I've been wondering how you knew I was here. You didn't, did you? It was Lachlan that brought you."

"Mike, stop yelling. I didn't come here to see Lachlan. We're going to see him in San Francisco. I came here because I had to find you. And the way I knew you were here is really quite simple. I couldn't find you in Las Vegas. I knew you'd be in one or the other."

I calmed down a little. "All right. But how did you find out *he* was here?"

"The detective agency. The one I've had working on it for the past year. I got a report from them just before I left San Antonio. Lachlan's here because he's trying to reach a property settlement with his third wife. She's staying at a dude ranch here, to divorce him."

"But how'd you recognize him? You don't remember what he looked like any more than I do."

Without a word she opened her purse, which was lying on the desk. She took out something and sailed it across to me on the bed. I picked it up. It was a snapshot. "From the detective agency," she said.

He was a powerfully built man who'd probably be in his late forties. It was a bold, self-assured face, and there was something about the way he held himself that gave you the idea he was one of those overbearing blowhards who's always telling and showing you he's just as good a man as he was twenty years ago. There wasn't anything of the simpleton about him, though. The eyes told you better than that. They looked sharp and tough.

"A hard nut to crack," I said, and sailed it back.

She smiled. "Not too hard."

"He's no fool. His record tells you that."

"I know," she said. "But that just makes it interesting." Her eyes were shining. She was in love with the idea.

"All right," I said. "But you still haven't explained that screwball remark in the elevator."

She smiled again. "It's really quite simple, Mike. It was a plant."

"A what?"

"Something that will stick in his mind. He heard it, because I saw him look around. It'll puzzle him for a while, and then he'll forget it. But the next time he sees us he'll remember it. And he'll be curious."

"He won't be half as curious as I am," I said.

She got up and began pacing the floor. She ran her fingers through her hair. "It's just what I've been telling you all these years, Mike, you Latin bird brain. We've found Lachlan, and you've got no plan of operation."

"No," I said. "But that's what we're going to do now. We're going to fig-ure one out."

"It won't be necessary, I assure you. I took care of that long ago. It's all set. With just a little help from us, Mr. Lachlan is going to dig his own pit, walk into it, skin himself, and pass us the pelt. Now, do you want to know how it's done?"

"How? What kind of flimflam is it?"

"The fixed race."

"Cut it out, Cathy," I said impatiently. "This is no time for joking."

"I'm not joking. That's the way we do it."

"Don't be a sap," I said. "Didn't you look at that picture? Don't you re-member his record? He's no idiot. He'll never go for anything as corny as that."

She blew a smoke ring and looked at it. "You think not?" she asked smugly.

"Of course not. You tell any six-year-old kid you're going to let him in on a fixed race and he'll laugh in your face."

"Yes. I know. That's the reason I'm going to use it. I want to make it as hu-miliating as possible. I want to rub his face in it."

"But it won't work, I tell you," I said angrily.

"Mike, you're being a little naïve. In the first place, you have no concep-tion at all of the depths of human credulity. And in the second place, you don't tell him you can fix a race. You convince him you can by telling him you *can't*."

"Now, that makes sense," I said sarcastically.

"It makes a lot of sense when you understand what I mean."

"If I ever do," I said. "Suppose you go back to that crazy thing in the ele-vator and start filling me in from there."

"All right," she said. She sat down on the side of the bed. "To begin with, one of the angles of the thing is the fact that we both speak Spanish."

"So does Lachlan."

She smiled. "Exactly. If he didn't, it would be utterly pointless. But he does, and he doesn't have any idea at all that we know it. And when we meet again, if he's curious about us, he'll never let us know he does understand it, and that's very important.

"Now, remember what I said. I mean, the way it would sound to somebody who understands both languages. I asked if there was going to be another 'one' at Hialeah. Hialeah, of course, is obviously a race track to anybody. And then, as I knew you would, you asked, 'One what?' Now, that could mean, of course, that you didn't have any idea what I was talking about, but since there were other people present it could also mean, 'Shut up, you damn fool.' So I apologized, very contritely, in another language, which I obviously hoped nobody listening would understand. You see how simple it is?"

"Yeah," I said. "You sound like Charlie."

"Oh," she said, "all that's elementary. The really dirty work is yet to come."

"All right, all right," I said. "But, Cathy, it looks to me as if we're both off the track in one thing, right at the beginning. And that is, we've never thought of any reason why Lachlan should go for any kind of flimflam. They all work on the sucker's desire to make a few fast bucks. And if Lachlan is already loaded, how can we interest him?"

"Because," she explained patiently, "nobody has plenty of it, and nobody ever will. And on top of that he's paying big chunks of alimony to two wives already, and number three is getting ready to push up to the trough. And don't forget the little matter of income tax. Who couldn't use a few hundred thousand that didn't have to show up on March fifteenth?"

"O.K." I shrugged. "But I still say this race thing is crazy. So we go to him and whisper in his ear that we've got a sure thing in the second at Belmont Park. So then he calls the cops."

"Dear old Mike," she said exasperatedly. "We don't whisper anything in his ear, now or ever. We try our best to avoid him. We don't know anything about races, fixed or otherwise. And when he comes around pestering you about it, you assure him, quite honestly, that to the best of your knowledge there is no such thing as a fixed race."

"I don't believe it."

"You will," she said.

Chapter Eleven

If the world had lost a great actor when Charlie became a crook, it lost a brilliant general when Cathy was born a girl. The next week was one of the busiest I'd ever put in in my life. When you looked at the thing at close range and out of context, it didn't make much sense; all we seemed to be doing was spending money in one mad shopping spree. But when you saw it in perspective and as part of the whole plan, it was all as carefully thought out as the Normandy invasion. We drove to San Francisco and registered at the St. Francis as Dr. and Mrs. Michael Rogers.

I went to a tailor and ordered five new suits and assorted tweed sports coats and slacks and went to a shirt-maker for a couple of dozen new shirts. She began looting the San Francisco shops. She'd always had wonderful taste in clothes, and for once in her life she didn't seem to care in the slightest what anything cost, so before long she began to stand out as a clothes horse, even in San Francisco. I'd meet her to take her to lunch and when I'd see her coming along the street in the spring sunshine she looked like an angel with charge accounts.

"Could I buy you this flower stand?" I asked.

"Silly, why?"

"We could throw flowers in front of the cable cars."

"You're nice, Mike, but impractical."

"What do we have to do now?"

"The Rotunda of the City of Paris. We're still looking for pictures for the apartment. Remember?"

"We haven't got an apartment. Remember?"

"We will have."

And we did. We got just the one we wanted in the Montlake, the big apartment hotel where Lachlan lived. It was six rooms besides the servants' quarters, with a view of the bay all the way from the Golden Gate to Alcatraz and a doorman who looked a little like Admiral Drake except that he dressed better. When I learned the rent I managed to keep from wincing.

"We'll be ready to move in in a day or two, Mike," she said excitedly that night in the room at the St. Francis. We had gone up to get cleaned up for dinner. A boy had brought up a bottle of Scotch and some ice, and I fixed us a drink. She had on a new robe about the color of moonlit fog and probably less than half as dense. She was something to see.

"You're something to see," I said.

"So I noticed, you Latin goat. Just hold some ice cubes on your wrist for a moment, or think of me as your ex-wife. We have to talk business."

"What now?"

"How would you like a Jaguar?"

"No, thank you," I said. "I used to be married to one."

"Idiot! I mean the car."

"Why?" I asked. "Are you turning in the Cadillac?"

"No. The Jaguar is for you."

"That's fine," I said. "That's just what we need. Two cars, I mean. Nobody's found space enough to park one around here since the Coolidge administration, so now we're going to circle the block with two."

She lit a cigarette and sat down in a big chair. "We need it," she informed me. "It's more window dressing."

"That brings up a point," I said. "Aren't we overdoing it a little?"

"No," she said definitely. "Not for Lachlan. He's the type of *nouveau riche* who thinks money's for show. You have to club people with it if you have it. I know all this is a little thick, but subtlety'd be lost on him."

I shrugged. "Maybe you're right. But if Lachlan doesn't go for it, it'll be an expensive horse laugh."

"Don't worry," she said calmly. "He'll bite."

It was one of the primary booby traps in her campaign. She'd explained it to me that day in Reno, in pointing out why we'd had to have so much money to tackle it. I didn't understand at first.

"It doesn't match up," I said. "Michael Rogers is a veterinarian. Well—I mean, they probably do all right, and maybe they even eat steak twice a week, but I never heard of one who had a private pipeline into Fort Knox."

"Well?" She smiled.

"Oh!" I said.

"You see? There it is. What would be your idea if you were a bank president and noticed one of your seventy-a-week bookkeepers or tellers was coming to work in a Mercedes-Benz and buying his wife a new mink every year?"

"I'd call the auditors. Or grab my piggie bank and scram before he got that too."

"In other words, you might have a faint suspicion that he had some other source of income?"

"All right," I said. "You don't have to draw me a picture."

It was fine that week—most of the time. I noticed, though, that the moments when she could relax and laugh or even pay much attention to my telling her how lovely she was were becoming more and more rare. She was completely absorbed in this Lachlan thing. It was becoming an obsession with her. We had to rehearse it by the hour. When we weren't talking about it, she was thinking about it, going through each of the moves in her mind.

And I began to catch myself thinking about Goodwin more than I had. I'd quit worrying so much about the police as time went by and we still seemed safe enough half a continent away, but I had a habit of suddenly—and for no reason at all—remembering Goodwin himself or his wife and their house in Wyecross. I wondered how he had raised the $65,000, whether it had taken everything he had. And then I'd curse myself. What did I care how he raised it? How much did I suppose he'd worried when he'd helped Lachlan ruin the rest of us?

And there was one other thing. I awoke one night to find her pounding on my chest and crying out that I was breaking her in pieces.

"Mike! What on earth are you trying to do?" she panted.

I was sweating. My pajama top was wet and my hands were shaking. I had to switch on the light and look at her to reassure myself. "It was just a dream," I said. "A bad dream."

"For heaven's sake, what did you dream about? Dinosaurs?"

"Donnelly."

"Oh, will you ever forget Donnelly?"

"No," I said. "And I just thought of something."

"What?"

"I shipped him out here. Remember?"

We moved into the Montlake the next day, and it must have looked like an Indian prince taking off for his summer palace. There were sixteen pieces of luggage, I think, besides all the packages and hatboxes and a fur coat or two.

The apartment was on the ninth floor. I stood by the big windows in the living room and looked out over the bay. It was sparkling and clear in the morning sunshine, and I could see a boat going out to Alcatraz. They've got a view over there too, I thought, but they don't like it. A whole rock covered with tough guys and wisenheimers who knew more than the cops. And just beyond, out of sight up the bay, was San Quentin, where the state of California kept its smart characters who could never be caught. I remembered that awful minute in the hotel room in El Paso when I'd opened the door and seen her standing there with the two men in white Texas sheriff hats. How many warnings did I need?

I shrugged it off, a little angrily. I was getting as nervous as an old woman. Either we wanted Lachlan or we didn't. And if we did, I couldn't spend all my time standing around shaking like a chicken. He'd taken his chances, and if we wanted a rematch we had to be as tough as he was.

We bought the Jaguar that morning and drove it over on Fillmore to try it out on a hill. After that we rolled it down Bayshore to San Mateo, went over to Skyline, and came back to the beach and to the Cliff House for lunch. For a while we were like a couple of high school kids with a new hot rod. We had a bottle of wine with the abalone and we laughed a lot and were very happy, watching the seals out in the kelp beds and the big ground swells heaving up to batter at the rocks. When we came back to the apartment there was a Chrysler station wagon with a lot of dust on it pulled into the loading zone ahead of us and the doorman and two bellboys were unloading luggage and an armful of heavy boat rods and salt-water reels like drums. The big bare-headed man in the suede jacket was wearing sunglasses, but I saw him turn and do a double take at her as we went past, and I knew we were closing in on him at last. It was Lachlan.

I got up early the next morning and made a trip down to the Skid Row south of Market. To put on this act of ours we had to have the help of one other person—just a brief appearance in the early stages—and he had to speak Spanish. She even had that all figured out. It had to be somebody with enough intelligence to swing his part and still not be a wise guy who'd ask too many questions or want to muscle in himself. And we had to be sure he'd disap-pear when his job was done. There was an answer to that, which I thought of almost as soon as she did: a wetback.

I took the cable car down to the foot of Powell and walked on over to Howard. It was another beautiful morning, even here among the flophouses and cheap taverns and hole-in-the-wall cafés smelling of grease and chili. A wino slept with his head against a fire hydrant with an empty bottle in the gutter beside him, and somebody had stolen his shoes. There were half a dozen employment agencies along here with big blackboards on the walls and men standing around listlessly as if they had even forgotten what they were wait-ing for. I tried the first one and didn't see anyone who looked promising. In the next one my luck was better. He was a young Mexican in clean khakis and a leather coat.

I went over to him. "Good morning. Looking for a job?"

He nodded, a little warily. The jobs came off the board he was watching, not from strangers wandering in off the street.

"You speak English?" I asked.

He nodded again. "I was born in San Antonio. I speak much English."

"That's fine," I said. "I was in San Antonio myself, during the war. Sta-tioned at Fort Lewis. You know where that is?"

"Oh, sure. I live near to it. I worked there."

He looked pretty good and as if he might do. He was a good liar, and a wet-back, and that's what we wanted. "It's all right," I said in Spanish, and grinned at him. "I don't care what part of Mexico you're from. I'm not an Immigration man." He was fast on the uptake, all right, for it took him only a second to see he'd gone into the bucket on that Fort Lewis thing. Lewis is in Washington.

"How are you called?" I asked.

"Juan Benavides."

He probably wasn't, but it didn't make any difference. "I'm glad to know you, Juan," I said. "My name's Rogers. Let's go get a cup of coffee. Perhaps I have a job for you."

We went over to Mission and found a restaurant a little cleaner than most. He was broke, so I ordered him some ham and eggs while I got coffee. While he was eating, I gave him the proposition.

"I'll give you an outfit of clothes, two hundred dollars American money, and a bus ticket to anywhere you want to go. The job won't take more than a half hour, with maybe two or three hours' coaching, but you may have to wait around a week or ten days till I get ready for you. Naturally, I'll pay for your room and meals while you're waiting. How about it?"

He stopped his assault on the ham and eggs for a moment to study me with grave Latin suspicion. "What class of job is this?"

"It's just a little joke I want to play on a friend of mine. I need somebody who speaks Spanish. Very good Spanish, too, not like just any peon."

"A serious joke?"

"No," I said. "Not serious."

"Maybe there will be trouble with the police?" He was a little suspicious of that "joke on a friend" angle, as I knew he would be if he was smart enough to be of any use to us. However, I had a pretty good idea as to what form his reluctance would take.

"No," I said. "This is not a joke that would interest the police."

"Nevertheless," he said, "I could not do a job of this class for less than three hundred dollars. As you can see, it would take great skill."

He'll do, I thought. He doesn't even know what the job is, and already it takes great skill and three hundred dollars. Maybe we should take him in as a partner.

"Two-fifty," I said.

"Two hundred and seventy-five, and a gold watch chain with the suit."

"Two hundred and sixty and a gold watch chain," I said. There really wasn't any sense to it, but you can never afford to lose face in one of those transactions by giving in on the first round. It isn't actually the money so much as a matter of personal honor.

"I accept your job," he said.

I took him over to a men's furnishing store on Market and let him pick out the whole outfit from the shoes up. He settled for a sort of semi-zoot affair in something that looked electric blue in the store and would probably be worse in daylight, and got a high-crowned snap brim hat to go with it. It was about what I'd had in mind, and it all fitted the picture very well. He had to look sharp. I paid for it and gave him the alteration slip for the suit and the Montlake address and apartment number.

"The clerk says it'll be ready day after tomorrow," I said. "As soon as you get it, come on up to this address and see me. Here's twenty dollars. Get your-self a room, and when you come up, be sure to bring me the hotel telephone number, or at least the name, so I can look it up. You understand all that?"

"I understand. Do you remember the gold watch chain?"

"It will be there."

We went out and shook hands on the sidewalk. "Until later," I said.

"Until later."

I watched him take off across the street. Of course he could always pick up his new clothes and lam, with all of it clear profit, but I didn't think he would. He'd probably show up.

I walked back to Powell. The usual crowd of tourists blocked traffic around the cable-car turntable, but I managed to climb onto the step as the car started clanging up the hill with people hanging on everywhere, like a subway car turned wrong side out. We only have two cars now, I thought; I have to do this. The trouble was I was just as big a sucker for the cable cars as the other tourists.

When we made the stop at Sutter some more people piled on till we looked like a bunch of grapes being dragged up a hill. Some tall guy made a landing on the step beside me and I tried to crowd over enough to give him something to hang onto. His arm was across in front of my face and our feet were so mixed up I didn't know whether I was standing on mine or his.

"A little crowded, eh, Belen?" a voice said in my ear. I turned, and Judd Bolton and I were rubbing noses like two Eskimos. Our arms were across each other's necks as we held onto the stanchions.

We stared at each other for a full ten seconds. There didn't seem to be any-thing to say.

"Do you rumba?" I asked.

Chapter Twelve

"Yes," he said. "But I sing better. Or maybe you'd rather have a little talk first."

The car stopped in the middle of California Street and he stepped down and nodded at me. I got down and we both walked over to the sidewalk. I still hadn't thought of anything. I'd known all the time this was going to happen, but maybe I just hadn't expected it so soon.

"How about the Top of the Mark?" he asked.

"All right."

It wasn't crowded, and we got seats by a window with empty booths on both sides of us. We ordered Scotch, and while we were waiting for the drinks I studied his face. The cuts were healed now. You couldn't see anything in the eyes; they were as noncommittal and hard and gray as ever. He was smooth and tough as they come, but somehow in a civilized sort of way— which made it worse, because there was no way on earth to guess what he was capable of.

Suddenly I was conscious of an odd sort of flashback to that night in the bar in New Orleans and the way he had cringed before Donnelly. It still puzzled me. The evidence didn't add up right.

The drinks came. "*Salud*," I said. And then, as soon as the waiter was gone, I went on quickly, trying to beat him to the punch. "Well, don't keep me guessing all day. I want to hear about it. How'd you get away? And what about Charlie? Did he—"

"Cut it out, Belen," he interrupted impatiently. "Let's dispense with the fairy tales and get down to business. Where's Cathy?"

I could see that routine was out. As she'd said, they'd known they were sold as soon as they took a look at the car. I had to try something else.

"Cathy?" I asked in surprise. "How would I know?"

"Oh, I see. She's not with you?" he murmured politely.

"No," I said. "I went off and left her in El Paso. She's lucky I didn't strangle her. Leaving me there in Wyecross to get away the best way I could."

"Two down," he said boredly. "Now, if you're sure you're finished with that one, we'll get on with it. You left Reno together just a week ago, if that's any help to you, so where is she?"

He had me. He knew all the answers. I lit a cigarette to stall for time. "You don't think I'm going to tell you, do you?"

"I don't know for sure, but I think so. As a matter of fact, you probably won't have to. If you'll just tell her you saw me and give her a message, she'll probably call me."

"She won't," I said. "But let's have the message."

"Tell her if I don't get my share of that money, I'm going to call Lachlan."

He had us. He had us right over the barrel. One word to Lachlan and the whole thing would blow up and drift away in a cloud of smoke before it even got started. I sat there looking at the wreckage of all our plans with a sort of numb helplessness, and it was a long minute before the full implication of it hit me.

"What do you mean, Lachlan?" I snapped. "What do you know about him?"

"Why, practically all there is to know," he said calmly. "After all, she and I were planning the deal together until she picked you up in New Orleans."

I felt the anger burning inside me. So nobody knew about it except us! Lachlan was ours.

"And just in case you think I don't know where he is now," Bolton went on smugly, "I'll dispel that little illusion. He's back at his apartment in the Montlake. He came in yesterday."

"All right," I said helplessly. "I'll tell her."

I'd tell her plenty, I thought.

"Just ask her to call me at the Sir Francis Drake."

"And you think she's going to split that money with you? After the way you and Charlie double-crossed us?"

It didn't bother him at all. "That was Charlie's idea," he said with urbane composure. "And as far as splitting the money's concerned, I don't see that she has much choice in the matter." He smiled. "Do you?"

I didn't. There was no use arguing about it. He held the cards. I wondered what she'd do. Nobody could make her give up that much money, and nobody could make her give up Lachlan. It was a variation of the irresistible force and the immovable object. Either way it was unthinkable. I looked out across the Bay Bridge with its cables shining in the sun. There was no use searching for a way out. There wasn't any. Suddenly I thought of something else, a question I'd never been able to get her to answer.

"By the way," I said, "since you seem to know everything, there's something I wish you'd clear up for me. Who is Donnelly?"

He glanced at me, slightly puzzled. "Don't you know?"

"Of course not. I wouldn't ask if I did."

"He's a hophead, for one thing. Used to peddle the stuff, till he got to using it himself, or maybe it's the other way around. Kind of a handyman for a gang around Chicago, and later in New York."

"How bad is he?"

He shook his head slightly. "It's always hard to say. You have to know how much of the stuff he has in him at the time, and a number of other variable factors. Unloaded, so to speak, and without a gun, he's about as harmful as the Easter bunny. He may be a little cracked at times, I think, and seems to hate women. Probably his hormones are out of kilter. I don't know. All you have to do is guess all these factors at any precise moment."

I felt a little sick. "But where does he get this dream that Cathy owes him some money? Out of the pipe?"

Bolton picked up the glass and looked at it, frowning a little. "No, I don't think so. I don't know for sure, of course, but it looks to me as if for the first time in his life he might be on the right side of something. It all depends on the way you look at the ethics of gambling debts."

"How's that?"

"Well, legally, they have no status, of course. Gamblers, I understand, look at the matter differently."

"They do," I said curtly. "But get to the point."

"All right. It's a simple thing. You knew Lane was a bookie, I guess, and that he was killed by a holdup man? Well, the day he was killed he accepted a bet from Donnelly for four hundred dollars on some horse named— I don't remember now. Silver Stream or Slip Stream or something like that. Donnelly's a terrific plunger and all the money he doesn't spend for dope goes to the ponies. But once in a while he gets hold of a good tip and makes a killing. This horse was one of them. He was a long shot, and maybe Lane took it and laid it off somewhere and maybe he didn't. Nobody knows, because that night Lane was killed right in front of his house in Connecticut as he and Cathy were getting out of the car. The horse had come in and paid a little better than twenty to one. She says Lane didn't accept any such bet as that. Donnelly says he did. Take your choice."

"Do you think Donnelly had anything to do with killing him?"

Bolton shook his head. "No. They caught the man who did it. Donnelly couldn't have had anything to do with it, anyway. He was in jail."

"In jail? Well, how'd he make the bet?"

"Earlier. The police picked him up on suspicion of something around noon that day, and it was several weeks before he was in circulation again. And that's the reason he didn't have the betting slip to back up his claim. He says the police lost it when they took all his stuff away from him at the jail."

"It sounds fishy to me," I said.

He shrugged. "As I say, I wouldn't know. The only thing I'm sure of is that I'm glad it's not me he's after."

I felt a little cold, thinking about it. "So Donnelly wants eight thousand. And how much is it you're after?"

"Thirty-two thousand, five hundred. I'm presenting Charlie's bill, too."

I stood up. "I wish you both luck," I said. "You'll need it."

"You think so?" He smiled coolly. "Just give her my message."

I went off and left him sitting there. Everything was ruined. And on top of that, she had lied to me. I was burning with anger as I stalked over to the Montlake.

She wasn't in the apartment. I waited, walking up and down the living room, smoking one cigarette after another. I don't know how long it was. It was the sound of bumpers clashing that finally took me to the window. I looked down and I could see her. She was trying to park the Cadillac. If it had been anyone else I'd have said she was drunk, but I knew she couldn't be because she never drank that much. She was trying to put the car in a parking space at least two cars long and she was as clumsy at it as a rhinoceros in a tearoom. She would bang into the car in front and then go slamming back to crash into the one behind, and she never did get close to the curb. I watched her coldly, wondering what it was this time. She could put that Cadillac anywhere a parking lot attendant could, and in half the time.

Then I saw what it was. Another car had apparently just pulled up a minute or two before, nearly up at the end of the block. It was a foreign car of some kind, and I could see the man getting out. Even nine floors up I recognized the Texas hat and the arrogant walk. It was Lachlan. He looked toward the bumper crashing and walked back to her instead of going in the doorway. I could see them talking, and then she slid over in the seat while he walked around and got in behind the wheel. He eased it into the parking place and they both got out. They were directly below me and I could see the white blur of her face, tipped up a little, thanking him and smiling. Then they came on inside the doorway.

In a few minutes I heard her key in the apartment door. I sat down on the arm of a big chair. She came in smiling, her eyes shining with excitement, and ran over to kiss me.

"Mike, darling. I was hoping you'd be back. I did it." I said nothing.

She went on, babbling with amusement. "It was easy. Just a slight variation on an old theme." She began to notice something was wrong. She looked at me questioningly.

"Darling, what's the matter?"

I reached out and caught her arm and pulled her toward me. "Nobody knows about Lachlan except us," I said roughly. "He's ours, our own private project."

"Darling," she protested, "of course nobody knows." She took another look at my face then, and I didn't have to spell it out for her. "So Bolton is in town?"

"Why'd you lie to me?"

I let her hand go and she sat down, looking at the floor. At last she glanced pleadingly up at me. "Please try to understand, Mike. Don't you see? I'd found Lachlan at last, after all those years. And I didn't even know where to start looking for you, to help me. I had to have somebody, because I couldn't do it alone, so I got Bolton."

What difference did it make? I thought wearily. The whole thing was washed up anyway. "Well, for your information," I said, "you've got Bolton. Right around your neck. Unless you want to hand him thirty-two thousand dollars."

"What!"

"He says if you don't call him, he's going to call Lachlan and tip him off."

She raised her head and stared at me. "Oh, he is?" she asked. She was getting that thoughtful look in her eyes again. "And just where is Mr. Bolton?"

"At the Sir Francis Drake."

"And he wants me to call him? Well, isn't that nice?" She stood up.

"What are you going to do?" I asked.

She smiled. "Why, I'm going to call him, Mike. That's what he wanted."

I just sat there and watched her. She picked up the telephone and asked for the hotel.

"Mr. Bolton," she said sweetly. "Mr. Judd Bolton. Would you ring him, please?" Then she looked at me, completely deadpan, and winked.

"Hello, Judd. How *are* you? This is Cathy," she said. What now? I thought. It was old college chum greeting old college chum after an absence of five years. "Mike just now told me you were in town and said you wanted to see me. Of *course*, dear. Come on over. Dr. and Mrs. Rogers. We're in Nine-A at the Montlake. Hurry over and we'll pour you a drink."

After she had hung up she called the desk and asked the clerk to send a boy up with some Western Union blanks. When they came she sat down at the coffee table and wrote out three or four telegrams. I merely shook the ice in my drink and waited. There was no use even trying to guess what was going to happen.

He came up about twenty minutes later. I let him in, we nodded coolly to each other, and I went out in the kitchen to fix him a drink. When I came back Cathy was still sitting at the coffee table with her telegrams and he was smoking a cigarette and smiling complacently from a big chair across from her.

"Lovely place you have here," he said. "Nice view."

"Yes, isn't it?"

"Nice of you to ask me over."

"Not at all," she said sweetly. "We're just sorry we didn't know sooner you were in town. I understand you were thinking of trying to get in touch with us through Mr. Lachlan."

I sat down at the other end of the sofa, stretched out my legs, and watched them. Bolton held all the cards. You could see that in the complacent and almost patronizing way he was beginning to put the pressure on. He had us, and he knew it. He'd sweat us for a few minutes first, though, just for laughs.

"Oh, I didn't really think that would be necessary," he said smoothly. "I was sure you'd agree to my proposition as soon as you had a chance to examine it."

"Why, certainly, Judd," she said. "But how can I agree to it if I don't know what it is?"

"Well, I've been thinking about it." He gazed thoughtfully at the end of his cigarette like a banker getting ready to grant a two-million-dollar loan. "It would be a shame to give up this Lachlan deal, now that you've got so much invested in it. So why don't we work out a deal along these lines? You turn over the thirty-two thousand, five hundred you owe me and Charlie, and then cut me in for half of this Lachlan negotiation."

I whistled softly. There was nothing bashful about Bolton when he started tightening the screws.

"Oh, I meant to ask you," she said smoothly, "do you know where Charlie is?"

He shook his head and smiled. "In the East somewhere, I believe. I'm not sure."

"Well, if you're collecting for him, how do you expect to deliver the money if you don't know his address?"

He smiled again. "That does raise an interesting question, doesn't it? But we needn't go into that. I'll be glad to accept full responsibility for delivering it, and relieve you of the worry. I know it's been bothering you."

"That's very nice of you, Judd. But what if we can't agree to your terms?"

"Oh," he said easily, "I think you can come around to my way of thinking. Life is essentially a series of compromises."

"But just supposing, for the sake of argument, that we didn't?"

"In that case, I'd have to call Lachlan."

"Would you, really?"

"Certainly."

She smiled. "I like your frankness. I'll be equally open with you. The telephone is right over there by the door."

I couldn't see what she was driving at. Neither could Bolton. He studied her face, trying to figure it out.

"You mean that?" he asked.

"Why, surely. And I'll even let you use it first," she said. "I'll send my telegrams after you're finished talking to Mr. Lachlan."

"Telegrams?" he asked. I hadn't got anything yet, but maybe he could hear the bomb beginning to tick.

"Yes. Oh, I didn't show them to you, did I? I wrote them out while we were waiting for you. Here." She shoved them across the table, all except one. "The first one is to the chief of police in Denver. And the other is to the bunco squad in Miami. They're still anxious to contact a Major Jarvis Ballantine, I understand. And, of course, as far as the police here in San Francisco are concerned, I could just call them on the telephone and suggest they check with Denver and Miami and that they might find you at the Sir Francis Drake or the airport."

He was the one who was sweating now. You could see it working on him. "You don't mean that," he said.

"I'll tell you an excellent way to find out. Call Mr. Lachlan and see."

"You couldn't." He was blustering a little.

"I've already suggested a way you can test it. You won't know for sure until you do. You say life is a series of compromises; in a way, it's also a series of uncertainties."

"Yes, but there's one thing you've forgotten," he said. "And that is that I could call the police in Wyecross and tell them where you are."

"But, why, Judd, for heaven's sake?" she asked innocently. "Or have you forgotten something? I didn't have anything at all to do with that, but you did."

She had him there, in this colossal game of bluff. There was no way Goodwin or the police could ever pin any of it on her. All she had was the money.

He ground out the cigarette in a tray and got up. His face was dark with anger.

"You're not going, Judd?" she asked. "Why, you haven't even finished your drink."

"What's in it?" he asked harshly. "Arsenic, or cyanide?" He stopped at the door and looked back, and I could see him beginning to get hold of an idea. Some of his assurance returned.

"You won't get away with it," he said, grinning coldly. "You really overlooked something, Cathy."

"And what is that?"

"I might—I say, I just *might* call Lachlan tomorrow or next week or ten days from now from Seattle or Los Angeles or Jersey City. And you wouldn't know it. Maybe you didn't think of that. There's an interesting little uncertainty for you. How would you like working on a mark who's been wised up and has the bunco squad sitting on the side lines waiting for you to make your pitch?"

I hadn't thought of that, and now that I got a look at all the deadly beauty of it I could feel the butterflies in my stomach. Wouldn't that be a setup? We'd never know whether Lachlan had been tipped off or not until the actual moment they closed in on us. It would be like trying to disassemble an unfamiliar land mine in the dark; the only way you'd know when you had the trigger was when it went off. She couldn't have any answer for that one. Or did she? I looked at her and she was smiling again.

"Oh, how stupid of me," she said. "I knew I had forgotten something. I didn't show you the *other* telegram."

"The other one?"

"Why, yes. This one." She held it out, but he made no move to take it. "It's to the Chicago police. Just a little tip that they might get in touch with you by contacting your mother out in Oak Park. Think what a revelation that'll be. To both the police *and* your mother. Can't you just see the headlines? 'Son of Prominent Committeewoman Sought.'"

I watched his face. It was the first time I'd ever been able to see very far into Bolton, and now that I did I didn't find it a very comforting sight. He looked at both of us with his hand on the door and said, "That's one I'd advise you not to send, Cathy."

That was all. He went out and closed the door.

Chapter Thirteen

He'd called it an interesting uncertainty, and that was probably the understatement of the year. Would he, or wouldn't he? It could drive you crazy. Who had out-bluffed whom?

Fortunately, I didn't have time to stew about it that night. I met Lachlan, at last.

We were going out to dinner and stopped in the cocktail lounge in the building. It was the usual chi-chi sort of place, with white leather upholstery in the booths, a girl playing a Hammond organ, and just enough light to grope your way around. The place was almost empty. We had just sat down at a booth and ordered our drinks when I saw him come in. He didn't notice us at first, and sat down at the bar. When his drink came he looked up and saw her in the mirror.

He didn't know me, and she hadn't asked him. He came over anyway, with his drink in his hand. "Hello, there," he said.

It was just the sort of break we'd been hoping for, but it still got under my skin. She looked up, pretending she had just noticed him, and smiled. "Why, hello. It's Mr.— ah—"

"Lachlan, folks," he said heartily. "Remember? The parking lot attendant."

She made the introduction. "This is my husband, Dr. Rogers. Darling, Mr. Lachlan. The man who helped me park the car."

I stood up and we shook hands. "Join us?" I asked, with as little invitation as I could get into it. I was supposed to play it very cold and close-mouthed, the way we had it worked out, but it wasn't any act.

He jerked his head for the waiter to bring a chair, and sat down at the end of the table. We'd hardly touched our drinks, but he insisted on ordering two more. "Doctor?" he asked. "Are you an M.D.?"

I shook my head curtly. "Veterinarian."

He dismissed that with a grunt. "Oh?" he said, and turned to Cathy. "You know, Mrs. Rogers, I could swear I've seen you somewhere before. You're not in the movies, are you?"

It was pretty crude, especially from a middle-aged goat who was old enough to be her father. I had a pleasant moment thinking of how, normally, she'd let the air out of any oaf who'd pull something like that, but now she took a bow on it, looking flattered and a little overcome, like a girl at her first prom. "No," she said, shaking her head and smiling. "I've never been any nearer Hollywood than right here."

"Well, that's a shame," he boomed. He turned and included me in the conversation again. "Doctor, I notice you drive a Jaguar. How do you like it?"

"Pretty well," I said. "I haven't had a chance to race it yet."

"They're not bad. I had one for a while, but I got rid of it and picked up that Italian job I've got now. There's a car. Of course," he added, with an offhand wave of the paw, "it costs a lot more." He was one of those people who manage to rub their money in your face like grating a nutmeg.

"By the way," he went on, "Mrs. Rogers said you lived a long time in Peru. You ever do any fishing around Cape Blanco?"

This was one of the ticklish parts of it. Cathy'd been to Peru with her mother one year, but I'd never been there. We were pretty sure he hadn't either, but weren't absolutely certain of it.

I shook my head. "No. I was mostly up in the mountains. Little trout fishing was all."

"Oh, trout." He consigned trout fishing to the category of sissy pastimes like making your own clothes or painting teacups. "I was hoping you might have tried it. Never been there myself. The usual places, Bimini, Acapulco, and so on, but somehow I always missed Blanco."

"Oh?" I said.

He brought us up to date on what kind of physical condition you had to be in to fight marlin, and asked us to guess his age. We both knew he was either forty-eight or forty-nine, so I said forty-one and Cathy said forty. He told us he'd played football in college, and that he could go out there right now and run through a scrimmage without raising a sweat. He knew several movie stars. He kept a forty-foot cruiser at San Diego. But I kept noticing he never mentioned Central America. That was good. Most of this was directed at Cathy, but occasionally he would remember I was there too and make an effort to work me into the conversation. "What kind of work do you do mostly, Doc?" he asked. "Horses? Dogs? That sort of thing?"

"I'm not doing any at all at the moment," I said.

Cathy took it off the backboard. "Dr. Rogers hasn't practiced for several years, though he used to work mostly with race horses. Lately, he's become interested in research."

"For the government?"

She shook her head. "Just for himself. You see, his father was a medical missionary in the Andes and as a child he became interested in the Indians and—"

I shot her a dirty look, trying not to make it too obvious, and she let it trail off rather lamely into something vague about high altitude and diet. While she was still floundering around with it, I glanced at my watch and said curtly we had to start to dinner. The whole thing was brusque to the point of rudeness. I shook hands rather coldly with Lachlan as we stood up, thanked him for the drink, and said with no sincerity at all that I hoped we would see him again. As we were leaving and were almost, but not quite, out of earshot, I snapped at her in Spanish, "Long tongue!"

That night after dinner we worked on the plan some more. We had an argument to begin with, but she finally won me over. I said her whole idea was too subtle for a meat-headed egotist like Lachlan, that he never stopped talking about himself long enough to be curious about anything or anybody.

She disagreed with me. "You're wrong, darling. He's just intelligent enough to get it, without being smart enough to see through it or be afraid of it. God knows you're right about his egotism, but you should cry about that. I'm the one who's going to have to listen to him. And it's in our favor, anyway. What could be more intoxicating to a conceited gas bag like that than the knowledge that he's outsmarted us and found out what you're doing—when he does, of course? And he's already put one thing over on us. He understands Spanish as well as we do, and we don't know that. I suppose you noticed that in all that monologue of his there was never anything about Central America."

"Yes. I noticed that."

"I was afraid he'd brag about it—the way he does everything else—before we had a chance to nail it down. He won't now. Your bawling me out for being a *lengua larga* has scotched that."

She coached me on the Peruvian angle until I felt as if I'd lived there for years. Complete saturation was what she was after, and nothing less would satisfy her. I protested, pointing out that Lachlan had never been to Peru and wouldn't know if I did make a mistake, but she paid no attention. I not only had to know everything about Dr. Rogers, I had to be him.

The next day Juan Benavides showed up and he went through the mill.

It was about two in the afternoon. The buzzer sounded, and he was in the corridor looking very sharp in his electric-blue suit and wide-collared shirt.

"Come in, Juan," I said. I took his hat and he looked around in awe, probably kicking himself for not having started his bargaining at five hundred instead of three hundred dollars.

I gave him a cigarette and called Cathy. She was wearing blue pajamas and a long robe with wide sleeves, and you could see he was much impressed with her. She shook hands and smiled, and then curled up in a big chair.

"We are very fortunate," she said, giving him an approving glance. "Already I can see that Juan is just the man for the job."

From then on he was hers. The two Spanish-speaking gringos were without doubt completely crazy, but this one was of unbelievable beauty and she thought highly of him.

She told him everything he was supposed to do and say, and then she told him again. She sweated him through it for an hour. I wrote down the telephone number of the hotel where he was staying. We told him to be there where we could reach him any afternoon after four, and then I went back downtown with him and let him pick out the gold watch chain.

"Where is your watch?" I asked.

"Perhaps someday I will have one," he said. "Who knows?"

I gave him some more expense money and asked him about the bus ticket. He thought it over and decided El Paso would be a good place to go. After I dropped him off I went around to the bus station and bought it. We were all ready for the next act.

On an impulse I ducked into a cigar store and called the Sir Francis Drake. Bolton had checked out and had left no forwarding address. It could mean anything at all, and probably meant nothing, but for a moment I felt a chill just thinking about it. He could tip Lachlan off from anywhere, and we'd never know it until they slipped the handcuffs on us.

When I got back to the apartment she was gone again, and she didn't get back until nearly six. She was elated when she did come in. She'd run into Lachlan and he had taken her down Bayshore to San Jose in that Italian car of his to show her how it performed. Or at least, that was his excuse.

It was good, but I was irritated. "Wait a minute," I said. "How much of this are we going to have, anyway? I mean, going off with him all afternoon—"

She laughed. "Mike, for heaven's sake, have you forgotten who he is? That's Lachlan, the man we both wanted to kill when I was ten years old. Stop growling and listen. We're doing wonderfully."

She'd got a pretty good line on his plans this time and we could set up some sort of timetable. Apparently they had talked a lot. He was going to be around San Francisco for at least another month, she said, before he went back to Mexico for some more fishing. His lawyers wanted him to stay around until they got this latest property settlement worked out.

But that wasn't the big news, she told me excitedly. "He actually stopped talking about himself long enough to ask me what you were doing. Incidentally, he was curious about me, too—his idea being, of course, that I must be the one with money, since you obviously couldn't be. I dispelled that by telling him my father was a bookkeeper for the Lima office of a mining company. I said we both grew up in Peru, but that we didn't meet until we were at Columbia. So now, if it's bothering his sense of logic any, he's right back where he started. You don't do anything resembling work, your father was a missionary, mine was a bookkeeper, and still we live like millionaires."

She jumped off my lap and starting prowling the living room, the way she always did when she was excited or thinking. She paused to light a cigarette, then waved it at me. "He asked me outright what kind of research you were doing—or had been doing. I was properly evasive about it, and vague. He wouldn't have to be a genius to figure out that you had given me unadulterated hell for talking too much the other night and that I still remembered it.

"I told him you'd been at the Hipódromo San Felipe in Lima as a veterinarian for the track, and then somehow"—she paused and grinned wickedly—"somehow we got onto horse doping and saliva tests, and I said that although they weren't part of your work, you'd become interested in them. Just chatter, you see. And then I shut up and listened to him."

We ran into Lachlan again that night in the cocktail lounge as we were going out to dinner, but declined his drink invitation a little coolly and eased out without talking to him. The following night we avoided the bar altogether. The thing to do was to let him rest a little.

The night after that, however, we went back and he was there ahead of us, sitting at a booth this time. He stood up and insisted we join him.

The drinks came. "How about having dinner with me tonight?" he urged.

"Why, we'd love to," Cathy said. "Wouldn't we, Mike?"

"Sure," I said, with scarcely any enthusiasm at all.

"Fine," he said. "I know a swell place down in the financial district. Never find it unless you knew this town like a book."

Cathy had her head down and was poking into her purse. "Oh, darn," she said. "I left my lipstick upstairs." She stood up. "If you'll excuse me. I'll only be a minute."

She went out and we sat down again. I wondered how the thing would come off. She had gone to call Benavides.

She was gone about ten minutes, stalling to give him time. Lachlan and I nursed our drinks and made an attempt at conversation. Without her there it fell apart like bricks without mortar.

I thought about him and tried to figure him out. Somehow he either wasn't the man I'd always expected or he was putting on an act too. The boasting and ostentatious show of money and bully-boy virility that characterized this middle-aged clown didn't seem to match up with the cold-nerved piracy of the man who'd engineered a coup like that one in Central America sixteen years ago. Maybe it was just a front, or maybe he was over the peak and softening up now, degenerating into a sort of propped-up wolf chasing girls half his age.

In the face itself there wasn't much evidence of breakdown. The eyes were steel-blue and sharp and a little too domineering, and the hawk nose and solid jaw gave him the look of a man who was able to take care of himself. Maybe it was in a number of small things. He was a little too loud. He dyed his hair to cover up the gray at the temples. You could see it—the reddish brown around the ears didn't quite match the rest of it. His clothes were too young for him. He wore double-breasted gray flannel suits with built-in shoulders and Hollywood drape, and topped them off with explosive ties and the modified Texas hat. It was funny, I thought; at first glance, when you knew his record, he looked dangerous, but when you got closer to him he began to sound a little hollow.

Was it an act? That was the bad part of it—there was no way to know until it was too late. But the thing we couldn't afford to forget for a minute was that he'd lived by his wits for a long time, and he'd always come out on top.

"Mrs. Rogers tells me you used to be with the Peruvian Jockey Club," he said, leaning back against the white leather.

I shrugged. "Not as a member, if that's what you mean. I worked at San Felipe as veterinarian for a while. A long time ago."

"How is the racing down there? Pretty crooked?"

"No," I said, a little impatiently. "Probably as clean as it is here."

He gave me a superior smile. "Whatever that means."

"It means it's pretty straight. Thoroughbred racing is one of the most rigidly
governed sports in the world, and they do a good job of keeping it clean."

"You think so?" He didn't, it was obvious. And he had the knack of implying that if I did I was a fool.

I shrugged it off and changed the subject, as if reluctant to talk about horse
racing. We got onto fishing, which wasn't much better. He had only amused
tolerance for fly fishermen. In a few minutes Cathy came back.

"More trouble," she complained with a wry smile as we sat down. "Sometimes I envy men. I had a run in a stocking and had to change it."

I ordered another round of drinks to make sure Benavides would have time
to get here. When we had finished them, Lachlan said, "We'll take my car.
It's already out front." We went out through the lobby with Cathy in the
middle chattering about something. It was after seven, and when we got out
the big doors in front it was dark except for the street lights and the glow from
the sign over the cocktail lounge. Fog was coming in across the hill and cutting off the tops of the buildings. Benavides wasn't in sight. He'd had plenty
of time, I thought angrily. Where the devil was he? Then I saw him. He had
just come around the corner of the building, walking very fast.

We turned and went down the sidewalk toward Lachlan's car. Just before
we reached it I could hear footsteps behind us, beginning to run now, and
then he called out.

"Señor Rogers. Doctor! One moment, please."

We all turned, just as he came up and put a hand on my arm. I shook it off
angrily, brushing at him with my hand. "Get away," I said irritably, continuing to walk toward the car.

He came after me, talking very fast in Spanish. "Please, you must listen. You
will tell me when there is another one, no?"

"What are you talking about?" I said coldly. I had him by the arm now, and
was hustling him away. "Shut up, you stupid idiot!" I hissed at him, still jock-
eying him along. I turned to Cathy and Lachlan and apologized in English.
"I'm sorry. I'll get rid of him in a minute. You go ahead."

They went on toward the car with Lachlan turning to look curiously over
his shoulder. I walked Juan back, being careful not to get completely out of
earshot.

"Now, you big-mouthed fool," I lashed at him, winking at the same time,
"what are you doing here?"

"Señor Barnes sent me away from Miami. He said he would kill me. But I must have money. I cannot live in this country without money. You will tell me when there will be a long race, no?"

"You're lucky Barnes didn't kill you," I said angrily. "I heard about it. You talked your stupid head off. There was so much comeback money at the track we didn't get five to one." I chopped it off suddenly as if just realizing I was talking too loudly myself.

"But, Doctor, how am I going to live?" he begged. "You must tell me when there is another so I can bet—" He stepped back, holding out his hands, as I made a step toward him.

I took out my wallet and handed him the $260 and the bus ticket, folded up between the bills. "Here," I said. "And you stay away from here. If I see you around here again, I'll call Cramer. You know what he does to long tongues."

He tried to follow me back to the car, still talking. I waved him off furiously, and he turned finally and shuffled away. He had done it nicely, and I hoped he'd use that bus ticket.

They were in the car waiting, and looked questioningly at me as I slid in beside Cathy. "I'm sorry," I said. "Damned nuisance. The only way you can get rid of him is to give him a couple of dollars."

"Oh?" Lachlan asked casually, easing the car away from the curb. "Do you know him?"

"He used to work for my father, in Peru. Dad brought him back to the States with him three or four years ago, but he won't work any more. Just a bum now."

He didn't say anything more as we drove on down the hill through the early evening traffic. I was eager for a chance to talk to Cathy, to find out how it had gone over and how much of it they'd been able to hear. All through dinner I was hoping to get a moment alone with her, but I never did. Afterward he suggested we go to the Fairmont, but Cathy begged off, saying she had a slight headache. We came back to the apartment about ten o'clock.

The minute we were inside the door she pulled my head down and kissed me. "You and Benavides should go on the stage."

"Was it all right?"

"Perfect."

We avoided Lachlan completely for the rest of the week, and then, as she said he would, he came to us. Early in the morning after the Benavides incident I went downtown to the hotel where he was staying, intending to build a fire under him if he was still hanging around. He was gone, however, and the chances looked good that he had taken the bus for El Paso. As soon as we got back to the apartment we packed a couple of bags and took off for Carmel. Everything was under control, and all we had to do was play hard to get and just wait.

It was wonderful at Carmel. I forgot the whole thing for three days, and stopped worrying about Bolton, and Donnelly, and whether the police were watching us. It was a fine time.

We hadn't been back in San Francisco more than a few hours when he called us. He had four tickets to a play at the Geary, he said. How would we like to join him and his date for it, and then go dancing afterward?

"We're beginning to click, darling," Cathy said, looking speculatively at a row of gowns hanging in a closet.

It was easy to see Lachlan had something up his sleeve when we met them downstairs in the cocktail lounge and I got a glance at his date. No aging buck on the prowl would want to be chaperoned by a married couple when he could have been alone with all those natural resources. She was a brown-eyed blonde who overflowed her gown to within a short drool of being arrested for blocking traffic. The gown itself was a plunging-neckline affair in a sort of ripe-avocado green, and above the timber line she looked like whipped cream squeezed out of a tube. Her name was Bobbie Everett and she was in radio, she said, and when I made the obvious and somewhat asinine observation that she ought to be in television she thought that was cute. This was odd, considering that she had probably heard the same remark ten thousand times since TV had taken the bosom to its bosom.

The strategy began to be a little obvious by the time we'd left the theatre and had gone to a night club. Really, I was the most interesting man she'd ever met. Honestly, I was. I simply must tell her all about myself. Working with race horses, imagine that. Didn't I think racing was just simply divine?

She had to have something to report to Lachlan, so I blossomed into a brilliant conversationalist under all this flattering attention and told her all about myself. I told her how to treat bowed tendons.

Of course, I didn't know anything about it, but since practically anything was news to her, I was on safe ground. It was about five dances before I was able to outmaneuver Lachlan and get a dance with Cathy.

"Well," she said, "and how are you and your little friend? You don't seem to be feeling any pain."

"I'm all right," I said. "A little snow-blind, but otherwise O.K."

"Yes," she said, "I thought you looked like a homesick skier. But remember, you're the close-mouthed type. What has she learned so far, besides the fact that your vision seems to be all right?"

"I haven't told her anything except the story Lachlan already has from you."

We compared notes as soon as we were back at the apartment. She was elated. There wasn't any doubt at all now that he was going for it.

"He's going for something," I said. "Maybe it's you."

"Don't be silly. Listen, Mike, we're turning for home now. I can tell. From the things he said tonight—when he wasn't playing the big shot, of course—

I've got a pretty good picture of just how much he's figured out. He knows you're mixed up in horse racing in some way, but he can't quite see where or how. I mean, you're not anywhere near an operating track, you're obviously not a bookie, and if you were an owner or trainer you'd say so. And that thing Benavides kept saying about a 'long race' is getting him. Why should long races be any different from any others? He hasn't quite enough information to complete the picture, but he will have, very shortly. I've got a date with him tomorrow. You don't know it, of course, but he's taking me out to lunch."

Chapter Fourteen

We didn't get up until late, and around noon she went out. She was enchanting in a whole new spring outfit, smart and very lovely from nylons to short-veiled hat, and when she came to kiss me she left a hint of fragrance that lingered in the apartment after she was gone.

"I'm off to betray you, darling," she said.

I prowled irritably around the apartment. Was he going for it, or was he just going for her? She was convinced he was rising to the bait, but just how sure were we as to what he considered the bait? Maybe, as far as he was concerned, she was it. Lachlan had money already. He didn't chase girls to get money; he used money to chase girls. And what if Bolton had tipped him off, as he'd threatened, and he was laughing about the whole thing, playing along with us while the police watched, just waiting to spring the trap? I shuddered.

I kept thinking about Bolton, and after a while I started wondering about Charlie and why we hadn't heard anything of him. After a while I couldn't stand my thoughts and the apartment any longer and went out and walked downtown. I had to locate a good bookie joint, and they weren't very plentiful any more. The federal tax and the clampdown by the police had driven most of them out of business. It took a number of telephone calls to some old friends before I got on the trail of one. It was in the rear of a saloon on the other side of Market. I finally got in, and sat around for a while reading a scratch sheet and watching the Santa Anita results go up on the board. I didn't need the place yet, but I wanted to get the telephone number and be sure I could get in when I did. I made a few random bets, and lost on all of them.

She still wasn't back when I returned to the apartment. I mixed a drink and sat around thinking of the fine time we'd had at Carmel and wondering if it could ever be like that all the time. Maybe when we finished with this.... I got up and started pacing the floor again. Maybe when we finished with this we'd be in separate penitentiaries.

It was a little after five when she came in, very happy, and ran to kiss me. They'd had lunch, and then gone for a long drive down toward Half Moon Bay.

I mixed her a drink, and she told me. "He has all the parts now, Mike," she said, talking very fast and excitedly. She had changed into lounging pajamas and a blue robe and sandals and was curled up in a big chair with the drink. "He got it out of me at last." She looked across at me and laughed. "I finally told him about the plant that had fascinated you ever since you were a child in Peru and how much research you had done on it. He'd never heard of coca, and the chances are he's down at the library right now, looking it up in the encyclopedia. And when he finds it, he's gone."

That was it. Coca was the detonator, the trigger on this booby trap she had rigged. She'd first learned of it when she was in Peru. Cocaine is derived from it, through an involved chemical process. The Andes Indians chew the dried leaves and it acts as a stimulant. They are able to get by on very little food and can carry tremendous loads for long distances when under the influence of it. Naturally, it's harmful, as is any system of trying to get something for nothing, but that wasn't the point.

The point was that this was one of a series of deadfalls he should have planted in his mind now, and if he followed the trail she had left he should stumble into every one of them. I was interested in the effect of coca, which was a stimulant; I had been a veterinarian at a South American race track and had become interested in something else that wasn't part of my job—the saliva tests they give the winners of races to check for illegal drugs or stimulants, and which are a chemist's job; Benavides had stupidly kept saying something about "long" races while I was trying to shut him up; and last but not least, I had brushed him off and denied very coldly that there could be anything crooked about racing the only time he had mentioned it. All that, plus the fact I apparently had a mysterious source of income I never talked about, was a very neat package.

It should be obvious to anyone who thought about it that if illegal drugs introduced into a race horse would show up in a chemical analysis of his saliva or urine, the same drug would always show up no matter in what form it was used. But with all the overwhelming weight of evidence pointing in the other direction, he could close his eyes to that and come to the only natural conclusion—the one he wanted: that I had worked out a method of getting some form of coca into a horse and giving him enough edge to win a long race at, say, a mile and a quarter or above, without its being detectable in the tests. That was it—that and the fact that he had got all this information out of her instead of from me, had got it because she was a frivolous chatterbox who didn't have sense enough to keep her mouth shut. He understood Spanish, and he had a way with the ladies. He had put one over on us.

We stayed away from him that night, and we both remained in the apartment until noon the next day. Then I went out alone, picked up the Examiner, and wandered into the bar. It was practically deserted except for the single barman on duty in the afternoon. I sat down in a booth, ordered Scotch and water, and spread the paper open at the sports section. I killed two hours there and then went on back to the apartment without ever seeing him. When I came in she said he had called, wanting us to go out with him and Bobbie Everett again. She had begged off, saying she didn't feel up to it.

"I think it's you he's after," I said.

"No," she said. "Wait. Give him time."

The next afternoon I did the same thing, sitting in the bar with a drink and the morning paper open, reading the racing news from Santa Anita and the Florida tracks. Just before I was ready to take down my props and go home, he came in.

"Oh, hello, Rogers," he said, with just a shade too much heartiness. "Mind if I sit down?"

I grunted an invitation of sorts and folded up the paper, giving him just a brief glance at what I was reading.

"How's Mrs. Rogers? Hope she's not feeling bad."

"No," I said. "Just a cold."

His drink came. "Well, here's to crime," he said. Maybe that's the latest thing, I thought. He set his glass down suddenly, as if he had just remembered something. "Damnit," he said, "I've been meaning to tell you something. Thought of it the other day. I remembered you were a fly fisherman, and a friend of mine that's here in town now has a big ranch up on the Rogue River. He's always after me to come up when the steelhead are running, but I don't care anything about that piddling kind of fishing. Thought you might like to meet him, though. I'll bring him around and introduce him. He'll fix you up with some fishing, come summer."

"Oh, thanks," I said. "Thanks a lot. I've heard a lot about the Rogue, but I never had a chance to fish it."

"Well, that's what friends are for, the way I see it."

"That's right," I said, without much enthusiasm.

He was silent for a few minutes, apparently thinking about something.

"Say, Rogers...."

I looked up. "Yes?"

"We hit it off pretty well. And we've both been around. I'd like to have a little talk with you. The barman can't hear us over here."

I tried to keep my face blank and lit a cigarette to cover up my nervousness. "Talk about what?" I asked.

He leaned forward a little and lowered his voice. "As said, we're not kids, so you can cut out the innocent talk with me. I know who you are."

The butterflies were swarming in my stomach, and it was all I could do to stare back at him without any expression at all. If he had our number, what was he going to do? Call the cops? Was it too late now to run?

"Would you mind explaining what you're talking about?" I asked, as coldly as I could.

"Cut it out," he said. Then he winked. "There's just the two of us here, so you can let your hair down. I've known all along you were cleaning up some way, but it took me a while to figure it out. How about letting me in on something good?"

I could feel the sigh of relief coming all the way up from the bottom of my lungs and choked it down before it got away from me. It had been a bad moment.

"Look, Lachlan," I said irritably, now that I had hold of myself again, "what the devil are you talking about, anyway?"

"So you're going to play it that way?"

"Play what?"

"That hard-to-get stuff. Good God, man, all I want is just a tip now and then. That's not much to ask, is it?"

"Maybe I'm a little dense today," I said wearily. "Or never did learn the English language too well. Would you mind drawing me a picture?"

He leaned back in the seat and watched me for a moment, and then the nasty smile began to spread across his face. He was getting ready to let me know he had me. "Yeah. If you insist, I'll draw you a picture, Rogers. You're a pretty slick customer, but there are others around. I'll tell you something you didn't know. I happen to speak Spanish as well as you do. And I heard your little argument with your friend the other night. You remember, the one who used to work for your father?" He chuckled.

I let it hit me in the face, just a glancing blow he would be able to see for an instant; then I went blank again. "All right," I said, "so you're a linguist. I still don't see what you're driving at."

He leaned on the table again. "The hell you don't. That boy was yelling something about 'long races.' I couldn't figure it out at the time, but I've got it now. We both know what you're doing, so why not cut it out and be a good guy and let me in? I know how to keep my mouth shut, if that's worrying you, and I won't bet heavy enough to tip anything."

"Wait a minute," I said. "Let me get this straight. You're suggesting I'm mixed up in horse racing? Is that it? That I'm getting information of some kind?"

He grinned again. "Now you're talking sense. Except that I'm not suggesting anything—I know. And I don't mean information. I mean fixed races."

I stared at him. "Don't be a fool. There's no such thing as a fixed race."

He shook his head. "Boy, you're a hard nut to crack. Look, Rogers, I not only know you've got a way to gimmick a race now and then; I even know the kind you gimmick and the way you do it without getting caught. Now, will you come off it?"

I sighed and put down my glass. "Are you really serious about this, Lachlan, or is it a gag of some kind?"

"Of course I'm serious."

"Well, look. I'll tell you a few things. I used to work round race tracks as a veterinarian, so maybe I know at least as much about racing as you do. And one of the things I do know is that there is absolutely no such thing as a fixed race. Did you ever stop to figure out how many different and unpredictable factors there are to contend with in just one race? In an average field of eight horses, say? There are eight jockeys, eight horses, eight pole positions, good racing luck, bad racing luck, jams on the turns, injuries, and a thousand other things. And if you were fool enough to try bribing riders, there never have been and never will be eight crooked jockeys in one race. The odds against it are astronomical. There might be one you could buy, or even a slim chance of two, but not eight. At least six, and probably all eight, would report you to the stewards, or at least laugh in your face. They make a living riding horses, and if they got caught in something like that they'd be out on their tails in ten minutes."

"Cut it out," he interrupted. "I'm not talking about crooked jockeys. Don't be so pigheaded. I know you hype 'em. Or your men at the track do."

"Doping, you mean?" I snorted. "Didn't you ever hear of the saliva test?"

"Sure." He had that wise grin on his face again. He looked at me and said slowly, "Sure. I've heard of it. And I happen to know you've got a way to beat it."

I got up. "Well, there's no use arguing with you. I can see that. Think any' thing you want, but"—I stopped and stared coldly down at him—"don't bother me with it any more. I don't go for it."

I went off and left him sitting there. As I was going up in the elevator it suddenly struck me, that thing she had said a long time ago in Reno. She'd said he would come to me, demanding to be let in on a fixed race, and that the way to convince him there really was such a thing was to deny it could even exist.

The next move was up to him, and he did exactly what she had said he would. The next morning the telephone rang and she answered it.

"Oh, how are you?" she asked, a little breathlessly. "Why, no, he isn't in. He went downtown this morning." She looked across at me and winked, with the deadpan innocence of a child. There was silence for a moment while she listened. "Well, I—I really shouldn't.... Oh, yes, it would be perfectly all right, of course.... Well, all right. I'll meet you there in the bar. But only this once. I'll leave a note saying I've gone to the movies."

She hung up and looked over at me and grinned. "El Prado, for lunch."

She was gone until nearly three, and when she came in she didn't say any' thing for a moment. I could see she was bursting with something, though, and after she came over and kissed me and rumpled my hair she opened her purse without a word and dropped a sheaf of bills on the sofa. I looked at them. They were century notes, and they came to a thousand dollars.

"All right," I said, waiting.

"It was just as if I had written the part for him and he'd spent all night mem' orizing his lines." She sat down and lit a cigarette. "Mike, it was so easy it was' n't even any fun. He said he knew what you were doing, and there was no use my trying to cover up any more. Oh, he was quite brutal about it. He had me, you see. I was slipping out and meeting him. I tell you, sweet, that conceit of his is something that has never been approached. It's awe-inspiring. So I broke down and told him everything. Then he turned on the Lachlan charm, which seems to consist largely of breathing on you and bugling and trampling the shrubbery, and said everything was going to work out fine. We're going to double-cross you, you see.

"I went on to explain that it wasn't quite as easy as that. A lot of times I never did know myself when you had a deal coming up or what horse it was. You see, you're very hard and mean, and you never tell anybody anything. I told him you actually shot at a man once, for talking too much. He should find that easy to believe, after the way you brushed him off yesterday. Oh, I gave him a good story about all the double-frammis times frammis-squared elements that went into it—how you never knew for sure until just a few hours before race-time that it was a deal because they had to wait to get a line on the probable odds, since they never dealt in short-priced horses, and because they didn't want too much money bet too soon, for some silly reason you had tried to explain to me but which I could never understand. I'm the bird-brain type, you see. Anyway, you usually get the telephone call from the track just in time for you to get your money bet, and most of the time I don't know anything about it until it's all over.

"I told him I'd do what I could, and that if I could possibly find out when one was coming off and what the name of the horse was I'd try to get in touch with him without letting you know. All very uncertain and iffy, you understand. Naturally, that wouldn't do at all, so then he came up with the perfect solution." She stopped and looked at me with her eyes brimming with laughter. She nodded toward the money. "I'm to get it bet, if I can."

"O.K.," I said. "We've got him. But there's one thing. You let him give you too much money."

"Why?"

"Well, he has to win this one, of course, for the come-on. And to make it look good we've got to set up a specific race—a long race, naturally, something a mile and a furlong or over—so you can show him what he won it on. Suppose a real long shot comes in? You may have to fork over fifteen or twenty thousand dollars. That's pretty big bait."

She shook her head, gesturing with the cigarette. "Naturally, I'm not going to bet all of it. I just couldn't get it placed, because there wasn't enough time. That's part of the tease, you see. So when I do figure out a way to get past you and make a really good bet for the Happy Conspirator, he'll unload like a dropped piggie bank."

"That's better," I said.

"But wait," she went on. "That's not all. We're going to carry your idea of a specific race one step further. I'm going to give him the word that I've got part of his money bet and tell him the horse, before the results come in over the radio."

"How?" I asked. "The only way you can do that is to call some bookie for the results. They usually have them a few minutes to a quarter hour before the radio station gets around to them, but it'd be fairly obvious. He'd see through that."

"Not if I'd been sitting in the bar with him for the past hour or two and he knew I hadn't called anybody."

"Fine," I said. "But if you'd been sitting there with him for that long, why hadn't you told him the name of the horse before?"

"Because," she said, grinning, "you were there too. And of course I couldn't say anything in front of you. The minute you leave, I tell him. And then in maybe ten minutes the results come in over the radio in the bar, and sure enough, the horse has won."

"It sounds wonderful," I said. "But how?"

"I'm working on it. The first thing we need is a telegram. You go downtown in the morning and send me one."

We worked out the details. It was a beautiful piece of skulduggery, but it was going to take very precise timing to make it work. I went down the next morning and sent the telegram, and when it came we steamed it open so the envelope could be resealed, and saved it.

To make the whole setup look good we had to make him wait, and the longer he waited, the better it would be. The tension started to build up again as I got to thinking of Bolton and the police, and I was growing jumpy and irritable. He called her twice, wanting to know what was happening, and she stalled him. I kept watching the papers for a spot that looked good, and on the fourth night, when the morning papers hit the street, I found one. The eighth race on the next day's card at Hialeah was at a mile and a quarter, a claiming affair for cheap horses. I bought a Racing Form and went back to the apartment to check on it.

It looked fine. The horses were a sorry lot, non-winners since the first of the year, and there was nothing that stood out. The public selectors didn't agree on anything, and unless the Miami papers all happened to hit on the same horse, there wouldn't be any outstanding favorite. This was fine, because if there was a standout at a short price and he accidentally stumbled home in front it wouldn't look too good. We were supposed to be dealing in long shots. It looked as if Country Mile, Sweet Bobo, and Dinny's Queen would get most of the play, but in a field like that anything could win.

"This is the one," I said. "Let's go."

"How many entries?" she asked.

"Nine. We won't get the scratches until too late, but we can handle nine all right."

We wrote them all down, with a code word consisting of a masculine name opposite each horse, and spent an hour memorizing them. There couldn't be any slip, for if she got the wrong horse the whole thing would blow up. Around ten she called Lachlan, but he wasn't in.

She tried again at midnight and got him. "Hello," she said very quietly. "No. He's in the bath. I just now got a chance to call. There may be something coming up tomorrow about—you know. He just got a phone call from Miami. No, I didn't hear much of it, but there won't be anything certain until morning, anyway.... Yes, I'll try." Then she added hurriedly, "I've got to hang up now. I'll call you."

In the morning we went downtown together around eleven o'clock. She was supposed to hurry back alone just before one, call him from the apartment, and tell him excitedly that she had wonderful news and to meet her downstairs at the bar. Posttime for the eighth at Hialeah would be between two-thirty and two-forty P.M., Pacific time, and this would put her in the bar with him about an hour and a half before the race was even run. And she was going to tell him the name of the horse she had bet his money on. The gimmick was that I had to walk into the bar right behind her, before she could say a word to him.

When we got downtown we checked to be sure he wasn't following us, and then went up to the Starlite Roof of the Sir Francis Drake for a drink and on over to a place on Geary for lunch. It was twelve-thirty when we came out of the restaurant. We parted and she walked on down toward Powell to get a cab in front of the St. Francis. I went the other way, intending to pick up a scratch sheet and see how many horses were out of the race.

It was just luck that I noticed him. He went by without looking at me at all, going in the opposite direction, the way she was headed. I froze up, not moving, waiting to be sure. Maybe he hadn't seen her. The hell he hadn't. He was following her. I turned and took after the two of them and when I caught up with him he was about thirty feet behind her. She never did look back. I grabbed his arm and wheeled him around.

"Looking for somebody, Donnelly?" I asked.

There was no expression on his face. "Well," he said. "It's Strong Boy. And still grabbing at people."

She had flagged a cab and was climbing in. I took a deep breath of relief, and then it cut off suddenly as a big hand descended on my shoulder from behind.

"You ought to grab somebody your own size, pal," a voice said in my ear, and I turned, realizing too late that Donnelly'd had a convoy. The big slab of a face on a level with mine was tough and the eyes were full of a sour humor.

"Old friend of yours, Monk?" he asked Donnelly.

"I was following the broad and he loused it up."

"Well, maybe he knows where she lives."

"Yeah," Donnelly said. "Yeah. Maybe he does."

"I tell you how we could find out," the humorist said. "We could ask him.

Maybe he talks."

"Yes," I said. "I know where the broad lives. She lives with me."

"Well, that's nice. And where do you live? With her, I suppose."

"That's right."

"You walk behind him, Monk, and I'll walk on his right. Come along, pal."

It was in the sunlight of high noon on Geary Street with a thousand people going by. They couldn't do it.

"You couldn't shoot here in the street," I said.

"I'll tell you how you can find out."

I went.

Chapter Fifteen

It was only about two blocks away, a small hotel with a potted palm in the lobby. We went up to their room. Donnelly took the gun out of the holster under his left arm and clicked the safety off. He sat down on the bed and lit a cigarette, tipping his head to one side to let the smoke curl up.

The big man rocked on his feet and slammed me in the stomach. I fell back against the wall with my left arm across the rickety dresser. I got up, feeling sick, and lost my head. I started for him.

Donnelly motioned with the gun. "Uh-uh." It was like something out of a gangster movie.

He hit me again and I slid down the wall to the floor, trying to get my breath.

"Ask him where the babe lives," Donnelly said.

"Where does the babe live?"

I couldn't say anything. I couldn't even breathe.

"Where's the babe live?"

I shook my head and he hauled me to my feet and hit me again. He must have been a pro at one time, because he didn't break his hands up hitting me in the face. He hit me in the belly.

"Where's the babe?"

It was the lunch, and the water I'd drunk. I was in agony.

He hit me again.

"He ain't going to talk," Donnelly said. "If we beat him up enough to make him sing he'll be too big a mess to get out of here without the cops on us."

"He'll talk, all right. I been saving that one."

"He'd just pass out. Leave him go."

"The hell."

"Leave him go."

"How about one for the road?"

"What did I say?" Donnelly asked.

"All right."

They waved me out the door. I could still stand up, and I made it. It didn't add up, but I was too sick to think about it. Then I was in the street and breathing again and I knew how crazy it was. He wanted to know where Cathy was and he wouldn't give up that easily. I walked to the corner before I arrived at the obvious answer. They were going to follow me. I looked back, but I didn't see them. I turned a corner, walked another block, and turned again, watching the people behind me for a repeater. By the time I got down to Market I had him spotted. It wasn't Donnelly or the big man, but someone I hadn't seen before, a middleweight in a tan topcoat and high-crowned snap-brim hat. He was following me, all right, and I couldn't go back to the apartment unless I could shake him.

Then suddenly I remembered, and I felt cold all over. I looked at my watch. It was five minutes of one. Cathy would be coming down to the bar to meet Lachlan and tell him the news she didn't have yet, depending on me to be there to queer it until we got the results of the race. If I didn't show up, the whole campaign was wrecked. What could she tell him? That she had bet his money, but she didn't know the name of the horse? I started to run, looking for a telephone booth, frantic with fear that I was already too late.

There was a drugstore on the corner and I hurtled in, side-stepping customers and plowing my way to the booth at the rear. There was a woman in it, and a man waiting. I started to turn and run back to the street to look for another one when I saw the woman hang up and reach for the door.

I beat the man to it. "Pardon me. Emergency. Wife. Ambulance."

He took one look at my face and stepped back. "Sure," he said.

I dropped a coin in and dialed. The line was busy. I dug out the coin and popped it back into the slot. I got another busy signal. God, did they have only one trunk out of that board? Was everybody in the building calling out at once? I dialed again.

"Good afternoon, Montlake Apartments."

"Dr. Rogers," I said. "Nine-A."

It was too late. She was certain to have started by this time. I could hear the telephone ringing. It rang again. And again. We were sunk.

Then it clicked, and I could feel the breath ooze out of me.

"Cathy?"

"Mike! I was just going out the door."

"Don't," I said frantically. "Hang on until you see me getting out of a cab in front. I can't explain now. But hold everything."

"All right. But hurry."

I went back out front. He was standing by a newspaper rack, reading the headlines and watching the door. I started down Market, walking slowly. When I saw a cab coming with no others behind it I waited until it was almost abreast and then leaped to the curb, waving my arm. He stopped and I climbed in. I could see my man standing by the curb, listening.

"Palace Hotel," I said.

"Right, Chief."

When we reached the next corner I leaned forward in the seat. "Never mind the Palace. Make it the Montlake." My stomach felt as if I'd been stepped on by an elephant.

I looked at my watch again as I hurried into the lobby. It was nine minutes past one. Lachlan would already be in the bar. Everything now depended on my finding the right bellboy. He was a smart kid named Barney, with an alert eye for the easy dollar. I spotted him over near the desk and caught his attention.

I got him off to one side, reaching in my pocket at the same time. "You've got to do me a favor, Barney. I've got a big bet on a horse in the eighth race at Hialeah," I said, almost whispering, and looking around the lobby like a criminal. "My wife'd raise hell if she knew it. So I want you to call the bookie for me and find out who won. Can you do that?"

"Sure, Doctor," he said, eying the ten spot in my hand. "Where'll you be?"

"In the bar. Or the apartment. Try the bar first. She'll be with me, so write it on something and say it's a phone call. No. Wait," I said, hauling out the telegram. "I've got a better idea. Write it on this. On the front side of the wire. And then seal it up again. Say it's a telegram that just came for me. You got that?"

"Sure."

"You know the phone numbers of any bookies?"

He shook his head. "I used to know plenty. They're hard to find now, though."

"Well, here." I handed him the slip of paper with the telephone number of the horse parlor I'd located.

I could see her stepping out of the elevator now. It was timed beautifully. She came toward us.

"Oh, there you are, dear. You're late. I want a drink before lunch."

"I'll be right with you."

She looked at us a little suspiciously. "What are you doing?"

"Just telling Barney I was expecting an answer to a wire, and where he could find me. You run along. I'll be right with you."

She started into the bar. Barney and I grinned at each other. "Remember, the race'll be off around two-thirty-five. Call that bookie right away, and keep calling until you get it. And bring it right in. I've got too much on this one." I handed him the ten.

"I know how you feel," he said.

She had gone through the door now. I gave her a few more seconds, walking very slowly. When I came she had just sat down at the booth with Lachlan and was talking eagerly, her face alight with excitement. She looked up and saw me and her eyes went blank as she cut it off.

I walked up. "I thought I saw you coming in here when I got out of the cab. What are we drinking?"

Lachlan and I nodded. Cathy recovered and began chattering about something to cover the awkward pause. I sat down in a chair at the end of the table and ordered Scotch.

It should have been amusing, sitting there knowing Lachlan was raging to find out what Cathy had to tell him and knowing there wasn't anything he could do about it. It wasn't, however, for I wasn't even thinking about it.

Not any more. I was thinking about the fact that Donnelly was in San Francisco looking for her, and knew she was here, and that he had help now. Our
time was running out so fast you could see it go.

San Francisco's not New York, and looking for somebody who's transient
and who would be living the way she would is easy. You just cruise around
Powell Street and Union Square and Nob Hill, and it's only a question of
time.

I tried to shake it off and get back to the matter at hand. We had to keep
Lachlan here because the thing would be pointless unless she was with him
every minute so he'd know she hadn't had a chance to get the results of the
race. There wasn't much chance he would leave, but I held the bait out where
he could see it.

"Have to get back downtown in a little while," I said to Cathy, pretending to be unaware of the tension around the table. "Just time for a drink or
two. Unless you want to have lunch?"

She glanced at Lachlan. "No, dear. I don't think so. Why don't you get
something downtown?"

I knew she was wondering what held me up and why I'd sounded so
strange over the telephone, but there was no way I could tell her. Time
dragged. I ordered another round of drinks. Lachlan stalled as long as he could,
hoping I would leave, but finally gave in and ordered.

"What time is your appointment, dear?" Cathy asked, making a good act
of being impatient and trying not to show it.

I shrugged. "Any time after two-thirty."

The conversation would flare up for a few minutes, then die out until somebody prodded it again. Two-thirty came, and then two-forty-five. The strain
was getting me now. What was keeping Barney? All the horse parlors should
have it by this time. We had to have it before the radio station put it on the
air.

I was just starting to sweat in earnest when I saw him hurrying in from the
lobby entrance. Paying no attention, I picked up my glass and started to take
a drink. "Dr. Rogers. Oh, Dr. Rogers."

I turned. "Yes?"

"Telegram," he said. "It just came, and I thought you were here in the bar."

"Thanks," I said. I handed him a dollar.

They were both watching me. I was at the end of the table, and of course
they couldn't see anything but the back of the telegram. I tore the envelope
open and pretended to read. Barney had written it in pencil down in one corner. "Devil's Toupee," it said. I was conscious of thinking it was an awful
name for a horse and it was no wonder he was running in two-thousand-dol-
lar claimers. There was no payoff price, so Barney must have got it right off
the griddle, before they posted it. I hoped it was official.

I stood up. They looked at me inquiringly. "It's from Carl," I said to

Cathy. "I'd better call him. I'll see you later."

I folded the wire, stuck it in my pocket, and went out. "Carl" was the code name for Devil's Toupee, and now she could tell him the name of the horse she'd bet his money on. They'd get the bartender to turn on the radio to the station that broadcast the race results between recordings.

It was a smooth trick. Of course, a sharper would probably see through that telegram stunt and would know I had told her some way, but the thing that Lachlan would never get past was the fact that she had started to tell him almost two hours ago, when I came in and she had to shut up. That was the snapper, and it was a good one.

I hurried across the lobby and went up to the apartment. Switching on the radio, I tuned in the station. There was music at first and then, after a commercial, the announcer came on with the results of the third at Santa Anita. Then there was another recording. I began to worry. Suppose it had already been broadcast? The whole thing would be like a joke without a punch line. I was curious about the price, too, because that was important. Devil's Toupee should have been a long shot.

There was another long-winded commercial. Then it came. It was Devil's Toupee, Country Mile, and Lady-boots. Devil's Toupee paid $26.80, $14.60, and $9.00. I whistled, and did a quick calculation. She was going to tell—or had already told—Lachlan she had managed to get $400 of his money bet, so she'd have to pay off $5,360. That was a lot of bait. But it was going to be irresistible— better than twelve to one on a sure thing.

It was. She came in full of excitement about twenty minutes later and told me how it had gone.

"He's got it," she said, perching on the arm of my chair. "That easy-money fever. You could see that look in his eyes, and his hands were trembling after the announcer gave the payoffs. It's not the money, Mike. It's a disease. He's helpless now, like a baby. I mean, the whole thing went off so perfectly. He'd fight you now if you even tried to tell him it was a gag.

"Just as I knew he would, as soon as I told him the name of the horse, he made the bartender turn on the radio so we could wait for the results. Then he dug up a newspaper that was around the bar and looked up the public selectors' picks. There are three of them, you know, and each one had three horses in that race, and not one of them even mentioned Devil's Toupee. I just smiled at that, of course. Then when the results came in—that's all, brother. He's a sitting duck."

She stopped to light a cigarette, and laughed at me through the smoke. "Then, of course, he started to cry because he didn't have more money on it. I told him it was just impossible; I didn't have enough time and bookies were too scarce now. And that I was taking a long chance, crossing you that way, even getting four hundred down. I said he had no idea what you were like when it came to letting out information—that you wouldn't let your own mother in on it, and so on. I said you were dangerous in a rage and I was afraid of what would happen if you found out. He climbed down then and became very apologetic. I'm too good a thing to alienate, you see, and he has to keep me buttered up. Of course it wasn't my fault. I'd done beautifully. The only thing was, he just had to figure out some way to get a real bet made the next time."

"O.K.," I said. "The thing to do is let him stew in his own juice for a while. He'll be desperate to get that bet down by the time you have a way figured out for him to do it." I stopped and looked at her. "There's just one catch. We haven't got much time."

She stared at me. "Why? We've got all the time there is."

"No, we haven't. Donnelly's here in town. Looking for you."

"Oh, Donnelly's foot!" she exclaimed impatiently. "I wish you'd quit worrying about that moronic pipsqueak." She broke off suddenly, just remembering. "So that's what it was? With all this other stuff, I forgot about it. What happened?"

I told her. She was furious at first. "Why, that chiseling little vermin! We ought to—" She stopped.

"That's it, exactly," I said. "We ought to—what? Call the police? He hasn't done anything—yet. And, if I might point it out, we're not in a very good position ourselves to be jumping into the lap of the police force."

She quieted down a little. "What do you suppose he's up to, Mike? I mean, having those other two men with him?" It was the first time she'd ever shown any inclination to regard Donnelly as anything but a stupid punk, and now she wasn't scared so much as curious.

"I don't know," I said. "But I don't like it."

It scared me to think about it, but there wasn't anything to do but sweat it out. We couldn't give up on Lachlan and run. That was unthinkable, even before, but now he had over five thousand dollars of our money besides. We had to stick, and every day my nerves would be drawing nearer the snapping point. There wasn't only Donnelly to think about; there was always Bolton. How did we know Lachlan wasn't putting on an act? If he had been tipped off, he'd know we would let him win the first one. The time the police would close in would be just after he'd handed us the money for the big deal.

She saw Lachlan nearly every day, at lunch or in the bar. He was getting the money together. He was thinking bigger all the time; at first it had been fifty thousand, and now it was a hundred thousand he was talking about. And she was needling him with the complete impossibility of it. How could they get that much money bet in the few short hours they'd have to do it? And suppose she didn't find out the name of the horse at all? She was slowly driving him frantic. She'd dangled the easy money there before him, and now she was keeping it tantalizingly just out of his reach, pulling it back bit by bit.

Raising that much cash wasn't easy. Of course, he had plenty of money, but nobody keeps amounts like that lying around in cash. And he had whopping alimony and income-tax payments to meet all the time. He was working on it, though, she said, and could put his hands on sixty thousand right now.

But how was he going to bet it? That was the thing she was driving him crazy with.

Monday night she broke it. She came in from a ride with Lachlan and said, "He's ready, Mike."

"He's not half as ready as I am," I said. "I can't stand much more of this."

"It won't be so bad now. There'll be plenty to do. Your trouble is that you can't stand inactivity and suspense at the same time."

"Doesn't it bother you?"

"Not that much." She smiled. "It's just a war of nerves. All you have to do is outlast the opposition and make him give way first. It's intriguing."

"Sure," I said. "So is Russian roulette. Don't you ever think about what Bolton said?"

"I thought you were a gambler, Mike. It's a calculated risk, with the odds on your side. A hundred to one he was bluffing."

"I'm just a piker," I said. "All I ever gambled with was money." I went on wearing the same old groove in the carpet. "But if he's ready, let's go. I'd rather be dead than alive and waiting for it."

She smiled again. "We're already off. You can start looking for the race any time."

"You've already told him, then? I mean, about betting the money?"

She nodded. "Just a few minutes ago. All I had to do was hint at it and he was ready to climb all over me like a big dog. He has eighty thousand dollars in a safe in his apartment and he's going to give it to me in the morning."

I tried to fight off the chill. That would be the moment. "Where?" I asked.

"In the bar. I'm going to meet him there around ten."

"That much cash would be in large bills," I said.

"Probably thousands, mostly. I thought about that—the serial numbers, I mean. That's one reason I suggested the bar, at ten o'clock in the morning. It should be practically deserted, and if there's anybody around I'm not sure of, I can always back out and not take it."

"They might be outside. Or in the lobby."

"I've thought of that. There's nothing I can do about the lobby except to look it over before I go into the bar. But you can watch the front of the building from here. If anybody shows up who doesn't look right, phone me."

I couldn't sleep at all that night, and in the morning, a few minutes after ten, when she started down to the bar I could feel the butterflies holding a death dance in the cavern where my stomach should have been.

I stood by the window and watched while time came to a slow crawl and died. What did a plain-clothes cop look like? Like sixty million other men. If anybody got out of a car and started into the bar or into the lobby, could I possibly get through that switchboard to her in time? Nobody came and nothing happened.

After a long time she came back up to the apartment. She had a brown Manila envelope with her and she took it into the bedroom and emptied it out on the bed like a bag of dirty clothes.

I looked at it. It was the first time I had ever seen eighty one-thousand-dollar bills, and the way I felt, I never wanted to see another one. A knock on the door would have sounded like a hand grenade going off.

Chapter Sixteen

The big act was coming up now, the ticklish one, the one that had to go just right. There couldn't be any mistakes from here on out. We had the money, but we had to get out from under without Lachlan's screaming for the cops. We knew how we were going to do it—we hoped.

The angle she had worked out for Lachlan to get his money bet was simple enough. Since there was no way of knowing for certain whether she'd find out when there was another race coming up and what horse was rigged to win it, the thing they had to do was to get me to bet the money when I bet mine. And of course it had to be done without my knowing it, since I was a hard guy who'd cut their throats in a minute if I suspected it. So she had told Lachlan she knew the three betting commissioners who handled my money for me, and had sounded them out on taking some for her. They had agreed, of course, and were willing to bet hers—the whole wad of it—when I telephoned my bets in. Lachlan presumably didn't know—and she was playing it like a dumb chick, pretending not to know—what would happen if somebody began trying to dump eighty thousand dollars on some long shot the morning before a race. That was the gimmick, the thing that was supposed to get us out of the fire.

Actually, Lachlan probably did know, or would if he stopped to think about it, but he had the easy-money fever now and a man isn't completely rational when he's under its spell. He had intimated he knew it, that day when he'd been trying to break down my resistance in the bar, when he'd said he wouldn't talk and he wouldn't bet too much. He was forgetting or ignoring it now, with the lure of the big killing leading him on, but if everything went off according to plan, he'd be reminded of it—but good.

What would happen is simple enough. Nothing scares a bookie like a lot of money on a long shot, unless it's more money on a longer shot. They get fat off favorites, playing the old percentage year in and year out, but they can be wiped out by getting caught with a big bet on some long shot that happens to win. Most of them won't pay track odds above twenty to one, but even that can be disastrous if they get caught with a wad, say a thousand or two thousand dollars' worth.

They'll take it in small amounts, but when somebody starts trying to shove chunks of it in on some horse that figures to go to the post at a long price, they get suspicious and scared and start laying it off—that is, betting it on the horse themselves with bigger bookies who handle that sort of thing. And a lot of it winds up back at the track, being bet through the parimutuel windows, which of course drives the price down. If the horse does win, then, they've saved themselves in two ways: they've hedged their bets, and they've driven the price down to where it isn't disastrous.

And she and Lachlan—so Lachlan thought—were going to unload eighty thousand dollars on the horse and not upset the applecart. It was a laugh.

She had to make several trips downtown to make all this look good, and of course I couldn't go with her, just in case Lachlan was keeping an eye on us. I'd be in the wringer every minute she was gone, thinking of Donnelly, and I made her take a taxi every place she went and keep the cab waiting for her.

We had to have the right race now. Tuesday night there was nothing that looked good. A mile-and-a-sixteenth was the longest race on the next day's card, and that was a handicap for high-class horses, which wouldn't do at all. Wednesday night we drew another blank, the only race at any distance being at Fairgrounds, and that wouldn't do because we were supposed to be operating in Florida. We had to get something soon. Every day of delay was an agony of sheer suspense. Thursday night I hung around the stand that sold the Form, waiting for it to be flown in from Los Angeles. It was late again, and didn't come in until around ten. I grabbed one and went back to the apartment. This time I found it. It looked fine.

Again, it was the eighth, a mile-and-one-half claiming race for three-thousand-dollar horses. There were only eight entries, and nearly all the public selectors liked Torchy and Smoke Blue, with Tanner's Girl getting a nod here and there. Tanner's Girl looked like what I was after. She was a seven-year-old mare who'd won only three out of nineteen starts last year and one out of eight so far this year, all of them in two-thousand and twenty-five-hundred-dollar claimers. But the race she'd won this year had been the last time out, a little over two weeks ago right there at Hialeah, just managing to hold on to take the winner's end at a mile and a furlong, and that was what I wanted. It meant she should have a lot of support at the track. A lot of horse players seem to have the idea that a horse that won last time should win again, an idea that helps in keeping them broke. What we had to have was a horse that would go at a comparatively short price and finish somewhere up the track, and Tanner's Girl looked as if she could do both.

Of course, we could have cut out the risk by not letting Lachlan know what horse it was until after the race was over, to be sure the horse we "bet" on didn't win, but that would spoil the whole plan. He had to know in advance which horse it was, and before we got through he'd know why she lost.

In the morning at nine o'clock we cut it loose and let it roll. She called Lachlan.

"Hello?" she said eagerly. "He just left. A few minutes ago.... Yes.... Yes. It's wonderful news. He got a telephone call from Miami at eight-thirty, and I heard it this time. It's a horse called Tanner's Girl in the eighth race. The minute he left, I called the betting people. They've already started. The only thing is...." She hesitated.

Then she went on hurriedly, and a little apologetically. "What I mean is, it all came up so suddenly I didn't get all the money placed with those men. There's ten thousand I was going to give to another one.... Martin, please. I couldn't help it. I tell you I did my best.... But— But Martin, can't you see? It's still all right. That's the reason I called you. You still have three hours or more. I'll bring it down and meet you in the bar and give it to you right now. And if that's the way you're going to act, you can bet your old money your-self," she wound up defiantly, like a little girl on the verge of tears.

She was silent for a moment, listening. "That's all right. I didn't mean it either. Of course I'll help. You wait in the bar, and I'll bring it right down."

She hung up and winked at me, grinning. "Let him get around that," she said.

That was another reason we had to let him know the horse in advance. She was giving back ten thousand dollars of it to make him bet it himself. It was costly, but she was buying a psychological advantage that would be worth it. Take your old money and bet it yourself. I don't want anything to do with it. And when it was coupled with the snapper ending she had worked out, it might get us off the hook. Might, I thought. San Quentin was full of guys who were sure they were off the hook.

She took ten of the bills out of the envelope and went down to the bar. In about ten minutes she was back. That was the way it was supposed to go. Once she was down there she suddenly remembered she couldn't go down-town looking for bookies because that's where I was and she might run into me. He'd have to do it alone.

I stood by the window and watched him leave. Unless he broke that wad into a lot smaller chunks, he was going to leave a trail of very suspicious book-ies behind him—that is, if he found any bookies. A man who appeared to be in his right mind trying to unload ten thousand dollars in one piece on a nag like Tanner's Girl might start them laying off what Tanner's Girl money they already held. Bookmakers have remarkably little faith in the inherent nobil-ity of man. And anything being bet back at the track would help to knock the price down.

We went over the timing for the last time, and then I left for downtown. It was a little after ten. The race should be off at around two-thirty-five. I bought a scratch sheet at a newsstand on Market and looked it over while I had a cup of coffee. Only one horse had been declared. The ideas of the pub-lic selectors were about the same as those in the Form, with Torchy and Smoke Blue getting most of the notice. Tanner's Girl was mentioned a few times, but never at the top.

I went over to the bookie joint. A few men were sitting around reading scratch sheets. Tanner's Girl was eight to one on the Morning Line, down in the fourth spot in a field of seven. Torchy was the favorite at three to two. I began to tighten up now. Too damn much depended on it. It wasn't money we were playing with now; it was freedom. Suppose Tanner's Girl won? We should have done it the other way and not told Lachlan the horse until after the race. But no, I thought, we couldn't get out of the fire that way. It would be too obvious. It would smell.

I started getting the jitters about Tanner's Girl. She had won the last time, hadn't she? For God's sake, I thought, I'm beginning to sound like a two-dollar horse player trying to make up his mind. I couldn't quit worrying, though, and bought another Form to check again.

She couldn't win. Any fool could see it. She was seven years old and she'd have lost any semblance of form she'd had two weeks ago when she won at a mile and a furlong. You couldn't keep a horse that old up to racing edge more than a few days. And God knows she hadn't had much then. She'd been losing ground all the way through the stretch and just managed to last. And this race was three eighths longer. It was ridiculous; she didn't have a chance. It didn't do any good, though. I'd been around long enough to know about the horses that couldn't win and the horses that couldn't lose. They ran in bookie joints, not on race tracks.

I couldn't sit still any longer. I looked at my watch. It was nearly twelve. The results of the first race at Hialeah were already posted. I went out to the bar and drank a glass of beer and then went to the telephone booth.

I looked up the number and dialed Pan American Airways. "Hello," I said. "I have to go to Japan. I wonder if you could tell me what I've got to have in the way of papers and shots and so on, and whether I have to get a military permit of some kind.... No, I'm sorry, I can't hold on right now. I'm late for an appointment. But would you call me at three o'clock sharp with the list? It's important. Dr. Rogers, at the Montlake.... That's right. Thank you."

Then I called Braniff and made the same request about Ecuador, and threw in two travel agencies, just to be sure. At least one of them should call right at three P.M. It didn't make any difference who it was, as long as the telephone rang.

I tried to eat some lunch, but it wouldn't go down. My throat was dry and I felt the way a matador does watching the door of the *toril* swing open and seeing the dust boil in the shadows inside as the bull lunges, ready to come out. This is not for me, I thought, staring longingly after the people hurrying back to their offices and desks. All they had to do was go back to work for four hours; they didn't have to stand still and wait while a bunch of little men braided their nerve ends into twitching coils.

I called Cathy. "Yes," she said. "He just called me. He's back. He got some of it bet. Don't worry, Mike. He'll be here. I've already told him you're staying downtown. Mike, please don't stew about it. Of course he'll be here."

He had to be at the apartment when the results came in. She had left the door open by telling him I'd be downtown and that she didn't feel like coming down to the bar or going out. He'd get around to inviting himself in so they could wait for the results together. Or at least, he was supposed to.

I went back to the horse parlor and sweated it out as the races at Miami slowly became history chalked on a blackboard in the rear of a saloon. The fourth, the fifth, the sixth. I watched them, telling myself Tanner's Girl couldn't win. At two-fifteen the betting on the eighth had begun at the track. I watched the first and second run-downs. Tanner's Girl was seven to one, then five to one, and the odds on Torchy and Smoke Blue were going up. Then Tanner's Girl was nine to two and it was five minutes before posttime. I had to move now, and move fast.

I flagged a cab. We got caught in a traffic jam crossing Market, and I kept looking at my watch and cursing. It was two-thirty-five now and they should be off. In ten minutes or less they'd have the winner. We crawled up Powell, got clear on California, and went on fast. I got out a block from the Montlake and went into the neighborhood bar I had picked out beforehand. It had a telephone booth, and it was only a minute's fast walking time from the apartment.

I ordered a Scotch and looked at the time again. It was two-forty-one. They wouldn't have it yet. They might not have got away before two-forty. I held the drink in my hand in the deserted quiet dimness of the bar, and then in spite of myself I was moving toward the telephone booth. I was dialing. "Naw. Naw," the voice said. "Nothing from Florida yet. They're off. That's all."

In the apartment Lachlan would be calling one of the places where he'd made his bets. I had to get it by the time they did and get up there within a minute or two. But that was assuming Tanner's Girl didn't win. If she did, then what? I clawed, for the dial again. The line was busy.

I waited while thirty seconds stretched into a year and tried again. This time I got it. "Yeah?" the bored voice said. "The eighth at Florida? Yeah, we just got it. Nag by the name of Seven Sharps."

"Tanner's Girl! What about Tanner's Girl?" I yelled. She hadn't won, but I couldn't seem to get my mind to accept it. Maybe I'd have to go down there and get him to draw me a picture.

"Out of the money. No prices yet. Y'welcome."

I was out in the street. Lachlan and Cathy would have it now and Lachlan would know he had lost close to eighty thousand dollars. A lot depended on how long it took for the initial shock to wear off and for the thing to begin to soak in, and I had to get there in a hurry. We had to put him on the defensive before he could get set to attack.

It was a minute and a half including the elevator, and I fought hard to get hold of myself. I came down the corridor whistling something and clicked the keys a little as I pushed one against the lock. It didn't fit, and I tried the next one, taking my time, fighting for coolness. Everything depended on the next few minutes and what I saw when I opened the door.

Chapter Seventeen

I turned the key and stepped inside, humming. "Where are you, baby?" I said.

She was standing in the center of the living room, alone, facing me, and when she winked I could feel the strain break inside me like a snapped violin string. She'd done it, as she'd said she would. She had hit him before he could recover, taking the play away from him and going panicky when they got the news, crying out that something had gone wrong and I'd be raging. And then, within a minute, they'd heard me outside the door.

"Mike—" You could hear her trying to cover up the terror in her voice. "Darling, I—I thought you were going to wait downtown. I mean, wasn't there a race?"

I went over and kissed her, pretending to notice nothing wrong. "Sure. Turn on the radio, will you? I want to get the payoffs."

She was staring at me with something like absolute horror. "The payoffs? Didn't you— I mean, haven't you—"

"I didn't go to the bookie," I said, as if I hadn't heard her. "Ran into George Carnovan in the Oak Room and we got to shaking dice and talking about the Army. You remember George. You met him at Aspen, that time we were up there when it rained and ruined the skiing for three days. He's got a travel- ing job now. Some paper outfit." I broke off and turned around to her. "What's the matter, Cathy? Turn on the radio. I want to find out what price we got. The results should be on in a minute."

"Oh," she said. "All—all right, dear."

I was feeling a little better now, but the sweat was still clammy on my face. The door to the master bedroom was on the right and it was open, but the one to the dining room, on the left, was just slightly ajar. Lachlan would be in there, then, and she couldn't make any move that would give it away for fear he was looking as well as listening. There was no way he could get out, so he had to stay and suffer. She'd built me up as a raging maniac when some- thing went wrong, and in about two or three minutes I was going to know I'd lost a lot of money on Tanner's Girl.

"You didn't get the results, then?" she asked, her voice very small and tight, as if she were out of breath. "You don't know if—if he won?"

"She," I said, struggling for just the right casual tone. "It was a mare, name of Tanner's Girl. Oh, she won, all right. But I want to get the price. Ac- cording to the scratch sheet she was eight to one on the Morning Line, but we'll do better than that. Should get twelve to one, anyway."

She didn't say anything. I turned and looked at her, as if just noticing for the first time that something was wrong. "What's the matter, Cathy? Don't you feel well? You look pale."

"I'm all right, dear. I—I mean, did you bet very much on the race?"

"Yes," I said, lighting a cigarette. "My whole quota. Five thousand dollars. But there's nothing to worry about. It was bet late and spread very thin. We'll do all right on the price."

"Your quota?" she asked blankly.

The radio was beginning to warm up now. It was playing music. "Skip it, Cathy," I said, a little irritably. "I've tried a dozen times to explain it to you. It's just a blind spot, I guess. But never mind. I want to hear this."

"Darling," she asked faintly, "could we go down to the bar? I think I'd like a drink."

"In a minute," I said impatiently.

"Please. Right now."

"I said in a minute, Cathy. I want to hear the results of that race."

Unless his nerve was very good, he should be getting the horrors. He might or might not have begun to get the implications of that stuff about the quota and betting late and spreading it thin, but he would as soon as that telephone rang.

"Darling, please." She was doing it nicely. You could hear the horror in it.

"Go ahead," I said. "I'll be down as soon as I get this. Wait." I broke off. The recording had stopped and the announcer was coming on. "This may be it now."

"We now bring you the results of the eighth race at Hialeah," the announcer began. Then the telephone rang. God, I thought wildly, both at once.

"Cathy," I snapped. "Answer that. I'm trying to listen."

She picked up the telephone and the clatter stopped. The radio went on: "The winner was Seven Sharps. In the place position it was Smoke Blue, with Miss Pouter third. Seven Sharps paid—"

"What!" I yelled. "What the hell does he mean, Seven Sharps?"

She had her hand over the telephone mouthpiece and was wailing, "Mike! Mike! It's long distance."

"The hell with that. Did you hear—" Then I did a double take on it. "Long distance? From where? Give me that!"

"It's Miami," she said faintly, collapsing into a chair. I grabbed it out of her hand. "Hello! Hello!" I snapped.

"Dr. Rogers? This is Pan American—" the voice on the other end said, just as I pressed down the arm and broke the circuit. He couldn't see it, the way I was standing, even if he were looking, and the noise of the radio would cover the click. I didn't dare leave it down, because it might ring again, but when I let it up I could hear the dial tone.

"Yes. Yes," I said. "This is Rogers. Go ahead. Carl? Is that you, Carl? Well, what the hell are you people— Yes, I just heard…. What do you mean, what am I trying to do out here? I haven't done anything but take your word, like a damned fool, and expect you to do what you're supposed to."

I still had the dial tone. The switchboard operator hadn't unplugged it yet, but she'd be on the line in a minute. I covered the mouthpiece with my hand, keeping my back toward the dining room.

"What!" I yelled. "Of course I didn't. Good God, do you think I'm crazy? I tell you it was five thousand, not a penny more. There wasn't a bit of it placed before eleven o'clock, and it was spread out everywhere. What do you mean, five to one? It couldn't have been.... What?... Listen, you know better than to ask me if I've been talking.... I don't care where the money was coming from, there was nothing leaked out here! San Francisco? I tell you it's impossible.... You did *what!* Why, you stupid idiot, I ought to— Hello! Hello!" I jiggled the hook savagely, then slammed the phone back into its cradle.

Cathy was huddled in a chair, watching me with terrified helplessness. I pretended I didn't notice her as I went raging across the room.

"Darling," she asked tremulously, "what—what happened?"

"What happened! I'll tell you what happened! One of those big-mouthed idiots back there got drunk and started talking, and now they're trying to blame it on me! Somebody dumped over fifty thousand on that horse, and every bookie in the country was flooded with Tanner's Girl money by post-time for the first race. They couldn't even get their bets placed. And then it started pouring back to the track. He said twenty minutes after the mutuel windows opened for the eighth race, Tanner's Girl was down from eight to one to five to one. So Carl sent the jockey out with instructions to run her into every blind switch he could find, even if he had to get clear off the track and chase her up an alley."

Of course, the whole thing was a dream. There hadn't been any big wads of money bet on Tanner's Girl and probably very little coming back to the track; what had driven the price down was the thing I'd figured on from the first—the old two-dollar bettors out there at the track betting on her because she won last time.

"But why?" she asked, her voice breaking with fright. "Why did they want her to lose?"

"Why? *Why?* Because they decided I was the one who'd talked! I wasn't there to defend myself, so I was the goat. They didn't have anything bet, so why should she win? They cut my throat. They left me out on a limb. They were going to teach me to keep my mouth shut! The dirty, rotten, big-mouthed—" I switched over to Spanish and ran through every dirty name I knew.

I whirled around to her. "Start packing. We're going back there, and somebody's going to have his tail in a sling when we get this thing threshed out. Trying to tell me that money was coming from San Francisco."

I stopped then, as if noticing for the first time the look of horror on her face.

I froze dead in my tracks, staring at her.

"Mike! Don't look at me like that! Mike, please."

"San Francisco, he said. Well, maybe somebody *has* been shooting off her little mouth."

"Darling! Listen! Please."

"Why, you little tramp!"

She pushed back in her chair, whimpering now. "Mike! I haven't done any-thing. Honest!"

"So you wanted to know the name of the horse, didn't you?" I grew very quiet and started to walk slowly toward her. "I remember now. You asked me what horse it was."

With a roar of pure rage, I reached for her. I got the front of her blouse and it ripped as I jerked her out of the chair. "Why, you rotten, double-crossing, blabber-mouthed little tramp, I ought to kill you! It see it now. When the filthy pig couldn't get anywhere trying to pump me, he got it out of you! So we've been going to picture shows, have we? Well, aren't we just too cute!" I let go, and shoved her, and she fell to the floor.

Still cursing, I ran to the desk and yanked open a drawer. There wasn't any gun in it, because I didn't own one, but there was a big metal paperweight the size of a .45, and I banged it against the drawer getting it out, and shoved it in my coat pocket.

She was beginning to scream now. "Mike! No! No! No!" She tried to get up off the floor, came up to her knees, and lunged desperately at my legs. "Mike! Please!"

I peeled her off, lifted her, and threw her backward. She crumpled to the floor again, whimpering. "I'll attend to you when I get back," I said savagely, and ran toward the door. I could hear her still whimpering with terror as I slammed it.

Lachlan's apartment was two floors above, but I didn't bother with the el-evator. I took the stairs two at a time, and was halfway up there before I sud-denly remembered there wasn't any necessity for acting, now that I was out of sight. The longer I was gone, the more time he'd have to get out of the apartment and run. I slowed down.

A Filipino boy in a white jacket answered the ring and I shoved past him before he could do more than utter a startled grunt. I plowed into the living room and looked wildly around. "Where's Lachlan?" I demanded, with my hand on the paperweight in my coat pocket.

He was scared. "He not here. Go out long time ago."

"Where is he?" I asked menacingly. I had to put on a good act because Lach-lan would get in touch with him or come back sooner or later, and the more I scared the kid, the better story he'd give Lachlan.

"No understand." He was taking refuge in pidgin English and pretending he didn't know what I was talking about. I switched to Spanish and chewed

him out, and he got that, all right. I went through all the rooms, pretending
to be putting on a big search, but just stalling for time.

I came back to the living room, still looking wild and scaring the houseboy.
I stood by the desk near the door, glaring around like a man who still hopes
to find somebody to shoot, and I don't know what made me glance down at
the mail lying there. There were two or three opened letters and one envelope with its end slit. Maybe it was the foreign stamp that attracted my attention. The return address was printed, some construction company in Be-
lize, British Honduras, and typed in above it was "Harold E. Goodwin, Supt."

Like a man in a dream, I reached down and picked it up and slid the letter
out. "Dear Mart," it began, "It's been some time since I've heard from you
and I just thought I'd drop you a line and see if you have any plans for coming back to our old stamping grounds any time soon...."

I slid it back into the envelope and dropped it on the table. I was numb. I
had forgotten Lachlan. I was thinking of a two-story house in a little desert
town on the edge of the sand dunes and a man named Howard C. Goodwin
and his wife. Suddenly it all balled up and hit me at once. I'd run up here as
part of an act, pretending to be in a murderous rage because she'd lied to me,
and when I got here I found out she had.

With an effort I pulled myself together. There wasn't time to think about
that now. We had to get out from under Lachlan. I shouted something threatening at the houseboy for the last time, and ran out the door. I'd been gone
five or six minutes now, and it should have been long enough for him to get
out of the apartment. And it was. When I got back, he was gone.

And so was Cathy.

I stood there, looking stupidly around the empty living room. Where could
she have gone? This wasn't part of the act. She was supposed to be here. The
radio had been turned off and it was unbearably silent after that crescendo
of violence, and I couldn't adjust myself to the abrupt letdown. I wanted to
make a noise of some kind, or run.

It had been only five minutes. She couldn't go anywhere in that time. I went
through all the rooms, idiotically, as if I were looking for a button lost off a
shirt. When I came out into the living room again the telephone rang shrilly,
knifing at the silence.

I answered it mechanically. "This is Inter-Continent Travel Service," a girl
said.

"I'm sorry," I said. "I've changed my mind."

Lachlan was gone, so she must have gone with him. But that was stupid. She
wouldn't do that. Everything had gone according to plan right up to the moment I left the apartment, and when I came back five minutes later she had
disappeared. Had Lachlan forced her to go with him? Had he been wise to the
whole thing? Maybe he was taking her to the police right now, or the police
had already been here and were looking for me now. I shook my head, trying

to clear it and think.

I ran down the corridor and punched the elevator button. The car was a long time coming, and seemed to descend with agonizing slowness, as if it were filled with helium and had to be pulled down. I looked wildly around the lobby, and then hurried out onto the sidewalk. She wasn't there. I went down the ramp into the garage. Both cars were in their stalls. I stared at them, and turned and ran out. I began to feel like a man in a nightmare. I thought about Goodwin, and then pushed him out of my mind. That would have to wait. The whole thing had blown up some way, and Cathy was in trouble. I looked up and down the sidewalk like a man in a trance.

I went back into the lobby. A man who was standing at the desk talking to the clerk turned and came toward me. "Dr. Rogers?" he said. "I'd like to speak to you for a moment."

"I'm sorry," I said. I had to get back to the apartment. She must be still in the building somewhere, and maybe she had gone back. I pushed past him, not even seeing him now.

"It's quite important," he said softly. "I think perhaps you'd be wise to listen to me, Reichert."

Reichert. I stopped abruptly as the name crashed through my thoughts and hit me like a bucket of cold water. I turned and stared at him. "What?"

He smiled. "Perhaps we could go into the bar. Would you like a drink?"

"You say it's important?" It was a stupid question. Even with Cathy going around and around in my mind, I could recognize danger when I saw it. It was there in the cool, incisive eyes and the probing intelligence behind them. He wasn't unfriendly or threatening; he was just efficient.

"I believe you'll find it so. Shall we go?"

We went. We sat down in a booth in the corner and ordered drinks. I tried to clear my mind to deal with this. Here was dynamite. And he wasn't a policeman; or if he was, they had begun recruiting their cops from Harvard Law School. He was around thirty, with a lean, alert face and crew-cut hair, and an unshined shoe or a piece of lint on the conservative Brooks Brothers suit would have been as sloppy as a tenement clothesline on a destroyer.

"Perhaps I'd better introduce myself," he said crisply. "My name's Sheldon Gerard. I'm an attorney. Winkler, Hartman, and Gerard, of El Paso. However, right at the moment I'm just more or less performing an errand for my uncle, who is a banker in a little town"—the probing eyes glanced up and went right through me—"called Wyecross. You may have heard of it."

The chill was spreading down my back, and I looked away from him until I could get control of my expression.

"My uncle," he went on with the cool efficiency of a professional executioner, "is ill at the moment, and wasn't able to travel, so he asked me to fly over here and take care of this for him."

There was no hope whatever, but I tried to bluff anyway. "That's too bad,"

I said, looking at my watch. "But I'm afraid you've made a mistake somewhere in your doctors. I'm not an M.D., so if you'll excuse me—"

"Nice try," he said, with something like approval in the sharp gray eyes. "But to get on—I'll be as brief as possible. To put it in four words, Reichert, the jig is up. My uncle, as you've probably already guessed, is a Mr. Howard C. Goodwin, of Wyecross. It might interest you to know that he suffered a nervous breakdown as a result of that expensive bit of hocus-pocus you and your friends sold him. Incidentally, it was a brilliant piece of work, and I believe you'd have got away with it entirely except for the thing that so often happens when a number of persons—some of them with police records—are involved. Around three weeks ago Mr. Wolford Charles fell afoul of the police in Florida on an old charge, and in the course of the investigation he let drop a few revelations concerning this particular bit of moonshine."

I couldn't say anything. I couldn't even move. I wanted to get up and run, but my legs wouldn't work. Charlie had been caught, and because she had beaten him and the double-cross and taken all the money, he'd spilled it to get revenge. All I could do was sit there and listen while this remorselessly efficient machine dictated the bill of indictment.

"Now, we're not interested in prosecution, for several reasons. One of them is that my uncle is a banker, and naturally the publicity wouldn't help the bank very much. The other reason, of course, is that Mr. Charles, the mastermind, is already in prison, or on his way there, on another charge, and we understand from some of his testimony that you and Mrs. Lane are more or less newcomers to the field of crime.

"So I have been empowered to offer you a little proposition. If you will return the whole sixty-five thousand dollars—which we understand from Mr. Charles's testimony you have—we will drop the case and not call in the police at all."

I grabbed at it. It was the only thing we had left. "All right. I'll give it back. But how do I know I can depend on you not to call the police?"

"You don't," he said coolly. "Except that you have my word for it. But on the other hand, what else can you do?"

"You tell me," I said wearily. I stood up. "Just wait in the lobby. I'll bring the money down."

"Very well," he said. "But I'd advise you not to try to run."

"Run where?" I asked.

"I see what you mean. All right, Reichert."

I went up in the elevator and walked along the corridor. My fingers were shaking as I fitted the key in the lock. Would she be back? And where did we go from here if she was? She had lied about Goodwin to get me to go into the thing with them. I opened the door and the apartment was empty. The silence rang in my ears.

I had to get hold of myself. There was no use trying to figure anything out now. I wasn't capable of rational thought, and there wasn't any time. I could look for her later. The thing I had to do now, before anything else, was get rid of that money. Give it to Gerard, get it into his hands before he called the police. There were seventy one thousand-dollar bills in the drawer, the money we'd taken from Lachlan, and by giving Gerard sixty-five of them to return to Goodwin we could stay out of jail. That was the only thing that mattered now.

I hurried across the room to the desk and yanked the drawer open, and then just stood there staring into it. The money was gone. I straightened up and rubbed a hand across my face, hard, and shook my head. The money's here, I thought. I'm just going crazy. I'm looking right at it and don't see it. I've just had too much of this. I'll be all right in a few minutes.

She'd put it there. Burglars don't read Poe, she'd said, putting it in there, slipping it into an old bank-statement envelope and throwing it carelessly in among a bunch of letters in this drawer. Not in some other drawer; in this one. I jerked it all the way out and letters and envelopes flew across the rug as I emptied it. I gathered them up one at a time and put them back. It wasn't there. It wasn't in any of the others.

This was the end of the line. She was gone, the money was gone, and I was holding the bag after the rest of the snipe hunters had gone home.

Chapter Eighteen

I was a bug in a tin cup. I was the only one left, and Gerard was waiting for me in the lobby. When he got tired of waiting, he would call the police.

I tried to light a cigarette. The lighter wouldn't work, and I crumpled the cigarette and threw it on the floor. It wasn't Gerard and the police I was try-ing to get away from in my thoughts; it was the awful knowledge that she had done this to me. She'd lied about Goodwin, and now she'd calmly cut my throat.

But wait. That was exactly the same thing I'd thought that awful afternoon in Wyecross, and she hadn't deserted me. Maybe it wasn't true. There must be some way out of it, some other explanation. If she had the money, why had she gone with Lachlan? *Had* she gone with him? But she must have; they'd both left here within five minutes. Maybe Lachlan had taken the money. Maybe he'd been wise to the thing all along, and had gone after the police. Maybe Bolton *had* tipped him off. I stopped suddenly.

What had Gerard said? I forced myself to stand still and think back over every bit of it, word by word, as well as I could remember it. Charlie had been arrested in Florida three weeks ago. That was it.

I grabbed the telephone and called the desk. "There's a Mr. Gerard wait-ing in the lobby. Would you page him and send him up to Nine-A?"

I could be wrong, but what did I have to lose? I was headed for San Quentin either way. When the buzzer sounded I opened the door and let him in.

He looked at me with raised eyebrows. "Really, Reichert, I must ask you to hurry."

I hit him. He just grunted like a rabbit and started to sway, and I hit him twice more on the way down. It was dirty, and he didn't have a chance be-cause I outweighed him by thirty pounds, but I wasn't in any position to be squeamish about it. He didn't try to get up. He just crawfished backward across the rug until he came to rest with his head against a chair. Blood ran out of the corner of his mouth.

His chest heaved as he fought to get his breath. When he could speak, he said, "That was a stupid thing to do."

"I do a lot of stupid things. I've been doing them for several weeks."

"I have no choice now. I'll have to call the police."

"I don't think you will," I said. "Where's Bolton? And Wolford Charles?"

He stared blankly. "Bolton?"

"You want some more?"

"Really, Reichert—"

I started toward him. "Come on. We haven't started yet."

He began to look really scared. "I don't know what you're talking about."

"Charlie, or Bolton, or both of them, sent you up here. They're still after that Goodwin money. You said Charlie was arrested three weeks ago and spilled himself. Didn't you?"

He put a hand to his jaw and stared at me, puzzled. "Yes."

"Well, he couldn't have told anybody three weeks ago that I was here and that the name I was going under was Rogers, because he didn't know it. He got it from Bolton. So where are they?"

He started to shake his head. I reached down for his shirt to haul him up, and he began to whimper. He didn't look so efficient now. I cocked a right to let him have it.

"All right," he said. "Don't hit me again. I'll tell you."

I heaved him into a chair and stood there watching him. My hand hurt and I was out of breath myself. "Let's have it."

"It was all their idea, but they needed somebody you didn't know to do it. Bolton called her and asked her to meet him downtown. That was to get her out of the way so we could work on you. They didn't think she'd fall for it, but maybe you would."

"Wait," I said. "When did he call?"

"About two-thirty. But she didn't come. I waited here anyway, thinking I might see her go out. And then I did. She went out with some man wearing a white Texas hat and they got in a car and drove off. I was just getting ready to call you when you came down."

I thought swiftly. The reason she hadn't gone down there to meet Bolton at two-thirty was that Lachlan was in the apartment, waiting to get the results of the race. She couldn't leave, even if she'd wanted to. But then she had, later, with Lachlan. But why? Had she gone to see Bolton then? And why had she taken the money?

"Where are Bolton and Charlie now?" I demanded.

"At the Sir Francis Drake. That's where she was supposed to meet them."

"Sit where you are," I said. I'd just started to reach for the telephone when the buzzer sounded. I leaped for the door with my heart pounding in my throat. But it wasn't Cathy. It was Bolton.

I watched his face as he looked toward Gerard sprawled back in the chair with blood on his face. There was only a flicker of regret, and then it was gone. I wondered why he had come; there was no way he could have known the thing had already failed, and he was taking a chance of wrecking it.

"If you're looking for your boy," I said, "you can have him."

But he had already forgotten Gerard. He was out of breath, as if he had been hurrying, and I didn't like the way his face looked. "Belen, have you heard anything from Cathy?"

It began to get to me now. I didn't like the way he asked it. I grabbed his arm. "What is it? Damn it, Bolton—"

He shook my hand off with savage impatience. We were about to snarl and pile into each other like two men who had suddenly gone crazy, and it wasn't from anger. It was fear.

"Where is she?" I was crowding him, forcing him back.

He put out a hand and shoved me and I got set to swing at him. Then he barked, "Get hold of yourself, Belen," and we both realized we were acting like fools.

"All right," I said furiously. "All right. But, good God, can't you say something? What is it?"

"I don't know. But I think it may be Donnelly."

"Why?"

"She was talking to me on the phone, and then— But I'd better explain. I called her about two-thirty and said I had to see her about something very important. She seemed to have something on her mind, and practically hung up on me. I was still waiting in the hotel room, hoping she might show up, when I saw her come down Powell with Lachlan in that foreign roadster of his. That was just after three. And a few minutes later she did call. From a pay phone somewhere. She was warning me. She had an idea I was up to something—that is, that Charlie and I were—and she'd tried to get you and you didn't answer."

That would have been when I was down in the lobby with Gerard, I thought. Wouldn't he ever get to the point?

"She said she was on her way back to the apartment. And then she suddenly quit talking. There was a gasp, as if somebody'd thrown water on her, and that was all. It was a pay phone, because the operator came on in a minute, while I was still and wanted another dime. Donnelly's here—"

"I know he's here," I said. "I know the hotel he's in."

Bolton caught up with me. "I'm going with you," he said. Then we both remembered Gerard. He got out of the chair, looking dazedly at us, not even knowing what we were talking about.

"You'd better go on back to the Drake," Bolton said to him. He came with us. We flagged a cab and went off and left him standing there on the sidewalk.

I didn't know the name of the hotel. I gave the driver the general location, talking too fast and having to repeat it. We shot down off the hill, weaving through traffic, while I prayed there would be something there. It was our only lead, the only thing we had to go on. I turned and looked at Bolton. His eyes were tired, and I could see the lines of strain around his mouth. Even in the mad confusion and the fear that had hold of me, some part of my mind noticed it and wondered. Why was *he* taking it so hard? An hour ago he was coolly trying to swindle her.

I spotted the hotel and yelled for the driver to stop. We got out and paid him and ran across the street. There was no one in the lobby except the clerk behind the desk. He was reading a Racing Form and looked up boredly as we hurried through and up the stairs. I didn't know the number of the room, but I remembered which one it was. Bolton was right behind me as I ran down the corridor.

It hit me then, but it was too late to do anything about it. There would be two, or maybe three of them, and they all had guns. We had nothing. But it couldn't be helped.

I pounded on the door. There was a sound of movement inside, and somebody was fumbling at the bolt. I got set to crash against the door when it opened, and then caught myself just in time.

It was a man I'd never seen before. He was wearing a pair of glasses and nothing else, and he was holding a highball glass in his hand and there was lipstick on his face. "'Shgoin' on?" he demanded. "You lookin' for shmack in the kisser?"

I stared blankly at him. "Sorry, Mac," I said dazedly. "I—I was looking for my wife."

"Whash she look like?" he asked. Then he drew himself up indignantly. "You gidda hell out of here."

We turned away. I felt sick. It was our only chance and now we didn't have that. Could it have been the wrong room? No. That was one hotel room I could remember. We ran down the stairs to the lobby.

The clerk glanced at me with surly disinterest. "What you want?"

"A man named Donnelly. Did he check out?"

"Nobody here by that name." He dismissed us and went back to his paper.

I reached across the desk and got his collar and heaved. When he was straight up and clear of the chair I let go and shoved. He bounced against the mailboxes. "Maybe we could have your attention for a minute," I said.

He stood up. "I tell you—"

"We're looking for a man who was here. I don't know what name he was registered under. He's a little guy who looks like he was made out of pipe cleaners and he's got the face of a forty-year-old baby. There was a big guy with him. Where are they?"

"They checked out."

"When?"

"Two days ago."

"Did he have a car?"

"I don't know. I think so."

We went outside. What chance did we have, in a city of eight hundred thousand, and not even a place to start? Bolton flagged a cab and we went back to the apartment.

"We've got to call the police," I said.

"We can't. She wouldn't have any chance then."

I waved him off wildly and reached for the telephone. He jerked it out of my hand. I was raging. I tried to swing at him. He caught my arm.

"Look, Belen. We can't call the police. Our only chance is to wait here. Don-nelly may call you. Or make her call."

"Why the hell would he call us?"

"I've got to tell you something." He had gone over by the window, and when he turned back I could see the strain in his face. "Maybe I can make you see what I mean. And stand back till I get through. Cathy's in a bad spot, and it isn't going to help any to have us swinging at each other. Donnelly's not what I said he was. I invented him."

I stared at him. We were all going crazy.

"Donnelly's not a gangster. He just thinks he's one. He's a punk, a cheap horse player with a warped mind. You described him when you said he had the face of a forty-year-old baby. Movie gangsters are his heroes. He goes to crime pictures and patterns his speech and clothing and mannerisms after movie killers."

That was it, the thing that had puzzled me for so long. Even in all this mad-ness I could remember the odd impression I'd had every time I'd seen him, that feeling that I was watching a killer in a B movie. But what was Bolton trying to say?

"He was a punk who always wanted to be a big-shot gangster and didn't have the nerve," he went on harshly, "and now he thinks he is one. I did it. I built him up. God knows I didn't intend it to end this way. How did I know how near the edge he was?"

"What are you driving at?"

"Shut up and listen! I'm trying to tell you. It was a game I was working on Cathy. I invented that story about the four-hundred-dollar bet and got hold of Donnelly to play the part. I pretended to be scared to death of him to scare her, to make her pay off the eight thousand she was supposed to owe him."

I went for him. I was wild, not even half seeing him, just asking for it. He rolled with the punch and countered. His fist crashed under my jaw and I slid down beside the chair.

He was raging. "Will you stop acting like a fool, for God's sake?"

I shook my head and tried to get up. The blow had knocked a little sense back into me. We had more on our minds than fighting each other.

"Maybe he's not so dangerous," I said.

"He is dangerous. Can't you see that? He's kidnaped a girl, and when his nerve goes back on him, how do we know what he'll do in a tight spot? That's the reason we can't call the police. If a patrol car pulled up alongside him he might fold up like a wet paper towel, and on the other hand he might start blasting away at everything. There's nothing crazier than a cowardly punk with a gun.

"I could see it beginning to get him when he looked me up in Los Angeles—after I was up here the first time. You'd already bounced him around and locked him in that freight car, remember? I told him the deal was off. He could-n't scare Cathy; it was useless. He began to pull that tough stuff on me and I could see he had begun to believe it himself, so I slapped him down. But it didn't do any good. He was already the Napoleon of the underworld, and he'd picked up a couple of hoodlums who think he's just what he pretends to be. What'll they do when they find out they've been sucked into com-mitting a serious crime by a crazy punk who'd cry at a parking ticket?"

"All right, all right," I said desperately. "But what makes you think he'll call? What the hell would he want to call me for?"

"Because that's just what a movie gangster would do. He wants money, and that's the way they do it in the movies."

All they had to do was take it. Just take the money and kill her, on a back road somewhere in the Marin County hills. I didn't want to say it, but I had to.

"He won't have to call to get it," I said. "She's got it with her."

He stared at me. "How much?"

"Seventy thousand dollars."

"Good God," he said. "Oh, good God." He went striding across the room. "Look, Belen, maybe they'll just take the money and throw her out."

"Yes," I said. "Except that he's crazy. And if we were crazy too, maybe we could guess."

I started for the telephone again, to call the police anyway, when something suddenly occurred to me. I stopped. "Didn't she say on the phone that she'd tried to get me? And she was warning you to lay off?"

"Yes. That's right," he said. Then he began to see it too. "Say—"

"Then maybe she hasn't got the money with her. It may be still here in the apartment." I had it now. It all fitted. That call from Bolton had put her on her guard. She had a hunch they were trying to get her out of the way so they could try some kind of sucker game on me to get their hands on that money. But there was no way she could warn me during that act in the apartment for Lachlan's benefit. And afterward she'd had to leave with Lachlan. That was the thing I hadn't been able to understand before, but I could see it now. We'd made it too convincing. He'd thought I was going to come back and kill her, and had insisted on taking her with him when he left. She had to go, to make it look right. But after she'd left him, downtown somewhere, she'd called Bolton and warned him to lay off, and had tried to call me. She would-n't have worried about it if she'd had the money with her. So it must be here.

"Well, that means he'll call here," Bolton said. "Extortion, because he knows she has the money from Goodwin."

My mind was working a little better now. And I was suspicious of Bolton again. "There's just one thing I want to know," I said. "What's your angle this time? How much of this junk can I believe? You've just told me you were trying to scare her out of eight thousand dollars with Donnelly. Two hours ago you and Charlie were trying to swindle her out of sixty-five thousand with that game with Gerard. What are you trying to pull now?"

He stopped his pacing and ran a hand through his hair. "Does this look like an act?" he asked harshly. "For God's sake, Belen, this is the truth. It's on the level. Sure, I'll admit I tried to swindle her. I'll try it again if I get a chance. She'd do the same to me, and love it. But having her hurt is something else. I couldn't stand it if anything happened to her."

"You couldn't?" I asked. It was too much for me. "You're lying."

"No," he said quietly, staring straight at me. "I'm not lying now, Belen."

And I believed him. He was as crazy about her as I was. There wasn't any way on earth to understand it, but there it was. Suddenly it occurred to me that they were just alike. I'd known her all my life and still I didn't understand her as well as he did—as well as they understood each other.

But what difference did that make now? The chances were that neither of us would ever see her alive again. It had been—God, how long *had* it been? Where was she? She couldn't be dead. She was so beautifully and brilliantly alive that you couldn't conceive of her ever being anything else. I wanted to go to the telephone and throw it against the wall to make it ring.

I would walk toward it, then away from it. I would go clear across the room and try to shut it out of my mind to make it ring suddenly and surprise me. I went into other rooms. I stared out the window. Without even bothering to think about it, I saw Lachlan's foreign roadster driven up from the garage and the Filipino and two bellboys loading it with bags, and then, suddenly, Lachlan leaping from a cab, climbing into the car, and driving away. He was gone. We had spent untold hours planning and rehearsing an act to make him do just that, and now that I saw him doing it, it meant nothing at all. I was waiting for a telephone to ring.

The sun was gone now, and fog was coming in over the hill. In a little while it would be dark. And in just a little while we could quit hoping.

I stopped abruptly and turned to listen. It was only a tiny sound, but it went through me like flying slivers of glass. It wasn't the telephone. It was someone putting a key into the lock on the other side of the door. The door swung open and Cathy was standing there, with Donnelly and the big man behind her.

"Darling," she said, "I hope you weren't worried about me."

Chapter Nineteen

Donnelly shoved her. She shot into the room and tripped on her high heels and fell. I started toward her. The two men were inside the room now, and Donnelly took the automatic out of his coat pocket. "Uh-uh," he said.

The humorist looked from Bolton to me with apparent relish. "How about these two clowns, Monk?"

"Shove 'em in another room so we can talk to the babe."

"Listen, you little punk—" I began.

He tilted his head sidewise and looked at me. "Yeah?" he asked. It was the motion-picture killer at his deadliest—detached, professional, utterly without emotion. And it was terrifying. Not because of that, but because he was as crazy as a loon.

Bolton tried it. "Donnelly, I think you've carried this stupid joke about far enough."

Donnelly gave him the same stare, as impersonal as death. "Well," he said. "A comic."

Cathy was struggling to her feet. Donnelly held the gun in his right hand and shoved her again with the left. She staggered backward and fell onto the sofa.

He jerked his head toward Bolton and me. "Lock these clowns in the bedroom, Brock."

The humorist took a sap out of his pocket and slapped it against his palm, listening to the meaty sound of it. "This way, boys." He nodded toward the bedroom. "The quiz show is going on the air in this studio."

I started for him. Donnelly jerked the muzzle of the automatic around. Brock feinted at my groin with a knee and as I doubled over involuntarily and swung aside, with my hands down, the sap flashed in the air.

I wasn't knocked out. I was just incapable of movement, lying on the floor with a red ocean of pain sloshing around in my head while the apartment tilted and wheeled. I could hear a voice saying, "—and take this chunk of meat with you." Then I was being lifted by the shoulders and dragged across the rug.

I was in another room. It was dark, but I could hear someone moving. A light switch clicked, and I saw I was lying on the rug beside the bed. My head was bursting and nausea was a snake uncoiling in my stomach. Bolton was bending over me. He had blood running down his face from a cut laid open on his forehead.

I pulled my way up the side of the bed and sat down. I was weak and shaking. And then I heard the sound from the living room, a sudden, sharp crack like a canoe paddle on water, and a gasp.

A voice I recognized as Donnelly's was saying, "All right. You been stalling long enough. Where's the money you took off the chump?"

Somehow I got off the bed and started for the door. Bolton caught me by the arm. I turned and looked at him. His eyes were terrible. I got to the door. It wasn't locked, because the bolt was on this side, in the bedroom, but it opened the other way.

He shook his head. "The sofa's against it," he whispered. I had sense enough to know what he meant. All we had to do was push on it and shove the sofa back, with two men waiting on the other side with guns.

I could hear Brock. "How about me taking a turn at bat, Monk? Maybe she needs to be lifted a couple times."

Pain was still pounding at my skull, but my mind was clearing a little so I could think. We had to keep our heads. If we let the sounds on the other side of the door push us over the edge and started going wild, we'd all be dead. She would break after a while and tell them where the money was, but maybe Brock wasn't interested primarily in the money alone. You could see he got his fun in other ways.

I moved shakily to the window and looked out. It was totally dark now, and fog pressed in on the building like saturated gauze. Nine floors down the street lamp was faintly visible, while below and to the left the neon sign over the cocktail lounge was a diffused and watery splash of orange. I reached for the light switch and cut it and looked again. Beyond me to the left one of the big casement windows in the living room was partly open. The drapes were drawn but a little light escaped to seep futilely into the fog and lose itself. I strained my eyes downward and could just faintly see what I was looking for, a narrow ledge perhaps five inches wide running across the front of the building just below the windows.

Could I make it? The windows were a good six feet apart and each opened from the center, so I'd have to go around the one on the other end to get inside it, but by spread-eagling myself along the ledge I should be able to span the distance from one to the other. Bolton was beside me in the darkness, peering out.

I flicked the light back on. He shook his head. We moved away from the window so they wouldn't hear us and he said, "Not with the two of them in there and the light on. They'd get you coming through the drapes."

I knew that, but there was still one chance. There was a reading lamp on the night table beside the bed. I grabbed it up and pulled the plug out of the wall outlet. There was the stinging, sharp impact of flesh on flesh from beyond the wall and again that strangled intake of breath like a gasp, and we looked away from each other. My flesh crawled, and I couldn't control the trembling of my hands.

I took the lamp in one hand and the cord in the other and jerked. The wires tore out of the base, one already bare on the end. I put the other between my teeth and bit down, yanking on it with my hands. It cut my lip, but a little of the insulation was gone. I twisted the two bare ends together.

Bolton looked at me and shook his head. "If the lights in there are on a different circuit, you're dead."

We could hear Brock. "This won't get it, Monk. I tell you. You want to hear her sing? Just yank off her blouse and that brassiere and hand me your cigarette."

I stood up. "Wait till I get on the ledge and around the end of that other window. When I start to climb in, plug it back in the socket."

"You're still groggy. Let me go."

"No," I said.

Then I was outside and had my feet on the ledge. I had to lean outward over nine floors of empty fog to get around the edge of the open window. Now I was past it and could stand up against the wall, my face touching the bricks and my left hand holding onto the steel window frame. It was dark and everything was wet with the fog. I edged outward toward the right, inching my feet along with my heels extending out over space.

My left arm was straight out now, the fingers just gripping the window. The bricks were cold against my face. I put out my right arm and felt the fingertips just brush the edge of the other window. I couldn't make it. I couldn't get hold of both windows at once. My arms weren't long enough.

I teetered precariously, trying to stretch out another inch, letting go a little with the fingers of the left hand until they were just braced against the window frame, balancing there with my face shoved against the wall. I still couldn't hook the fingers of my right hand over the edge of the other one. I strained, trying not to think of the hundred feet of space between me and the fog-shrouded sidewalk below.

Then from inside the room I heard the sound of cloth being ripped and the little cry of terror torn from her as she began to break. I let go completely with the left hand, pushing, and swung across the wet, dark surface of the wall like an inverted pendulum. The bricks pushed at my chest, forcing me outward over nothingness, while I clawed wildly with my right. My fingers closed over the upper edge of the steel frame just as I started to drop and then I was hanging from it and pawing for the ledge with my feet. One of them hit and I pushed up with it as I pulled myself up and I was standing again, leaning outward to get around the edge. In a second I was around, with the angle of the steel frame behind me. Every muscle in my body was trembling.

I looked back and I could see Bolton in the light from the open window. He was watching me, and when I nodded, his head disappeared. I tried to pray. If the lights of the two rooms were on different circuits I didn't have a chance. The bedroom fuse would blow when he plugged in the shorted wires, but I'd have to go through the drapes into the living room in full view of the two of them with guns.

I could hear the faint but terrible rustlings of impotent struggle and I could hear her beginning to cry. And then the lights chopped off. I clawed my way inside, fighting through the drapes.

The darkness was impenetrable, as black as the bottom of a mine. I heard Brock curse, "What the hell," and I moved toward the sound of his voice with my hands out in front of me. I collided with somebody and we went down in a threshing tangle. All hell exploded at once. I heard a crash that sounded like glass breaking somewhere in the darkness and then the scraping as Bolton, fought at the bedroom door, shoving back the sofa. I knew it was Brock I had when a big fist crashed against my head. I swung wildly and hit the rug. I located his face with one clawing hand and swung at it with the other. He managed to land on me again, and then we were locked in a writhing mass of arms and legs. I got him by the throat and hung on, raging, not even feeling the blows battering on my face and chest.

Suddenly there was a light. I managed to swing my head a little and saw it was Cathy holding a cigarette lighter. "Put that out!" I screamed. "Donnelly! The gun!"

"He won't shoot anybody," she said, and just then Bolton came running past her. He appeared to take something out of her hand and then he was kneeling beside me. His arm swung, there was a meaty crunch, and Brock went limp. I looked at it. It was Donnelly's gun.

I got unsteadily to my feet and held onto a chair. I'd taken a beating and I was weak. In the faint light I could see Donnelly lying on the rug with a broken table lamp beside him and Cathy herself holding up the cigarette lighter. Her hair was wildly tousled, her blouse was torn, and I could see the stinging red on her face where she'd been slapped, but she was unmarked. She swayed a little and tried to smile.

"I socked him," she gurgled ecstatically. "I hit him with the lamp."

I caught her just as she started to fall. The darkness closed in around us and I heard Bolton saying something about the fuse box. I sat down on the floor and just held her in my arms. I knew it was the last time I ever would.

It was a half hour before things quieted down. We got the lights on again, and when Donnelly and Brock started to come around Bolton pointed toward the door with the gun.

"In just three minutes, I'm going to call the police," he said. Donnelly was crying, and Brock was looking at him with contempt as they left.

Cathy had changed clothes. We sat in the living room with drinks in our hands. She rattled the ice in her glass and glanced across at me and smiled.

"Mike, darling," she said happily, "do you realize we've done it? At last. After all those years."

"Yes," I said. I got up and walked over to the window and looked out at the fog.

"You don't have to worry about it, Mike. He was so scared when he left here he'll never see through it. It was beautiful, wasn't it?"

"I know," I said. "He's already gone."

I didn't feel anything about him at all. I don't know what I had expected, but there just wasn't anything. What he had done couldn't be wiped out by what we had done. I didn't feel any remorse for having swindled him. Not him. And I didn't feel any pride in it, or satisfaction. I tried to think of some reaction, but the only thing I could come up with was that I was just tired of him. I was sick of the sound of his name, and I didn't even want to think about him any more.

"It was beautiful, Judd," she was saying to Bolton. "When we have time, I want to tell you just how we did it."

It had been coming ever since I'd picked up that letter on Lachlan's desk. I didn't want it to. But there wasn't anything I could do about it. The confusion and excitement and the worry about her had kept putting it off, but it was here now. I turned around and faced her. "What do you think we ought to do now?" I asked.

"Why don't we go to Acapulco for a few weeks?"

I shook my head. "I mean after that. Remember, we haven't got Lachlan to look forward to any more."

"Oh," she said cheerfully, "I've got loads of ideas. Some even better than this one. But this was beautiful, wasn't it? It was just so *perfect*, Judd. I mean, for Lachlan. You see, Lachlan is essentially a wise-guy type, a pseudo sophisticate, and the thing we had to do—"

I walked slowly over and stood in front of her. Bolton stopped listening to her and watched me. "Cathy," I said, "where did you hide that money?"

She smiled. "In one of your suitcases."

"How about bringing it out here?"

She looked at me questioningly, but got up and went into the bedroom. She came out in a minute with the envelope in her hand. Bolton was staring now.

"What are you going to do, Mike?" she asked curiously.

Without answering, I sat down at the coffee table, slid the bills out, and began counting. It took quite a while. All seventy of them were there. The room was very quiet when I had finished. I put them in two piles, sixty-five in one and five in the other. Then I passed the five to her.

She was staring at me. "Mike, what on earth—"

I put the sixty-five one-thousand-dollar bills into the envelope and shoved it in my pocket. "You spent a week in Wyecross, investigating, didn't you?" I asked her. "And you told me Howard C. Goodwin was the one who'd worked for Lachlan."

"Yes." She was hardly breathing as she watched me.

"Well, I spent a lot longer than a week there, and I went ahead and helped swindle him. So I guess neither of us has very much to be proud of. Do we?"

"What do you mean?"

"It makes you a liar, and it makes me stupid for believing you."

"No," she said defiantly. "I tell you—"

"It's no use, Cathy," I said. I told her about the letter in Lachlan's apartment.

"All right," she said hotly. "I *did* know it. But, Mike, I went out there in the first place because his name *was* Goodwin, and because Elaine said he had been in Mexico."

"And you found out he wasn't the one. But when I asked you, that night in New Orleans—"

"But don't you *see*, Mike?" she said frantically. "I had to tell you that. We had to have you. Could I give up the chance at Lachlan we'd waited for all our lives?"

That was it, I thought. I felt rotten as hell. It was always Lachlan, and still it wasn't Lachlan at all—or it hadn't been for a long time. He was an excuse, or maybe he had started it in the beginning, but he really didn't have anything to do with it any more. She had needed him, maybe, to rationalize it up until now, but that was all over.

It was a game. It was the most fascinating game in the world, and it was the money. I thought of the way she had been ever since we had started to work on Lachlan, the preoccupation, the tense excitement showing in her eyes, and the way she would sometimes forget I was there. It had been there all the time for me to see, and now that I couldn't evade it any longer I knew I had been seeing it in spite of trying so hard to look the other way. She had smiled with that hard, bright look in her eyes when I'd warned her Lachlan was no sucker and that it wouldn't be easy. She didn't want it to be easy. The more difficult it was, the better. It was a challenge. That was what made it fun.

She'd not only been willing to swindle a man who'd never done anything to her, knowing he wasn't the Goodwin we were after, but she had made up that story about Elaine Holman for the sheer pleasure there was in knowing she had swindled Charlie too. She didn't stand to get any more money out of it that way; it was just the secret satisfaction there was in outfoxing the fox, of getting him to do the work, and of being able to laugh at both him and Bolton afterward, because no matter what happened, the police would never be able to touch her, because she hadn't taken any part in it.

It was strange, as I thought about it now—about the way she had lied to me about Goodwin—that there wasn't any anger. When I'd left her in El Paso I'd been in a rage, on the ragged edge of hurting her, but now there wasn't anything except a sort of sadness. She couldn't help it. Maybe she'd been made that way by what Lachlan had done when we were children. But there wasn't anything she could do about it now.

I tried to straighten out the way I felt about it, but it was all mixed up, and the only thing I was sure of was that I didn't want any more of it. I was just sick of confidence games. I was sick of double-crosses and double double-crosses and of wondering who somebody really was and what he really meant when he said something. I reminded myself that I wasn't in a very good position to be pointing the finger at her from a moral standpoint; I hadn't had any qualms about helping to swindle Lachlan, and I didn't have any now. All I needed was to have the other fellow do it first. Maybe that was the exact point at which we divided. I had to have that justification, or that excuse, and now she didn't any more.

I sighed. I knew there wasn't any use, but I had to try. The twenty-three years were talking.

"You know what I'm going to do with the rest of it, don't you?" I asked.

"No," she said. She did know. I could see it in her face. "I'm going to send it back to Goodwin. Do you want me to, or don't you?"

"Send it back to Goodwin? Mike, are you crazy?"

I stood up. "I just wanted to know how you felt about it," I said. "And I think you know you can't stop me, so let's don't make this any rougher than we have to."

I went into the bedroom and pulled my two old suitcases out of the closet and started packing them. I didn't get half my stuff, and I didn't pay any attention to what I did pack because I was in a hurry. I was started now, and if I kept going, fast, without thinking too much about it, I could do it. She could go with Bolton; they understood each other. That was the way it had to be. But there wasn't any fun in thinking about it or in knowing that someday she was going to wind up in prison. When I came back out into the living room she had quit raging at me and there were tears in her eyes. She turned to Bolton.

"Can't you stop him from doing a crazy thing like this?"

Bolton shook his head, and looked at me and smiled. We both knew what he meant, and maybe she did too. If I wanted to cut my throat, why should he try to stop me?

He lit a cigarette and said with urbane amusement, "Belen appears to have done a little soul searching and come up with the decaying remains of some sort of peasant morality. I think you'd do better to leave him with it before he starts trying to share it with you."

She turned abruptly away from him before he had finished. "Mike," she said, "please—"

"Maybe you'd both better come with me," I said, "so there won't be any doubt as to what I did with the money. It won't take long."

I carried the bags and we went down front and got a cab. She sat between us as we rode down the hill. We were all very silent. We stopped at the air-line terminal while I took the bags in and checked them and bought a ticket to Las Vegas; then we went on down to Market.

We got out in front of the branch bank that stays open at night. They came in with me and watched, saying nothing, while I bought a cashier's check for $65,000, made out to Howard C. Goodwin. Bolton didn't want to stop me and she couldn't, because a scene would only bring the cops. We walked over to a drugstore and I bought an envelope and a stamp. I addressed it at the counter, put the check in, and sealed it. In the upper left-hand corner I wrote one word: Reichert. We went out on the sidewalk.

It was foggy down on Market now. We walked slowly along the sidewalk, with Cathy in the middle, and none of us said anything. There was a mailbox on the next corner. I handed her the envelope. When she looked up at me I saw she was crying. She shook her head and handed it back to me.

"No," she said. "I'd rather you did it. Maybe it means something to you. I'd only feel like an idiot."

I dropped it in the slot and let the metal lid clang.

"You're a fool, Belen," Bolton said.

"Shut up," she said tonelessly. And then, "Get a cab. And wait in it. I'll be there."

He flagged one and got in. She stared at me silently for a moment. And then she said, "I guess you know now, Mike, why I kept putting you off when you asked me to marry you again. I knew this was going to happen sometime, and it's simpler this way, isn't it?"

"Do we have to do it?" I asked.

"Yes," she said. "You know that."

"Why?"

"Because it just wouldn't work any more. We both know it, don't we?"

"Yes. I guess we do."

"But it's been a long time, hasn't it? Remember?"

"I'd rather not." I wanted to get going while I could.

She tried to smile. "Let's don't kiss each other good-by. I'll just go now. But, Mike, we did get even with Lachlan, didn't we?"

I thought about Lachlan. He had ruined more than Dunbar & Belen when he pulled off that scheme sixteen years ago.

"No," I said. "But if I were you I wouldn't worry about it any more."

She had started toward the cab, but now she turned and looked back.

"Why?" she asked.

"Because we never will," I said.

THE END

RIVER GIRL
by Charles Williams

Chapter One

It was three in the afternoon and hot. Tar was boiling out of the black-top paving around the square and heat waves shimmered above the sidewalks. I drove on through town and down the side street to the jail with the Negro boy. He was about nineteen and looked scared to death.

"I ain't done nothing, Cap'n," he kept saying.

"O.K.," I said. "Relax. Nobody's going to hurt you." My head still ached from last night and his talking got on my nerves.

I turned him over to Cassieres at the jail. "Stick him in the county tank. Did Buford call you?"

"No," he said. "What's he booked for?"

"Assault," I said. "Attempted assault. I don't know. He took after another boy with a knife. Buford said pick him up."

I drove the car around to the garage and left it and went back to the square. The courthouse was stifling and smelled of sweeping compound and old dust and cuspidors. Buford wasn't in the office.

"He's out for coffee," Lorraine said. "Though how anybody could drink coffee in this weather...."

She looked at me and smiled. We both knew he was in the back room of Billy Barone's drinking gin rickeys. She had worked in the sheriff's office about six years.

I shed the gun and tossed it into a filing cabinet. "I'm going home," I said.

"Oh, I almost forgot. Louise was in. She said to tell you she picked up the car."

"O.K.," I said. "Thanks." I'd have to walk. Louise was probably playing bridge somewhere.

I went out and my head started to throb again with the glare. Cars went by, hissing on the soft tar as if it were raining. I started to walk across the square to get a Coke before I went home, and then remembered Buford had asked me to stop by and see Abbie Bell.

Abbie's hotel was out on Railroad Street, toward the planing mill and the freight depot. It was a run-down section, not over a half-dozen blocks from the square but tough and full of cheap beer joints. I could hear the shriek of the planer and the slap of dropped planks across the afternoon stillness and smell the heat.

It was different a long time ago, I thought. I walked this way to school before the old one burned down, and there were some good houses along here then. I was center on the fifth-grade football team and in love with a girl named Doris or Dorothy. At night I used to lie awake and rescue her from burning buildings and capsized boats and bullies big enough to be in the seventh grade.

A Negro girl was sweeping the lobby. I went down a dim hall and knocked. Abbie herself opened the door and looked out, then stood back for me to come in. There were two electric fans going and the blinds were pulled to keep out the sun.

"Hello, Jack," she said. She must have been around thirty-five, quite short, with very sharp brown eyes and closely cropped black hair in tight curls close to her head. She always wore ridiculously high heels to make herself look taller, and now she had on a blue dressing gown of some sort of filmy stuff.

"God, this heat. How about something cold to drink?"

"Thanks," I said. I sat down under one of the fans.

"Tom Collins?"

I nodded. She called out the door to the Negro girl. While we were waiting for the drinks she went into her bedroom and came out with a white envelope in her hand. The girl brought the drinks in and left them on a tray in front of the sofa. Abbie sat down and we lit cigarettes.

"Know any new toasts?" she asked.

"No," I said. "It's too hot to think. Here's how."

She put the envelope down on the table. "I don't know what the hell I get for this," she said.

I shrugged. "Ask Buford. I just work here."

She looked at me levelly. "You sure you want me to ask Buford?"

"He sent me," I said. I could bluff too. Buford didn't get all of it, but I didn't think she'd take it up with him. He didn't want to see her, anyway. Elections were tough enough without having to carry Abbie Bell on the ticket.

She spread her hands. "Oh, what the hell, you pay it anywhere. You always pay somebody. But I get tired of having my car tagged for overparking uptown."

"Take it up with the marshal's office," I said. "We've got a police force."

"Don't I know it? I have to support 'em. And you people too. My God. And when I get a drunk in here that wants to tear the joint down, I have to bounce the bastard myself. It's enough to make you cry."

I took another sip of the drink. It was too sweet, but it was cold.

"Cheer up," I said. "Suppose you worked here."

"Well, I've worked in better places than this," she said, and grinned. Somehow she looked like an impish kid when she did that. I liked her. And still I'm chiseling her out of twenty-five dollars every two weeks, I thought, and wondered if the headache was getting worse.

"You never do any business here, do you? Except this."

"No," I said. "What the hell, you think I'm crazy?"

"Cut it out, Jack. My girls are clean. You can take my word for it."

"Yeah, I know. And they'll give you your money back if a parachute doesn't open, too."

"Well, it's a good thing all married men aren't as cautious as you are. I'd
go broke."

I shook the ice in the glass. "Buford asked me to give you a message, Abbie. He says for Christ's sake don't let any more kids in here."

She took a deep drag on the cigarette and exhaled smoke into the blast from
the fan. "Is he still crying about that?"

"Look," I said. "He's been sweating blood for a week, and so has the so-
called police force. That kid was Buddy Demaree, and Buford's really had the
heat put on him."

"I know, I know. I've heard enough about it. Look, Jack, I try to keep those
lousy high school punks out of here, but Jesus, I can't watch the door every
minute. I don't want 'em in here any more than Buford does. I'd rather have
a skin rash. They smell of a cork and they're drunk, like that dumb bunny.
And they never have a crying dollar on 'em—all they want to do is to feel
up all the girls and then go out chasing their lousy jail bait."

"Well, try to keep 'em out. Buford may not be able to smooth it over the
next time one of 'em gets plastered down here and wrecks his old man's car.
And that preacher is getting worse all the time."

She looked at me. "Yeah, how about that guy? I'm paying you people to do
business here—why don't you keep him off my neck? God, I never know but
what he may come in here some night with an ax like Carry Nation and chop
the joint up. Can't you muzzle him before he closes the whole town up?"

"Maybe Buford'll think of something." I stood up and started for the door.
"I'll see you, Abbie."

She waved the drink. "Tell Buford the girls are working for him."

I walked across town in the heat, thinking of the lake and of trees hanging
over water very quiet and dim back out of the sun. It had been months since
I'd been fishing. The car was parked in front of the house, and as I went past
I noticed the white sidewalls were black again. I grinned sourly, thinking of
Louise and curbs.

She wasn't in the living room. I went down the hall. A cold shower, I
thought, and a bottle of beer out of the icebox, and maybe this headache will
go away.

"Is that you, Jack?"

I looked in the bedroom. "You'd be in sad shape if it was somebody else,
wouldn't you?" I said, smiling.

She was lying on the bed in nothing but a pair of pants and a brassiere, reading the latest copy of *Life*. The electric fan was running on top of the dresser.
Louise was very pretty, a taffy blonde with long, green eyes and a stubborn
round chin. She took a great deal of pride in her clear, pale skin, and didn't
go in for suntan because she always blistered.

"You're home early, aren't you? I called the office to ask you to bring in some steak, and Lorraine said you'd already left."

"I had an errand."

She reached out a slim arm for a cigarette and looked at me questioningly. "You did? Where?"

"Abbie Bell's."

She flipped the lighter and took a deep puff, letting the magazine slide to the floor and looking at me quietly through the smoke.

"Well, that's nice. How were the girls?"

I sat down and started taking off my shoes, thinking of the shower. "All right, I guess. I didn't see them."

"Well, then, how was Abbie?"

"Cut it out, Louise. You know what I was there for."

"Men are always on the defensive, aren't they? Really, dear, I'm not accusing you of anything. I was just asking about them. After all, I don't get much news. The husbands of most of my friends never go to whore houses."

"At least not on business," I said.

"You've got a dirty mind."

"O.K.," I said.

"I don't see why you have to go there in broad daylight. Suppose somebody saw you?"

"Nobody did."

"Well, it seems to me Buford could send somebody else."

"You know why I don't ask him to send somebody else."

"Yes, it's nice, isn't it?"

"It's being done," I said, feeling too rotten to argue.

"Maybe she'd raise your cut if you went down there and worked as a bouncer or something after hours."

"Maybe so. You want me to ask her?"

"And your father was a judge."

"You tried to buy anything with that lately?" I asked.

"Maybe I should go down and help Abbie out on Saturday nights."

"Oh, cut it out," I said.

She slapped the bed with an arm. "Oh, why do we always get in these arguments?"

"I don't know," I said. "I wish we didn't."

She was silent for a moment. I went on undressing for the shower and started into the bathroom in my shorts when she said, "Cathy and Mildred are going down to the beach for a week. They asked me to go with them."

"How can you?" I asked.

"After all, it's only for a week."

"I don't know where we'd get the money."

"Well, it certainly wouldn't take any fortune."

"With those two? You know how they throw it around."

"They do get a little fun out of life, if that's what you mean."

"And you don't?"

"Sometimes I wonder."

Here we go again, I thought, off on the same old rat race. We were strapped with payments on a new Oldsmobile we didn't need just because Cathy bought a Cadillac. In January we had to go to the Sugar Bowl because Mildred was going. Cathy's got a new Persian lamb. Mildred's getting a Capehart for Christmas. They could afford it. Cathy's husband was Jim Buchanan, who was vice-president and a stockholder in the bank, and Mildred was married to Al Wayne, who was in the real estate business.

"Sometimes I get a little fed up with those two," I said.

"Yes. I guess you *do* seem to prefer Abbie Bell."

"Oh, for God's sake—"

"If you'd like, we could ask her over for bridge. After all, we're practically in business with her. She could bring over one of the girls for a fourth."

"You could ask Mildred," I said. "Al Wayne owns the hotel and that whole block."

"I doubt if many people know it. And he doesn't have to go down there in broad daylight to collect the rent."

"All right," I said. "I'll quit going down there and to all the other places. We'll live on my salary."

"Your salary!"

"Well, there you are."

"You could have had Buford's job if you'd run against him last time."

I sat down in a chair and lit a cigarette, forgetting about the shower. "I couldn't beat Buford, and you know it. He's been sheriff for twelve years. And I haven't got his personality. Nobody in the county could beat him."

"You were in the war."

"Who wasn't?"

"Buford," she said impatiently.

"He was over draft age. I'm telling you, if I'd run against him I would just have been beaten and then I'd be out of a job completely. I thought about it plenty, but it can't be done. He's just one of those people. Even people who know he's crooked like him."

"Well, I wouldn't be too sure he's going to be there forever," she said.

"How's that?"

"You know what I mean. Or *who* I mean. That new minister, the Reverend Soames or whatever his name is. I tried to get you to go to church with us yesterday. You'd have heard plenty."

"Well, before you crow too much, remember that if they get Buford over a barrel I'll be right there with him."

"Yes. And isn't that something nice to think about? And for the crumby few dollars you get out of it. Think of what he's made."

"My God, Louise, do you want me to take it, or don't you? I can leave it alone."

"So you'd like to blame it on me, would you? Well, I like that!"

"I'm not trying to blame it on anybody. But, for Christ's sake, if I'm going to take it the way Buford does, let's take it and shut up about it."

"You can do whatever you want to," she said coldly. She reached out and smashed the cigarette with a vicious stab at the ash tray, long slim legs sprawling as she lost her balance on her elbow. "I'm going to the beach. I'll cash a check."

"Don't make it over seventy-five," I said. "That's all we've got in the bank."

"That's fine. That's just fine. I'll stay at the YWCA."

I got up and took the envelope out of my clothes. "Here," I said, tossing it. "There's a hundred and twenty-five in there." It landed on the bed next to her naked midriff. Well, it's gone full circle, I thought. That's where it came from—a girl on a bed.

"What about Buford?" she asked.

"I'll stall him. I've done it before. He knows he'll get it."

"You won't mind batching for a week, will you?"

"No." Suddenly I was fed up with everything—the quarreling, the heat, money, the job, all of it. I wanted to go fishing worse than I'd ever wanted anything. "I think I'll go to the lake."

"I may not have to spend all of it, Jack. I'll take it along, just in case." She had the money out of the envelope and was looking at it. She hadn't heard me.

I went out in the hall to the telephone. After trying the office and Billy Barone's, I finally located Buford at the Elks Club. He sounded as if he had a pleasant glow on.

"This is Marshall," I said. "I just wanted to tell you I'm going fishing. I guess you can struggle along without me for three or four days." The way I felt, I didn't care whether he liked it or not.

Nothing ever flustered Buford. "Fine, Jack. It's all right, son. You need a little vacation. Bring me back a channel cat."

Chapter Two

I began to feel better the minute I turned off the highway onto the old log-ging road. It wound up through the pine and then dropped off toward the lake bottom country to the east, very rough and full of chuckholes and not used for anything any more. The highway crossed the south end of the lake some five miles farther down, where there was a general store and restaurant and a place that rented boats, but I always went in here, as it was less used and saved that five miles by boat if I wanted to go very far up the lake. It was about fifteen miles from here clear in to the upper end of it, up in the swamps, but I'd never been that far. It was rough country, with unnumbered miles of sloughs winding all over the bottom, and you could get lost in it if you didn't know your way.

It was still two or three hours before sunset when I eased the Ford pickup and boat trailer down the last quarter mile of the old road and stopped un-der the big oaks at the end of a slough. The minute I cut the motor, absolute silence closed in on me and I felt at peace with everything.

It took only a few minutes to launch the boat, load it, and clamp on the mo-tor, and then I was under way. The slough was about a quarter mile long, and when I rounded the turn I was in the main channel of the lake itself, wind-ing off toward the north and northeast. It was about two hundred yards wide with dead snags and cypress clumps here and there and dense timber hang-ing out over the east bank. There were occasional weed beds and I knew the bass would be feeding in them around sunset, but I had four whole days and wanted to go on up toward the head of the lake, farther than I'd ever been before.

Two or three miles up I met another boat coming down, with two men in it. They waved and held up a string of bass, then they were gone behind and I was alone again. At times the channel was so narrow the trees almost met overhead, and it was cool in the shade with the breeze blowing in my face. At other places it widened out into long flats full of dead snags and stagnant, dark water, not muddy but discolored from rotting swamp vegetation, with the lowering sun slanting brassy and hot across it. Now and then a grindle would roll just under the surface, making a big, spreading ring on the water, and two or three times I saw big gars swimming by very close to the top. In-numerable arms and sloughs wound off on both sides into the timber, but I knew the main channel here and stuck to it. In another half hour, however, I was beyond the country I was familiar with and was going only on a sense of direction and sticking always to what looked like the larger channel.

It was late when I rounded a long turn and saw just the place where I wanted to camp. The lake was about a hundred yards wide here, with an open bank under a towering wall of oaks on the right, and dead snags and big patches of pads along the left. The sun was gone now and the water lay still and flat like a dark mirror except for a boiling rise where a bass smashed at something near one of the snags. I cut the motor and started drifting in, and silence seemed to pour out of all the vast solitude and came rolling over me like a wave.

I worked fast in the daylight there was left, stringing the trot line between two of the old snags and baiting it with the liver I had brought, then went ashore and built a fire to cook supper. After I had eaten I washed the dishes and sat down on the bedroll in the darkness, smoking and looking at the fire. The big bullfrogs had opened up their chorus and I could hear the whip-poorwills' lonely crying up in the swamp, reminding me of the nights I had camped on the lake when I was a boy. The Judge and I had fished a lot in those days. My mother was dead, and there had been just the two of us for a long time. He taught me to use the fly rod, how to drop a cork bug forty feet away beside a sunken log and to set the hook when the surface heaved, exploding with the strike, and how to release a bass after it was whipped. He never kept them. Tomorrow, I thought, I might catch one the old boy had in the net and then released to fight some other day, and then I knew it wasn't likely. He'd died six years ago, while I was overseas. It would have to be a very old bass to have fought the Judge.

I took off my shoes and clothes and lay down on the blankets, but it was a long time before I got to sleep. I kept thinking of the fights with Louise and the endless bickering over money. Nothing had seemed to have any point to it after I came back from the Army, I had just seemed to drift aimlessly, taking the path of least resistance. I was twenty-three when I came back, and for a while I'd thought of going back to school under the GI plan, for I had finished two years at the state university before the war, but that had gradually fizzled out when I started going with Louise. Then Buford offered me a job as deputy as a favor to some people who had been friends of the Judge, and, before long Louise and I were married. We had gone into debt for the house, and then there was a new car, a Chevrolet, and before that was two years old we bought the Olds. It wasn't too hard, after a while, to start taking money from the same places Buford was taking his.

Maybe it's just as well the Judge isn't here any more, I thought. He never cared that much for money.

It was a beautiful morning, very still and cloudless, with patches of light mist hanging over the lake in the early dawn. I got up and picked up a towel and ran down to the boat. Stepping into it, I pulled out into the channel with the oars, took off the shorts, and dived in. The water felt warm, but it was clean,

and I swam down until I felt the bottom under my hands and then came shooting up, bursting clear of the surface like a seal playing. Beyond the wall of the
oaks along the bank I could see the sky in the east growing coral now, and
across the vast and breathless hush of early morning I heard the explosive
smash as a bass hit something among the pads along the other shore.

I pulled hurriedly back to camp and got the fly rod and some bugs and came
back, letting the boat drift silently among the snags. Tying on a cork bug with
a dished-in face, I began working out line with false casts and dropped it thirty
feet away in a pocket at the edge of the pads. It lay cocked up jauntily on the
surface with its white hair wings erect, perfectly still like some big green-and-
white insect trying to make up its mind what to do next. I twitched the line
and the face dipped down and gurgled with a bubbling sound and little rings
spread outward from it toward the pads. I twitched it again, quite gently,
then the water bulged upward and swallowed it. I raised the rod tip and felt
the weight that meant the hook was in, then he came out of the water glinting green and bronze in the early light and shaking his head to throw the hook.
Bugs aren't so easy to sling as big plugs, however, for there isn't the lever-
age, and when he went down he still had it. He didn't like it a bit, and made
a run for the pads, but I managed to get him turned in time, and began taking in line as he came nearer. He jumped twice more, tiring himself, and in a
little while I had him close up to the boat. I was reaching for the net when
he saw me and was off again, making the reel sing. The next time he came in
he was about done for and lay weakly on his side as I slipped the net under
him. I lifted, and he flapped in the net in the bottom of the boat, a beauty that
would go three pounds. Slipping the hook out, I lifted him over the side into
the water. He lay quietly for a moment, then flipped his tail and swam out.

I missed a few strikes, and then they quit feeding. Going over to the trot
line, I ran along it, pulling hand over hand along the line. There were three
catfish on it, one small one that would be just the right size for breakfast, and
two others of two or three pounds each. I was wondering if I would be able
to keep them alive until I went home, when I heard an outboard motor suddenly break the silence of the lake.

It surprised me, for I hadn't thought there was anyone else up here. I looked
up and saw it coming around the bend, three or four hundred yards distant.
It was coming fast, and as it approached I saw it was a big skiff, probably sixteen feet, with only one man in it, and that he apparently had no intention
of stopping to swap fish stories. As he came abreast I waved. He looked at me
once, lifted a hand in a gesture that was almost curt, and went on past. Then
his motor sputtered and died.

I had started to row back to camp when it quit on him, and I watched the
boat drift along on its momentum for a little way and then come to rest. He
was looking at the motor. I turned and started over.

"Trouble?" I called out.

I could see him shake his head. "Just out of gas."

As I came up alongside I saw the motor was a big Johnson with a lot of power. He was filling the tank from one of those Army surplus jeep cans, and I looked at him, wondering if he might be anyone I knew. He glanced up briefly and went on pouring gasoline. I didn't know him, but for just a fraction of a second I had that feeling there was something familiar about his face; then it was gone. Maybe I just ran into him on the street sometime in town, I thought.

He didn't look as if he lived in town, though, or even went there very often. His face was deeply tanned, almost black from the sun, and the dark and graying hair was long above the ears and growing down his neck into the collar of the sweaty blue shirt. It was the lean, bony face of a man somewhere in his forties, with haze-gray eyes faintly bloodshot, as if he had not slept, and full of an infinite sad tiredness like those of a man who has been looking for too long at something he doesn't like. The face was tired, too, and intelligent, but completely expressionless, and it was frosted along the jaws and chin with a beard stubble that was grayer than his hair. He wore a floppy straw hat and faded overalls rolled halfway to his knees, and I could see he was barefoot. His shoes, however, were up in the bow of the boat out of the inch or so of water sloshing around in the bottom. Lives up here, I thought. Probably makes a little whisky and traps some during the winter. His hands were shaking badly and he was spilling some of the gasoline.

"How's fishing?" I asked.

"All right." He screwed the cap back on the gasoline can and set it up forward by his shoes. Then I noticed the tow sack in the bottom, under the seat, and wondered if it didn't have whisky jars in it until I saw the dorsal fin of a catfish sticking through.

"Taking them down to the highway?" I asked. I knew the restaurant at the foot of the lake specialized in fried catfish and that they bought the fish from the swamp rats who lived up here in the sloughs.

He nodded.

"Here," I said, glad to find somebody who could use the ones I had. "Take these along. I've got more than I can eat and they won't stay alive until I go home."

He glanced up briefly and shook his head. "Don't need 'em." Then, as an afterthought, "Got all he'll take. Thanks."

I shrugged. "O.K."

He was ready to go and was about to crank the motor when he paused. "Pretty far up the lake, ain't you?"

"Yes," I said. "Why?"

"Nothing. It's easy to get lost up here, though." The motor caught and he was gone.

I kept thinking about him as I cleaned the catfish for breakfast. His face was familiar somehow, I thought, but I knew I'd never seen him before around here. And there was something else I couldn't get out of my mind. He looked like a swamp rat and dressed like one, but the speech didn't ring true. He used the right words but he said them differently, the way they would sound if you were reading dialect out of a book.

I wondered how far up he lived, then suddenly remembered the odd way I had first noticed the sound of the boat. He must have just started it when I heard it, which meant he hadn't come from much farther away than around the next bend, possibly half a mile.

Chapter Three

I probably would never have gone up to the cabin if it hadn't been for the accident.

It was one of those stupid things that seem to happen only when you're fishing alone. It was about midmorning and I was casting a white streamer fly for crappies near an old windfall at the edge of the lake along the other shore when I must have let my backcast drop too far and touch the water. At any rate, when I came forward with the rod I felt the line slap my back and then the sting of the hook.

I untangled the line from around my neck and tried to reach the fly. It was between my shoulder blades, and I could just touch it with my fingertips. Thinking it had only nicked me, I tried to shake it loose by jiggling the leader, but it stuck. I cursed myself for a clumsy fool, getting tangled up in a fly line like somebody who'd never had a rod in his hand before. After trying to dislodge it by poking at it with a small stick, I began to realize I was solidly hooked. It didn't hurt much, but any movement of my arms irritated it, because the shirt would move and shift the hook.

I cut the leader with a knife so I wouldn't have the fly line dangling from me, and sat there while I smoked a cigarette and thought about it. I hated the idea of starting back down the lake looking for somebody to get it put for me. On a weekday like this I'd probably have to go the full twenty miles to the highway before I met anyone. Then I thought of the man who had gone by early in the morning, but I knew that even if he went down and straight back he'd be another three or four hours at least, and might not be back until night. Suddenly I remembered again the way I had first heard his boat, as if he had started it up just around the bend. Maybe his cabin was nearby and there might be somebody there.

I went back to camp with the hook digging painfully into my back with every stroke of the oars, and got out the small pair of diagonal pliers I carry in the tackle box. Then, clamping on the motor, I started up the lake.

At first glance the long reach of the lake above the bend seemed to be empty and deserted, a continuation of the miles below it. There was the same wall of oaks, the weed beds and gaunt dead trees, and the water flat and brassy in the sun. A big slough led off into the timber on the right and I was almost past it before I saw the small boat landing just inside the entrance.

I wheeled about and turned in, cutting the motor and drifting up alongside the landing, which consisted of two big floating logs with boards nailed across them. There was a live box made of rabbit-wire netting alongside the float, and I could see a few catfish swimming around in it.

I tied the boat to the logs and went up the trail through the timber. There was a long clearing, with bunch grass and weeds, dead and brown now in the late summer, with a dust-powdered trail going back to the frame shack at the other end. The house was small, not over two rooms at most, with a sagging porch in front, and covered with old oak shakes the color of tarnished silver. It sat up off the ground on round blocks, and under it I could see the big black-and-tan hound lying in the dust. He rose and stalked dejectedly out as I approached, but there was no other sign of life. Grasshoppers buzzed in the warm morning sun, and there was a peaceful, almost drowsy stillness about the place that made you think of a painting or some half-forgotten fragment of a dream.

I stopped in front and called out. "Hello. Hello in the house."

There was no answer and no sound of steps inside. I could see a feather of blue-gray smoke curling from the stovepipe and drifting straight up in the motionless air, and knew someone must be around nearby if there was still a fire in the cookstove. I tried again.

"Hello in the house."

The old hound looked at me sadly and gave a listless wag of his tail, but the silence remained unbroken. I could feel the hook pulling at my back and began to wonder impatiently if I would have to go down the lake after all. Damn, I thought. Turning, I walked around the side of the house on the bare, hard-packed ground. Someone had tried to grow flowers in a little bed along the wall, but everything was dead and withered now except the lone morning-glory winding along some white string stretched up past the window. The ground at the base of the vine was damp, as if it had been watered last night.

There was nothing behind the house except a privy with its door hanging crazily open on a broken hinge. There was no barn, for there were no animals except the dog, and not even a well. They must get water from the lake, I thought. A black walnut tree shaded the corner of the house, and on beyond the privy there was just the dead bunch grass stretching out toward the wall of timber closing it all in. I heard a squirrel chatter across the stillness, and inside the kitchen the fire crackled once inside the stove.

I was just turning to go back around in front when I saw a sudden flash of color in the edge of the timber and a girl stepped out into the clearing. What I had seen was a blue bathing cap, and now she came on toward me along the trail in the wet bathing suit, seeing me standing there but not changing the unhurried gait. It was a beautiful walk, and I watched her, trying not to stare, conscious of the crazy thought that she could be modeling a bathing suit instead of walking across a backwoods clearing.

It wasn't one of those two-piece Bikini things, or even the fancy and highly colored ones usually worn around beaches, and even though it was very small and tight and clung to her like nylon with a static charge, there was still somehow a suggestion of modesty rather than display about it, probably because it was of the kind professional swimmers wear, smooth and black, and cut down for utility rather than advertising. You had an idea, watching her, that she was a good swimmer.

"Hello," I said.

"Good morning." She stopped, with water still dripping from the suit into the powdery dust at the edge of the trail. She was a little over average height, with square shoulders, and quite slender, with long, smooth legs, not deeply tanned, and the suit pulled tightly across her breasts. Her eyes were deep blue and faintly questioning, and there was something incredibly quiet and still about the face. There was no way of knowing what color her hair was under the bathing cap. She might be any age, I thought, from twenty to twenty-eight.

I knew I had been staring and tried to smile to cover it up. It was awkward, because she somehow gave the impression she didn't care whether I stared or not, and didn't care a great deal, as a matter of fact, whether I was even there.

"I was just looking for a little help," I said.

"Yes? If there's anything I can do...." She let it trail off, still looking at me quietly, and I was conscious of that same puzzling impression I had had about the man. The speech didn't fit, somehow. It wasn't what you would expect to hear up here in the swamps.

I turned around so she could see the fly sticking in my back, feeling like a fool because it was such a stupid thing to have happen. "I can't quite reach it," I said.

She stepped closer and examined it, touching the shank of the fly gently with her fingers. "I can't tell because of the shirt," she said, "but I think the barb is caught."

"I think so," I said. "It's not hard to do, though. The thing to do is push it on through, cut off the barb, and then back it out. I brought some pliers."

"I think I can do it," she answered. "Will you wait a minute until I change clothes?"

"Oh, sure," I said. "Go ahead. I'll wait out here."

I turned back around and she unfastened the chin strap of the cap and peeled it off, running her fingers through her hair and shaking it out. It was straight and dark brown, almost black, falling in beautiful disarray across the side of her face, and I stared at it with almost the same sense of shock or outrage you might have at seeing a beautiful painting defaced, for it had been badly mangled by some clumsy attempt at cutting it. Whoever had cut it must have used a lawn mower, I thought. She shook the cap to get the water off it and went in the kitchen door, straight-backed and unhurried. The door swung shut and then I heard the front one close.

I lit a cigarette and squatted on my heels in the shade of the walnut tree, listening to the ratcheting buzz of the grasshoppers and thinking of the way she had looked and of that strange stillness about her face. It wasn't the blank emptiness of stupidity or the quietness of inner serenity—there was something about it that made you think of the dangerous and unnatural surface calm of a city under martial law.

In a few minutes the door opened and she came out with the wet suit, which she threw across a clothesline. She had on a shapeless old cotton dress too big for her and hadn't bothered to put on any make-up or comb her hair, and she was barefoot like any backwoods slattern. She couldn't have made herself look any worse if she'd tried, I thought, and got the impression somehow that she *had* tried.

"You can come in now," she said.

I followed her through the small kitchen into the front room. The floor was bare except for a small rag rug, rough pine planks worn white with scrubbing, and there was a small mud fireplace neatly swept. There were a couple of rawhide-bottomed chairs, and an old iron bedstead standing in the corner by the fireplace, and across on the right between the window and the front door there was a dresser with a milky and discolored mirror. The air was hot and still inside the room, and I could hear the ticking of the tin alarm clock on the mantel above the fireplace. There was a photograph of her next to the clock, apparently taken not too long ago, but at least it was before her hair had been butchered up like that.

"Do you have a razor blade or a pair of scissors?" I asked.

"Yes. Do you want me to cut the shirt away?"

I nodded. "That'd be best. Then we can see what we're doing."

She got a small pair of manicure scissors out of the dresser and slit the shirt around the hook. I unbuttoned it and slid it off, and turned my back to the mirror to look over my shoulder. I was deeply tanned from the waist up and wore no undershirt. The streamer fly was a vivid slash of white and silver tinsel against the sun-blackened hide, and as well as I could tell, the barb was deeply embedded. I caught a glimpse of my face in the mirror and for the first time remembered I hadn't shaved since yesterday, and wondered what kind of thug I must look like to her, big, with the flat, sun-darkened face rasping with black stubble.

I motioned with a hand and passed her the diagonal pliers. "Pinch the muscle and skin up with your fingers and run it on through as if you were baiting a hook," I instructed.

"It'll hurt," she said quietly.

"Some," I said.

I turned my back toward her and felt the slight, trembling pressure of her fingers pinching the skin. There was a fiery bite of pain, and when I looked in the mirror again the barb was through in the open and a thin trickle of blood ran down my back. She snipped off the barb and backed it out.

"Just a moment," she said. She pulled open one of the dresser drawers and brought out a bottle of iodine and a Band-aid and applied them to the punctures.

"You should have been a doctor," I said. "Thanks a lot."

"Don't mention it."

I am six feet one, and the top of her head came up just a little past my chin as she stood there when she had finished. She'd be taller in high heels, I thought. Barefoot! Why? And why, in God's name, did she ever let somebody hack her hair up like that?

I reached for the cigarettes in my shirt hanging over the back of a chair. "Do you smoke?"

"Yes. Thank you." She took one and I broke a match on my thumbnail and lit it and then mine.

The blue eyes were devoid of any expression as she looked at me through the cigarette smoke. "You can put your shirt on," she said.

You couldn't get behind her voice any more than you could behind the eyes. The way she said it, it might have been only a reminder that I had forgotten to put it on, or it might have been a flat command. I thought about it, remembering that she had wanted to change out of the bathing suit into that hopeless sack of a dress before she would take the hook out for me. She turned and looked out the door as I slipped it on and tucked it inside the trousers.

The room was perfectly quiet except for the same monotonous ticking of the cheap clock and the faintly drowsy hum of summer insects out across the sun-baked clearing, but there was nothing peaceful about it. Somehow, the whole mood of the place seemed to come from her, as if the air itself were charged with that same tension you could sense behind the contained, set stillness of her face.

"My name's Jack Marshall," I said.

She turned back from the doorway and stood just inside it, leaning slightly against the frame, looked at my face for just an instant with an odd, intense glance as if she were trying to remember something, and then resumed the expressionless blankness. "I'm Mrs. Shevlin."

"Have you lived up here long?"

"About a year."

"I guess you swim a lot?"

"Every day. Except in winter."

"You must like swimming," I went on, in spite of the fact that it sounded more like a police investigation than it did a conversation.

"Yes. I like it. Fortunately."

"Fortunately?"

"Yes. There isn't much else to do."

"I guess you're pretty good at it. I'm not much myself. I just dog-paddle."

"Oh?" It was polite and nothing more. Why does she want me to get out of here? I thought. You can hear the loneliness screaming there inside her.

There was no way I could keep from staring at her hair. We faced each other across six feet of hot, explosive silence in the room and I could not look away. It wasn't any of my business and I had no business here at all now that the hook was out, but it was like one of those terrible compulsions in a dream where you can't stop whatever it is you're doing.

"Who did that?" I asked.

"Did what?" She knew, though, what I meant.

"Cut your hair that way," I said, still with that feeling of being unable to stop myself.

"Are you a barber?" she asked coldly.

"No. But I could do a better job than that."

"I wouldn't dream of troubling you."

"I'm sorry," I said. "I know it isn't any of my business. I just couldn't help it."

She shoved a hand through the dark confusion of the hair and turned abruptly away from me. "It's all right," she said. "I—I guess I'm just nervous." She walked over in front of the fireplace and threw the cigarette in it, remaining there with her back to me.

"I guess I'd better run along," I said tentatively. There was no answer except the ticking of the clock as my words hung and died in the stillness of the room. I turned toward the door.

"Thanks again for taking the hook out."

She said nothing at all and didn't even turn around. I went on out, across the clearing in the hot sun, and down the trail to the boat.

It wasn't until I was all the way back to camp that I suddenly remembered the pliers. I had left them there.

Chapter Four

I should have broken camp and got out of there, but I didn't. Fishing had lost its magic and I was only going through the motions, but still I stayed. I kept seeing that disturbing picture of her coming across the clearing in the wet bathing suit with that deadly stillness in her face. Who was she? And what were they doing up here?

I awoke once during the night, and for an instant I could have sworn I heard the rhythmic beat of someone's swimming past out in the channel, and then I knew I must have been mistaken. I lay on my back looking up at the stars, and then for some insane reason I couldn't understand I suddenly saw that forlorn and pathetic morning-glory vine before me in the darkness, its base freshly watered, and the girl walking up that long trail from the lake carrying bucket after bucket of water to pour on it to keep it from dying like the rest of the pitiful flower bed. I'm going nuts, I thought.

It was the second night before I would admit it to myself. I was waiting for him to go back down the lake. Why? I thought. I never did a thing like that before.

Friday morning I awoke at dawn, determined to pack and leave. I'll get out of here before he goes down the lake again, I thought, and never come this far up again. I was still lying there twenty minutes later when I heard the sudden cough and sputter of his big motor up the lake. The boat came on around the long bend and then it was going past the camp, and when I looked up I saw him sitting with his big floppy hat in the stern of it, turning his head to stare at me. Neither of us waved. I lay there listening to the sound of the motor going farther away, getting fainter and fainter in the distance, and even after it was miles down the lake I kept imagining I could hear it. I should have gone, I thought.

I fought it until ten o'clock before I knew for certain I'd never leave here until I saw her again. I tied the boat up at the landing and went up the trail and along the dusty path through the grass. She wasn't swimming this time. As I came near the house sprawled dejectedly in the hot morning sun I could hear her inside, making some repetitious, scraping sound that rasped across the drowsy quiet of the clearing.

"Hello," I called out, as I had before.

There was no answer but that same sound, that *whusk, whusk, whusk* from the front room. The old hound came around the corner and looked at me with listless indifference and then went back to the shade of the walnut tree. I stepped up on the porch and looked in the door. She was down on her hands and knees in the center of the floor of the front room with a bucket of soapy water and a stiff brush, scrubbing the floor with such an absolute fury of concentration she hadn't even heard me. She had on the same old sloppy dress and was barefoot again, and the wealth of lovely, dark, and mutilated hair swung untended and forgotten down the side of her face. There seemed to be something of fanaticism or driving anger in the way she swung the brush, as if she were determined to wear out the floor or herself.

I stepped back softly so as not to frighten her and called out again from the edge of the porch.

The *whusk, whusk* ceased. "Come in," she said.

I stepped up to the door. She had half straightened and was upright on her knees, and now she brushed the hair back out of her face with the back of a hand.

"Hello," I said, smiling. She's beautiful, I thought. Even like that she's beautiful. I had a strange and almost overpowering impulse to walk into the room and pick her up bodily, out of that mess of soapsuds. Cut it out, I thought. Cut it out.

"Hello," she said, nodding slightly. She made no effort to stand. There was no surprise in her face, and I wondered if she had been expecting me. Then on second thought, I realized there wasn't anything else in it either—no hostility, welcome, friendliness, anger, or anything. The curtains were drawn completely.

"I forgot my pliers the other day," I said as the silence stretched out.

"They're there in my dresser drawer." She gestured with a hand.

"Thanks." I stepped inside to the dresser and started to pull open the nearest drawer, the one on the left.

"No," she said hurriedly, gesturing. "The other one." But I had already pulled it out before I could stop. As I shoved it back I couldn't help seeing what was in it—some khaki shirts, two or three bottles of whisky, and the cold, slablike bulk of a Colt. 45.

Well, practically everybody up here in the backwoods has a gun, I thought. I gave no sign I had seen it as I opened the other drawer and got out the pliers.

"Would you like a cigarette?" I asked.

She was still on her knees with one hand on the bucket. She shook her head. "No. Thank you."

I lit one for myself and threw the match out the door. She made no move to ask me to sit down or to get up herself. It was awkward, and I knew I should go.

"How is your morning-glory vine?" I asked. Realizing how stupid it sounded, after I had said it, I went on lamely, "I got to thinking about it the other night. You carry water up from the lake for it, don't you?"

She looked at me oddly. "You noticed it?"

"Yes," I said. "The other day. It had been watered."

She stared down at the floor. "I water it at night. But I guess it will die, like the rest of them. Maybe the soil isn't right. I don't know."

Suddenly I didn't want to talk about the vine any more. It was strange, but I had a queer feeling it was more than just a flower to her, that it was a personal tragedy of some kind and not for me to go blundering into.

"How does it happen you're not swimming today?" I asked, to change the subject.

"I was busy. And sometimes I swim at night."

I looked at her, somewhat startled. "You do? In this swamp? Isn't it dangerous? I mean—well, can you see where you're going?"

"You can see all right out in the middle of the lake."

"Where do you swim?" I asked. Suddenly I remembered that odd sensation the other night when for a moment I had been sure I had heard someone going by out in the channel.

"Up the lake, mostly. Sometimes down this other side, all the way around." She gestured off toward the right, in the direction of the slough. "This is an island, you know."

Devil's Island, I thought, for no reason at all. Maybe it was the way she said it. "It is? You mean the slough connects with the lake on both ends?"

"Yes."

"Do you ever swim down the lake?" I asked.

She looked up at me. "Yes. Sometimes."

"I think I heard you one night."

"The day you were up here?"

I nodded.

"Yes," she said quietly. "I swam by your camp that night. I could see the remains of your fire."

"Do you think you'll go swimming tonight?" I asked.

I was standing there by the dresser, still holding the pliers in my hand, and I could feel that strange, tight stillness there had been in the room before, as if the air itself were charged with some meaning that never showed itself on the surface.

"I don't know." She was staring straight ahead, not looking toward me. The hand on the bucket was white-knuckled, as if she were clenching it. "Yes," she went on, softly, almost as if talking to herself. "Yes. I might."

That was all there was to it. In a minute she returned to her scrubbing and I went on back to the camp.

It was late. I lay on the bedroll near the still faintly glowing remains of the campfire and looked up at the night sky through the openings in the trees. I had been there a long time, sleepless, waiting, and had watched the constellations swing as the hours dragged by, and had strained my ears toward all the night sounds of the swamp. I heard the deep bass *garo-o-om, garo-o-om* of the bullfrogs out at the edge of the lake and the whippoorwills calling far away in the night and once in a while a faint whisper in the leaves overhead as a small breeze stirred. I rolled over on my side and held my watch out toward the embers of the fire. It was almost midnight.

There hadn't been any use trying to make myself break camp and go on home that afternoon. I knew I didn't have any business here, waiting for a man's wife to come up this way just in the hope of seeing her again, but there didn't seem to be anything I could do about it. I knew it was a foolish and very dangerous thing to do, but I had to see her. Why did her husband let her go swimming around late at night alone in an immense swamp full of old snags and weeds and water moccasins? Did he know it? Or didn't he care? Who was he, anyway, and why did his face look familiar? Who was *she*, in fact? She was just as foreign to the swamp as he was. And why had there been that clear and unmistakable but still unnamed tension in the air both times I had been up there? I went around and around with the same old questions, hour after hour, getting no nearer to an answer than I had ever been.

Suddenly I raised myself on an elbow and listened. Was that the sound I had heard, or imagined I had heard, the other night? It came again, a quiet ripple on the water and a rhythmic swishing that could have been an arm swinging forward and sliding into the water. I sat up. I was sure I heard it now, coming from up the lake, between here and the bend.

I got up and walked down to the boat. The surface of the lake was dark and still and powdered with stars, and I could see nothing except the black loom of the tree wall along the other shore. I stood still and then heard her quite plainly. Turning in the direction from which the sound came, I studied the darkness intently, and in a moment I could see the reflected stars heave drunkenly and drown in the broken surface. She was almost abreast of where I was.

"Hello," I said quietly. I took out a cigarette and lit it, knowing she would see the flame of the match. After the light went out I was totally blind for a moment and couldn't tell whether she was going on by or not.

Then, suddenly, I heard a splash right in front of me and there she was not ten feet beyond the boat, her head and shoulders out of the water as she stood up.

"Hello," I said again.

"Mr. Marshall?" she asked. "You're up late."

"Yes. I was hoping you might come by."

"Why?" I couldn't see her face at all, just the white blur of it under the bathing cap.

"I just wanted to talk to you. Why don't you come ashore and have a cup of coffee with me? I've got some made."

She didn't answer for a moment. "Well," she said hesitantly at last, "all right."

She waded ashore and we went up to the fire. I handed her a towel and she dried her arms and legs while I pushed the coffee bucket up against the embers. I threw a couple of small sticks on the fire, and when they caught and flared up the flames highlighted her face and the lines of her figure.

"Don't you want to take off the cap?" I asked.

She shook her head. "It's all right."

I was squatting down, poking at the fire, and I looked up at her. "Please do."

She stopped rubbing with the towel and looked at me with that odd stillness in her face. "Why?"

"Because your hair is beautiful."

I could feel the silence tightening up around us again and knew I shouldn't have said it. But hell, I thought, a girl isn't that touchy unless she's afraid. And it isn't me she's afraid of—it's herself.

"Beautiful!" she said bitterly.

"It is."

She said nothing. I took the other towel and spread it on the bedroll. "Sit down here," I said. "The coffee will be hot in a minute."

"But my suit will get your blankets wet."

"No. Not with the towel. Please do. It's more comfortable."

She sat down with her legs doubled under her and I handed her a cigarette. The coffee began to sizzle around the sides of the bucket, making a comforting sound in the night. I poured two cups and handed her one. "Do you like cream and sugar in it? I have some canned milk."

"No. Black, please."

I sat down across from her, on the ground. "What's your name besides Mrs. Shevlin?"

"Doris."

"You know," I said, "you shouldn't swim in that swamp at night. It's dangerous."

"It's all right. I know all the water and it's safe enough. I'm a good swimmer."

"Doesn't your husband ever swim with you?"

"No. He doesn't care for it."

"I can't understand his letting you do it," I said, and again I was conscious of walking on ground where I didn't belong. "I mean," I went on hurriedly, "I realize it's none of my business, but doesn't he worry about you?"

"No—" she said, cutting it off as if she had started to say more and then had changed her mind.

"Do you go to town very often?" I asked.

"No. I've never been to town since we came up here."

"Not in a whole year?" I asked in amazement. "Doesn't your husband take you at all?"

"He doesn't go either. He goes down to the store at the foot of the lake twice a week, and that's all."

"What days does he go?" I asked, and after the words were out I knew why I had asked, and wondered if she did. She probably had noticed that I'd waited three whole days to go back after the pliers.

She knew, all right. She looked at me with that intense stillness and made no reply. It occurred to me then that I knew anyway, for he had gone first on Tuesday and this was Friday.

"No certain days," she said, and then I knew she had realized the same thing and that she wasn't telling the truth. "Just whenever they ask him to bring some fish."

I began to understand a little about her then—a little, and, as I found out later, I hadn't even begun. Loneliness was driving her mad. She wanted to talk to me or to somebody, but she was afraid to. She didn't know, if she started something like that, whether it would get out of control. But, as I say, I didn't know half of it then.

"Look," I said, "I come up here fishing quite often. Would you like me to bring you some magazines? I'd be glad to do it."

She shook her head and smiled a little. It was the first time I had ever seen her smile, and it made her look even younger and prettier. I felt again that powerful desire I had this afternoon to pick her up in my arms. "No," she said. "Thank you. But he brings me things to read from the store. It was nice of you to offer, though."

"It wasn't as nice as you think it was," I said, leaning forward a little. "It was partly because I wanted an excuse to come and see you again."

"You know you can't do that, don't you?" she asked quietly.

"No," I said.

"You can't. Is it because I stopped here? Did that give you the idea—"

"Nothing gave me any idea. I just want to see you again."

She stared at the ground. "Don't say that!"

"Why not?"

"I'll have to leave if you're going to talk like that."

"All right. I won't say it. But there's no way you can stop me from think-ing it."

"You can't. I shouldn't have come here. It's crazy."

"Of course it's crazy," I said. "Does that change it?"

She put down the coffee cup, still looking at the ground, and made that same desperate gesture, that utterly hopeless quick movement of the hand across the side of her head and down her neck, that she had made the other day—only now it wasn't through her hair, because she still had on the rubber cap.

"Don't come back," she said, staring.

"Why not?"

"You can't."

"You don't want me to?"

"No."

"Are you sure?" I asked.

"Are you enjoying this?" she asked. Her face was white and she had for-gotten to smoke the cigarette. It burned slowly up toward her fingers, the long gray ash precariously clinging.

I wanted to reach out and put my hands on her arms, to take hold of her, but her eyes held me away. I could see the battle going on behind them.

"You came down here to tell me to stay away, didn't you?"

"Yes."

"But I hadn't said anything then. Before you came tonight."

"Do you think I'm blind?" she said harshly. "Don't you think I could see, there at the house?"

"Yes," I said. "And you weren't the only one who could see. There were two of us there."

"Stop it!" she lashed at me.

I threw the cigarette in the fire. "Tell me," I said quietly. "Where is he?"

"He's at the house."

"He knows you're here, doesn't he?"

"No."

"How could he help knowing it?"

The face was as white and still as smoke. "Because he's drunk. He's passed out."

"You can't go back—"

"Why not? I'm used to it."

I leaned forward and took her wrist in my hand and lifted the cigarette from her fingers. "You're going to burn yourself," I said, and threw it in the fire. She pulled back on the arm and I could feel my fingers shaking as they tight-ened. She hit me with the other hand, across the mouth, and stood up with her face held together only by an effort of will, and I could hear the dry sound of the crying in her throat.

"Listen," I said. "Doris—"

She jerked away from me and ran through the darkness toward the edge of the lake. Before I could get there I heard the splash as she went in, and when I got down to the edge of the water she was gone. I could hear her swimming away in the darkness.

Chapter Five

There was no use trying to sleep. I built up the fire enough to see by, packed everything and stowed it in the boat, and went out and picked up the trot line. It must have been around two o'clock when I started down the lake on the oars. After about five miles I could see light in the east, and when the darkness over the water had begun to wash out to the thin gray of early dawn I cranked the outboard. She's back at the house, I thought, lying there beside a passed-out drunk, looking up at the oak shades and waiting for another day to start.

I was back home by eight o'clock. Parking the old Ford and the boat trailer in the back yard, I went in through the back door, taking a long time to find the right key. Louise wouldn't be back until the middle of next week. I noticed she had left the light on in the kitchen, and when I went into the bedroom her nightgown and robe were dangling from the back of a chair and the bed was unmade. I undressed and went into the bath. There were some pants and a pair of nylons hanging on the curtain rod in the shower. I grabbed them off and threw them in on the bed. After a hot shower and a shave, I dressed and went out in the kitchen, remembering I hadn't had any breakfast. There were some unwashed dishes in the sink, and I couldn't find any orange juice in the refrigerator. The hell with it, I thought. I'll eat in town. I got a bottle of whisky out of the cupboard and poured myself a big stiff drink for a bracer because I hadn't had any sleep.

I sat down at the kitchen table as I drank it, trying to put her out of my mind. I've got to stay away from there, I thought. Somehow I've got to do it.... There's no way out of a thing like that. Without any way that I could stop it, my mind was thinking, this is Saturday. There's Sunday, and Monday, and Monday night.... I won't go back, I thought. And then I could see the white, unhappy face and hear the dry sound of her crying.

I went out and backed the Olds out of the garage. Forty-five-fifty a month from now until the time we need a Cadillac, I thought. It was already hot in the square and the town was beginning to fill up with people coming in for Saturday. I parked and started into the courthouse and met Buford coming out.

"Hello, Jack," he said, smiling. "Catch any fish?"

"A few bass," I said. "No catfish, though," I went on, lying, because I had promised to bring him one and hadn't.

"How about a cup of coffee?"

"Fine," I said. "I haven't had any breakfast yet."

"Come on. Let's go over to Barone's."

Buford was a handsome man somewhere in his forties, but he looked younger than that. He was big, about my size, with coal-black hair graying at the temples and very assured gray eyes and a quiet, poised demeanor that made women crazy about him. He was a college graduate and smart, but he always wore a big white hat with the brim turned sharply up at the sides like any ham politician, and he would lift it clear of his head in a courtly-gesture to every woman of voting age that he met, even when he was driving a car. Men liked him just as well, and people who must have known he was crooked would vote for him.

We crossed the square, dodging cars, and went down the street to the big neon sign that said, "Barone's." It was full of chrome and big mirrors and the clattering sound of dishes, with a counter and a row of booths upholstered in imitation leather. In the back, next to the swinging doors going out into the kitchen, a heavy oak door bore a sign reading, "Members." It was supposed to be a club, and I guess in a way it was, but the membership was limited to anyone who could prove he had the price of a drink.

We went on in, and it was quieter here and the lights were less garish. The room had a small bar along one side and some more booths, with a stand at the back holding a half-dozen slot machines. Up front there was a juke box. There was no one in the place except the bartender and a large blonde in a tight black dress talking to him. It was the owner herself, Billy Barone.

She turned and smiled. "Good morning, Sheriff. Hello, Jack." Her hair was waved, and looked as if it had been carved out of lemonwood and buffed down with wax.

We sat down in the last booth and she came over. "What will you officers of the law have this morning?" she asked, still smiling, and giving Buford a long, lazy glance.

"Black coffee for me," Buford said. "With a shot of Bacardi rum on the side."

"You've been a bad boy, Sheriff," she teased. "And how about you, Jack?"

"Breakfast," I said. "Ham and eggs and some coffee."

"It wouldn't be safe to take all that on an empty stomach," Buford said. "You'd better have something."

"All right," I said. "Bourbon."

The bartender brought the drinks over, and in a minute a girl came in with Buford's coffee. He pushed two nickels across the table toward her. "How about putting those in the juke box?"

I knew he detested juke boxes and their canned noise, aside from the money they brought him—he owned a part interest in the outfit that controlled them and the slot machines and pinballs. It wasn't hillbilly music he wanted; it was privacy.

"Here's how," he said. We drank. The juke box hissed, then commenced its blaring.

He took out a cigar and lit it, then removed it from his mouth and looked at it in the manner of a man who loves good cigars. He's an odd one, I thought, a queer mixture, and not somebody I'd want to tangle with unless I had to. That nineteenth-century courtliness fronted for a lot of toughness you could see sometimes looking out at you from behind the noncommittal eyes.

When he talked business he never wasted words. "The grand jury convenes next week," he said quietly.

"And—" I said. It had met before.

"We've got trouble. There's talk. And too many people that a month or so ago would have been asking me for something just happen to be looking in store windows now when they meet me on the street. Most of it is Soames. He's got his teeth into that business about the Demaree kid, and he knows where the kid got drunk. The word is going around now that he's going to blast the lid off everything Sunday, and everybody's going. He's been doing a lot of looking around. Normally, it wouldn't amount to much, but just before the grand jury it's dangerous as hell. Soames, unfortunately, isn't just another crackpot, and he's no windbag. People are beginning to listen to him, people who don't usually pay much attention to rabble-rousers and crusaders with ants in their pants."

"All right," I said. "What do we do?" I knew what I wanted to do. I wanted to get out of the whole stinking mess and get a job washing cars or digging ditches, but that's the bad part of that kind of business—it's not easy to get loose, especially when the heat starts.

"We do just what anybody else does with gasoline on his clothes—we don't light any cigarettes. I want you to tell Abbie Bell and that woman out on Cypress Street to keep the lid clamped on those places, because if we have any more trouble down there I'm going to run them out of town before we all get caught in the wringer. And slip the word to all the rest of them. Sometime today drive out to Moss Inn and tell Carpenter he'd better start looking his customers over a little more carefully before he lets them go back where the games are. There's no telling who Soames is getting his information from, but he's getting it straight. However, it's the cat houses he's got his guns leveled on right now, and particularly Abbie Bell's. But the whole thing's dynamite, at least until after the grand jury adjourns."

"O.K.," I said. "I'll tell 'em." It didn't show much on his face, but I knew he was worried.

As it turned out, I didn't get a chance to tell anybody anything. Trouble started almost before we got back to the office. The telephone was ringing as we walked in the door. Lorraine picked it up.

"Yes? Yes. He's here now. He just came in. Hold on a minute." She handed it to Buford.

"Yes, speaking," he said. He listened for a moment. "All right. Just keep your shirt on. Yes, Marshall. Of course I'll send Marshall. He'll be there before you can stop screaming." He hung up.

"You can get your coffee if you want, Lorraine, I'll stick around." She looked at him, grabbed her purse, and left, knowing it was an order.

When she was out the door he turned to me. "It's that Bell woman. Yelling her head off. Some big sawmill hand's gone berserk and is trying to kill one of the girls. She wants you. For God's sake, try to get it quieted down with- out anybody getting hurt."

I knew what he meant, and didn't even get the gun out of the filing cabi- net where I'd left it Monday. I don't like guns anyway; I had enough of them during the war. I was out the door before he'd finished talking.

I took my own car because there wasn't time to go to the county garage af- ter one. Traffic was snarled in the square, as it always is on Saturdays, and I had to creep through it, cursing. When I got clear of that I shot down the next six blocks giving it the gun all the way. All we needed now was for somebody to be killed in one of those places and the county would blow up right in our faces. I slid to a stop in front of the chili joint and ran across the street to the hotel. The street was quiet except for the wailing of a juke box in one of the beer joints, and fortunately there wasn't any crowd gathering. I could hear a noise as of someone hammering in the back of the building.

Abbie let me in the door and then slammed it shut, fast. She had the filmy blue robe clutched around her with one hand and was waving an empty gin bottle in the other. The tight curls seemed to strain outward from her head as if she carried an electrical charge.

"Stop the crazy fool!" she was yelling. "He'll kill somebody!"

"All right, relax," I said. "Where is he?"

"Upstairs. At the end of the hall. My God, stop him!"

I went up the stairs on the run, still hearing the pounding. The hallway had no windows at the ends and was dimly lighted with one small, unshaded bulb, and all the doors were closed. I could see him down at the end and ran toward him. He was a big devil, naked except for a pair of shorts and one sock, and he was swinging a small table by one leg like a footstool, hammering on the door with it. He had one of the upper panels already knocked in and was work- ing on the other. Inside the room I could hear a girl's voice, high-pitched and on the edge of hysteria, not crying or pleading but dredging up obscenity I'd never heard before in twenty-seven years.

"I'll get you, you lousy little slut," he yelled, smashing the table into the door again and splintering the other panel.

"All right, knock it off, Mac," I said. "You've had your fun."

He paused, with the table pulled back for another swing, and looked around at me. I was still ten feet away, moving toward him. In those things you can never let them see any hesitation or you're a dead duck, but I did- n't feel too sure about it. He was as big as I was, or larger, and crazy with rage, and he appeared to be only around twenty, an age when you haven't found out yet that you can be hurt.

"Drop it," I said roughly.

He stood poised to swing. "You a law?"

"Yes," I said. "Give me that." I reached for the table.

I don't know whether it was because he could see I was alone and didn't have a gun or whether he was so wild with rage he didn't care, but at any rate I saw his face go wild again and he swung. I tried to get inside it, but the table caught my arm and shoulder and I fell over against the opposite door. I could hear somebody scream down at the other end of the hall, and realized Abbie had followed me up the stairs.

"I'll show her! I'll show the chippy!" he yelled, swinging the table at me again. I was down on my knees with my left arm numb, and I lunged at his legs, hitting him low and taking him off balance. He came down, and the two of us and the table rolled in a pile on the floor. I could hear the table give up the ghost as one of us rolled over it and the legs started caving in. He landed a big fist on the side of my head and made it ring. I slid clear of the tangle and got to my feet before he did, and as he tried to scramble up he was wide open for a second. I got my feet set and swung, catching him under the jaw, and his feet slid out from under him. He bounced up, too insane with fury to re-alize he was leaving himself open in exactly the same way he had the first time, and I hit him again. We went through the whole, identical procedure two more times before he finally quit and lay there on the floor.

"I'll kill her! I'll get her!" he was saying over and over and beginning to cry.

I was winded and my left arm felt as if a car had run over it. I had to lean against the wall to steady myself while I fought for breath. He sat up, still cry-ing, and I kicked the wrecked table out of his reach.

"Sit right where you are," I said.

He had his chin down on his chest and the big shoulders shook with the silent retching of his sobs. I felt sorry for him even if he had tried to brain me with the table, and wondered what the girl had done to him.

"Where are this guy's clothes?" I called out, and looked behind me. Abbie was coming back up the stairs again. Apparently she'd run down when he floored me with the table.

"Get his clothes," I said.

She was still waving the gin bottle as if she had forgotten she had it. "Je-sus, I don't know where his lousy clothes are," she began, when suddenly one of the doors opened.

It looked like a sequence out of a movie comedy. The door flew open ap-parently of its own volition and a pair of blue serge trousers sailed out to land in the middle of the hall. A shirt followed it, then two shoes at once, and a tie. Just for an instant, the white, staring face of a girl appeared around the frame and then ducked back inside and the door slammed. She hadn't said a word.

That's odd, I was conscious of thinking; he's trying to beat up this girl, but his clothes are in another girl's room. He must not have been with this one at all.

I picked up the clothes and tossed them to the boy. Now that I had time to get a good look at him, I saw he was a big blond kid who needed a haircut and that there wasn't anything vicious about his face.

"Put these on," I said. "You going to behave yourself?"

"All right," he mumbled. "Ain't no use fightin' laws."

"You took a hell of a long time finding it out," I grumbled, but glad he was getting some sense at last.

I could still hear the girl inside the room cursing obscenely and shrilly with the monotonous repetition of a phonograph record with the needle stuck. Afraid she would get him started again, I stepped over and stuck my head in through the smashed panels.

"Pipe down," I said. Then I saw her, and began to feel scared for the first time. She was sitting on the bed in a sleazy-looking kimono with her blonde hair rumpled as if she'd just got up, and if she was a day over sixteen, I was sixty.

Chapter Six

She saw me. "Who the hell are you?"

"Never mind," I said. "Just stop that noise."

"Why, you jerk!"

I heard the boy behind me and turned around. He was putting on his clothes, stuffing the shirttail inside his trousers. He had quit crying, but his face was white and trembling and I could still see that wild look in his eyes.

"Move down the hall," I said, trying to get him out of earshot of the girl. "Then put your shoes on. We're going for a ride."

He looked for an instant as if he wanted to jump me again, then he thought better of it and walked down toward the stairway.

"What are you going to do, Jack?" Abbie asked. "Ain't you going to lock him up? My God, I don't want the crazy ba—"

"Yes," I said roughly, still thinking about the girl. "I'm taking him out. Give him a chance to get his shoes on. I'll be back here in about ten minutes, and while I'm gone don't let that girl out of here! And don't let anybody in."

"All right, but—"

"Look," I said. "*Don't let anybody in!* And I mean *anybody.* Tell 'em you're dead, or the girls have gone to summer camp or the country club, or anything. But keep 'em out."

I motioned for the big kid to go on ahead of me and we went out and got in the car.

"Where we going?" he asked.

"Jail," I said, turning the car around.

I could see his face begin to harden up again. "I reckon I'll get worked over when you guys get me in there—for fighting a cop. I've heard about that."

"You won't if you keep your big mouth shut," I said.

"You mean you ain't going to tell 'em?"

"No," I said. "Just keep clammed up and don't say anything to anybody. Especially about that girl."

"I'll get her yet," he said, with that tight sing to his voice.

"Shut up," I said. "Look. That's probably the stupidest thing in the world, making a statement like that. If anything *ever* happens to that girl, you'll go to the chair for saying what you just said if anybody can prove it. What'd she do to you, anyway?"

I shot a quick glance at him. His face was all screwed up as if he couldn't make up his mind whether to fight again or to cry. "She's a lousy, chippy little—"

"Never mind *what* she is. What did she do?"

"Me and her was married about eight months ago. We run off. Then her old man caught us and had it un-nulled because she ain't but fifteen."

"She's what!"

"She ain't but fifteen. I told her I'd wait around till she was old enough to get married proper and they couldn't un-null it on us, but she run off with another fella, an old guy twenty-five or thirty that didn't want to marry her."

"You're sure that's how old she is?" I asked.

"Yeah. Of course. Ain't I knowed her since she was a little girl? I always figgered on marrying her."

"All right," I said, easing through the traffic in the square. "You just keep your mouth shut and you won't get in any trouble."

I turned him over to Cassieres and called Buford from the jail. "Lorraine back yet?" I asked when he answered.

"She's just coming in now. How'd you make out? Did you get it straightened out?"

"Part of it," I said. "Can you meet me in front of the jail? Right now?"

"I'm on my way." He hung up.

In about two minutes his car pulled up behind mine. I went back and leaned in the window.

"What is it?" he asked quietly, looking worried.

"I've got the guy in there," I said. "He's just a kid about nineteen or twenty and he's all right, but he's off his rocker about the girl. I think I've got him shut up so he won't do any talking. But here's the thing. It's that girl. She's fifteen."

"Sweet Jesus! If Soames ever—"

"I know. And it's straight, too. The kid says he's known her all his life. We've got to get her out of there. You got any money on you?"

"A hundred or so. Can you handle it all right?"

"I think so. I'll take her down the highway and put her on a bus."

"She'll just wind up in another cat house somewhere else. So you know about not buying her a ticket into some other state, don't you?"

"Yes," I said. "I'm not going to buy her a ticket of any kind if I can help it. I think I know a way to handle it."

"So she won't come back?"

"There's no way to guarantee that. If I work it right, though, she probably won't."

He took out his wallet and handed me a couple of fifties and some twenties. "There's a hundred and sixty. Jack, I'm glad there's somebody around that office can use his head."

"Now's as good a time to tell you as any other," I said. "I'm quitting as soon as this stink blows over. I don't like it."

"No," he said. "You think it over. I don't want to lose you."

"I've already thought it over. But we haven't got time to argue about it now. I've got to get back down there."

"That's right. I'll have that kid booked on a vag or something, and as soon as we get the girl out of town we'll tell him to beat it."

"O.K."

I went back to my car and drove down to Abbie Bell's. The Negro girl came to the door, still looking scared. "Ain't nobody heah," she said, trying to close it. "Miss Abbie say ain't nobody comin' in heah."

"I know," I said, pushing past her. Abbie heard me and came out of the parlor into the hall. She'd got her hair straightened out and had a drink in her hand this time instead of the empty bottle.

"Come on in, Jack," she said, and then to the maid, "Bring this man a Collins, Kate. And put some gin in it; he's not a customer."

We went into the parlor and I closed the door. "God, I'm glad you got rid of that big gorilla, Jack," she said.

"Never mind. Where's the girl?"

"Up there in her room still bitching her head off. Did you ever hear such a foul-mouthed little bag in all your life?"

"How did she get in here, Abbie?" I asked curtly. "And how long ago?"

She took a sip of her drink and looked at me with puzzled innocence. "What do you mean, how did she get in here, Jack? She just came in through the front door and said she was a hustler."

"Do you know how old she is?" I asked.

"How old? Lord, no. Why should I?"

"She's fifteen."

"No! Is that all? She *looks* older than that."

"Yes," I said sarcastically. "She looks sixteen."

She lit a cigarette and stared at me with amiable exasperation. "Well, what am I supposed to do, Jack? Send her back to get ripe? She—"

"Didn't you even ask her how old she was?"

"Of course not. Why the hell should I? Look, Jack, this is a cat house, not a girl's boarding school. Jesus, if they're old enough to give it away, they're old enough to sell—"

I cut her off. "How long's she been here?"

"I don't know. Three, four days."

"Well, she goes out. I'm going to take her clear out of the county and put her on a bus."

She looked at me and saw I meant it. "Oh, O.K. She's a pain in the neck, anyway. Stays plastered about half the time, and she never makes any money. She's so foulmouthed even the roughnecks can't stand her."

"Well, tell her to get her stuff packed."

"She hasn't got any stuff. All she had when she came in here was the clothes she was wearing, and that'd better be the way she leaves, too."

"She had on a kimono a while ago."

"I gave her that to keep her from running around here naked. It stays. And, by the way," she went on, "who pays for my door?"

"You do, I guess."

"I'll see Buford about it and get him to make that big ape—"

"You'd better stay away from Buford. The way he feels right now, about that girl being in here, he'd just as soon shoot you."

She rattled the ice in her glass and shrugged. "God, *men!* What a bunch of muttonheads! Why don't they let women write the laws?"

"How did all that fuss start, anyway?" I asked.

"I don't know, exactly. He was here all night, and as near as I can get it from Bernice—the girl he was with, the one who had his clothes—everything was all right and peaceful until this morning he opened the door and started out in the hall for something. I guess he must have seen this other little bag then— she must have been going down the hall. She'd been swacked to the ears all night in her room, and I guess he hadn't seen her before. Anyway, Bernice said he let out a roar like a stuck pig and lit out down the hall, yelling at every jump."

The maid brought in my drink. Abbie went out, leaving the door open, and in a moment I could hear her going along the hall on the upper floor. There was the sound of shrill feminine argument and after a few minutes she came back.

Picking up her drink from the table where she'd left it, she sat down, shaking her head. "She'll be down in a minute. I'd tell you what she said you could do, but I can't repeat it."

I took a sip of my drink. "And that big kid's completely off his nut about her. How do you figure a thing like that?"

"It's men, I tell you. They should never let 'em out alone."

In a minute the girl came down the stairs and stood in the doorway. She had combed her hair, which was dirty blonde, and had on a blue summer dress with a wide, dark-blue patent-leather belt and high-heeled white shoes with no stockings. She might have been pretty if she hadn't shaved off all her eyebrows except a thin line and painted them on with black grease or something. She had rebuilt her mouth, too, the upper lip an exaggerated cupid's bow that went a third of the way up to her nose. She looked at me with edged contempt.

"Sit down," I said. "We'll be going in about half a minute."

"Who says we'll go anywhere?"

"I do," I said, lighting a cigarette.

"Why, you stupid jerk! You know what you can do?" She told me what I could do.

Abbie smiled at me. "She's a dear little thing, isn't she?"

I got up. "Come on, kid. Let's go."

"And what makes you think I'll go?"

I shrugged with elaborate indifference. "You either go where I'm trying to take you or you go to jail. And you won't care for our matron. She'll like you, but you won't like her," I said, making it all up. The matron at the jail was all right.

"Oh." She hesitated. "And where do you think you're going to take me?"

"I'll tell you about it on the way. You going?"

"All right," she said harshly. "It can't be any worse than this dump."

We started out. "Good-by, dear," Abbie said, still smiling sweetly. The girl stopped in the doorway and told her what she could do.

"You *are* a dear," Abbie said. The girl told her some more.

"How about knocking it off before we get out in the street?" I said. "There might be men present."

We went on out to the car. I had it all pretty well thought out by this time. It was about seventy miles down to Colston, and if I remembered correctly, the New Orleans bus went through there around one in the afternoon. It was a little after eleven now. We could make it. I threw the coat with my wallet in it into the back seat and got in.

The girl climbed in, crossing her legs with her dress up over her knees. "How about a cigarette?" I gave her one and we started out. "God, what a jerk burg this is," she said. "Anything would beat this."

We skirted the back streets to hit the highway without going through town, and when we got out on the road I opened it up to about sixty.

"Where's your home?" I asked.

She took a drag on the cigarette, and threw it out the window. "I haven't got any."

"You must have come from somewhere."

"Wouldn't you like to know?"

"I'm not trying to take you home."

"Where are we going?"

"Oh, you'll like this place," I said. "It's just outside Bayou City, kind of like a farm, you might say. Only not a real farm. And it's not a reform school, either. I mean, when you see it, reform school would be the last thing you'd ever think of. It's run by a man and his wife, by the name of—oh, nuts, I know their name as well as I know my own. It's—ah— Look in my coat, back there, and get my wallet out, will you? I think there's a card with the address and their name and everything."

"It sounds like a crumby dump to me," she said, but in a minute she turned around in the seat and lifted up the coat, slipping the wallet out. "Here," she said.

"Look and see if you don't find a card in there," I said.

She looked through it. "I don't see anything."

"I must have lost it, then," I said. "Well, it doesn't matter. I know how to get there. Just throw the wallet back in the coat."

She put it back. "You don't think I'd go to a joint like that, do you?"

"Well, if you'd rather go to jail—"

She was silent for a moment. "What do they do down there?" she asked.

"Oh, it's a nice place. They work in the vegetable gardens and milk the cows, things like that—lots of outdoor exercise. Have movies, too. Once a week, travelogues and science stuff, you know. The girls like it. No boys there, of course. It's for girls only."

"Jeezus!"

I didn't say anything. After a while she turned to me with a smile and said, "You know, big boy, maybe you're not such a sticky creep, after all. You *have* got a good car, and you're kind of good-looking, in an ugly sort of way. Why don't you and me just go on to Bayou City and go on a little party? I could show you a good time."

"Relax, kid. Put it away. I've been on parties."

"God, what a jerk!"

She shut up after that and was silent the rest of the way to Colston. It was about five minutes of one when I pulled up and parked across the street from the bus station.

"Well, what are we going to do here?" she asked with that same insolence.

"I thought I'd better phone ahead so they could get a ce—I mean a room ready for you. Probably have a phone in the bus station over there. You stick here in the car and I'll be right back."

It was Saturday afternoon and cars were jammed in the streets and hordes of people roamed about. I took out the car keys and walked across to the bus station.

"What time does the New Orleans bus go through?" I asked the girl at the ticket window.

"Due here in about three minutes. And it's only a five-minute stop. You want a ticket?"

"No," I said. "I'm expecting somebody."

I went back to the car. She looked at me without interest. "They didn't have a pay phone. There's a drugstore just around the next corner. I'll try there."

"Well, don't drop dead of anything. It would just kill me."

"I won't be gone more than ten minutes," I said. "Don't you try to run off."

"Now that I've thought about it, you can drop dead." I went around the corner to the drugstore and bought a pack of cigarettes, then went over and squeezed in at the fountain and ordered a lemon Coke. When the boy brought it I heard the big air horn of the bus down the street and knew it was on time. I drank very slowly and looked at the clock. It was four minutes past one. Then I heard the blasting roar of its exhaust in low gear, and saw it go past the corner, headed for New Orleans. I paid for the Coke and went back to the car.

She was gone. I reached in for the coat, hoping she had left the wallet. It wasn't a very good one, but it was my only one. It was still there. She'd just taken the money.

I locked the car and went up the street to a beer joint, taking my own money out of my watch pocket and putting it back in the limp wallet. It was dim inside and I found a place at the bar. "A bottle of Bud," I said, wondering why I always got these headaches in the afternoons.

Oh, hell, I thought, she's probably stolen plenty of things before. You could see what she was like, couldn't you? You didn't teach her anything; nobody could. She was born that way.

It'll be all right now, I thought. At least, until something else starts to break loose. Suddenly I wanted to get in the car and just go on driving the way it was headed, go so far I could never find my way back. And it wasn't only Buford and the grand jury I could feel behind me.

What was she doing now? Was she down on her knees in soapy water trying to beat all desire out of herself with a scrubbing brush, or was she looking for another withered leaf on that scrawny and pitiful vine?

Chapter Seven

Sunday morning I went to church to hear the Reverend Soames, and after I was there I wished I'd stayed away. There was something about him that made me uneasy, gave me that same feeling an escaping prisoner must have when he hears, far behind, the first baying of the hounds as they pick up his trail. He was a big, impressive man with a manner about him that kept reminding me of Buford, and his voice had a quality of persuasiveness and irresistible power that you could not escape no matter where your mind would turn. It brought you back and held you there and made you look at what it had to show.

He didn't rant or raise his voice, but he talked, from information. "If the law enforcement officers of this community will come to me, I will be glad to tell them where to find these places that have so far eluded their vigilance and that apparently only boys in their teens can find. I will point out the slot machines and gambling places, and give them the addresses of the brothels operating openly in this town, and give them the names of the women running them."

The church was packed, and I glanced around at the people sitting near me. They were completely absorbed, their faces serious. How many of them will be on that grand jury? I thought. When it ended I went home. People were standing around in front of the church in little groups, talking. Maybe it was only my imagination, but I thought I could feel their curious, cold glances on my back.

I switched on the light at the side of the bed and looked at my watch. It was two in the morning. I had been lying there, smoking one cigarette after another, for three hours without ever approaching sleep. At every turn of my mind she stood there before me, still-faced, unspeaking, very beautiful in her shapeless, terrible clothes. There was no way to get around her; she blocked every path of thought, every escape I tried. I could shut my eyes and see her, and when I opened them she was there looking at me from the darkness.

I've got to stop it, I thought. I can't go on like this. I'll be as crazy as that big kid. She's just a woman who is being killed by loneliness in that swamp, and what woman wouldn't be? What's different about her? Is this going on and on until I go back there and see her again? And would it stop then, or get worse? I cursed, and got up to go into the bathroom to find Louise's sleeping tablets. I took two of them and lay down again. I tossed and turned for what seemed like hours. It must have been about three when I finally got to sleep.

Monday was an endless flat plain of heat, and of hours that seemed to go on forever. I walked through stagnant time like a man in a dream, hoping the day would end and dreading the night that had to come when I would have nothing to do but lie in the darkness and fight it again.

Buford had been tickled with the way I had got rid of that girl. "That was a good job," he said. "She won't be back."

"You can't tell," I said. "A girl like that is capable of anything. You don't know what goes on in her mind." I didn't want to talk about it. Everything irritated me. I sat eating lunch in Barone's café without knowing what I ate and not even caring.

I went to a movie after supper and walked out before the end of it. I went home because I couldn't think of anywhere else to go. I sat there in the empty house, turning off the radio because I couldn't stand the noise, and then turning it on because I couldn't stand the silence.

I went out in the hall and looked at the telephone. I could call him, I thought. Call Buford. Just tell him I might not be in tomorrow. I wouldn't have to go up the lake. I could still show up for work even though I'd said I might not be there. It wouldn't mean I was going, would it? No. It didn't make any sense. I wouldn't call him. Then I had the telephone in my hand.

"Elks Club," a voice said. I couldn't even remember asking for the number.

"Is Buford there?" Maybe he wouldn't be. That would be fine. Then I would have that on my side. If I didn't locate him I couldn't go.

"Just a minute." There was a long silence. She was crying when she said he was drunk, I thought, crying with the dry sound of tearing something inside her throat. She didn't want to tell me. "Hello. No, he's not here."

That settled it. That settled it once and for all. I couldn't go because I couldn't find Buford.

I called Barone's.

I called the Eagles.

I was sweating, and cursing under my breath. I shook the telephone like a woman with a sick baby trying to get a doctor late at night. I put it down and sat there looking at it, feeling my nerves jumping. I wanted to tear it loose from its wires and throw it down the hall.

Lorraine! I thought. Maybe I could get her.

I could hear it ringing. She's not at home either, I thought, and began to have the crazy idea that all the rest of the human race had disappeared and I was left here alone to go mad beside a telephone that didn't go anywhere or connect with anything.

"Hello," a girl's voice said.

"Is this Lorraine?" I asked stupidly.

"Yes. Oh, is that you, Jack? What is it?"

"This is Jack Marshall," I said, and then realized she already knew who it was.

"Yes. What is it?"

"I—ah—" What the hell did I want with Lorraine? Then, suddenly, I had the crazy idea she must think I was calling her up to ask for a date because Louise was out of town. Why would she think a crazy thing like that? I thought angrily. Had I ever done—

I began to function again. "Oh. I just wondered if you'd tell Buford in the morning that I might not be in. I can't locate him."

"Why, yes. I'll tell him."

"Thanks."

It wasn't until I had hung up that I realized I hadn't given any reason at all. Well, what of it? I thought. What difference does it make? If you're going twenty miles back in a swamp because you can't stay away from another man's wife, why worry about a little thing like not making up a lie for your employer?

I stood there for a minute in the hall and then, without even thinking about it, as if I had planned it for a week, I took a flashlight and went out in the yard, along the wall of the house where the vines were growing. There were some morning-glories, and when I found a young, small one I dug it up with a butcher knife, taking a lot of dirt with it, and packed it in a small cardboard box. I went back inside the kitchen with it and poured some water on the soil, then stood there looking at it with a sort of stupid and unaccountable happiness like a kid who suddenly feels good for no reason at all.

What the hell am I doing this for? I thought. Am I losing my mind?

The sun was coming up now. I could see shafts of yellow light filtering through the dense canopy of timber like those in the pictures of the interiors of dim cathedrals. I sat very quietly in the boat, drawn far back under the overhanging trees where the slough came out and joined the main body of the lake. From where I was hidden I could not see up the lake at all, only a short section across and down, toward the south, but there was no reason for looking—I would hear his motor long before he came into sight.

I looked at my watch. He must have left up there over an hour ago, at least, which meant he should be down here in less than an hour. With his motor he could make it in that much time; it would take me at least three or a little over. I lit a cigarette and smoked it in fierce, quick puffs, impatient at the slow dragging of time. A water moccasin swam across the flat mirror of the slough, an undulating dark head at the apex of a spreading, V-shaped ripple on the water. It came up past the boat, paused, looking at me for an instant with the cold, unwinking, incurious eyes like little chips of stone, then submerged, dropping from sight without effort into water the color of tea.

Maybe he wouldn't come. Maybe she had been telling me the truth when she said he had no certain days for going to the store. I looked at the watch

again; less than five minutes had passed. Why hadn't I brought at least a semblance of fishing tackle with me? What would I look like if I met someone up
here, a man going up the lake in a boat for no reason at all, not fishing because
he had nothing to fish with? Suppose I met him, or he saw me? There was
nothing in the boat except that ridiculous cardboard box of moistened earth,
shoved as far back out of sight as possible under the seat in the bow. I'm crazy,
I thought. I'm insane. No man in his right mind would be doing this.

A half hour passed while I smoked cigarettes chain fashion and listened for
the motor. Then I heard it, or thought I did, and held my breath to listen. Yes,
there it was, still far up the lake. I waited while the sound grew in volume,
and pulled farther back under the overhanging limbs into the shelter of the
leaves. The boat came past the entrance of the slough, and then for a moment
I could see him, less than fifty yards away, sitting up straight in the stern with
the big floppy straw hat set exactly level on his head and looking neither left
nor right as he went on down the channel. My boat rocked gently in his
spreading wake and then he was gone, the sound of his motor dying away in
the distance down the lake. I pushed out from under the trees and started up.

It was after ten and the sun was brassy on the water when I went past the
place where I had camped. As I came around the bend I wondered if I would
see her swimming in the long stretch of the lake above, but there was no sign
of her, the water flat, unbroken, and shining like a mirror in the sun. I throttled the motor down and turned into the entrance of the slough, feeling my
heart beating and conscious of the tightness in my chest. Without even
thinking of it, I went on past the boat landing, around a swing of the slough,
and pulled up at the bank under the low overhang of a tree. Even before you
will admit to yourself that you are a criminal, I thought, you begin to act like
one without conscious thought. I tied the boat up and stepped ashore with
the cardboard box cradled in my arm.

Pushing through the timber and underbrush because the trail was below me,
to my left, I came out into the clearing, seeing the brown, dry grass and the
weathered ruin of the house squatting in the sun. I was out of breath and had
a feeling I had run for miles. Would she be swimming? Or would she be at the
house? What would she be doing?

I went on across the clearing in the hot sun like a man walking across an endless plain in a nightmare he cannot stop. Why, it hasn't changed at all, I
thought. It looks exactly as it did before, and then the realization came that
it hadn't been years since I was here last. It had been four days.

I stopped in front of the porch, not seeing the old hound this time, or any
sign of life. A grasshopper sang in the still, bright heat, and out at the edge
of the timber a crow cursed me with raucous insolence and flew away.

I stepped up on the porch. "Hello," I said. "Doris, where are you?"

There was the soft sound of bare feet from the rear of the house and I
stepped to the door. She had come into the front room, apparently starting

to the door to see who it was, but when she saw me she stopped. She had on a different dress this time, of another color at least, but an identical shapeless sack of cheap cotton too large for her, and she was still barefoot.

"Doris," I said. "I—" The words quit on me and I stood there foolishly with the clumsy box in my arms.

She said nothing at all. Still standing unmoving in the center of the room with her arms down at her sides, she stared at me with the fixed intensity of someone in a trance.

"I brought you another vine, Doris," I said idiotically, not knowing what to do with it now that it was here. "You see, it's very green and fresh. I think it'll live." When she still made no move, I shifted it awkwardly to my hands and set it on the dresser.

She spoke then, though her voice was still little more than a whisper. "Why?"

"Well, I—I mean, the other one was dying."

"No," she said in the same strained and tightened voice. "Why did you come back?"

I stepped toward her and still she did not move. She watched me with that tortured intensity of the eyes, like someone suffering pain or grief and trying not to show it. The dark hair, uncombed but still lovely in its disarray, framed and intensified the paleness of her cheek, and her face, tipped slightly up to look at me, was blank, tightly held, as devoid of emotion as the hot, choking, and explosive silence about us in the room was devoid of sound.

"I came back," I said quietly, "because I had to. It wasn't because I didn't try. There wasn't any way I could stay away from you. You don't have to tell me what I'm doing. I know what I'm doing."

I reached out and took her by the arms and then began to go wild. I had my arms around her and was kissing her. She held onto me like someone drowning, and I could feel the trembling of her arms about my neck.

Her face was against my shoulder and her voice was muffled, but through the wildness of it I could hear her say, "Not here. Please, not here," the voice breaking as if she were crying.

Chapter Eight

We lay on old leaves in mottled shade, very close together, touching but not talking, the lake a sheet of stainless steel seen here and there through openings in the trees and time arrested and held motionless across the dead center of noon. Her head was on my arm, her face turned toward mine with her eyes closed, and I brought up a hand and ran it spread-fingered through the dark disorder of her hair.

There had been little talk between us, no need for talk, or thought of it. There were still the thousand things about her I wanted to know, but they seemed far away, things I could ask her later, after we had been pulled out of the spent and languid backwater and caught up again in the running current of time. Lying there, I thought about it and tried to remember if it had been real or only a dream, that fantastic and unbelievable thing of two people supposedly or at least otherwise sane, walking without a word or a sign, woodenfaced, not even holding hands or whispering, straight out of the house and across the clearing in silence and white sunlight without any cajoling or pleading on the one part or that age-old simulation of reluctance on the other, without any necessity for communication, as if the whole thing had been planned and discussed for months and rehearsed like a big wedding. And when we had reached this place she had stopped and turned. That was all.

I thought of a fire burning for a long time inside a house with all the doors and windows closed, consuming the interior but still contained, until at last the roof caved in and it burst out with uncontrollable fury. Why? Was it just the loneliness?

There had been no reproach afterward, no silent accusation in the eyes or any mention of my coming back after she had told me to stay away. She had cried once, but only for a minute, with her face muffled against my arm, and then it had gone away, unmentioned and unexplained.

She opened her eyes. They were very near, and looked enormous and deeply blue and quiet while she studied me as if she had never seen me before. Reaching up a hand, she ran soft fingertips across my face. "I'm sorry I hit you. The other night."

"It's all right," I said. "I knew then I could come back. It wasn't me you were trying to stop."

"You knew that all the time, didn't you?"

"Yes. You were fighting yourself so hard you might as well have been carrying a sign."

"I know," she said quietly. "I thought then it would matter. But it doesn't. I guess it's like pain when you have it long enough—before you reach the point you can't stand it any longer you go crazy, or die, and it's all changed. I'm either crazy or dead."

"No," I said. "Just beautiful."

"You like my hair-do, don't you?" It was a joke, but she didn't laugh. There were just those enormous eyes, very close, watching me.

"Yes. The first time I saw it I thought that whoever chopped it up like that should be horsewhipped. But now I like it."

"I guess there are some things you can't stop," she said quietly, more to herself than to me.

"There's no way we could have stopped it."

"It's like it was sometimes when I was out there swimming in the lake at night. There'd be just the black top of the water with the stars reflected on it, and I'd wonder why I couldn't swim down until I drowned, just stay under, as if the water was a black sheet over me. You can't, though. If you can swim you can't drown yourself. When I began to hurt I always came up."

I could feel the anger begin to flame up inside me. "What did he do to you? Does he get mean when he's drunk?"

"No," she said hesitantly. "Only once. We had a fight. But I don't like to talk about it."

"I've got to know," I said. "Can't you see I have to know?"

"It was just the loneliness. I was beginning to go crazy with it, I guess."

"It was more than that," I said.

"No. It was mostly that. We were all right until we came up here."

"What did you come up here for, anyway? Neither of you belong in this swamp."

"We know that now, but it's not easy to get out."

"But why? I mean, in the first place."

"Running," she said woodenly. "It was a place to hide."

Somehow, I had known that. "Him?" I asked. "Or both of you?"

"Just him. It's something that happened before I met him."

"What is it?"

"I don't know. He never did tell me. But, as I said, it was all right before we came up here. Between us, I mean. The moving around was bad, all right, and we never had much because he was always changing jobs, but he was good to me and I guess we were still in love with each other. But this place was too much for us. I guess it was more my fault than his, but I couldn't stand it. We got on each other's nerves and began to fight, and then he started drinking like that. He won't leave here because this is the first place we've ever found where he didn't sooner or later see somebody who might recognize him so we had to move again. And it's getting harder for him to get any kind of job. He looks older than he really is, and of course he can't ever give any references or say where he worked before."

"But," I said wonderingly, "why didn't you leave?"

She looked at me. "How?" she asked simply.

"Good God, you mean he won't let you?"

"In a way."

"But," I protested, "how could he keep you from it?"

"I said in a way. He won't take me down to the highway, or let me have any money. Where could I go?"

"But why?" I asked. "Why does he want to keep you here if there's nothing between you any more except fighting?"

She was silent for a moment. "I'm not sure," she said at last. "I think I know, but I don't like to talk about it."

"You have to tell me," I said.

"As I said, I'm not sure. But I think he suspects I'll turn him in. I guess it must be the law he's running from, and it has preyed on his mind so long he suspects everybody. Maybe you crack up after just so much of that. Anyway, I think that's what he believes—that if he let me get away from here I'd report him to the police because we've fought so much. Especially after he found I was trying to run away. I quit asking him after a while because it always caused trouble between us, and I began to steal from him."

"Steal?" I said. "How could you steal from your husband?"

"Stealing is what I mean," she said. "You could call it anything you like, but I prefer to call it that. When he was drunk, or asleep, I would take money out of his clothes. Not very much, because he never had much, but just a dime now and a quarter the next time so he wouldn't miss it. One day he found it, where I had it hidden, in a baking-powder can, and knew I was planning to leave someday when he was down the lake. He led me down to the edge of the water and made me watch while he threw the coins out in the lake, one at a time, and then made me throw some, and when I refused at first—" She broke off. "Are you enjoying this?"

I felt sick. "I can stop that," I said. "I'll take the—I'll take him in."

"No," she said. "Can't you see that's exactly what he's accusing me of? Not in words, of course, but in his mind. I can't do that. All I want to do is leave."

"How long has this been going on?"

"Four months. Maybe five. You lose track of time."

Yes, I thought, I guess you would.

I sat up and got two cigarettes out of my pocket and lit them, passing one down to her. She lay back with her head on the leaves, smoking the cigarette and looking up at me. The shapeless old sack of a dress was pulled down demurely across her knees, giving her an odd aspect of completely defenseless innocence, like a little girl. The bare legs below the hem of the dress extended down past my side, smooth and faintly tanned, and I turned around a little so I could see the feet. Suddenly, for no reason at all, I slid down there and gathered them up in my lap.

They were slender feet, quite small and beautifully formed, but rough and calloused on the soles from going barefoot, and they were dusty from the trail. Very carefully, with my fingers, I brushed all the dust from them, as if they were very old pieces of fabulously valuable and very fragile jewelry I had found gathering cobwebs in an attic. Then I turned them slightly inward, pressing the soles together up near the toes, and held them, thinking how small and breakable they looked, like the delicate feet of a china doll, in the big, dark hands. I looked up and she was watching me with a misty softness in her eyes.

"Why are you doing that, Jack?" she asked.

I shook my head. "I don't know," I said.

I looked up again and she was crying, quite silently and without any movement of her face.

Time came back for us without any warning. It was the sound of a motor. We sat up. "Jack—" she said.

It was an outboard, a big one, and coming nearer. He must have had it throttled down for it to get that near before we heard it.

"Where is your boat?" she asked in an urgent whisper.

"It's all right," I said. "It's hidden. I'll get off here after dark. But I've got to see you again. Tonight. I'll be down there where I was camped. You've got to come."

"I—I don't know," she said. Her eyes were scared. "But I've got to go." We both stood up.

I kissed her. "It's all right. There's no hurry." We heard the motor quit and knew he was drifting up to the landing. "But you have to come. Promise me you will."

"I will if I can. There's no way to know."

I had my face down against her cheek, holding her very tightly, not wanting to let her go. I knew what she meant. She would come if he got drunk and passed out. Isn't that wonderful? I thought.

"I—I ought to go, Jack."

"It doesn't matter," I began.

"Oh—oh, God!" She pushed away from me and I could see the terror in her eyes. Then I remembered it too. It was that vine, in its box—sitting right there on the dresser in the front room. It would be the first thing he saw when he walked in the door.

She broke away from me, turning, and ran. I could see the color of the old dress flashing through the trees along the trail. I ran after her until I was near the wall of timber along the edge of the clearing and then stopped, knowing I could go no farther. I could feel my heart pounding as I saw her, still running, coming up directly behind the house so he couldn't see her from in front.

He had come out of the trees by the boat landing, carrying a big paper bag in his arm. I saw her go in the back door while he was still a hundred yards away, and felt so weak in the knees I could hardly stand and wanted to sit down there and rest.

So this is the way it is, I thought.

I walked through the trees to the upper end of the island, where the slough came back into the lake. It was nearly half a mile, through heavy timber, and I knew he wouldn't find me up here, but hiding like that gave me an uneasy feeling.

As soon as it was dark I eased back down the slough to where the boat was. I didn't dare go down past his boat landing, so I took the boat clear around, back up the slough and down the far side of the lake on the other side, pulling it very carefully with the oars and taking care not to bump the oarlocks.

I didn't like it. But what am I going to do? I thought. To say I won't come back up here any more to see her is silly. I know I will. There isn't anything that could keep me from coming back, not the dirty feeling or the uneasiness, or even being actually scared. By the time I get back to town I'll be counting the hours until I see her again.

Chapter Nine

With my back against the trunk of a big oak, I sat waiting in the darkness where I had camped before. A few mosquitoes buzzed, for there was no breeze, and night lay hot and sticky across the swamp. I smoked endless cig-arettes, and once I remembered—and immediately forgot—that I hadn't eaten anything for twenty-four hours. I hadn't brought anything except an extra pack of cigarettes.

Would she come? For the twentieth time I struck a match to look at my watch. It was eleven-fifteen. It's about the time she came before, I thought. She'll come. I just haven't given her time. She has to. I got up and walked down to the water's edge and listened. There was nothing, no sound.

I began to imagine things. He had found the plant there. She hadn't had time to hide it. He had beaten her. Maybe he had killed her. Who knew what he would do? I could see her against the wall in yellow lamplight, being held and struck, the helplessness and terror in her face, and for an instant it was so real I wondered if I were going to be sick. If she doesn't come before long, I thought, I'm going up there. I won't go back without knowing. I'll go up there. And what? I thought. Walk into a man's house and demand to know if his wife is all right, tell him I have to see her? I threw down the cigarette and ground savagely at the red coal with my heel.

I heard her then. I wanted to run out into the water and meet her, but I stood there on the shelving bank and waited. She came up out of the water, wading, and I could see the pale gleam of her face and arms.

"Jack?" she whispered.

"Here," I said. I picked her up in my arms, wet bathing suit and all, and car-ried her up the bank.

"I'll get your clothes all wet."

"Hush," I said. "Hush." I kissed her, not putting her down.

"We have to talk, Jack," she whispered urgently.

"Yes," I said. "In just a minute."

I put her down, standing, still holding her. "We've got to talk," she said.

"I know. I know what you mean. But not right now. I can't let you go or think of anything right now. I've been crazy, sitting here, imagining things. He was beating you."

"You're hurting me."

"I'm sorry."

"It's all right, Jack. I don't mind."

"It was terrible," I said. I unfastened the chin strap of the cap and pulled it from her head, loosing the darker-than-night disordered riot of her hair.

Everything began to go then, rushing outward in the night, and after a long time the swamp came back and became again the dark, familiar trees, the ground, and stars.

"We can't do this, Jack," she said after a while. "This afternoon, when I was running—"

"I know. But what can we do?"

"You felt it too, didn't you?"

"Yes. But maybe not as much. When I had to go up there and hide."

"It will always be that same way—that same feeling."

"Yes. I know. We've got to go away."

She told me a little about him that night, about how they happened to be married and how it was before they came to the swamp.

"It was during the war, Jack. I was living in a little town with my father. He's a minister and we'd always lived in a succession of little towns like that, and during the war they were heartbreaking in a way, they were so lonely. You were probably overseas and don't know what they were like with all the young men gone. Even the ones who were Four-F went away to work in ship-yards and things like that. I was working in the office of a lumberyard and he came to work there. That was the first time I saw him. He was about thirty-five, I guess, and I was only twenty, but I was attracted to him in some way, partly because of the loneliness, I guess, and the fact that I knew he was lonely too. He didn't look nearly so old then and was rather good-looking. I used to wonder why a man that age and as well educated as he was would be doing common labor around the lumberyard, and I guess I built up quite a mystery about him. Girls do that, you know. After a while we began to go to movies and things like that.

"It was about a week before we were going to be married that it happened. We were sitting in the drugstore drinking a Coke one night after the movies when a man came in, a man I'd never seen around town before and who looked like a sawmill hand or laborer, in overalls, and all of a sudden I noticed how Roger—he had another name then—how Roger was looking at him. And when the man happened to face in our direction Roger turned his head suddenly, pretending to look for something in his coat. That night we left town on the bus. He didn't explain anything; he just said he was going and that I didn't have to, he wouldn't expect it of me. But I went. I was in love with him then. We were married in another town.

"It was that way for years. I knew after the first time that he was running from something, and it wasn't just that man, because another time it was a different one he saw. It was an awful way to live, worse than the way my fa-ther had always moved around from church to church, but I didn't mind too much. It was only after we moved up here that he began to go to pieces like that and drink.

"Before that he was always good to me. But now that thing has been preying on his mind so long he's changed and isn't like he used to be at all. The way he looks sometimes—almost as if he thinks people are hiding out there in the trees trying to catch up with him...."

I went back to town in the early morning, leaving the boat and trailer hidden in the underbrush near the end of the slough because there was no question any more about not going back. Louise hadn't come home, but there was a letter from her. They were going to stay another week, she said, and couldn't I send her a hundred dollars? I poured a big drink and sat looking at the letter in the kitchen while it grew light outside and the heat began.

My pay check was in the office and I endorsed it and sent it to her. The drink had made me lightheaded because I hadn't eaten anything for so long, and I was conscious of the wild thought that if I could keep on sending her enough money maybe she'd never come back. In sickness and in health, I thought, looking out the post office door at the sun blasting into the street.

Buford said nothing about the money he knew I owed him, the pay-off from Abbie Bell. "I turned that kid loose," he said. "I told him to get out of town, and if he ever came back we'd throw away the key."

"O.K.," I said. I couldn't get my mind on anything. With the grand jury coming up we were walking through spilled gasoline with cigarettes in our hands and I couldn't even think about it. All I could see was an empty flat ocean of time to be crossed before I would see her again. And what do you suppose she goes through, I thought, out there with that crazy bastard and never knowing what he knows or what he'll do? We've got to get away. But how? And using what for money? And if I run now there'll be an investigation for certain. It would look like guilt; why else would a man run off and leave his wife and home? And if they brought an indictment she'd just be moving around over the country with another fugitive. From what little she'd told me I could see what it had done to him, and I didn't want any of it.

Thursday I had to go with one of the other deputies to take a prisoner to the state penitentiary, and we didn't get back until late Friday afternoon. I was jumpy and on edge, and drove like a madman. When I got back in town I found out from Buford that the grand jury session had been moved back to Monday. After nightfall I slipped out of town and headed for the lake. There was still no moon, but by now I could run the channel in the dark.

There was nothing to do but pray she would come. She did. At eleven or a little after she came swimming down the channel and waded out of the water where I stood waiting for her.

"I almost died, Jack. I thought something had happened when you didn't come. We can't go on like this."

"I know," I said.

"Can't we go away tonight?" she whispered. "Now. Just take me away somewhere."

"In a bathing suit?" I said. "With no money? We can't."

"We could go back in your boat and get my clothes, what few things I have."

I held her tightly, wanting to tell her yes but knowing we had to wait. "I know," I said. "But it won't be more than a few days more. I've got it all figured out. I can sell my boat and trailer and all the fishing and camping gear. I think I can get two hundred for it. And the old Ford will take us. We'll go to Nevada; that's far enough away. I can work at something, and we can get divorces and be married."

"All right," she said slowly. "But please make it soon." Suddenly, I felt her shiver as if she had a chill.

"What is it, baby? Are you cold?"

"No," she said. "I guess I was just trying to shake off a feeling I keep having, a sort of premonition that we haven't got much time. It's like one of those dreams you have—you know, when you're trying to catch a train and can't get out of the waiting room because somebody has locked the door. You see the train pulling out and you keep on tugging at the door...."

"Don't do that, honey. It's going to be all right."

"Yes. I know. Only—"

"Only what?"

"I keep remembering something that happened a long time ago. I thought of it just then, when I had that chill."

"What is it?"

It was one of the strangest things I had ever known in my life. I began to know what she meant almost before she told me. She'd hardly said a word before it was all right there before me.

"It's a silly thing," she said. "But it's so plain, even after all these years. I can hear the school bell, and see the street corner in the early morning with the sun shining, and that big woolly-looking dog going by with the newspaper in his mouth—"

"Wait!" I said, wondering. "What dog? Say that again!"

"You made me late for school," she went on slowly, almost as if to herself. "It was the first time in my life I'd ever been late. But you were carrying my books, and you stopped to chase the dog to get the paper away from him."

"No!" I said. "Let me think. Doris.... Doris.... And your father was a minister, you said. I know now!"

"Doris Carroll," she said. "Didn't you know who I was, Jack? But then, with a different name.... And it must have been more than fifteen years ago. I knew you though, as soon as you told me your name."

"We were in the fifth grade," I said. "You were the first woman I ever loved. I remember you moved away the next year and I was heartbroken."

"For a week, anyway?"

"For almost a month," I said.

We talked about it for a long time that night, and after a while I guess I forgot what it was that had brought it to her mind in the first place. I don't think
she did, though. The last thing she said when we had to go was, "Please, Jack.
Get us out of here. And don't let it be too long."

I knew what she meant. Don't make us late again.

We raided all the places. The delegation, headed by Soames, came into the
sheriff's office Saturday afternoon and Buford heard them out with that grave,
deferential courtesy of his. "Gentlemen, this office is at the service of the cit-
izens of this county. That is what it is here for. Get the warrants, Jack."

He asked Soames to come along. The Moss Inn was first on the list, and
when we got out there all the dice tables were gone out of the back room and
the slot machines had disappeared. The next two places were the same. It was
dark by the time we got to Abbie Bell's, and when we went in all the girls
except two were gone. One of them was embroidering a doily and the other
was sitting in a big chair in the front room reading *Better Homes and Gardens*.
Abbie was wearing steel-rimmed glasses and working on a set of books.

"Can you tell me what this is all about, Mr. Buford?" she asked coldly.
"Don't I have enough trouble trying to make a living out of this rooming
house, with the government and all the XYZ's and ABC's making me fill out
forms and tell them what I did with every nickel I ever made, without you
trying to drive away what few roomers I do have?" She followed us upstairs
and we looked in all the rooms, finding no one. The beds were neatly made
and the rooms clean, and in one of them a canary in a little wire cage was
singing cheerfully. Abbie kept up her outraged scolding, but once when the
two of us were alone in the rear she looked at me with the deadpan innocence
of a child and said quietly out of the corner of her mouth, "Jesus, I hope the
laundry don't come back while you guys are here."

I watched Soames to see what he thought of it, and wondered if he could
be taken in by a trick as old as this. He said nothing at all during the raids,
and afterward he thanked Buford with a courtesy that equaled Buford's own,
but once I saw in his eyes the look of a man who has just drawn the other ace.
It made me wonder.

I awoke before dawn Sunday and lay there thinking about it, unable to go
back to sleep. I could get her out of there. I couldn't leave for a few more days,
or maybe a week, until we saw which way the grand jury was going to jump
and whether Soames had anything else up his sleeve, but I could take her away
to wait for me somewhere. It wouldn't be safe to bring her into town, but I
could take her down to Colston and get her a room there. Anything to get
her out of that swamp and away from him before something happened or we

got caught.

I made a pot of coffee and then drove out, picked up the boat and trailer at the end of the slough, and brought them in. I didn't want to sell the stuff in town if I could help it, because that in itself might look suspicious, as if I felt the heat and were getting ready to run, but there was a man over at New Bosque, the station agent there, who had been trying to buy my motor for a long time, and I thought he might take it. I loaded up everything, fishing tackle and all, and went over there with it. I was going to give up fishing, I said, if I could get the right kind of price for the stuff; there were too many arguments with my wife about it. He laughed and said he knew how it was, he was married too; and we began. I knew I was going to take a beating on it that way, and I did; it was worth four hundred, even secondhand, and I finally got two-twenty-five. The worst part of it was giving up the Hardy rod the Judge had given me on my nineteenth birthday, but after taking it out of the case and looking at it once I handed it over and left.

I cashed his check the first thing Monday and waited. The grand jury convened that morning, and we sat through the long day wondering what would happen, but nothing did. It was quiet.

To get up the lake to where she was I'd have to go clear down to the south end and rent a boat and motor, now that I'd sold my own, but that was all right. I had it all figured out.

Tuesday morning I didn't say anything to anybody. I just went. And that was the day that everything fell in.

Chapter Ten

I was at the store on the end of the lake by daybreak and rented a skiff and a big outboard. After buying a bucket of shiners from the man who ran the place, I rented one of his cane-pole fishing outfits and said I thought I'd go up the lake a way and see if I couldn't catch a few white perch. He'd never seen me before, and merely grunted something and looked at me with the casual and almost contemptuous indifference with which fishing-camp proprietors regard all fishermen. By the time it was light enough to see, I was on my way. I wanted to try to get nearly halfway up before I had to duck in somewhere and wait for Shevlin to go by. He would be coming down with his catfish, headed for the store, and with all the turns in the channel he might be right on me before I saw him. I should be able to gauge it within a half hour, for I knew about what time he left.

But something went wrong. Either he had left earlier than usual or I had tried to cut it too fine, tried to get too far up before I turned off into a slough and waited. Suddenly, I came around a bend in the channel and saw him up ahead, less than half a mile away. I looked wildly around, but there wasn't anyplace I could hide. He would have seen me by this time, anyway.

The lake was a little less than a quarter mile wide here, with acres of big weed beds off to the left. I cut the motor and swung hard left into one of the openings through the pads, getting as far out of the main channel as possible, and when I had come to the end of it I dropped the square concrete block of an anchor and grabbed up the cane pole. Not even bothering to bait the hook with one of the shiners, I swung it out, and sat there staring intently at the cork float like all the fishermen in the world.

He came on past, looked toward me only once, very briefly, answered my wave with a curt gesture of his hand, and then was gone. It's all right, I thought. Even if he saw me duck over here like that, he won't know me. This is a different boat. Mine was painted green, while this one, like all the rental boats down there, was a dirty white with a number on the bow.

I sat there waiting, listening for the sound of his motor to die out down the lake. When it was gone completely I pulled in the anchor and started up again. All the rest of the way I kept a sharp eye out for other boats, praying I wouldn't meet any fishermen, for I didn't want anyone to see us as I was bringing her out. There were none. Now that he was gone, I had the whole swamp to myself. I must have been more than halfway up when I met him, for it still wasn't ten o'clock when I turned in at the entrance of the slough by his boat landing. Not bothering to hide the boat now, for I didn't want to waste the time, I tied up at the landing and went up the trail, feeling that same suffocating excitement I always felt when I was coming nearer to her, and now there was added to it the knowledge that we would have to hurry. We had to be back down the lake before he started home.

She wasn't in the house. I walked right in and looked quickly around, and then out the back. She's swimming, I thought. But no, her suit was on the line. "Doris!" I called out. There was no sound. Beginning already to feel that cold, greasy sensation of fear in my belly that I always had whenever I thought of the two of them up here alone and of what he might do if he knew, I turned and ran along the trail toward the timber. Maybe she was out there toward the lake. And then I saw her. She had just come out of the timber and was carrying something shiny in her hand.

She saw me and started running. "Jack! Jack!" she cried out, and then I saw what it was she had. It was the gun, that Colt .45, held out in front of her away from her body as if it were a dead snake, her fingertips grasping it by the end of the grip so it tilted slanting toward the ground. As we met, there in the open, sun-drenched clearing, she stooped and placed it carefully on the ground beside the trail, lowering it very gently as if it might explode, and then straightened, looking at me with eyes wild with relief and ecstasy and half crying and trying to smile at the same time. "Oh, Jack!" she said, her voice muffled against my shirt.

"What are you carrying that gun for?" I asked. "What is it?"

"I was looking for another place to hide it. Are we going away today, Jack? Now? Isn't that what you came for?" She looked up at me pleadingly.

"Yes. Right now. I'm going to take you out of here as soon as you can get ready."

"Oh, thank God!"

"But tell me about that gun."

"I've had it hidden out in the woods. For days now. One night he was drunk and I was out of the house, and when I came back way after midnight he was passed out, and the gun, which had been in that drawer ever since we came up here, was lying on the table just beyond where his hand was. I didn't know what he had intended to do with it. But I was so scared I took it and ran out in the woods and hid it. Then, yesterday, he was out there a long time and I began to have the horrible thought that he had managed to find it and was just letting me go on thinking he hadn't. So I thought about it all night and decided to throw it in the lake. And then this morning after he was gone I changed my mind and thought maybe I was just being silly, and that I'd hide it somewhere else."

Holding her and feeling the shaking of her body, I knew she wasn't telling me all of it. She was afraid of him and had been bringing it back to hide it in the house where she could get it if she had to. I thought of the way she had been carrying it and felt a little sick, knowing just how much good it would have been to her if she'd had to use it. She wouldn't even know how to shoot it.

I picked it up and we walked back to the house. I put it on the dresser, thinking we would take it with us and drop it in the lake, and then I turned and
looked at her standing there with her face flushed and her eyes shining with
the thought of leaving and wanted to take hold of her again and knew there
wasn't time. There was never any stopping when we started that, and we
could both feel the minutes slipping past, hurried and driven by the re-
morseless ticking of the clock.

"No," she said. "I want to go, Jack. We've got to go."

"I know," I said. "Where are your other clothes, and your shoes and stockings?"

She went to the dresser and opened the bottom drawer. They were all
wrapped in newspapers, the white, high-heeled shoes, the one pair of nylons,
and the underthings. The little summer dress had been ironed and then folded
inside a newspaper clipped together around the edges with pins. She carried
them over and put them on the bed.

She looked down. "I'll have to wash my feet before I can put on the stockings."

"Wait." I went out in the kitchen and brought a basin of water from the
bucket and found a bar of soap. She sat down in one of the rawhide chairs and
washed her feet. I watched her, smoking a cigarette and listening to the hot
dead silence of the room being chopped off in sections by the clock. I'll buy
her stockings, I thought, and bathrooms with tile floors, and clothes, and....
We'll be gone from here and she can live like other women and somehow I'll
make her happy.

"I'll wait out in the kitchen," I said when she had dried her feet and was
ready to put on the stockings. I went out and sat down by the table, throwing away the cigarette and lighting another. She didn't bother to close the door
and I could hear her changing clothes, the soft rustle of cloth as she pulled off
the old dress and put on the new one and the sound of the shoe heels against
the floor.

"I've sold my boat and outfit," I said. "The one I'm in is a rental boat from
the foot of the lake. I have to take it back, but this is the way we'll do it. I'll
turn off down there at the slough where I used to launch mine, and leave you
there. We'll wait there until he goes by, going up the lake, then I'll go on
down and take the boat back and pick up my car. Then I'll come back by the
old logging road and get you. That way nobody'll see us. Then I'll take you
down to Colston and get you a room. You can wait there until I can get away
and then we'll leave for Nevada."

"All right, Jack," she said quietly. "I'm about ready. You can come out
now."

She had gone over to the dresser and was combing her hair at the mirror. I
stood behind her, looking at her reflection in the glass. The dress was a blue

one with short sleeves and trimmed with white at the collar, and I thought it was almost the color of her eyes.

"I just want to look at you," I said, and turned her part way around, holding her there at arm's length. My back was toward the door and she was facing it, looking up at me with her eyes shining. Suddenly I saw them change and could feel my back go cold as I saw the terror in them. I heard her little indrawn gasp, as if ice water had hit her from behind, and at the same instant I heard the heavy shoe rasp against the flooring of the porch.

His eyes were crazy. He stood framed in the doorway, not moving or saying anything, just looking beyond me as if he saw only her and didn't even care that I was standing there, and I'll never live long enough to forget his eyes.

"Get back!" I yelled. "Stand back!"

He didn't even hear me. Suddenly he made a lunge for the gun, still lying on top of the dresser. I beat him to it with my right hand and threw up the left to shove him back. He slid back against the wall and then I heard her run from behind me, going toward the other side of the room, and the scream that had been trying to fight its way out of her throat came free at last, going up higher and higher in, a thin knife-edged column of sound slicing into the silence. He came off the wall and started for her and she stopped and turned to face him, helpless, with her legs against the bed. I felt the gun kick in my hand and he stopped then as if he had seen me for the first time, and put his hand up to his chest, still looking at me, and started to fall. The scream cut off as if the noise of the gun had chopped it in two, the way they blow an oil well fire with nitro, and then she began to sway.

I looked at him lying on his face with the little searching trickle of blood running out from under his shoulder and curling indecisively across the incredibly clean, silvered white planks of the floor she had scrubbed so long, and then I put the gun down on the dresser and went out the front door into the yard and was sick.

Chapter Eleven

There was just the humming of insects in the drowsy heat and the old hound watching me sadly with his red-rimmed eyes as I clung to the post at the corner of the porch. The noise and the violence had washed back like a receding wave and left me stranded here in the sun-drenched peace of the clearing while I fought down the sickness and tried to get hold of myself enough to go back inside the room. I had to snap out of it; she was going to be bad enough without both of us going to pieces. If she waked up lying there like that and looking at what she would see not three feet in front of her eyes.... It wouldn't be pretty.

I straightened up and retched again and spat, trying to get the taste out of my mouth, and walked back into the room on unsteady legs, looking across and beyond him to where she was lying. She had almost fallen onto the bed, but her legs had bumped it as they doubled under her and pushed her out and away so she had crumpled to her knees and then slid down, and now she lay partly on one side with an arm under her face like a child asleep. I knelt down beside her with my back to him but still feeling him there behind me as if I were looking at him out of the back of my head. The blue dress had slid up as she fell past the bed and the long legs were bare above the stocking tops, smooth and ever so faintly tanned, even fair now against the sand-colored stockings and the dress, and I looked at them, but not in that way, not even conscious of the loveliness of them, only busy at shutting him out of my mind. Her eyes were still closed as I rolled her on her back, and I noticed, in the fury of concentration of trying to see only her and not him there behind me, how long and dark the lashes were against the wax-candle paleness of her face. I smoothed the dress down very gently and picked her up.

The sickness rolled over again in my stomach as I had to step across him to go toward the door, and then I was in the open with her. I put her down on the porch in the shade, and as I was easing her shoulders back against the floor she stirred. Her eyes opened.

For an instant she stared at me blankly, not remembering. "Jack," she whispered. "What happened?" Then, as I had known it would, it hit her. I could see it come pushing up into her eyes and she cried out, grabbing my arm. "Where is he? Jack, where is he?"

I knelt with my arm still around her shoulders and held her with her face against my chest while the crying shook her body. This is what I've done to her, I thought; I was going to make her happy and this is the way I've done it. I could feel the helplessness and time going by and the trap closing around us, and all I could do was kneel there in an agony of numbness with only that one little corner of my mind still working, telling me over and over that I had ruined her. When the shaking subsided I took a handkerchief from my pocket and wiped away the tear stains as well as I could.

"It'll be all right," I said. "Don't cry, Doris. It'll be all right."

I could see her fighting to get hold of herself. "We've got to go," she whispered frantically. "We've got to get out of here! Oh, Jack!" She started to break up again and I shook her a little, holding her very tightly until she stopped.

"I'm sorry," she said weakly. "I'll be all right in minute so we can go."

"No," I said, not wanting to do it but knowing I had to. "We can't go now."

She stared at me as if I'd lost my mind. "We can't go? But Jack, we've— we've got to."

"It won't do any good to run now," I said. My mind was working enough to see that.

"But it's the only thing we can do."

"No," I said. "You saw what it did to him; being hunted, I mean. We can't do it. We wouldn't have a chance of getting out of the country, in the first place, and if we did we'd just be running the rest of our lives or until they caught us."

"But what are we going to do?" she cried out piteously. "What *can* we do now? Isn't he—?" I could see in her eyes the question she couldn't ask.

"He's dead," I said bluntly, trying to get it on the line so we could look at it and know where we had to start.

"But you couldn't help it, Jack! You couldn't! Wouldn't they see you had to do it, that you were trying to protect me?"

I shook my head, not wanting to do it, but knowing there wasn't room enough for even one of us in that fool's paradise. I hadn't done it because I had to. I'd done it because I'd lost my head, gone completely wild when I saw him start for her. No jury on earth would ever believe I'd had to shoot an unarmed man twenty pounds lighter and fifteen years older than I was just to keep him from hurting her or to defend myself. I could have stopped him with one hand. And if by any stretch of the imagination they could ever manage to swallow that, there was still the fact that I was in his house, where I had no business, and that she was his wife. I gave it up and tried to close my mind on it. There wasn't any way out in that direction.

I fought at the numbness in my mind like a drunk trying to sober up enough to think. The trails ran outward from here in all directions, crossed and crisscrossed and tangled, and if we took any of the wrong ones we were finished. We couldn't run without being fugitives the rest of our lives. I couldn't go back to town and report it, because no matter how you tried to dress it up as something else, it was going to come out as murder. But wait! Suppose, I thought, grabbing at everything, suppose I had been fishing out there and had heard her screaming and had come to help and found him beating her. I'd tried to stop him and he'd got the gun out and in the fight over it I'd killed him. I was a deputy sheriff and I'd be within the law in butting into something like that. Would it work? Maybe, I thought.

And then I thought of her on the stand and the district attorney tearing her to pieces the way I'd seen them do it. A woman as beautiful as she was, and her husband killed by another man under peculiar circumstances? He'd start to tie it up into a triangle killing before he'd finished looking at her legs. Had she ever seen me before? Was she *sure* she hadn't? Wasn't it rather odd that a man who hadn't been fishing for months should suddenly go four times in two weeks and to the same place every time, even neglecting his job to run off up there? I was beginning to think a little more clearly now, and in my mind I could see the succession of witnesses and the facts. And wasn't it a little odd, also, that I had sold all my fishing gear to the station agent at New Bosque because I'd given up the pastime, and then two days later I was up the lake again with a rented outfit, a cane pole and live bait, according to the testimony of the fishing-camp proprietor, and this in spite of the testimony of the other witnesses that I hadn't used an outfit like that since I was a boy in grammar school? And consider this other strange coincidence, ladies and gentlemen of the jury, the fact that somehow this man was always up the lake fishing on just the days that this woman's husband happened to be away at the store. Are you sure now, Mrs. Shevlin, that you never saw this man before in your life? No, I thought. That isn't it; we'd just be walking right into their arms.

I thought I had her quieted down, but now she started shaking again and pushed back on my chest with her hand. She got to her feet, swaying unsteadily, and then ran off the porch before I could stop her and started across the clearing toward the boat landing.

"Doris!" I called out. "For God's sake!"

I ran up behind her and caught her arm but she didn't even notice I was there. I gave up trying to stop her then; maybe if we got completely away from the house she could get hold of herself.

In spite of the high heels, she was walking faster and faster. We left the bright sunlight of the clearing and then suddenly she jerked away from me and started running down the path through the trees. Both the boats were drawn up at the float, one on each side, and she stopped at the end of the trail and stared at them wildly.

I caught her arm again and then for the first time she noticed me.

"Let's go, Jack," she cried out frantically. "Start the boat!"

I swung her around and caught hold of both arms. They were shaking as if she had a chill. The touch of lipstick she had put on her mouth, hardly noticeable a while ago when I had held her in exactly this way to look at her, was now a violent slash of carmine across the dead pallor of her face, and her eyes were staring with shock. I wanted to take her in my arms and just hold her until it wore off, but there wasn't time for that any more. I shook her almost roughly, and then when she screamed I let go of her arm with the right hand and slapped her, hard. It was like kicking a puppy.

The scream cut off and she put a hand up to her mouth, backing away from me. "Doris!" I said. "Listen! You've got to listen to me. Are you all right now?" Then I thought of that old football question. "Listen, what day is this?"

She stared at me as if I'd gone crazy. Maybe I have, I thought.

"Doris, do you know what day this is?" I asked again.

She moved the hand from her mouth around to her cheek where I'd slapped her, still looking at me. She was beautiful and she was hurt, and more than anything in the world I wanted to reach out for her and just pick her up and take her away from here, but I had to keep my head. It was losing it that got us into this mess in the first place.

I took out a cigarette and lit it and handed it to her. She accepted it mechanically. I led her over and made her sit down with her back against a stump while I squatted in front of her, taking her chin in the palm of my hand so she'd have to look at me.

"It's Tuesday," she said suddenly. I had already forgotten about it.

"All right, now," I said. "I think now you know why I asked that, and why I slapped you. We're in a jam, and if we run without using our heads we're going to be in a worse one. I'm trying to think, and I want you to help me. Can you answer some questions for me?"

The wild stare of the shock had gone out of her eyes now. She was rational, but I hated to look at the misery in them.

"Yes," she said dully. "But what difference does it make now, Jack? Everything is ruined."

"No," I said, almost roughly. "It's not. Just keep thinking that it's not, and after a while you'll see it. It wasn't your fault; there was no way on earth you could have prevented it. If anyone is to blame, I am, for losing my head and getting panicky when I saw he was after you, and even that was an accident. Neither of us wanted to do it." I stopped for a moment, and then went on, talking faster. "And in the end it won't make any difference. He's better off now than he was living the way he did. Nothing matters now except us. Nothing matters with me except you, because I love you, and I want to find a way out of this so we can always be together. Now, will you listen and try to help me?"

She had forgotten the cigarette and let it roll from her fingers. I picked it up and took a puff on it, fighting to steady my nerves and to think. "Yes," she said quietly. "I'll try, Jack."

"All right. Good. Now, tell me, and I want you to think hard. Do you have any idea at all what he was running from?"

She stared at me, puzzled, then shook her head. "No. He never did talk about it."

"And you never did ask him?"

"Only once. And after the way he looked, I never did again."

"But you think it was the police? I mean, that was always your impression, wasn't it?"

She nodded.

"Why did you think so? Try to remember."

She looked at me helplessly. "I don't know, Jack. I—I guess it was just be-cause I couldn't think of anything else a man would run from. There could-n't be many other things, could there?"

"Yes," I said. "Probably dozens of them. A woman. Some man who was af-ter him. The draft, during the war. A scandal of some kind. Blackmail. But the chances are that it was the police. Didn't you tell me once that when you had to run like that, it was usually after he'd seen someone you thought he was afraid would recognize him, and that it wasn't the same man each time?"

"Yes. That's right. It happened at least three times. I mean, that many times that I saw the man myself. And it was always a different one."

"Do you remember anything about these men? How did they look, and so on? I mean, was there anything special about them?"

"No-o. Except that they didn't seem to be policemen themselves. The first one looked as if he might be a sawmill hand or something like that. Another time it was a better-dressed man standing in a line at the post office. And—oh, I don't know, Jack. They looked just like anybody else."

I tried to add it up. There wasn't much to go on. These people he kept try-ing to dodge didn't make much sense except that the chances were they were ex-cons. An ex-convict can be anybody, and you won't know it or notice him unless, of course, you happened to be one yourself and were there with him and knew him. But why the running? Of course, a man who's served time and is trying to forget it isn't anxious to run into any of his old friends who might expose him to the community, but he's not that afraid of them, at least not to the extent of throwing up his job every time and dragging his wife all over the country. If that was all it was, he'd have probably told her anyway. An escaped convict? A good chance, I thought. And there was still that im-pression I'd had that I had seen him somewhere before.

I sat still, thinking. My mind was perfectly clear now and I could see all the angles. It'll have to do, I thought. There's a good chance that he's wanted for something pretty bad, in which case we're in luck. And if he's not on the lam from something, at least we're not any worse off than we are now. The thing to do is go back to town and find out. And then, if he is, come back here after him. Killed, resisting arrest.

No, I thought. It won't work; not that way. It would be tomorrow before I could get back, and by that time he'd have been dead too long. It'd never fool anybody. But I began to see it then, the other way, the perfect setup I'd been looking for. It was a long-shot bet, and it all depended on what he was wanted for and how badly, but if it worked we were out of the woods forever.

"What is it, Jack?" she asked, staring at my face. "What are we going to do?"

"I've got an idea," I said. "I think I know the way now. There isn't anything you can do, so you just wait here for me, and when I get through we can go. I'm going back to the house."

"Back there?" she asked with horror.

"I have to," I said. I leaned forward and kissed her, holding her face tightly between my hands. "I'll be back before long."

Without waiting for her to say anything, I got up and went back along the trail toward the cabin. As I neared it I saw the old hound lying under the porch, and suddenly I realized I had forgotten about him altogether, or had never thought of him at all. What were we going to do with him? We couldn't just leave him here to starve on this island. Oh, hell, I thought, he can swim. He'll get off.

I stepped up on the porch, dreading it. It had looked good when I'd thought of it back there at the boat landing, but it wasn't going to be easy to do.

Chapter Twelve

Putting it off wasn't going to help any. I stood in the center of the room looking down at the man I'd have to live with now for the rest of my life, then I started searching for the things I needed. There was an extra bedsheet in a little locker out in the kitchen, but that wasn't heavy enough. I had to have something thicker than that so he wouldn't drip blood all over me and onto the trail while I was carrying him down to the lake. In a minute I found it, an old canvas hunting coat in one of the dresser drawers.

Feeling the nausea swell up and turn over in my stomach, I reached down and touched him, rolling him over onto his back. The eyes were open, staring up at me, and I would have lost it then if there'd been anything left inside me. Sweating, fumbling, in a near panic, I slipped the canvas coat over his arms, backward, then rolled him again, away from the pool of blood, and pulled the coat together around his back and buttoned it. It was big, like all hunting coats, and there was slack enough to make it reach around that way.

I stood up, thinking. It was nearer to the lake if I went straight out beyond the side of the house, on that path she used when she went swimming, rather than going clear down to the boat landing. And, too, if I took him out that way and went down and brought the boat around to him, it would keep her from having to see him and possibly becoming hysterical again. Stooping, I put my hands under his waist and lifted. He was limp and awkward to handle, but not as heavy as I had thought he would be. Maybe the fright and the urgency gave me extra strength. Anyway, I managed to get him across my shoulder without too much trouble. Stepping carefully around the blood so I wouldn't get my shoes in it, I went out through the kitchen and across the clearing. The trail through the timber was dim, and cooler than the sunlight, and for an instant I remembered that other day when we were out here and how we had come running back when we heard his boat. Suddenly, that reminded me of the fact that we hadn't heard the boat at all this time, and I knew he had cut the motor far down the lake and used the oars. He had known I was up there, or had thought I was. What was it she had said—"After so much of that running maybe you start to crack up and suspect everybody"? There couldn't have been much reason for his thinking I was up here, unless he had recognized me down the lake, but he had, and now he was dead. It wasn't a pretty thing to think about—the way you had to live when you were on the run like that. And now, unless this idea of mine was good, we were the ones who would be running.

I put him down at the edge of the trees along the lake and walked away a few steps so I wouldn't have to see him and stopped to get my breath. While

I was doing that I suddenly remembered something else I had forgotten. I had to have something heavy to weight him with. In this warm water he'd come to the top in a few days. That's too much forgetting, I thought uneasily. I've got to stop that. Once you start something like this, you can't overlook anything.

I tried to think of something I could use. It had to be some object that wouldn't be missed if anybody searched the place, as of course they would. There was his big outboard motor, but that would be missed right away. And I couldn't use part of the kitchen stove for the same reason. Well, Christ, I thought, the thing to do is go back there and look—not stand here worrying about it like an old woman.

There was nothing under the house, no rocks or bricks. In the kitchen I found a flatiron, but only one, and it was too light. I stood there looking around, cursing the delay and feeling my nerves beginning to jump again. There had to be something. In desperation, I bent down and looked under the bed. And there it was. I hauled it out, another outboard motor, a small one he probably used for trolling. It was a two-and-a-half horse, and would weigh about thirty pounds, which was heavy enough. When I picked it up I heard a little gasoline splash around in the tank. I started to drain it out on the ground outside and then decided it wasn't worth the trouble, and started looking around for some wire. I looked at my watch. It was a little after eleven.

It had to be wire. Cord or rope would rot after a while. I finally found some tied up in the walnut tree, and went back out to the lake carrying the outboard, hurrying now to get it over with. I put the motor down beside him and went back across the clearing to the other end, to the boat landing. She hadn't moved.

"Are you all right now, Doris?" I asked gently.

She looked up. "Yes, I'm all right. Can we go now?"

"Not for a little while longer. You know what I'm doing, don't you?"

She shuddered. "Yes. I think so."

"Can you handle a boat?" I asked.

I could see the horror begin to come back into her face. "You want me to—to—"

"No," I said. "Not with me. I just want you to take the other boat up there to the bend and keep a lookout. There's not much chance anybody will come along, but we still can't risk it."

"Yes," she said quietly. "I can do that much. I'm sorry, Jack."

"It's all right," I said. "You're doing fine."

I helped her into the rental boat and gave it a shove. Then I got in his, unclamped the motor and lifted it out onto the float, and followed her out of the slough, using the oars. When I got out into the lake I thought of something and looked under the seat for the tow sack he carried the fish in. They were still in it. So he *hadn't* gone on to the store. I didn't think he'd had time, even with that big motor, to get clear down to the store and back since the time I'd met him. I didn't like it, because the man who bought the fish down there would remember it, remember he hadn't shown up when he was supposed to. Well, I thought, there's nothing I can do about it now.

I rowed up the lake shore to where I had left him, then waited until she reached the bend and got in position. When she got there I took a good look up the lake, in the other direction, to be sure it was clear. There was no bend up there and I could see for a mile or more, the lake deserted and glaring in the sun. I backed in to the bank and got out. Pulling the stern up a little so it would rest on the beach, I picked him up again and laid him across the big seat, on his side with his legs doubled up, then brought the motor over and started fastening it to him with the wire. It was hot and breathlessly still now and the surface of the lake was like a sheet-metal roof blazing in the sun. The shaking and revulsion began to take hold of me again at having to touch him and move him around like that, but I kept on until I had done a thorough job of it.

It was harder to shove the boat off now, with him across the stern, but I worked it loose, still standing on the ground and holding it, and moved it around with my hands until it was parallel and I could get in without having to climb over him. Sitting on the middle seat, I splashed water with an oar until I had obliterated the mark the boat had left on the beach, took one more look down the lake to where she was and up the lake to see that both directions were clear, and started pulling out into the channel. When I got out toward the middle I turned around and sounded with the anchor rope. It was about twelve feet deep. Stepping back to the stern, I took hold of the coat and rolled him off. There was a splash and the boat rocked, and then he was gone. A string of bubbles came to the surface, and then at last one big one that made a bulge in the water like a bass feeding. My knees gave way on me and I had to sit down.

She saw me head back to the landing and started rowing in herself. I tied up at the float and dumped the catfish out of the wet tow sack into the water. They were still alive. After looking the seat over carefully to be sure there was no blood on it, I put the motor back on the stern. She came alongside in a few minutes and I made the boat fast and helped her out.

"I've just got one more thing to do," I said. "It won't take more than about twenty minutes."

She came very close to me there on the float and looked up. "I'm sorry I went to pieces on you," she said quietly. "But I'm all right now, Jack. Hold me for just a minute before you go back and I won't cause you any more trouble."

When I reached out for her and tipped her face back I could see that a little of the color had come back into it and that the dead, washed-out agony was leaving her eyes. "Jack," she whispered, pleading. "It'll be all right with us now, won't it? Tell me it will."

I knew what she meant. It wasn't the police she was thinking of. I kissed her, holding her very tightly, then ran a hand along her cheek and through the straight, dark hair. "Yes," I said. "It'll be all right. It'll be just like it was before."

"For always, Jack?"

"For always," I said.

There were two water buckets in the kitchen. I found a big dishrag and a scrubbing brush and set to work, spilling some water on the floor where he had lain, mopping it up with the rag and wringing it out into the bucket. When I had used up all the water I went down to the lake shore for more, throwing the dirty water out into the lake. Then I used soap and the stiff scrubbing brush over a wide area and carefully mopped up all the soapsuds, wiped the floor as dry as I could get it with the cloth, dumped the soapy water in the lake, washed out the buckets, filled one of them with water, and brought them back to the kitchen.

I stood there in the front room for a minute, looking around. The floor would be dry in a few hours and everything else was in order. I saw her purse lying on the dresser where she had left it, and picked it up. Then I gathered up the gun, wrapped the wet cloth around it, and stuck both in a pocket so I could throw them in the lake. It was as I was just starting out the door that I again felt that disturbing and uneasy awareness of having forgotten something absolutely damning. It was picking up the gun that reminded me of it. The gun was an automatic, and somewhere in this room was the ejected cartridge case, which I had completely forgotten. I stopped, feeling the hair prickle along the back of my neck. I was too slipshod about things like that.

It wasn't anywhere. I looked all over the floor, under the dresser, under the bed, and on top of it, and I couldn't find it. It had to be here, and it wasn't. You couldn't lose anything as large as a .45 case in this bare room, I told myself. It's impossible. I stood still by the dresser, sweating, afraid again, hearing the ticking of the clock beat its way up out of the silence and the dead, empty air and the heat. Frantically I jerked the gun out of my pocket and unwrapped it, and pulled the slide back until I could see the cartridge in the chamber. It was unfired, as I had known it would be, for the gun hadn't jammed. The empty case had come flying out, as it was supposed to, and now it was gone. Had one of the dresser drawers been open, I wondered? Maybe it had flown in there. I yanked them open, one by one, and pawed through them. It wasn't there. Hold onto yourself, I thought. Don't start coming apart like an old maid with the vapors. You've already lost your head once in this room and killed a man, and if you lose it again you may kill yourself. There's a good explanation for it if you'll just cool off and look for it. Nobody's been here, so it's still here. It has to be.

He was there, I thought, coming off the wall and going toward the bed, and I was right here in front of this dresser. The gun would have been along a line like this, with the slide over on this side.... Christ, I thought, the door! Shoving the gun and the cloth back in my pocket, I hurried outside. It was lying near a clump of dead grass, glinting in the sun. I took a deep breath.

When I came back to the boat she said nothing, but I could see the question and the pleading entreaty in her eyes. "Yes," I said. "We can go now. It's all finished." She gave a little cry and caught my arm. I helped her in and shoved off. When we were well out in the lake I tied the gun up securely in the cloth, which would still show bloodstains in a laboratory, and dropped them over the side.

This was the part now that scared me. There were fifteen miles of lake between here and the slough where I would leave her, and at any turn of the channel we might come across a party of fishermen in a boat. There wasn't much chance of it, for it was a weekday, and there had been none when I came up, but I still didn't like the risk. It would be dangerous to have anybody see me taking her out. But there wasn't any other way to do it. I had to take the boat back, and if I kept it up here to run her down the lake after dark I wouldn't get back with it until midnight or later, which would cause dangerous talk later when the story broke. So there was nothing for us to do except go ahead and pray we wouldn't meet anybody.

Our luck held. I ran the whole fifteen miles with the motor wide open and my heart in my mouth as we came around every turn in the channel, and we didn't meet a single boat. As I swung into the entrance to the slough where I used to launch my own boat, I breathed freely for the first time and lighted a cigarette, conscious of the way my hand had stiffened around the tiller. It was only then that I realized that neither of us had said a word since we left the landing. At the end of the slough I cut the motor and drifted up to the bank. I looked at my watch. It was five minutes of two. That was good time, I thought.

I helped her out. "It'll take me a little over an hour to take the boat back to the foot of the lake and get my car and get back here," I said. "You can sit down here, or if you want to you can start walking out toward the highway on that logging road and meet me. You won't meet anybody on it because it's never used any more. Can you walk in those shoes?"

She nodded eagerly. "Yes. I'd rather walk. I'd go crazy sitting here. I can't get lost, can I?"

"No," I said. "There's only one road and it doesn't branch off anywhere. But if you get to the highway before I get back, don't go out on it. Wait for me in the timber."

I refilled the fuel tank of the motor again from the can in the bow, and dumped most of the shiners in the lake to make it look as if I'd done a lot of fishing. They were dead because I'd forgotten to change the water on them. Of course, I didn't have any fish to show for my day, but fishing-camp proprietors never expected you to catch anything anyway.

I shoved off and started the motor, and as I went down the slough I swung around once and looked back. She had turned and was walking along the ruts of the old logging road, very straight and lovely and alone, and suddenly I knew, more than I ever had before, how much I loved her, and that if anything ever happened to her, everything would end for me.

I'd driven the Olds down this morning instead of the old Ford, and after I returned the boat I blasted it back up the highway to where the logging road turned off. It was slow work there, however, because of high centers, and I'd gone barely a quarter mile before I met her. After she'd climbed in and I turned around I passed her the cigarettes and asked her to light me one. As she handed it over, she said, "You haven't told me yet what we're going to do, Jack."

"I'm not sure about all of it yet myself," I said, swinging out of the ruts to get past a high spot in the road. "A lot of it depends on what I find out in town. But right now I'm going to take you down to Colston, where you can get on a bus without being seen by anybody around here and where we won't be seen together."

"But what are you going to do?"

"I'm going to meet you in Bayou City. Day after tomorrow, or that night."

On the way down to Colston I stopped at a small town and bought a cheap suitcase and three or four Sunday papers to stuff in it so it wouldn't feel empty. "You'll need that to check into a hotel," I said. "They probably wouldn't give you a room without it."

As I started to get back in the car I suddenly noticed her hair. I mean, I noticed it in the way that someone else would, the way I had when I had first seen it. I had grown accustomed to the way it was chopped up, and to me it was beautiful and I always wanted to get my hands into it and it made my breath catch in my throat to look at her, but everybody else who saw it was going to notice it and remember the girl who'd had her hair cut with a dull butcher knife.

She saw me looking at it and for an instant the tension went out of her face and her eyes were tender. "You're still fascinated with my hair-do, aren't you?"

"Yes," I said. "But I wasn't thinking of my reaction to it. The idea, for the next thousand miles or so, is to blend into the herd, or at least as much as a girl with your looks can do it, and you might as well be leading a couple of pandas on a leash."

She looked at herself in the rear-view mirror. "Can you run back in the drugstore and get me a package of bobby pins?"

She worked on it while I drove. It was long enough to roll into a knot on the back of her neck, and when she got through none of the ragged ends showed. "How do you like it now?" she asked, turning to lean toward me.

"Fine," I said. "Now you're just another beautiful girl. Women will look at your clothes and men'll look at your legs. You're safe enough."

"Do you like it better this way? I could wear it like this."

"No," I said. "I liked it better the other way. Somehow, it was easier to imagine being lost in it and never finding my way out."

She looked over at me with her eyes soft and reached out to pat my hand on the steering wheel.

"Warn me when you're going to do that while I'm driving," I said. "You'll get us both killed."

When we got to Colston I pulled off into a quiet side street under the big trees and stopped. Taking out the wallet, I handed her a hundred and fifty of the money. "I'm going to tell you good-by here," I said, "because I'm going to drop you off a block or so from the bus station and run. There will be a bus for Bayou City sometime this evening, around seven, I think. You'll arrive there a little before midnight. Go to the State Hotel. It's a small one, quiet, and not too expensive, but still not crumby enough for the cops to have their eyes on it. Register as Mrs. Crawford and just wait until I show up. Try to buy yourself a few clothes, but make the money go as far as possible, because we're going to have to travel by bus. I won't be able to bring the car the way things are going to work out. And be sure to remember this: When I get there, don't recognize me. It may be safer for us to travel separately until we get clear out of the state. You can slip me the number of your room on the quiet, but don't let anybody see that you even know me."

I took her face in both my hands. "I won't see you for forty-eight hours, and after that we'll be together for the rest of our lives. So this is two days' worth of good-by, and then there'll never be another one."

She held onto me, and when she finally stirred and pushed back on my chest her eyes were wet. "Jack," she whispered, "I'm afraid."

"There's nothing to be afraid of," I said. "Just hang on."

"But you're up to something."

"No," I said. "It's not anything dangerous. Not as dangerous as running now would be."

"But what is it? Don't you see I have to know?"

"All right," I said. "But it may not pan out. That's the only reason I didn't want to tell you. It all depends on what I find out in town. I'm going to try to make it look as if *he* killed *me*."

Chapter Thirteen

It was nearly seven when I got back to town. The sun was down, but the air was still and heat lay stagnant and suffocating in the streets. I started to go on up to the courthouse, but remembered it would be closed now, and since I'd have to get the custodian to let me in the building there was no use in hurrying. He probably wouldn't be there to start cleaning up until nearly eight. Impatient and savage at the delay but still trying to tell myself there was no hurry, that I had all night to find out what I wanted to know, I turned in at the house. At least I could get out of the sweaty fishing clothes and take a shower.

As I was turning the key in the back door I heard the telephone ringing inside. The key stuck for a minute, and while I worked with it I could hear the ringing going on with that shrill, waspish insistence a telephone always has in an empty house. Just as I got the door open and started through the kitchen it quit. Well, the hell with it, I thought.

There was a postcard from Louise, the usual picture of a yellow beach covered with parasols and a Prussian-blue ocean in the background. "We're having a fine time," she said. I threw it in on the bed and started to undress for the shower. At least, I thought, she didn't ask for money this time. The shower felt wonderful. I turned it on hot, then cold, then hot again, feeling my nerves begin to unwind and a little of the tightness go out of me. And then, in the middle of it, the telephone started in again. Oh, for Christ's sake, I thought, and let it ring. It went on, seeming to grow shriller and more angry as the seconds passed, and finally I turned off the water and reached for a towel. Just as I came out of the shower stall it stopped.

I dried myself, wrapped the towel around my waist, and went out in the kitchen. Getting a couple of ice cubes out of the refrigerator, I poured a glass half full of bourbon and ran a little water in it. By the time the first two swallows had gone down I could feel myself settling like a punctured balloon. I hadn't realized how taut I'd been now for hours. It'll be all right in a few days, I thought. It'll wear off, and I won't think about it. I know I won't. The telephone started again.

This time I got to it, still carrying the drink. "Hello," I said impatiently. "Marshall speaking."

"Where have you been?" It was Buford, and I could hear the cold anger in his voice. "I've been trying to get hold of you for hours." I could feel the tightness coming back. Something had happened.

"I had a little private business to attend to," I said. I knew I had a bawling out coming to me for going off without telling him, so if he wanted to give it to me now, this was as good a time as any.

"Well, next time how about letting me know about it? I might have to get in touch with you."

"Right," I said. "I see what you mean."

"No. You don't. You don't know *how much* I mean. I want to see you right away."

"All right. What's up?"

"All hell's broken loose. But I can't talk about it over the phone. Get over here as fast as you can."

"Where are you?"

"A friend's place. That four-story apartment house on Georgia Street. Apartment Three."

"I'll be there in a couple of minutes." I hung up.

I had an idea about the "friend's place," but I'd never been there or even known where it was. Buford was a bachelor and lived with his mother in a big ugly gingerbread house built by his grandfather back in the eighties, but I'd always been pretty sure he had another place somewhere, for he could disappear right here in town at times and nobody could find him. It wasn't any of my business, however, and I'd never thought about it much except to wonder once or twice why he didn't marry the girl, whoever she was. Maybe he didn't believe in marriage.

I finished the drink and went into the bedroom to throw on some clothes. The car was still in the driveway, and I backed out and headed across town. Apartment 3 had a private entrance. I pressed the buzzer and the door clicked. There was a short hall at the top of the stairs, and the door to the living-room was on the left. It was a big room on the corner of the building, looking out into both streets, but the curtains were drawn now and the lights were on, for it was dusk outside.

It was beautifully furnished, with a beige rug and blond furniture, a big console phonograph, and shelves full of record albums and books, but the two things that would hit you in the eye as you walked into it would be first the girl, and then the guns. She was on the sofa with her legs curled under her, and as I came in she uncoiled and stood up with the connected flow of movement of a cat turning on a rug, a small girl with a vital, somehow reckless face and short-cropped hair in tight rings close to her head like curling chips of copper. She was wearing a blue dressing gown that just touched the floor under her feet and was pulled chastely together at the base of a creamy throat with a large silver pin in the shape of an Oriental sword. I had seen her around town a number of times, driving a Lincoln convertible, but never had known who she was except that someone had said she was married to an Army engineer working on something in Alaska. The story had probably been started by Buford.

"Mr. Marshall?" she asked, smiling. "I'm Dinah."

"How do you do?" I said.

She saw me looking around inquiringly. "Mr. Buford is out in the kitchen mixing a drink. He won't let me do it; he says no woman should ever be trusted with a loaded gun or a cocktail shaker."

I nodded, and looked around at the wall. She must have seen the wonder on my face, for she laughed. "How do you like my gun collection?"

I looked back at her and saw the amusement in the gray eyes. Somehow you got the idea that the very incongruity of it tickled her probably as much as it did Buford, this idea of a girl's apartment—traditional in every other respect, secluded, anonymous, tastefully furnished—with one whole wall covered with guns. There were expensive shotguns, which he used during the bird season, rifles all the way from .22's to large caliber things I'd never seen before, and a beautiful collection of antique firearms probably going back to Revolutionary days.

"They're nice," I said. Any other time I would have gone over and looked at them more closely and probably would have paid more attention to her, this amazing flame-haired figurine who found amusement in sharing a love nest with an arsenal, but right now I had too many other things on my mind. Impatience was making me jumpy and I wished Buford would come on and tell me what he thought was so damned important and get it over with so I could go on with what I wanted to do, get over to the courthouse and find out what I could about Shevlin.

He came in then with three highballs on a tray. "Hello, Jack," he said, quite calmly, and I knew that if he intended bawling me out any more about running off that way he wasn't going to do it in front of the girl. He was always an odd one; he was dangerous enough to kill you if the necessity for it ever arose, but there wouldn't be any breach of good manners.

We sat down and he got right to it. Lighting a cigar, he looked at me across the coffee table. "Don't worry about Dianne," he said, which meant we could talk freely in front of her.

It seemed to me she had said her name was Dinah, but I let it go. "What happened?" I asked.

"It's your friend Abbie Bell. She's in the hospital. In bad shape."

"What!" I put down the glass. "What happened to her?"

"Some man jumped her with a knife and chopped her up pretty badly. She's in serious condition; they think she has a chance to pull through, but nobody can see her yet."

"Who did it? Did you get the—" I caught myself, thinking of the girl.

"That's the funny part of it, and the part that's got me worried. We've got him in jail, but we don't know who he is or why he did it. No identification of any kind on him, and as far as we can find, he hasn't got a record."

"Was he drunk?"

"No. Cold sober. And he shut up like an oyster when we arrested him. Not a word out of him.'"

"And now?" I asked.

"It's dangerous. If Abbie dies, there'll be an awful stink, naturally, for allowing a place like that to operate. And the man'll have to stand trial, of course. And it isn't just what's on the surface here that worries me. Something tells me there's a lot more underneath."

"Who picked him up?" I asked.

"Hurd." Bud Hurd was the other deputy here in town. "It was about three this afternoon. The phone rang, and it was some Negro girl who works down there at Abbie's. The maid, I guess. She was screaming her head off, not saying anything but, 'Miss Abbie! Miss Abbie!' over and over, so I shot Hurd down there to find out what the hell was going on. He said the place was a madhouse. The Negro girl and a white one were screaming out in the hall, and when he went in the room where the rest of the racket was, Abbie was folded up across the end of a sofa with her clothes half torn off and a cut down one arm and another bad one in the back. The man was still waving the knife and swearing, and when Bud came in he made a break for the door but Bud collared him and hit him once with the sap to get the knife away from him. He called the ambulance and they took Abbie to the hospital. We can't get in to see her, and he won't talk, so we don't have any idea what it was all about."

"How about the girls?" I asked. Somebody should know what started it.

"They had disappeared. I guess there was only the one white girl left there, besides the Negro maid, and they both lit out while Bud was getting the man calmed down. They didn't seem to have taken anything with them."

"And they didn't come back?"

"No. Bud went back later and couldn't find them."

I stood up. He looked at me questioningly. "You got any ideas?"

"I'm not sure," I said. "But I think the girls will come back, if their clothes are still there."

Dianne, or Dinah, looked at me across the rim of her glass, the reckless gray eyes alight with interest. "Yes," she said, nodding. "They'll probably come back now that it's dark. Can I go too? I'd like to see the inside of one of those places."

"No," Buford said shortly.

She said nothing, but the eyes shifted, studying him thoughtfully, and then she shrugged. You got the impression she'd never spent a great deal of time in her life asking permission of anyone, or paying much attention to refusals.

"I'll be back in a little while," I said, glad she wasn't going and anxious to get started.

So far it was just a confused mess in my mind. I hadn't had a chance to sort any of it out, and as I got in the car and started down there my mind was busy with it. I was sorry about Abbie, of course, and hoped she would pull through, but there wasn't anything I could do about it. And, of course, the main thing was trying to figure out what bearing it was going to have on what I was trying to do. On the surface of it, it would have none, for if I had any luck and found out what I hoped I'd find about Shevlin, I'd be gone tomorrow and they could have this load of grief all to themselves from now on. But when you looked at it again, it wasn't quite that simple. With this thing flaring up and a grand jury investigation a very real possibility, my disappearing the very next day was going to make the long arm of coincidence look as if it had been pulled out at the socket. I didn't like it. And I wasn't just running from a bribery charge now. If they got to sniffing around too much over the place where I'd disappeared, it would be Shevlin they'd find.

The square was full of people joy-riding to escape the heat and heading for the movies. I shot down the side street and stopped the car a block away from Abbie's. The beer joint was an island of light and juke box noise, and beyond it the hotel was completely dark. A drunk came out of the saloon and lurched past me, headed across the street for the chili place, but there was no one else around. I went softly up the steps and opened the door, standing very quietly for a moment in the front room. Maybe the girl and the maid had already been there and gone. I could tell by turning on the lights and looking in the rooms upstairs to see if any clothes were left, but that would mean that if they started to come back now they'd see the light and run again. I was trying to make up my mind about it when suddenly I heard a footstep and the click of a switch in the hall on the second floor and I could see the reflection of light above the stairs.

I went up them, trying not to make any noise, and had reached the top before I heard a sharp cry of fright, and the door to the room slammed shut. This left me in total darkness, for the light had been inside the room, but I could see the thin crack of it under the door and walked toward it. The door was bolted.

"Who is it?" the girl inside cried out. Her voice was scared.

"Marshall," I said. "Open up. I'm not going to hurt you."

"Who?"

"Jack Marshall. From the sheriff's office."

"I didn't see anything! Honest, I didn't."

I knew why she had run. She was afraid of being called as a witness in the trial in case Abbie died, and she didn't like the idea. In her profession, she probably figured the less she had to do with the courts and police, the better off she was.

"I know," I said. "I'm not trying to take you in as a witness. I just want to talk to you."

"How do I know you're telling the truth?"

"You don't. But you can't get out as long as I'm standing here, so you might as well open up and see."

"All right," she said hesitantly. I heard the bolt slide back, and pushed the door open.

There was an open suitcase on the bed and she had just started to put her clothes in it. She stood near the dresser, still holding a pair of stockings in her hand, her face pale and the large brown eyes watching me uneasily. I suddenly remembered this was the room that boy's clothes had been in.

"You're Bernice, aren't you?" I asked, trying to calm her a little.

"Yes. But I didn't see anything down there. You don't want me for any-thing, do you?"

"No," I said. I came on into the room. "Would you like a cigarette?"

She took it and I lighted it for her. This seemed to ease her mind a little, and she sat down in the chair near the head of the bed, sitting up straight on the front edge of it as if she might fly away any minute. Her hands turned nerv-ously in her lap and I wondered if she'd burn herself with the cigarette. She must have been around twenty-eight, not a very pretty girl, but with a rather docile, not too bright face, which must have been pleasant and good-natured when she wasn't scared like this, and her eyes had something of the timid-ity and shy friendliness of an old dog's. Her hair had been very dark at one time and was now hopelessly fouled up in some shade between maroon and black as a result, apparently, of some attempt to dye it red.

She saw me looking at it. "Miss Abbie thought one of us ought to be a red-head, so I told her I'd try it," she explained bashfully. "It didn't come out very good, did it?"

I was conscious of wondering somewhat crazily if I didn't have anything better to do than sit here and talk about this girl's hair problems, but got hold of myself enough to make some sensible and halfway civil reply. Maybe it would get her to relax enough to tell me what she knew about that mess down-stairs.

"I think it looks all right," I said. "But why red?"

"Well, you see, there was already a blonde here and two brunettes, and Miss Abbie thought maybe a redhead would be nice."

Christ, I thought, what the merchandise in one of these places goes through. But I wanted to get back to what I'd come here for.

"I guess you're leaving," I said, looking at the suitcase.

"Yes." She nodded. "Now that Miss Abbie's hurt...." She looked down at her hands in her lap. "There won't be nobody to run the place now. And I was afraid they'd arrest me for a witness. You're not going to, are you?" The big eyes regarded me apprehensively. "You promised."

"No," I said. "I just want to ask you a couple of questions. Did you see what happened down there? The first part of it, I mean."

"No," she replied. Her eyes avoided me and kept looking down in her lap. I knew she was still afraid and was lying.

"Well," I said, "that's too bad. But you go ahead packing and I'll give you a lift up to the bus station with your suitcase. Have you got enough money to get away on?"

"No-o, not very much," she said hesitantly. "I don't know for sure just how much a bus ticket to Bayou City is, but I might have enough. You wouldn't like to—to—" We had started to be friends now, and she had a little trouble getting back suddenly to the strictly commercial plane.

"No." I shook my head. "But I'd be glad to lend you twenty or twenty-five if it'd help any. It's kind of tough for a girl—"

"You would?" She looked at me with surprise.

"Sure," I said. I took out the wallet and removed a couple of tens from it and handed them to her. I can get it back from Buford, I thought. "Now, you go ahead with your packing."

I smoked a cigarette and watched her get her meager clothing together, making no more reference to the fight. She knows something, I thought, and she's just about convinced I'm not going to get rough with her or take her in.

In a minute she paused, looking down at the suitcase. "Thank you for the money. It was right nice of you. Not many people...."

"It's all right," I said.

She went on, still not looking at me. "I didn't see much of that down there. It scared me. You know how us girls have to live. The least little thing, the po-lice—"

"Yes. I know. It's a tough racket," I said, waiting and trying not to seem impatient.

"It wasn't Miss Abbie's fault." She turned away from the suitcase and looked at me now, the big eyes very earnest and full of loyalty to Miss Abbie. Now we're getting somewhere, I thought. "She kept telling him she didn't know where the girl was."

"He was looking for some girl?" I prompted casually, trying not to be too insistent.

She nodded. "Yes. He was looking for his daughter. That young kid that was here, the one that talked so mean."

She didn't have to draw me a picture. I knew what girl the man was looking for, and I knew just how quiet this whole thing was going to be the minute he decided to open his mouth.

Chapter Fourteen

There was a lot of it that didn't make sense. How had he known the girl had been here? And why had he shut up like that the minute he was arrested? I lighted another cigarette and ground the old one out on the floor.

"Look, Bernice," I said, trying to be as offhand as possible, "why don't you sit down and tell me all about it? You've got plenty of time before your bus leaves."

"All right." She sat down on the bed and I stepped over and took the chair.

"Try to remember what this man said," I went on. "You were there when he came in, weren't you?"

She nodded. "Miss Abbie and me was both downstairs. This man come in the front door and looked at me first and then at her and said, 'Are you Miz Bell?' He wasn't a very big man, kind of scrawny, with his face all brown and wrinkled up with the sun grins, like he was a farmer or something, but he was dressed up in his town clothes, a kind of shiny old black suit and tan shoes, but he didn't have no tie in his shirt collar. It was buttoned, but didn't have a tie. But that don't matter, I reckon. I do remember, though, that he had a kind of wild look in his eye. Anyway, when Miss Abbie said she was Miss Abbie, they went in that other room, the one in back of the lobby, a kind of parlor. At first I didn't hear 'em, because they wasn't talking loud, and then his voice kept getting stronger. 'Ain't no use you lying,' he kept saying over and over. 'I know she was here.' Then he was cussing and yelling something awful and I begin to be afraid he'd have the police after us. 'I'll show you how I know she was here,' he says. 'This is how I know. Jest look at that and then tell me you ain't seen her.' Miss Abbie was beginning to yell by this time, and I could hear her telling him she didn't have no idea where the girl was."

"Hold it a minute, Bernice," I interrupted. "You couldn't see them from where you were, could you?"

She shook her head. "No. They was in that other room. The door wasn't more than half closed, but I couldn't see 'em."

"Did you go back in the room after the police had been here and gone? I mean, after they took Abbie away?"

"No. Kate and me run down the street. First, Kate called the shurf's office, and then later, when the shurf got here, we run."

I nodded. It must have been a letter the man was showing Abbie. But where was it? If he'd had it on him when Hurd brought him in, they'd have found it when they searched him, when they took his money and belt and things. And Abbie couldn't have been carrying it when she left, for she wasn't in any condition to be carrying anything. Could it have been on the floor down there? If so, why hadn't Hurd seen it?

I stood up hurriedly. "You finish up your packing, Bernice," I said, "and I'll drop you off in town. I'm going down to that room and have a look."

I went down the stairs in the dark and along the lower hall until I found the door. When I was inside I struck a match to locate the light switch, closed the door, and snapped on the light. There wasn't much evidence of a fight, but when I thought about it I realized there couldn't have been any great struggle, as small as Abbie was. He'd just chopped her with that knife and she'd fallen over onto the sofa, and now she might be dying. There were blood spots on the rug, but they weren't what I was looking for. There was no sign of a letter.

I went across and looked at the sofa. There was blood on one end of it, on the arm. It sat in the corner, with the arm only about a foot from the other wall. Leaning over, I looked down. There it was. I squatted on the floor and reached an arm in after it and pulled it out. It was typewritten, on good stationery, and when I glanced down at the signature I could feel a draft blowing up my back.

> Dear Mrs. Waites:
> It is with extreme reluctance and with sadness and an almost overpowering sense of futility that I am forced to write you this letter. It appears that I have failed—at least so far—in all efforts to locate or get in touch with your daughter, and the only information I can pass along to you is that she has indeed been here in town but has now departed and I cannot even tell you where she has gone.
> It goes without saying that I was pleased to receive your letter—apart from the sad tidings that occasioned it, of course—for it is always gratifying to be remembered by the members of one's former congregations. And, believe me, my dear Mrs. Waites, I have left no stone unturned in my efforts to locate your daughter, for I believe that if I could find and talk to her I could help her to see the right way of life. You must believe me when I say that I know she is a good girl at heart, for I remember her quite well, and had I been able to get in touch with her I could have prevailed upon her to return home to you.
> But she is not here. I made arrangements to visit personally, with the police, of course, that establishment of which you spoke, that Miss or Mrs. Bell's, and can assure you she is not there. I wish that I could also, with honesty, tell you that she had never been there, but I am afraid that this is impossible. I have reason to believe—from other sources, not from the police—that the information given you by young Mr. Elkins is quite accurate, though I can but wonder at his motives in bringing a sorrowing mother any such additional burden of sadness as

that. I do agree, however, that you both were wise in keeping the information from your husband. I feel that he has been far too harsh with the girl in the past, and any further rashness on his part would only make a bad matter worse than it is now.

Rest assured that I have not given up, that I shall continue to do everything in my power to get in touch with your daughter if she is in this part of the country at all, and that my prayers are with you both in this trying hour.

With deepest regret that I have not been able to bring any better tidings, I am, as ever,

Your obedient servant,
RICHARD SOAMES

I read it over again and folded it up slowly and stuck it in my pocket. Buford was going to be interested in seeing this. Well, I thought, he had an idea there was more here than showed on the surface.

It wasn't too hard to piece it all together. Elkins must be that big crazy kid, the one who'd gone berserk when he found the girl down here. So as soon as he got out of jail he went back home, wherever it was, and told the girl's mother about it, or she had got it out of him some way. And the mother, knowing what a violent hothead like her husband would do when he heard it, had made the kid promise not to tell him, or maybe the kid hadn't because he was still sore at the old man. The mother had written Soames, knowing he was in the same town, and asked him to find the girl and talk to her, try to send her home. And then the old man had got hold of Soames's reply and headed for here with blood in his eye. It all added up, all right. The only trouble with it was that no matter how many times you added it, you couldn't get any total you liked.

Soames knew, then, that the girl had been here. He knew, and Waites knew, and the whole country was going to know as soon as this thing had time to explode, that a brothel operating with police connivance had been harboring a fifteen-year-old girl, that a woman was dead, or might be, and that the girl's father was likely to be tried for murder as a result of it. The smell of bribery and police corruption was going to be so powerful the grand jury wasn't going to be able to ignore it any longer.

Just then I heard Bernice coming down the stairs. She had the suitcase in her hand and was ready to go. I flipped the light off and we went out.

"The car's up in the next block," I said. "Just stand here out of the street lights while I go get it."

I brought it down and stopped and she climbed in. No one had seen us, or paid any attention, apparently. Dropping over one block to miss the square, I headed back to town, stopping on a quiet street a block from the station. I ought to get a job driving a station wagon at a girl's boarding school, I thought. How many times have I done this?

"So long, Bernice," I said, and held out my hand. "Just forget everything you told me and don't ever tell anybody else and you'll be safe enough."

"I won't," she said. "I don't want to get mixed up in nothing." She thanked me again for the money and got out. I saw her walk up the street toward the station. What a life, I thought. Cat house behind, cat house ahead. Then I snapped out of it. I was in a hell of a spot to be feeling sorry for her.

I drove around and parked in front of the courthouse and sat there for a minute, trying to think. Cars lazily circled the square, boys out riding with their girl friends; and something about it, maybe the summer night or the hissing sound of tires or the quick, musical laughter of a girl, suddenly made me think of how it had been before I went off to the Army all those years ago in 1942, how it had been to be home from college in the summer, out riding in the Judge's automobile, a Chevrolet somehow forever five years old. God, I thought, that was a long time back.

I shook my head, trying to clear it, like a fighter taking a beating. Get up there, I thought. Get up to the office and see what you can find on Shevlin; Buford can wait a little while. But what about this other mess? It was going to blow wide open, tomorrow or the next day. If I tried to disappear now, wouldn't everybody know it was a phony? And, knowing it was a fake, they would do a lot of looking into the place where I had disappeared, a place I didn't ever want anybody nosing around because that was where Shevlin was. I'd be better off to stay here and take the rap on the probable bribery charge than to direct any attention toward Shevlin. But, then, there was no use trying to kid myself that Shevlin's disappearance was going to continue unnoticed forever. Somebody would miss him and start looking into it. I shook my head again, and ran a hand across my face. It was like being at the bottom of a well.

I started around again, taking up all the obvious facts and examining them, and when I almost completed the circuit I suddenly found the one I sought, the one that had escaped me until now. Waites hadn't talked; he'd never said a word about why he was down there at Abbie's and why he had attacked her. Why? I wondered. Probably at first it was a natural enough disinclination to go shouting to the world that he was looking for his daughter in a whore house—that was understandable. But when he had a little while to think it over and see what a mess he was in, that he might wind up charged with murder.... Had anybody been in to see him? A lawyer?

I climbed quickly out of the car and started across the street to the drugstore to call Buford and ask him, and then suddenly remembered I didn't know the telephone number of Dianne's, or Dinah's, apartment, and that I didn't even know her full name. I stopped. It adds up that way, I thought. I know what's going to happen tomorrow or the next day, but Soames and the grand jury and everybody else connected with it has every reason to believe

I don't know a thing. But it was only a guess. Maybe they *hadn't* sent a lawyer to the jail to see him and tell him to keep his mouth shut until they got ready to close in on us. There wasn't any way to know for sure until I saw Buford.

But first, I thought, I'm going in that office and do the thing I've been try-ing to get to for the past nine hours. I'm going to find out about Shevlin. None of the rest of it means anything if I'm wrong about him. I wheeled and went up the front steps and banged on the door until the janitor came down and let me in. "Got to get in the office for a little while," I said, and went on past him up the stairs. I had a key to the office itself. When it closed at five-thirty all the telephone calls were switched to the office at the jail, but the files I wanted were up here.

I went in and switched on the lights. Getting out a cigarette, I turned to the bank of filing cases along the wall. It was going to be a long, tedious job, for I had no idea at all of how to begin, since there was obviously no point in trying to look him up by name. Shevlin was probably just the last of a series of them. I started in, riffling through the circulars and bulletins and notices, looking only at the ones with pictures. Ten or fifteen minutes dragged by. It was oppressively hot in the room with the big lights on and the windows closed, and I began to sweat. There was no sound in the building except oc-casionally the ring of a bucket somewhere down below as the janitor went about his mopping.

I slammed a drawer shut and paused, lighting another cigarette and think-ing. I wasn't getting anywhere this way. It would take a week to go through all this stuff. The thing to do was to sit down and try to analyze it logically. What was I looking for, anyway? Well, obviously, a "wanted" notice out on Shevlin, with the picture on it. But there were two facts about it that did-n't jibe: It would be a very old one, but still one that I had seen fairly recently. It would be an old one because Doris had been living with him for over five years and he hadn't committed any crime in that time; and it would be one that I must have seen fairly recently because there was still the fact that I had noticed something familiar about his face that day when I had run into him up the lake. I knew I had never seen him before, so I must have seen his pic-ture somewhere, and the most logical place to have seen it was here. There-fore, it really must have been some old notice that I had looked at not too long ago. But why? In which cabinet, and what had I been looking for at the time?

I smoked the cigarette out to the end in sharp, vicious puffs, sitting there at the desk with my chin on my hand, trying to remember, to concentrate. Im-patient, and conscious of the passage of time, with all the other events of the night gnawing away at the edge of thought, I struggled for the key to it. It *must* have been here that I saw the picture. I was more sure of it than ever. Some memory, some faint recollection of a thing that had happened here in the office lingered teasingly just beyond my grasp. I had looked at it not too long ago, and something outside the regular routine of office had made me do it. But what? I reached out for it desperately, almost knowing it, and it ran, laughing, off the edge of memory. It had something to do with Lorraine and the filing cabinets, some remark she had made. That was it! It was a joking and rather stupid observation she had made about the picture. And then I knew what it was.

It had happened three or four months ago. Lorraine had been filing papers in the cabinets and forgotten that one of the drawers had a broken stop. When she pulled it open it flew out on the floor, spilling papers all over the office. I was there at the time and had helped her gather them up. And it was while we were bent over the disordered jumble that she had picked up a picture that had caught her attention and held it out admiringly.

"Boy, but he's good-looking! If I ever get murdered, I hope it's by somebody as handsome as that!"

I jumped up from the desk. Well, I thought, I know what drawer he's in. And I know what he's wanted for.

Chapter Fifteen

It took only a couple of minutes to find it now. With a grunt of satisfaction, I jerked it from the file and put it on the desk, and stood looking down at the picture of Lewis Farrell, alias Roger Shevlin, wanted for murder and escape.

The picture had been made a long time ago, apparently in 1940, and Lorraine had been right in saying he was a handsome man, but the identity was unmistakable. Looking at it now, I could see why I had still noticed the resemblance when I saw him that day on the lake. It was the deep set, rather brooding eyes and the well-formed bone structure of the face, which the lines of the years and that grayish stubble hadn't been able to hide.

I read it hurriedly. He had been tried and convicted of killing his wife in 1939. There was no information about the crime itself, or the trial, but apparently it hadn't been first degree murder, for he had drawn a life sentence instead of death. He began serving time in the state penitentiary in 1940, was transferred to a farm as a model prisoner in 1943, and had escaped the same year. So far, so good, I thought, and very good.

The picture stared up at me. Year after year of running, I thought, and terror, and nights of looking up at the ceiling in the dark while he wondered who had seen him during the day. He'd had years of this and then wound up lying face down in his own blood in a backwoods cabin, and I had been the one who had killed him, so now I had bought my own ticket on the merry-go-round. I straightened up and ran a hand across my face. There was no use getting morbid about it now. I stuck the notice back in the file.

I closed the office and went back out into the square. It all depended now on what I found out from Buford. If he said that a lawyer or someone else had visited Waites after his arrest, we could be pretty sure they believed we didn't know what had really happened down there, or what was behind it, and that they were taking pains to keep us in the dark. Bernice was gone, and they wouldn't know we had the letter, and.... I stopped. The letter! My God, why hadn't I thought of it sooner? If Waites hadn't already told them that he'd lost it down there, he would sooner or later, and they'd go look for it.

I crossed to the car as fast as I could walk, backed out of the parking place, and shot down the street toward the hotel. Parking in the same place I had before, I took a look up and down the street. The hotel itself was still dark and no one was in sight.

I went up the steps. Slipping softly into the lobby, I walked down the hall by feel until I came to the door of the room. Once inside, with the door closed, I struck a match and looked around. It appeared to be just as I had left it. Walking over to the sofa, I took the letter out of my pocket and dropped it carefully down against the wall where I had found it. Then I went back out and got into the car, breathing easily again. It would have wrecked everything if they had found out, after I was gone, that I had read that letter.

I was beginning to feel like a man being chased through some horrible dream. How many hours ago, I thought, did I stand there in that cabin and turn her around facing me so I could see how she looked in decent clothes and with her hair combed, stand there feeling proud of the loveliness of her? Was it months ago now? I looked at my watch as I went past a street light. It was a little after nine. It didn't seem possible it could still be the same day.

Suddenly, I was conscious of a consuming desire to get back to the girl's apartment and find out the only other thing there was left to learn. Somehow, that seemed now to be the goal toward which I had been running since eleven o'clock this morning, the final knowledge that at last I had my hands on all the loose ends of this thing so I could know definitely, once and for all, what I was going to do. It seemed that for a length of time beyond all measuring I had been running across the surface of a lake on treacherous cakes of ice that sank under me as fast as I stepped on them. When I got one thing straight-ened out in my mind, something else would explode in my face and change it.

I parked and hurried up the walk to the entrance. The door clicked as soon as I pushed the buzzer. They're anxious too, I thought. I must have been gone a long time.

Buford looked up as I came in. "I just called the hospital. They think the Bell woman will pull through all right. They won't let anybody in to see her yet, though."

I was glad to hear it, in spite of the fact that I knew the grand jury would probably subpoena her. She was a bandit, but a cheerful one, and I liked her.

Buford went over and turned off the radio and came back to sit down on the sofa beside Dinah. She looked at me with interest.

"What did you find out?" Buford asked. He might have been asking me who won the Tulane-Alabama game, but I knew what was going on in his mind.

I sat down. I reached for a cigarette, and found the pack was empty. Dinah pushed a silver cigarette case across the table toward me, smiling. "Before I start," I said, "I want to ask a question. Did Waites have any visitor after he was arrested?"

"Waites?"

"That's the man you've got in jail. Maybe he gave some other name when you booked him, but that's his right one."

"Then you found out about him?"

"Quite a bit. And it's all bad. But first, did anybody go in to see him?"
He nodded. "Yes. Holloway."

I knew then I'd been right. Holloway was a lawyer, and a good one. He was also a member of Soames's congregation and active in church work.

"All right, let's have it," Buford said quietly.

"Well, hold onto your hat," I said. "That fifteen-year-old girl Abbie Bell had down there is Waites's daughter."

Buford put down the cigar and whistled softly. As rapidly as possible I gave him the whole thing, what I had found out from Bernice, what the letter had said, and what I had been able to figure out from it. He got the whole picture as fast as I gave it to him. There was nothing slow about Buford.

"So now we've got Waites in jail, where he'll be very handy for the grand jury any time they want to listen to him," he said. "And that Bell woman's in the hospital, where they can get her story as soon as she's able to talk."

"Yes," I said. "And you can't do a damned thing about either of them. You can't move Abbie Bell; and you can't run Waites out of town because he's under a serious charge, or will be, and you'd never in God's world explain it if he turned up missing. It's just about as near perfect as anything can be."

Buford picked up his drink and looked at it. "Sweet Jesus," he said.

"They know they've got us," I went on. "Mrs. Waites probably got in touch with Soames again when her husband took off for here with his hot head and his knife, asking him to try to head the old man off before he got in trouble. It was too late for Soames to do anything about it, but of course he knew who it was as soon as he heard there'd been trouble down at Abbie's place. So he had Holloway take the case to defend the old man, and in return they asked him to keep his mouth shut for another day or two until they could get their facts ready for the grand jury. I don't doubt that Holloway even told Waites he'd be in danger of having something happen to him if we found out who he was and what his testimony would do to us."

Buford got up from the sofa and walked slowly over to the wall where the guns were and stood there for a moment looking at them with his back to us. I sat looking at him, waiting to see what he would have to say, and then the rest of it began to fall into place for me. It was a part of the idea that had never occurred to me until this minute, and as I turned it over in my mind I was conscious of a warm feeling of elation and the knowledge that I had all the loose ends taken care of at last. This last piece fitted into it as perfectly as the final section of a jigsaw puzzle.

I turned back and noticed abruptly that Dinah had been watching my face with that speculative interest I had seen in her eyes before. Now that I thought of it, I remembered that every time I had looked around her eyes had been on me, not with anything flirtatious in them, but only with that intense and fascinated interest, as a child might watch grownups getting ready for a hunting trip.

The gray eyes smiled at me over the top of the highball glass. "You've got an idea, haven't you?"

"I think so," I said.

"I'll bet it's a good one."

"I don't know," I said. "I hope so."

Buford turned back from the gun collection. He had lifted down one of the shotguns, an English double barrel, and as he turned he brought it up and swung it in an arc, mounting the gun and swinging it through all in one fluid motion the way a good wing shot gets onto a covey of rising birds. Then he took it down, looked at it once, and replaced it on the rack.

"I like expensive guns," he said.

And expensive women, I thought, wondering how many other custodians of the gun collection there had been before Dinah. But I couldn't quite follow him at the moment. I knew he was down there at the bottom of the well, where I had been, looking up at the smooth, unscalable walls, and he wanted to talk about guns. But maybe guns just happened to be a good opening subject. I'd never underestimated him, and didn't intend to.

He reached down and picked up his drink off the coffee table. "You have any expensive habits, Jack?"

I began to have a strange and unaccountable hunch then, a feeling that we were both working our way around to the same idea. I lit another of Dinah's cigarettes. "No," I said. "None except staying out of jail. That may be a little expensive at the moment."

"It might be, at that." He sat down across from me on the sofa and looked at me. "You have any ideas? Don't worry about Dianne. Where information is concerned, she's a one-way street."

"Good," I said. "I wasn't worried about her." Actually, I didn't like this talking in front of her. Not that I didn't trust her, or had any reason to believe she talked too much, for after all he trusted her and he was no fool, but in something like this you increase your risk a thousand times for every additional person who knows what you're up to. However, there wasn't much I could do about it. If I insisted on talking to him alone, he'd probably tell her all about it later anyway, and it would be the same except that that way she might be angry about it and more likely to talk.

"All right," I said. "We're in the middle. We might as well admit it. Sometime tomorrow or the next day they're going to start issuing subpoenas by the dozen to find out what's been going on here. And you know as well as I do that that thing about the Waites girl is going to stir up a hell of a stink. It isn't anything that can be hushed up, especially now that her father will probably go to the pen over it. And Abbie Bell won't have any choice in the matter but to tell the truth when they get to her. She'll be under oath, and she's been around long enough to have heard of the perjury laws. 'Why, I've just been paying the sheriff's office for protection,' she'll say. 'Doesn't everybody?'"

Buford nodded. "But we know that. Let's hear something new."

"That's right. But I just wanted to be sure we were both starting from the same place. Now, here's where we split. As top man, you're going to be the one they turn to for the answers. But balanced against that is the fact that I've been doing the collecting, at least for a long time now; that is, they've never actually given you anything direct. They gave it to me. And that'll be what they testify. However, the people investigating the thing will know who got the money unless you're able to show them otherwise. What you need is a goat."

He nodded again. "I'm still with you."

"However, you can't make a goat out of me without my consent. It's too easy to tell the truth on a witness stand, as we both know. But, on the other hand, if you had a goat who wasn't here to take the stand, you might get by with it."

"In other words, if you ran."

"That's right. And running is expensive."

He took the case out of his pocket, selected a cigar with extreme concentration, bit the end off it reflectively, and flipped the lighter. "How expensive, Jack?"

"Five thousand," I said. I looked across at him and then at Dinah. She had her elbows on her knees and was staring at my face almost enraptured.

"I haven't got that much," he said. "But disregarding the figure for the moment, let's look at this running angle. Just how long do you think you could keep from being caught? You ever look at yourself in a full-length mirror? Put you in any group of a hundred people and you'd stick out like a platinum blonde with two black eyes and a French poodle. You're six feet two, or thereabouts, you weigh over two hundred, your face is as flat as an Indian's and two shades darker, and you've got coal-black hair with a curl in it you couldn't take out with a Negro's antikink solution. You wouldn't be away a week."

"Yes, I know," I said. "But if they thought I was dead, they wouldn't look very hard. Not in that way."

It startled him. He had the drink in his hand, and now he put it down and looked at me. "All right," he said. "Let's have it."

"There's a man up there in the head of the lake where I was fishing the other day who's wanted for murder and escape. I ran into him, thought his face was familiar, and tonight I looked him up in the files. You can verify this by looking yourself. His name is actually Lewis Farrell, but he's going under the name of Shevlin now. He's been on the run since 1943. Now, if I took one of the county cars tomorrow morning, drove down to the foot of the lake, rented a boat and motor, and went up the lake to arrest him and never did come out, what would be the natural conclusion after your searching parties found the abandoned boat floating around in some God-forsaken part of that swamp? Remember, this man is dangerous, and he's wanted for murder, not petit larceny or crap shooting."

I could see the idea take hold of him. "By God, that sounds all right, Jack." And then doubt began to show itself in his eyes, and he shook his head. "It's good, all right, but it's going to look like too much of a coincidence. Two weeks ago, or even last week, it would have worked all right. But now—"

"No," I said. "You haven't looked at all of it yet. I couldn't be running from anything that's going to happen here, because I don't have the faintest idea anything *is* going to happen. Bernice is gone, Waites has never said a word because they told him not to, the letter is down there where he dropped it, and I've never seen it."

"Say, you're right!"

"Of course he's right," Dinah said excitedly. "Mr. Marshall, that's good."

Buford thought about it for a minute. "But how about this Farrell or Shevlin, or whatever his name is? If he gets caught—"

"There's practically no chance of it," I said, wondering just how much he was guessing now. "The man's no fool, or he couldn't have dodged everybody all these years. And if I get careless and let him give me the slip as I'm bring-ing him in, do you think he's going to hang around for me to make a second run at him? He'll be clear out of the country in less than a day. And then, when he reads in the papers that he's being hunted for killing me, he *will* make himself scarce."

Buford nodded his head approvingly. "You're right about that, too. That would take care of you, all right, but how about me? So I tell them that this deputy of mine who just got himself killed was a crook, that I'm sure he was because he's not here to defend himself, so everybody has a good laugh."

"Yes, I know," I said. "There has to be more to it than your unsupported word. That can be taken care of."

"And there's Louise. Do you think she's going to hold still for it? Obvi-ously, in a setup like this, you can't take her with you, unless you expect the grand jury to believe that she was both clairvoyant and a practical believer in suttee. So she'll be here, yelling her head off to get on the stand and deny that you ever took anything."

"Yes. I'm coming to that." I leaned forward in the chair and looked at both of them, and particularly at Dinah. I didn't know how she was going to take this. "But suppose Louise suddenly lost interest in defending my good name, if she has any anyway. Remember, she doesn't *know* I turned any money over to you. All she knows is that I didn't give it to her. Suppose it turned out that all this time I had been paying the apartment rent and buying Lincoln convertibles for a girl friend named Dinah."

Buford put down his drink. "Well, I'll be damned!"

But I was more interested in Dinah's reaction. Her eyes met mine very gravely except for a flutter of humor far back in the depths, and she inclined her head. "Mr. Marshall was *such* a nice gentleman and I appreciate every-thing he did for me, and I'm *sure* I never had the *faintest* idea he was mar-ried."

Chapter Sixteen

Buford went to the kitchen to mix another drink. After he had gone out the door I looked across at Dinah and said, "I hope you didn't mind my suggesting that. I mean, there's no reason you have to get dragged into it."

The gray eyes crinkled up in a smile. "I don't mind at all. I'd love it."

She puzzled me a little. I hadn't paid much attention to her, under the circumstances, with that thing this afternoon eating away at the back of my mind and the rest of it in a whirl from trying to cope with all this other mess, but still I was conscious of something a little disturbing about her each time she got mixed up in my thoughts. The different sides of her you saw didn't add up to anything you would normally expect, and it made you wonder where she had come from and what made her operate. Small, chic, and smooth, completely feminine and disturbingly good-looking with the clear skin and slender face and the hair like polished copper rings, she looked like the classic example of what you would collect if you had the true collector's spirit and plenty of money, but when you looked at her again you were aware of the vitality and the restlessness and the audacious spirit in the eyes. You got the idea in a little while that she took excitement the way some people took drugs, and you wondered how she liked this bird-in-a-gilded-gun-collection existence she was living now.

Buford came back in a minute with the drinks. As he handed me mine he asked, "Where did you say this Shevlin lives, Jack? How far up the lake?"

"It must be about twenty miles up from the store," I said. "There's not much of anything except swamp above where he is."

He looked thoughtful for a minute. "That's over the county line, I think. Most of that swamp is in Blakeman County."

I shrugged. "Well, it doesn't make any difference. I don't think that anyone will ever take the trouble to look into whether I went a little beyond the line without knowing it."

"No. I guess not. Well, here's luck."

We drank, and then got back to the question of money. I asked for five thousand again. He insisted he couldn't get hold of it on short notice, especially without attracting attention, but that he could put his hands on three thousand in a safe deposit box at the bank the first thing tomorrow morning.

"O.K.," I said. That would do. After all, I had originally planned on having to do it on the two hundred odd I got for my fishing equipment.

I stood up. "I'll see you in the morning. It'll be better if you bring up this Shevlin job in front of the others. But then, you know how to handle it."

He nodded. "Leave it to me." He got up from the sofa and held out his hand.

"I won't be able to tell you good-by tomorrow, so here it is. Good luck." He paused, and then went on quietly, with his eyes directly on mine. "And remember, I'm buying a one-way trip. Don't come back, or we'll both be in trouble." It wasn't until later that I knew just how he meant that.

I didn't go directly home. I was too restless to go back to the house. And in a way, though I didn't want to admit it to myself, I knew that I was a little afraid. Ever since eleven o'clock this morning I had been going at a full run and my mind had been furiously intent on this problem, to the exclusion of everything else, but what was it going to be like when I lay down in the darkness with the problem solved and the movement stilled, with Shevlin putting his hand up to his chest in that terrible gesture and turning to look at me as his knees gave way under him and he started to fall? Was that what I would see when I tried to close my eyes? Or would there be nothing?

I turned and drove out north of town, past the lake where we used to swim in summers a long time ago when I was a boy. The bathhouse was gone now and the lake was filled with weeds, but as I sat there in the car in the summer night I could see the dazzling sunlight and hear the splash and the laughter as the sixteen-year-old Jack Marshall did a belly-buster trying to jack-knife off the high board to impress a girl, coming out of the water stinging and crimson from the impact. Circling through streets that were quiet now and almost deserted, I went past the high school and the football field, remembering October afternoons and the sweat and the dry taste in the mouth like copper pennies and the way the ground jarred, tilting crazily against your face. The old grammar school had burned, and there was a box factory there now, but I could see the corner where she had waited while I chased the dog, trying to get the paper from his mouth, and I could hear the school bell ringing, telling us we were late. I'll never see any of this again, I thought, but it's all gone now anyway.

It was midnight when I put the car in the garage and walked through the hot, dead air in the kitchen, hearing my footsteps echo through the house. I had changed into pajamas and was sitting on the side of the bed smoking a cigarette and wondering whether there would be any use in trying to sleep when it suddenly occurred to me that I hadn't eaten anything since breakfast. I padded barefoot out into the kitchen and started looking through the refrigerator, finding nothing except a bottle of milk that had been there for two weeks and was sour. In a cupboard I came across a can of salmon. I opened it and had started to dig it out onto a plate when the telephone rang. I started a little, surprised at the unexpected sound. Buford, I thought. My God, has something else happened? I went down the hall to the stand.

"Hello," I said.

"Mr. Marshall?" It was a girl's voice.

"Yes. Who is it?"

"Dinah Weatherford. I tried to get you a while ago, but I guess you were out. You haven't gone to bed, have you?"

"No," I said. "Not quite. Has something happened?"

"Not exactly. But could I come over for a minute? There's something I want to talk to you about."

"Why, yes," I said, wondering. "Do you know how to find the place?"

"I think so. You're sure it's all right?"

"Sure. I was just opening a can of salmon. I'll find you a clean fork."

She laughed. "I'll have you know I'm not a cat. Or am I?"

She hung up and I went back to the bedroom and put on a dressing gown and some slippers. It was hot, and I turned on the electric fan in the kitchen, sitting under it with my elbows on the table. What did Dinah have on her mind? I wondered if Buford had asked her to tell me something.

Glancing up at the clock, I saw it was nearly half past twelve and knew Doris would be at the hotel now. I thought of her alone and scared and tried to imagine what she would be doing at this moment. Was she trying to sleep, with a light on in the bathroom to drive away the dark? Was she standing at the window staring out into the streets at busses and neon signs and the hot bright lights of restaurant fronts and the people going home from shows, feeling the strangeness of it after a year of living burial in that swamp? Was she counting the hours, as I was? Tomorrow, and tomorrow night, I thought, and part of another day....

I heard the car pull up and stop in front of the garage. When I went outside she had cut the lights, but I heard the car door slam shut and she came toward me out of the darkness in the yard. I followed her into the kitchen. She had changed into a white linen skirt and a Russian-looking sort of blouse with long, full sleeves quite tight at the wrists, and when she turned under the light and smiled at me her eyes were alight with that excitement I had seen in them before.

"Let's go into the living room," I said.

She shook her head. "This is all right. I just wanted to tell you something."

I pulled out a chair and she sat down at the table. I sat down across from her, watching the play of light against the burnished copper hair and the audacious tilt of the head. "What's up?" I asked.

"I think I can help you."

"Thanks," I said. "How?"

"I got to thinking about it after you left and after Buford went home. This thing you're doing, I mean. It interested me." She stopped, her elbows propped on the table and her chin resting on her hands, looking at me. "You interest me."

"Why?" I asked. I didn't see what she was getting at.

"Imagination. You shouldn't have any, but you do. Imagination, plus the gambler's instinct. Don't you see?"

"No," I said. "All I see is a chump who got in over his head and is trying to wiggle out."

"Maybe you're not looking from where I am." She smiled, and then went on, "But let me tell you what I had in mind. Tonight when you told Buford what you were going to do, you didn't make any mention of what was going to happen after you abandoned the boat there in the swamp. Have you thought about that? You don't mind my asking, do you?"

"No," I said. "Not at all."

"Good. You realize, of course, don't you, that you're going to be afoot and that when you get out to the highway you won't be able to flag a ride because whoever gives you a lift will remember you. And, naturally, you can't take your car. Also, even if you walked to the next town, you wouldn't dare get on a bus there. They might remember you."

"Yes," I said. "I know that. It's not very good, that part of it, but it can't be helped."

Actually, I had an idea about it, but I didn't see any point in telling her. It wasn't that I didn't trust her, but there just wasn't any reason she had to know. There was a railroad across on the far side of the swamp, and at one place a water tank and siding where freights went in the hole for passenger trains. I planned to hang around there tomorrow night and get on a south-bound freight.

She leaned a little across the table. "Well, there's where I can help you. You'll be afoot, so I can pick you up on the highway after dark."

"Why?" I asked. "I mean, I appreciate it a lot, but it would be risky for you, and there's no reason you have to get mixed up in it."

"Yes," she said eagerly. "Don't you see I want to do it? Listen, Jack! I can call you Jack, can't I? It would be so easy. You just tell me where you'll be, say at nine o'clock, and I'll come by very slowly. I'll flip my headlights up and then down a couple of times so you'll know who it is, and then stop. If there are too many cars in sight, I'll go on and turn around and come back for you."

"And then what?" I asked.

"I'll give you a lift to Bayou City. You can get a bus there without attracting attention. That'll be far enough away. I'll tell Buford I just went down there shopping. I do it quite often."

"He doesn't know about this, then?"

"No," she said quietly. "He doesn't know about it."

I was thinking. This was a lot better way of getting out of the swamp than the other. I'd get to Bayou City the same night, and I wouldn't have to go to the hotel looking like a tramp from having ridden all night on a freight, providing I even got on one. It was just what I needed, but I still hesitated a little. Nobody does anything for nothing. What did she want to get mixed up in it for?

"What do you think?" she asked, watching me intently.

"It sounds good."

"Then it's a deal?"

"I'm still wondering what you get out of it."

"Excitement," she said simply.

"Is that all?"

"I think so. I'm not sure. But isn't that enough?"

"I don't know," I said. "I'm not that fond of excitement."

She studied my face. "You just think you're not. You don't realize yet what you're capable of."

"Look, Dinah," I said. "I'm not looking for thrills. All I want to do is get the hell out of here before I get thrown in jail. And I don't care if I never see any more excitement the rest of my life than a good, fast checker game."

"All right," she said. "But where do I meet you?"

What the hell, I thought. She just wants to help me for the laughs she gets out of it. Why not? It'd be a way out of that swamp.

"O.K.," I said. I was trying to get the layout of the roads and the lake straight in my mind to give her a picture of it. "Excuse me a minute. I want to get a pencil."

I found a pencil and an old envelope in the dining room and came back. She slid her chair around alongside mine, pressing gently against my shoulder and watching me as I drew the map.

"Here's town," I said. "The highway runs east along here, and then turns south, toward the end of the lake. You know where that store is down there, don't you? The highway goes across the south end of the lake on the big earth dam, and just beyond the east end of the dam there's a store and a boat place and a honky-tonk beer joint."

She nodded.

"Well, about two miles beyond that bunch of buildings a secondary road takes off to the left, going north. This runs up the other side of the lake. It isn't much of a road, but there's not much travel on it, which is good for our purpose." I paused, trying to remember landmarks. It had been a long time since I'd been over there.

The railroad was over there, running parallel and probably a quarter mile beyond the secondary road. I'd want to leave the boat at some place that would indicate Shevlin had headed for the water tank to catch a freight. There's a small creek, I thought, along there somewhere. And then I remembered.

"Look, Dinah. It would be about fifteen miles after you make the turn off the highway onto that country road. You hit a stand of big pines very close to the road on both sides, a half mile or more of them before they taper off into second-growth stuff again. Then there's a gravel pit with an old loading platform, off to the right, where I've marked it. Then, just about a half mile beyond the gravel pit, you'll cross a small concrete bridge. It won't be the first one, for there are some more below it, but I can't remember whether it's the third or fourth. Anyway, that's the reason I've put these other landmarks on here, so you'll know you have the right one. I'll be waiting just beyond the bridge. Blink your lights as you go over it. Think you've got it?"

"Yes. It's easy. Now, what time?"

"How about eight o'clock? It'll be dark by then."

She put her hand on my arm and smiled. "Wonderful. Can I bring anything for you, any clothes from here that I could put in the car now? Naturally, you won't be able to take anything extra in the morning."

I shook my head. "No. I won't take a thing. Just the clothes I'll have on. It wouldn't look right otherwise."

"Yes. That's right." She got up from the table. "Well, I've got to go and let you get some sleep."

I walked out to the car with her and opened the door. She stood very close to me for a moment, looking up, then she said, "Good night, Jack." I pretended not to notice the warmth in her voice.

"Good night," I said, and watched her back out of the driveway.

I took three of Louise's sleeping pills, and still it was a long time before I got to sleep. Doris was there, just beyond me in the darkness, and when I would start for her Shevlin would be there too, putting his hand up to his chest and looking toward me as he started to fall to the floor.

The pills made me oversleep a little. I got up and shaved and dressed and then looked around the house, not knowing why I did it, for it didn't mean anything at all. I'll never see it again, I thought, or Louise, and it doesn't mean a thing. I stood for a moment in the front door, then closed it and went on down the walk. Four years were just overnight in a hotel room.

I had breakfast at Barone's and got to the office about half past nine. Buford was already there, with Hurd, and Lorraine was looking for something in the files. Buford nodded abstractedly, and then Lorraine put the paper on his desk. I went over and sat down and started looking at the morning newspaper.

"Say, Jack," Buford said, turning around in his chair, "you ought to know your way around that lake pretty well, the number of times you've been up there fishing. You like to take a trip up there today?"

"Sure," I kidded. "Can I take my fishing tackle?"

"Not today." He sobered. "I just got a tip this man is up there near the end of the lake somewhere. You ever see him?"

He handed me the notice on Farrell. I looked at it. "No-o. I don't think so. Wait a minute, though. Maybe I have, at that. When I was fishing up there yesterday. Man was having trouble with his motor. No, he was older than this. Must have been forty-something and much thinner."

"That picture was made ten years ago. It was probably him, all right. The dope I got on him is that he's living in a shack pretty far up the lake. Take this along, and make sure you've got the right man before you bring him in.

The tip may be a false alarm. You know how it is."

"O.K.," I said. I went over and got the gun and a pair of handcuffs. "I'll rent a boat and motor down at the store."

"Watch yourself, in case he is Farrell. He's wanted for murder. You want Hurd to go along?"

I looked at Hurd and winked. "Not unless he wants to handle the motor while I troll for bass."

"O.K., then. You'd better get started. It's a long trip." He reached for his hat. "Wait and I'll walk down with you. I want to get a cup of coffee."

At the bend of the stairs there was no one in sight for a moment. He took an envelope out of his coat and handed it to me and I shoved it in my pocket. "Good luck," he said. "And remember what I told you."

Don't come back, I thought.

Out on the sidewalk there were several people standing around and we couldn't say any more. "I'll see you tonight," I said, and he waved and started across the square toward Barone's.

I went down to the garage for one of the county cars. While I was waiting for it I ducked into the rest room and checked the envelope. It was all there, in hundreds, fifties, and twenties.

The boy brought the car down and I got in and headed up past the square. It was beginning to be hot now, and I could hear the pigeons cooing up under the eaves of the courthouse.

You remember Jack Marshall? I thought. Big fellow, lived around here a long time. Quite a football player in high school. Daddy was a district judge, but he never did amount to much. Got to be a deputy sheriff and was killed out there in the swamp somewhere. Never did find his body.

Marshall? Jack Marshall? Name sounds familiar. What ever became of him, anyway?

I swung around the courthouse, and then I was headed out the street going south toward the highway.

Chapter Seventeen

As I drove down toward the south end of the lake, I was busy with the fact that Shevlin hadn't gone all the way down there yesterday with his fish. It wasn't a very big thing, but I knew it could lead to talk. When I had parked the car by the boat place I walked across the road to the restaurant and ordered a cup of coffee. The proprietor himself, a sour looking man in his fifties, was on duty behind the counter. He brought the coffee and then went back to looking at the morning paper.

"You know anything about the people who live up the lake?" I asked.

He turned a page, glancing up at me once and seeing the gun and the white hat. "Ain't many up there now. Used to be a few trappers, but most of 'em are gone the last few years."

I took out the wanted notice and shoved it across the counter. "Ever see this man around?"

He studied it for a moment, then shook his head. "No. Don't think so. Looks a little like a man up there I buy fish from once in a while, but he's older than this."

I knew he had recognized the picture, all right, but was reluctant to get mixed up in anything involving the police. He said nothing about the fact that Shevlin hadn't shown up yesterday.

"This is an old picture," I said, rambling on like a fool. "It's probably the right man, all right. I was up the lake about ten miles yesterday, and ran into him. His motor was broken down. Something wrong with the ignition, I think. I offered to give him a hand with it, but he said he was going to row back to the house and work it over."

"Oh?" He said nothing further, but I was pretty sure I'd cleared up Shevlin's failure to appear, in case it came up later.

"You don't have any idea where he lives up there, do you?" I went on.

"Nope." He shook his head. "Except that it's pretty far up, I reckon."

I bought a couple of sandwiches from him for lunch and went back across the road. The man with the boats recognized me from yesterday, and looked in surprise at the gun and the deputy's badge.

"Going to try 'em again today?" he asked.

"No," I said. "This is just business. I'm looking for a man who may be living up the lake."

I rented a boat and motor and shoved off. "I'll be back sometime this afternoon," I called out as I pushed away from the dock.

It was a little after eleven. I had nine hours between now and the time I was supposed to meet Dinah out there on the road. Handling the boat almost au-

tomatically on the broad areas of the lower lake, I tried to think it all out logically to see if I had taken everything into consideration. It was necessary, first,
that I go all the way to the cabin. This was principally to make sure that there
was no one fishing near it. It would be bad if some fisherman testified later
that he had been just below the place all day and had never seen me go past,
for it had to appear that I had gone to the cabin, taken Shevlin into custody,
and started out with him.

There were a few boats on the lower part of the lake. I passed three or four
before I got up as far as the slough where I had always launched my own, some
five miles up from the store. After I passed that point I began to tighten up
and worry. I could feel the tenseness growing inside me as each mile slipped
back in the wake of the boats and I stared with apprehensive eyes as I
rounded every bend in the channel. Of course, if I met anyone fishing, the only
thing I could do about it would be to remain above him until I was sure he
had gone back down the lake. Obviously, I couldn't have someone see me
come back down alone. And if someone testified that he had been fishing fifteen miles or more up the lake all day and had seen me go up, but never come
back, it would lead to the conclusion that Shevlin had probably resisted arrest and killed me up near his cabin, which I didn't want at all. That would
lead to a concentration of the later search for my body around the cabin itself,
where Shevlin was buried in the lake. If they started dragging the lake
around there, they might find him. Buford, after all, had to make some pre-
tense of trying to solve the mystery. And, too, the newspapers would be full
of it, with dozens of conjectures as to what had happened, and the swamp
would be full of volunteer searchers for a long time. If, on the other hand, no
one saw me go up or come down, the searchers would have no idea at all in
which part of the thousands of acres of sloughs and channels and marsh
Shevlin had disposed of my body. And since there would be no evidence of
a struggle around the cabin, the theory would be that I had started out with
him, got careless, and let him jump me somewhere below, after which he disposed of my body in some out-of-the-way backwater, went back for his wife
after it was dark, and then escaped. That was the way I wanted it.

Another thing I had to do was to be sure I knew where to turn off to the
east to get into the slough that led far across the bottom toward the road and
the small stream where I would meet Dinah. I had been up it once, years ago,
and thought I knew where it came out into the channel of the lake, but I
wouldn't be able to waste much time looking for it. As I went up I kept a
sharp watch, trying to remember what had distinguished it from the dozens
of other inlets and sloughs leading off on that side. As I recalled, it was a little larger than the others, and where it came out into the lake the point of land
between it and the lake itself had a narrow shelf of sandy beach instead of the
mudbank and the tangle of underbrush characteristic of most of the lake shore.
By the time I was a little more than halfway up to the cabin I began to look

for it in earnest, wondering if I had already passed it, for as I remembered, it was about ten miles up from the store. The slough itself led out across the bottom in a generally northeasterly direction and the small stream that flowed into it crossed the county road over on the east side of the swamp some fifteen miles above the highway, as I had told Dinah. After another mile or two went by, I began to worry, fearing that I might have my landmarks wrong and had passed it without recognizing it. Then, at last, I rounded a turn in the channel and saw it. I looked around carefully at the general location after I had gone by, to be sure I would recognize it without trouble on the way down. Of course, I could still be mistaken, but I was pretty sure that was it.

I had nothing to worry about except meeting another boat. I looked at my watch. It was a little after one, and I should be there by two or shortly after. In an attempt to relax and relieve the tension that grew with every bend in the channel, I unwrapped one of the sandwiches and tried to eat it. It was dry and tasted like cardboard, and I threw it into the lake. It's not much more than five miles now, I thought. There's not much chance I'll meet anybody this far up. But still, you never can tell. And right here would be the worst possible place, this near to the cabin. Turn after turn unfolded ahead of me, the lake flat and empty in the midday heat. I came up past the place where I had camped, rounded the last bend, and relaxed all over with a deep breath of relief. There was no one anywhere.

I'd better go up to the house, I thought, just to make sure everything looks all right and that nobody has been there. I had just swung the boat about, to head into the slough toward the landing, when I noticed it. There was something odd about the surface of the lake just above, a peculiar sheen or color to it that did not look right for the position of the sun. It seemed to have the appearance calm water sometimes has at sunset. I turned to look at it again, but the view was cut off by the trees as the boat entered the slough. Just imagination, I thought. Too much strain, and my nerves are beginning to play tricks on me. Then, for some crazy reason, "the multitudinous seas encarnadine" ran through my mind. For Christ's sake, I thought, I'm getting as jumpy as an old woman.

I was still thinking about it, though, as the boat nudged against the landing. I made it fast with the anchor rope, and then remembered I should refill the gasoline tank of the motor from the can of fuel in the bow. I took off the cap and found the funnel, and when I was unscrewing the cap of the can I spilled a little of the gasoline oil mixture into the half inch or so of water in the bottom of the boat. I looked down at it, indifferently at first, and then, as I watched it spread, with growing horror, while I turned cold all over as with a sudden chill.

Frantically I pushed the boat off and started the motor. Swinging hard around, I headed at full throttle out into the lake, terrified, already knowing what it was and cursing the stupidity that had ever let me fall into such a ter-

rible blunder. No wonder the surface of the lake had looked odd! I swung right
as soon as I was out of the slough, heading up the lake toward the spot where
I rolled him from the boat. I was at the outer edge of it now and plowing toward the center, looking all around me at several acres of water covered with
the microscopic and iridescent film of oil.

It was that outboard motor. I had started to empty the fuel I had heard
splashing around inside the tank, and then had changed my mind, thinking
it not worth the trouble. There hadn't been much more than a pint of it, but
now, lying on the bottom of the lake, it was being forced drop by drop out
of the airhole in the cap and was coming to the surface to spread out into a
monstrous and inescapable marker over his grave. There was no faintest breath
of air to form a ripple on the water, the surface lying as still and unmoving as
glass, with the result that it had spread out evenly over an incredible expanse
for so slight an amount of oil, so thin it would be completely invisible except
for the sheen of color reflected from the sky and sun.

I cut the motor and let the boat drift, trying to get hold of myself enough
to think. The oil was going to be here; there was no current in the lake to move
it, and there was nothing I could do about it now. Nothing, I thought desperately, except to find the spot where the motor was lying and see if more
was still coming to the surface. If there was, I had to stop it. But how?

Taking up the oars, I pulled slowly along, watching the surface of the water. There was no way to tell exactly where it was, so I turned and rowed back
toward the shore to get my bearings. Bringing the boat up near the bank just
off the place where I had beached it yesterday to put him aboard, I lined it
up and started pulling very slowly, stern first, out toward the center of the
lake. When I thought I had come almost far enough, I quit rowing and let the
boat come to rest, not moving about in it to set up any motion of water. Sitting dead still and swinging only my head, I began a minute scrutiny of all
the area for twenty feet or more around the boat, on both sides and in front.
The film of oil was slightly heavier here, and I knew I was very near the spot.
Two or three minutes went by and my eyes began to ache with the bright sunlight and the staring. Maybe there isn't any more, I thought. Maybe it has
all leaked out by now. Then I caught it, a glimpse of changing color seen out
of the corner of my eye, some ten feet ahead of me and to the left. I stared
fixedly at the spot, waiting, almost afraid to blink my eyes. They began to
sting, but I held them there, and in a moment I saw it again, quite plainly this
time. A drop of oil had come up out of the dark, tea-colored water and spread,
shining and iridescent in the sunlight, the colors changing as it thinned out
across the surface. With my eyes fixed un-waveringly on the spot, I picked up
the oars, gave them one shove, and then reached around for the anchor and
dropped it. I was right over it.

Now what to do? I looked up and down the lake, afraid again of other boats
or fishermen, but the long reach was devoid of any form of life or movement.

I was alone in the whole immensity of the swamp here in the bright heat of the middle of the day, but still I could feel the stirrings of panic within myself. Perhaps it was because already, without thinking about it, I knew what I was going to have to do and I was afraid of it. The oil on the surface of the lake was something I couldn't do anything about, except possibly to spread and scatter it by running through it with the boat and motor, but the oil in itself might not be too dangerous. After all, it would eventually disperse, collecting on the big leaves of the pads and the old snags and growth along the banks, and whoever saw it would probably believe that someone had spilled some fuel while refilling the gasoline tank of his motor, and think no more about it. But this other thing, this oil bubbling up here in one spot, a drop at a time and maybe going on for weeks, putting more and more on the surface, would be sure to arouse curiosity and eventually somebody would start dragging for whatever was down there. I had to stop it.

I sat still, thinking. The valve was probably shut off. There was very little chance that the fuel was leaking out there. That meant, then, that when the motor had come to rest there in the mud on the bottom it had been nearly upright, or tilted in that direction, and as air escaped from the tank and water forced its way in, the water naturally pushed the fuel up into the top of the tank, where it was escaping now, drop by drop, and might go on indefinitely.

I had been trying to evade it in my mind, dodging around it and never coming face to face with what I knew; but now, with all other escape cut off, I turned and faced it. I had to go down there. But could I? I could feel the weakness and revulsion take hold of me at the thought. He had been down there a little over twenty-four hours, in that warm water, and I knew that by now he wasn't alone. I shuddered. I just couldn't do it.

Was there any other way? I knew there wasn't. The water was twelve feet deep and I couldn't reach it with an oar. Trying to drag the anchor over it would be a futile waste of time. It had to be that way or not at all. It wouldn't take four seconds, I thought. All I would have to do would be to locate the valve, make sure it was shut, and then tip the motor down so the water and fuel inside the tank would change positions. I could do it in one dive. And it's either that or go away and leave it the way it is, knowing that sooner or later somebody is going to get curious about the source of all that oil bubbling out of the bottom of the lake. I stood up in the boat and started unbuttoning my shirt.

The water was warm. I lay in it, naked, alongside the boat, with one hand on the gunwale, trying not to think of anything except the motor. I can't wait all day, I thought. If I don't do it now I'll lose my nerve. Shutting my mind to everything, to all thought, I took a deep breath and dived. I seemed to go on for a long time, pulling myself down with powerful strokes of my hands, wanting to turn back but forcing myself to go ahead. It must be twenty feet deep instead of twelve, I thought wildly, and then I felt the soft mud under my arm. I was against the bottom. This was the terrible part of it now. Pulling upward against the water with my hands to keep myself flat against the mud, I groped around with them, feeling for the motor. There was no use in opening my eyes to try to see, for at this depth in the discolored water there would be no light at all. I swung my arms around wildly and felt nothing. My lungs were beginning to hurt and I thought of the boat above me, knowing I had to come up carefully as I approached the surface or I might bang my head into it. I couldn't wait too long. Putting my feet against the mud, I sprang upward, bringing my arms up over my head to feel for the boat. I missed it and came out of the water gasping for breath.

I can't give up, I thought, my mind still focused with that terrible intensity on just one thing—the motor. I gulped a deep breath and dived again. When I was against the bottom I started sweeping it again with my arms, and then my left hand brushed against something just at the ends of my fingers. I turned toward it, feeling my skin draw up tightly with revulsion. It was a shoe. Bringing my right hand around, I groped with it, moving a little, and felt the canvas coat. I was fighting desperately now to keep from being sick here twelve feet under water and drowning myself with the retching. I had my hands on the frame of the motor, and with some detached portion of my mind that still hadn't quite given itself up to the wildness I was able to orient myself. It was tilted against his doubled body in an almost upright position, just as I had thought it would be. Fighting at the panic, I ran my hands along the frame, feeling for the valve, and found it. It was tightly shut. Bringing my feet under me, I squatted upright alongside the motor and lifted, rolling the whole wirebound and terrifying mass of his body and the motor over 180 degrees until he was lying on his other side with the outboard upside down and its tank stuck into the soft and sucking mud. It wasn't until then, until I had started to shove upward toward the air and clean sunlight, that I felt the final horror, the thing I had feared more than all the rest. It brushed against my naked leg, hard and solid and cold, and then when I threshed wildly it was gone somewhere into the darkness. It was a turtle.

I held weakly to the boat, and in a minute I was able to climb in and collapse naked and dripping on the seat, waiting for the wildness to go away.

Chapter Eighteen

When I had dried a little in the sun I put my clothes back on, felt for the envelope that contained the money to be sure it was still safe, and sat looking out at the surface of the lake. No more drops of oil came up, and I felt sure I had solved it. As for that already spread out over the water, there was nothing I could do about it. I decided against trying to spread and disperse it by running through it, on the theory that it would do more harm than good. It would look more like an accidental spillage if it were all in one place.

I started the motor and headed back to the boat landing. After tying up at the float, I finished the job I had started before, filling the gasoline tank, and looked at my watch. It was three-fifteen. I went up the trail through the trees and out into the hot sunlight of the clearing. The old hound was nowhere in sight. When I went into the house, nothing had changed at all. It was all exactly as I had left it, except that the spot on the floor that I had scrubbed was dry now. I walked out into the kitchen and looked around there, finding nothing out of place. There wasn't a chance anyone had been here.

Going back into the front room, I stood there for a moment before the dresser, remembering the day she had taken out the hook for me and how beautiful she had been even in that terrible dress and with the roughly cut hair uncombed. I could almost feel her there with me in the intense, hot stillness, and I wanted suddenly with an almost overpowering longing to see her now. It's only until tonight, I thought, or early tomorrow morning. I'll see her then. And then, all at once, I was conscious there *was* something different about the room. Something that had always been there before was gone now, and I missed it. Then I knew what it was. I no longer heard the ticking of the clock. It had run down and stopped. It doesn't matter, I thought. I'd better get out of here now, before I start seeing *him* instead of her. I took a last look around. There was nothing that could do us any harm, and I went out, leaving the door open, and walked back to the boat. I should have taken another look.

From now on it's got to be good, I thought. I stepped down off the float into the rental boat and sat down on the seat. Taking out my knife, I slashed a small incision on the side of one of the fingers on my left hand. When the blood started, I picked up one of the oars and smeared it rather sparingly up near the round, heavy end just below the hand grip. It would be dry by the time I was ready to abandon the boat. Then I let a little of it drip into the water in the bottom, and smeared some on the seat. That took care of it, except the bailing can. Very carefully I put a set of smeared and bloody, completely unrecognizable fingerprints *inside* it, just where the fingers would normally be as a man grasped it to dip water out of the boat.

I was ready to go. Wrapping the cut finger in my handkerchief so it would-n't bleed any into his boat, I switched to Shevlin's, tied the rental boat on behind with the anchor rope, and was under way down the lake. Now it starts again, I thought. This makes three times, and if I had to do it once more my hair would be gray. Only now, if I meet somebody, it's the end of everything. But the miles ran back behind me, turn after turn, one empty and deserted reach after another while I sweated it out, and I saw no one at all. At four-forty-five I was down to the sandy point where the slough turned off, the one I had marked in my memory this morning. I wheeled and turned into it and in a moment I was out of sight of the lake, cut off and hidden among the trees on either side.

I had to throttle the big motor down here, for the channel was narrow and twisting, winding its erratic way across the bottom. And two or three times in every mile there would be big trees down in the water. These had to be carefully worked around, sometimes forcing me clear up against the opposite bank. After I had gone about three miles I stopped, pulled the rental boat alongside, and cut the anchor rope up near where it was made fast to the bow. Coiling it up so there would be no free end to float around in the water, I tied it all up in one bunch and dropped it into the slough. The anchor was a con-crete block that would weigh about fifteen pounds, and I knew that when they found the abandoned boat with it missing, the inference would be in-escapable. Shevlin had used the thing that was handiest, and what was left of Jack Marshall was lying on the bottom somewhere in all these thousands of acres of lake and slough with it tied fast to his body. I dropped the deputy's badge and the gun and handcuffs into the water along with the an-chor and sat for a moment watching the little rings recede where they had dis-appeared. There, I thought, goes the last trace of twenty-seven years of Mar-shall.

I got under way again, pulling the rental boat along with the short section of anchor rope still left fast to the bow. After about another mile I found the place I was looking for. A small stream came out into the slough on the right, its entrance choked with a rank growth of reeds. I stopped and pulled the rental boat alongside and got into it, setting the anchor of Shevlin's boat in its stern so it wouldn't get away. The blood I had smeared on the oar and the boat seat had dried solidly now, and I wet the bloody handkerchief I had had about my finger and set about washing it off. The way to do it, I knew, was to wash it just as clean as a man would who was anxious to leave no trace but at the same time was working under tremendous pressure. There would be no indication that it had been planted, but rather that it had been thoroughly searched for and washed off with just a slight smudge overlooked here and there. The gory fingerprints inside the bailing can I left just as they were, for they were completely invisible as the can was lying now. Then I took the small handcuff key out of my pocket and dropped it so it bounced under one of the slats in the wooden grating on the bottom of the boat, invisible unless someone lifted the grating. I wiped the motor all over with the handkerchief to remove fingerprints, rolled the wet cloth into a ball, and threw it far out among the reeds.

Taking one of the oars, I poled the boat back among the reeds, then pulled Shevlin's boat in after it until they touched. Lifting the anchor back into his boat, I climbed over into it myself and poled it back out of the growth into the slough. I turned and looked back. It was a good job. The boat was hidden, but it could be found. It looked exactly like the kind of job a man would do at night and in a hurry, not knowing, because of the darkness, that just a little white was visible through the shield of greenery. It's done, I thought. It's all done except getting out of here. In a few more hours I'll be with her. The past ends here, and from now on everything is ours.

The sun was almost down now and twilight was thickening here in the heavy timber of the bottom. I knew I had to hurry and get up to the head of the slough before it was completely dark, for it would be impossible to negotiate a small, twisting, log-blockaded waterway like this at night. Starting the motor, I got under way, sure it couldn't be more than another mile or two out to the road.

The going became worse and worse, and in a few minutes I had to cut the motor and take to the oars, picking my way carefully around down timber and logs. In another ten minutes I could see it was going to be impossible to take the boat much farther and I began looking around for a place to leave it. I wasn't long in finding it, a dead log projecting out into the water where I could step out and get on dry ground without leaving any tracks in the mud around the water's edge. I stepped out onto the log and gave the boat a shove, taking no pains to hide it. It made no difference how soon they found it.

There had been no rain for weeks, and above the water's edge the ground was hard and dry, with no danger of leaving tracks. It was almost totally dark now and it was slow walking, pushing through the underbrush. Then, almost before I expected it, I ran into the fence. The road was just beyond, and I was out of the bottom. There were no cars in sight, so I stepped out on the road, looking for the bridge. I could see the pale gleam of concrete just below me, and walked that way, squatting down just off the road where I could watch for the headlights of cars and get under the bridge to hide if necessary. I struck a match and looked at my watch. It was seven-forty.

At five of eight I saw the headlights down the road. The car was coming slowly, and when the lights began to break against the bridge I saw them drop and lift, and drop and lift again. The car pulled to a stop and I walked up the embankment and onto the road.

She grinned, the gray eyes alight in the soft glow of the instrument panel. "Jack, darling, I'm right on time. Here, I want you to drive." She slid over in the seat.

"All right," I said. I walked around and got in on the other side.

She curled up in the corner of the seat with her legs doubled back under her, and smiled at me. She was wearing a short gabardine skirt and another of those exotic-looking blouses, this one gathered up some way over her left shoulder with long diagonal folds running down across her breast. There was a bunch of violets pinned to it. "This is wonderful, isn't it?"

"Yes," I said. "Thanks a lot, Dinah."

I drove up the road a short distance, found a place to turn around, and headed back, gathering speed. "What's the news in town?" I asked, wondering if the storm had broken yet.

She shook her head. "I don't know, Jack. I saw Buford for a few minutes at noon, but I haven't heard anything since. I told him I was leaving at one o'clock."

I nodded. That made sense. She couldn't very well start down to Bayou City at seven o'clock at night. It would look crazy.

"You haven't had anything to eat, have you?" she asked.

"No. But we'd better not stop anywhere within a hundred miles. As Buford says, I'm too easy to see."

"Yes," she said quietly from the corner of the seat. "I've noticed that about you."

I let it pass, pretending I hadn't caught the inflection of it. It worried me a little, though, and at the same time I was conscious of feeling slightly ridiculous and uncomfortable. And then I remembered last night and the way she had looked up at me as she was getting into the car. I didn't think I had ever been one of those chumps who was convinced that every girl who came along was making a pass at him, but now I was beginning to feel that way. This made twice she had rolled the ball squarely in front of me, and twice I had refused to pick it up. She didn't strike me as a girl who had ever had to be that obvious, with her looks and charm, and she must be convinced I was incredibly stupid. That I didn't mind, but I didn't want her jumping to the only other conclusion a woman is ever able to see when the bait remains untouched. Absolutely nobody was ever going to know about Doris if I could help it. It would be too dangerous for both of us now.

I shook it off. Maybe I was mistaken, I thought. And it's a small thing, anyway. I'm beginning to have the worry habit; that's the trouble. Here I am, in the clear at last, on my way to Doris, with three thousand dollars in my pocket and an entirely new life ahead of us, and I insist on getting into a sweat about this thrill-chasing girl. By the time we get to Bayou City she'll probably have decided I'm just another Mortimer Snerd and be interested in something else.

"This is a nice car," I said, to change the subject and to keep the silence from stretching out.

"Yes," she replied absently, as if it didn't interest her much. "It rides nicely at a hundred and above. Why don't you let it out?"

"On this road?" I asked incredulously.

She grinned. "Why not? It's heavy."

"So's a granite headstone, but I don't want one," I said.

We came out onto the highway in a few minutes and I turned east onto it, headed toward Colston and Bayou City. She lit two of those king-sized cig-arettes she smoked and handed one to me. Almost unconsciously, the way a man always does when a woman lights a cigarette for him, I looked at the end of it before I put it in my mouth.

She rested her cheek against the back of the seat, smiling. "You're not afraid of a little lipstick, are you?"

I grinned lamely. "No. I didn't mean it that way. It was just a habit."

"And," she asked softly, "whose lipstick have you been avoiding?"

"Jesus, I don't know," I said, almost irritably. I wished we could get those bedroom overtones out of the conversation. "After all, I've been married for over four years."

"But you're not any more," she said. "Your wife's husband is dead. By the way, I hope you didn't carry any life insurance. And not because I have any-thing against your widow."

"No," I said. I knew what she meant, because I'd already thought about it. "It lapsed a long time ago. We needed a new car worse."

"That's good. For you, I mean. You can fool the police sometimes, but no-body ever got rich trying to make suckers out of those insurance investigators."

Again she puzzled me. How did she know things like that? And how did she get that way? Was she convinced she was some sort of dilettante crimi-nal, breaking laws for excitement? Or had she just been reading too many de-tective stories? I didn't believe either one was true. There was too much ed-ucation and native intelligence showing at times in between some of the crazy things she said.

Then she jarred me again. She could keep you off balance better than a pro-fessional fighter. "You don't like obvious girls, do you? I should have known."

"Why?" I asked, playing it dumb again. "What do you mean?"

"You're rather confusing to a girl. It's because you look like one thing and are something else. You look like a football player or a professional fighter, but somewhere along the assembly line they got mixed up and gave you a mind that works. That's what I mean I should have known. No moronic muscle man could ever have figured out all that mess the way you did."

I was beginning to feel like a chump again. "If all this is a gag, Dinah, how about knocking it off?"

I glanced around at her. She took a long puff on the cigarette and stared back at me without the usual humor in her eyes. "It's not a gag."

"What is it, then?" I knew it was a stupid question, and one I shouldn't have asked, but I couldn't think of anything else.

"Well, since I've decided not to be obvious, I'll be shameless. Or outright predatory. It's not a gag, because I'm in dead earnest. You couldn't give a girl a little help, could you?"

Lord, I should have taken the freight, I thought. This is a mess, and that's not the half of it. It could get to be dangerous. This girl knows too much to run any risk of getting her angry.

"You're kidding," I said lamely.

"I've just told you I'm not kidding. And you must think I have a queer sense of humor. Maybe I should go into burlesque and undress myself before a bigger audience."

"All right," I said. "You're not kidding. And I'll admit you're devastating, if that's what you're out to prove. You're good-looking and you're smooth, and I'd be eating out of your hand in a minute if it weren't that just at the moment I happen to be looking in the other direction—back over my shoulder."

She relaxed a little. "That's partly what I'm talking about, darling. I want to go with you. Look. I have most of my clothes in five bags in the back of the car, and a little odd change I've managed to save here and there, and this Lincoln with fancy leather upholstery and a surprising power plant under the hood, in case you'd care to investigate it. And I might be a little surprising too, if you'd take the trouble to try to become acquainted with me. I'm not really as dumb as you think I am, to be going at you this way. It's just that I haven't got time to follow any traditional feminine tactics. Bayou City is too near. And I'm not always too conventional, anyway. I get bored with it—"

"Dinah, cut it out," I said uncomfortably.

"I want to go with you."

"In God's name, why?"

"Well, to spring something entirely new, maybe it's biological. But that's not all of it. Jack! Will you get this car off the highway and stop the damned thing? I can't talk to you while you're driving. It's like trying to talk to a machine. Get it off the road. Jack! Please!"

I couldn't argue with her and drive at the same time. There was no telling what she might do, and I was convinced by now that she was capable of anything. I saw a dirt road up ahead, leading off into the timber on the right, and slowed to swing into it. Maybe I could talk or shake some sense into her.

Chapter Nineteen

I stopped the car and looked around at her in the dim light of the instrument panel. She remained curled up in the corner of the seat, staring moodily at me with the long cigarette in her fingers like some precocious and highly orna-mental child.

"It's all right. I'm not going to attack you," she said. "And you could prob-ably defend yourself. I weigh a hundred and ten."

"Now, look, Dinah—" I began.

"You can drop the fatherly attitude. You're twenty-seven, and I'm twenty-four."

"I don't get it," I said, shaking my head. "You're acting like some nitwit high school girl, and it doesn't fit you."

"I know. I know," she said impatiently. "For heaven's sake, darling, I know the manual of basic maneuver just as well as the next one. I could sprain my ankle. And I just *adore* Hemingway. And I just *love* to putter around in a kitchen. And I don't think for a minute that people *really* have to go to ex-pensive places to have a good time, do you, dear? But, for the love of heaven, don't you see there isn't time for that? Can't we dispense with that bird-with-a-broken-wing routine? Aren't we old enough, and intelligent enough—"

"But Dinah," I objected, "what the devil are you after?" I might as well be dumb to the last. I couldn't think of anything else.

"Now who's stupid?"

"All right," I said. "But why? What for?"

"Does there have to be a reason? Is it like geometry?"

"But for God's sake," I protested. "Of all the men in the world, why some crooked ex-deputy sheriff on the run from the cops?"

"Well, if you really think we have time for me to draw a diagram, it's be-cause I happen to be crazy about you. Or had you already managed to guess, from some subtle little hint I've given you?" She laughed, but there wasn't much fun in it. "It's just because I want you more than I ever wanted any-body or anything in my life. Right from the moment you walked into that liv-ing room which the cultured and sardonic Mr. Buford provides for me and his gun collection. Before you opened your mouth and started to talk, I thought you were just some magnificent thug—which wasn't too bad in it-self, for I *do* have all of a normal, wholesome girl's interest in thugs. And then I began to see a lot of other things about you. Imagination. Daring. And ex-citement. Always excitement. Don't you understand, Jack? To me you're the world's only defense against dullness. You're the personification of excite-ment."

"The personification of horse saliva," I said roughly. "Stop acting like a high school girl. I told you it didn't fit you. It's not your type."

"I know it sounds idiotic when it's put that badly," she cried out. "I can't explain it to you, not in a hurry like this. But, Jack, can't you see we belong together? Can't I go with you?"

"No," I said desperately, trying to think of something. I couldn't just brush her off. I didn't know how, in the first place, for I'd never had enough girls chasing me in my life to get any practice at it. And there was another and more important reason. She knew too much, and if she got furious there was no telling what she would do. "Look, you've got everything—"

"Except you," she interrupted.

"—everything a girl would want. And you'd like to throw it all away and go chasing around over the country with some man on the lam. Do you have any idea at all what it's like, hiding from the law?"

"Can't you see it doesn't matter? I don't care what it's like."

"You think it'd just be exciting. Well, let me tell you. The thrill wears off fast."

She threw the cigarette out the window. "Wait, Jack," she said softly. "You think I'm still some idiotic adolescent, just because I don't like boredom. Well, I meant what I said about excitement, but running from the police wasn't the only excitement I was referring to. I don't appear to have much success in trying to put what I feel into words, so maybe I could show you." She slid over a little in the seat and looked up at me with the gray eyes very large. "Jack. Look here at me. Just bend your head down—a little...."

The next thing I was conscious of was a soft, wild mouth, and the importunate, tightening arms about my neck, and the knowledge that, even with somebody else on my mind, I couldn't take too much of that. I got hold of myself and straightened up.

She slid back on the seat a little with her shoulders slumped, not looking up. "All right," she said. "You don't have to draw me a picture."

"I'm sorry, Dinah," I said. "Maybe we'd better go."

"Yes. But you *could* have told me, before I made a fool of myself. Is that where she is, in Bayou City?"

"Where who is?"

"Look. You've insulted me once. Don't do it again."

"There's not—" I began.

"If you don't mind, let's go! I told you I was going to take you to Bayou City, and I'm going to!" She grew quieter then, and went on, "If you'll slide over, I'll drive."

If I'd had any sense I'd have stayed behind the wheel, but I was too relieved at getting started again to heed any warning signs. By the time we were out on the highway, though, I knew what I was in for.

She was doing forty by the time she straightened out, and then I heard rubber scream, in high gear, and knew what she had meant by looking under the hood. The highway ran straight here for six or eight miles, and I sat back in the seat lighting a cigarette and watching the speedometer climb. I thought she would begin to flatten it off at ninety, but she didn't. At a hundred and five I quit looking.

It was a good road that would have been reasonably safe for eighty, in broad daylight, and there was very little traffic, but it was the cows I had the most trouble with. They have a bad habit of finding holes in fences and wandering out onto the roads at night, and I wondered if anybody would be able to separate enough of us from the hamburger to make burial worth while in case we found one tonight.

I thought that after the first blaze of anger burned itself out she might take it a little easier, but I was wrong. She apparently knew the road, for she cut it down before we came up to the turns and then gunned it again for traction as we started into them. Of course, it wasn't all as fast as that first straight-away, but she managed to stay pretty close to thirty miles per hour above what would be considered an absolute limit for night driving. Seeing, in a little while, that it was going to be like this all the way to Bayou City, I began to worry about patrol cars. We'd run across one sooner or later, and I thought hopelessly about my idea of getting clear out of the country without being seen by anyone who might remember me. Of course, a speed cop would never remember us, I thought bitterly—just a big overgrown gorilla and a hundred-pound dream of a flame-headed doll doing ninety-five at night in a souped-up Lincoln. He'd never give us another thought.

She slowed down going through Colston. I had to give her credit. She didn't want to kill any defenseless bystanders. When we hit the city limit on the other side, the speedometer began winding up again.

"All right, Dinah," I said. "I'm impressed, and I know you can drive. So how about knocking it down a little before we pick up a cop?"

"They can't catch me with one of those Fords unless it's souped up. And it won't stay on the ground if it is."

She was right. We picked up a patrol car just after we hit the first of the seventy-five miles of four-lane pavement. He never had a chance. Why they didn't set a road block for us, I'll never know. Maybe they'd chased her before and had just decided the best plan was to leave her alone and let her kill herself without any help.

I had thought we'd be in Bayou City around two in the morning. At a quarter of twelve we were rolling into the downtown section. Traffic was beginning to slacken off and people were going home from the late movies.

"Is there any particular place you want out?" she asked.

"No," I said. "Anywhere will do. I wish you wouldn't go off angry, Dinah. I appreciate this, and I think you're a nice guy."

"You've already told me what you think, if you'll recall."

She pulled up at the curb. I got out, and then leaned back in the open window, holding out my hand. "Don't go away like that, Dinah."

At first I thought she was going to ignore me. Then her face relaxed and she reached out and took it, her hand very soft and warm and almost lost in mine. "Good luck, Jack," she said quietly. She started to say something else, but choked on it; the face turned away, her hand jerked back, and I got out of the window just as the tires shrieked. I stood on the curb watching her disappear down the street. It's not too good, I thought. But what could she do? She was smart enough to know that after hauling me down here she was implicated in the thing herself, and that if she had any regard for her own safety she'd have to keep her mouth shut. There was one serious flaw in this, however, and I knew it. She wasn't exactly the overcautious type.

I shook the worry off impatiently. I had other things to think about than that wild-haired girl. Luggage, for one, I thought. Of course, I could check into the hotel without any, but the room clerk would be more likely to remember me that way. From now on I had to be careful always to do nothing in the slightest degree odd or out of the ordinary. I couldn't do anything that would make me stick in people's memories.

In the next block a chain drugstore was still open. I went in and bought a cheap overnight bag and some shaving gear and a toothbrush. Across the street at a newsstand I picked up two heavy magazines and an out-of-town Sunday paper. As I went back out into the street I snapped the bag open and slipped them inside. So far, so good, I thought, but I still don't know what room she's in. She'd be in bed now, and obviously I couldn't ask the room clerk.

I ducked into an all-night café and went back to the telephone. Looking up the number of the hotel, I dialed and waited.

The fan didn't work and it was stifling inside the booth. "State Hotel." It was a girl's voice. The operator was still on duty.

"A Mrs. Crawford, please. Is she registered? This is United Airlines."

"Just one moment, please." She paused. "Yes, sir. I'm ringing."

"Thank you," I said. I waited, feeling the tightness growing inside my chest as I realized how near I was to her at last. How long had it been since I had let her out of the car in Colston?

"Hello." It was Doris.

I wanted to cry out, "Darling, this is Jack!" Instead I asked smoothly, or as smoothly as I could, "Mrs. Crawford? This is United Airlines, the reservations desk." Would she recognize my voice and not say anything wrong? "We're very sorry, but so far we've been unable to confirm your reservation west of Salt Lake. I think we'll have it in another hour or two, however. Shall we call you then, or wait till morning?"

I heard a barely audible gasp and then she came through beautifully. "Thank you. Tomorrow morning will be all right. Just call me at Room Three-twelve here at the hotel."

"Thank you," I said. I hung up.

It was still hot in the street where the neon was beginning to die. A street-cleaning truck went by, swishing water into the gutters, and the traffic lights were flashing amber along the emptying canyon. Two yellow cabs stood idle at the stand up by the corner.

"State Hotel," I said, feeling the rasping of impatience.

I didn't have any name. I was nobody. I didn't exist. I stood with the pen in my hand, sweating, poised above the blank white card while the man behind the desk regarded me with the supercilious detachment of all hotel clerks. It had never occurred to me until this moment that if I was no longer Jack Marshall I must be somebody else, and that everybody had to have a name.

I had to put down something. He was watching me. "J. K. Mallard, Nashville, Tenn.," I scrawled across the card. He hit the bell.

The boy would never leave. He turned on the light in the bath. He turned on a floor lamp. He looked inside a closet. What does he expect to find? I thought. Ten million boys have looked inside ten million closets searching for something they've never found. I took two quarters out of my pocket and tossed them in my hand.

"Will there be anything else, sir?"

"No," I said, waiting.

He went out and I heard his footsteps going away. Give him two more minutes, I thought, to get out of the corridor. The way he moves.... I put the key in my pocket and went out and closed the door. My room was on the fifth floor, but I bypassed the elevators and walked down the two flights of stairs. I went along looking at the numbers on the doors, going softly on the carpet through the quiet, dim, impersonal tunnel that is the same identical corridor of a thousand different hotels. I walked past doors bearing the numbers 340 and 338; I was going the wrong way. I retraced my steps and started down the other way. I found 308, then 310. I stopped before the next door. I knocked softly, twice, and then once, the sound lost and absorbed in the empty, noise-proofed tunnel walled in by darkened cubicles of sleep.

"Jack?" The whisper was very faint, barely reaching me through the door.

"Yes," I said.

I heard the night latch click and the door opened a minute crack. "Give me just a minute," she whispered.

I waited. She doesn't have a robe, I thought, and not even a nightgown unless she's bought one. I pushed open the door, stepped quickly inside, and latched it. The room was dimly lighted by a single small bulb in the floor lamp in one corner, and she sat up in bed with the sheet clutched to her breast. The dark hair fell down across her shoulder and she was very beautiful and all at the same time a little afraid and full of yearning and inarticulate happiness as I came across the room. It's the same with her as it is with me, I thought.

We've both dreamed of this minute for all this time, and we don't know—there isn't any way we can know—what it will be like with us now. Would we ever be alone again? Had we escaped from Shevlin, or had we tied him to ourselves forever? I stood looking down at her, wanting to tell her how beautiful she was and what I felt, but no words would come. She forgot the sheet and lifted her arm up to me, letting it slide unnoticed from her breast and the cheap, peach-colored nightgown she had bought. I sat down on the side of the bed and gathered her up to me with my face down against her throat. And then when I raised my head and looked at her I knew that neither Shevlin nor anybody, nor anything, could ever reach us as long as we were together.

"You're not afraid now, are you?" I asked.

"No," she whispered. "It's all right now."

"Everything is just the same."

"Yes," she said simply. She was silent for a moment, looking up at me with eyes incredibly large, and very close and still. "I haven't been in the dark since then. But you can turn the light out now."

I went across the room and turned it off.

Chapter Twenty

There was no way to tell what time it was because she was asleep with her head on my arm and I couldn't move it to see the watch. Light was growing, though, beyond the drawn slats of the Venetian blinds, and I could make out objects inside the room. I lay very still for a long time, not wanting to disturb her, and thought about the two of us and the things we would do now that we were free at last. When there was more light I turned again and looked at her. She slept as quietly as a child, lying on her right side with her face against my arm and the hair very dark across the pillow. The strap of the nightgown had slipped off her left shoulder and the breast was exposed, rounded and very smooth, rising gently with her breathing. I smiled, thinking of the confusion in her face when she awoke and discovered it. I didn't want to disturb her sleep, but still it was somehow lonely being awake without her. Even being this near and seeing and touching her wasn't the same without the eyes open and looking at me. I leaned my head down and kissed her and she stirred. The eyes came open, and just for an instant I saw in them the awful awareness and the terror that I had feared. Then she saw me and it went away and she smiled. It will gradually disappear with time, I thought. For a while there will be these moments just at waking or just at dropping off to sleep when the mind has no defense at all and she is alone, but they will go away.

"You are very beautiful when you're asleep," I said.

"It's the first time I've slept since—"

"Yes," I said. "I know."

"You didn't mind, did you, Jack? I wanted to stay awake, but after a while I just seemed to melt and run together. I guess it was because you were here where I could touch you and I wasn't afraid any more."

"It's all right," I said. "I slept too."

She looked down at the gown slipping off her breast and quickly pulled it up, the confusion very becoming on her face, and would have drawn up the sheet but it had fallen to the floor.

"You haven't noticed my gown," she said reprovingly, to cover her embarrassment.

"I'm afraid not. You'll have to admit, though, that it has competition."

She smiled, and then her face sobered and she looked across at me with her eyes full of an almost childlike earnestness. "I—I bought it with some of the money you gave me, Jack. It didn't cost very much; it was the cheapest one they had. I can do without something else. But it's just that I wanted one so badly."

I could feel the tight constriction in my throat. It isn't even a wedding ring she's talking about, I thought, just a cheap, lousy nightgown she probably bought in a ten-cent store, bought looking back on being made love to in the leaves under a tree in broad daylight and looking forward to sleeping naked beside a man like a common prostitute. The only shred of respectability or common decency she would even ask me for was this sleazy, peach-colored misfit of a bargain-basement nightgown, and she was even anxious that I wouldn't think she had wasted too much money in buying that. For some unaccountable reason I was growing angry, and at the same time humiliated and ashamed, thinking of this pathetic attempt to clothe herself in at least some scraps of dignity.

"What else did you buy?" I asked.

"Just some—underclothes."

"And I suppose you got them at the dime store, too? The best they had?"

"Well, not exactly in a dime store, but they didn't cost very much." She looked at me uncertainly. "I know we don't have very much to spend. Remember, you told me."

I had forgotten that. And now that I was suddenly reminded of it I felt even more ashamed and angry. Then I remembered I hadn't even told her of the three thousand dollars we had.

"Do you know what we're going to do today?" I asked.

"Get on the bus?"

"No," I said. "We'll take the bus tomorrow night, after we've got a little better organized. I think we're safe enough here, at least for the moment, and we've got to get some luggage and I need another suit. Today, though, we're going to take you shopping. We're going to buy you some clothes, and I don't mean cheap junk." I sat up in bed and looked at her, aware that I was beginning to sound like a wild man and that I probably didn't make much sense to her. "Do you know what I'm going to do? What I've wanted to do for a long time? What I've wanted to do every time I thought of you going barefoot like a sharecropper's child and thought of those misfit abortions of dresses you wore around that house? I'm going to see you dressed in the kind of clothes you should have. We're going to start at the bottoms of those feet. Let me see your feet. Where are they?"

"Well, Jack, where would they be?"

I slid down along the bed and gathered them up in my hands, turning them inward and pressing the soles together the way I had once before. "We're going to start right here with the sheerest nylons ever made and the most expensive shoes in town and gradually work up."

I looked up and she was watching me with an amused tenderness in her eyes. "But Jack, what are we going to use for money?"

I had forgotten it again. Leaping off the bed, I went over to where I had left the coat. Slipping out the envelope, I took it over to her, pulled out the thick sheaf of hundreds and fifties and twenties, and spread them along the sheet in front of her.

She looked at it, dumfounded, and then up at me. "Jack, where on earth did that come from?" I could see the fright and anxiety begin to come back into her face and she went on, "What have you done?"

As rapidly as I could, I told her all that had happened. She listened quietly, not even touching the money, and when I had finished all she said was, "I'm glad it's all over. There won't have to be any more of that, will there? I know it's too late now to think about the way it could have been, but at least we can try to live the way other people do, can't we? We can both get jobs and we'll get by all right. I used to work in an office."

"Yes," I said. "Only you won't have to any more. I can get a job without much trouble. We'll go to Washington—the state, I mean. I was there when I came back from the Pacific in 1945. It's beautiful country, and you'll love it—mountains and rivers and green forests...." I happened to think then that perhaps she'd already seen all the green forests she'd ever want to, and went on hurriedly, "And Seattle is a nice city. You'll love it."

"It sounds wonderful. But I don't care where we go, Jack. Just so we're together, and maybe we'll be able to live in peace."

"Yes," I said. I bent down, placed a hand alongside her cheek, and kissed her. "All that other is finished now. It's past and gone."

Her arms went up around my neck, softly at first, and then they tightened and she cried out, "Oh, Jack! I hope it is. I hope so!"

"Of course it is," I said. "We're in the clear now. They'll believe I'm dead, and they'll never bother to look for you except as part of the hunt for him. There isn't a chance that anything will go wrong. But we can't sit here all day moping like a couple of old women. We've got to get started shopping." I stopped a minute, thinking, and then went on. "Look. Here's what we do. Today and tomorrow we'll go on just as we are now, not even knowing each other as far as anyone else is concerned. That may be a little overcautious now that everything has turned out so well, but it's just in case our descriptions are broadcast. Two people answering a general description are a lot more likely to attract attention than one alone. So we don't want to be seen together around the hotel. I'll meet you—" I looked at my watch. "I'll meet you at ten-thirty in the cafeteria up in the next block. We'll have breakfast together and then start buying your clothes."

I went back up to my own room, tore the bed apart a little so it would look as if I'd at least been in it, shaved, and went down in the lobby for the morning papers. I worked through them very carefully, starting at the front page and going back to the want ads, and there wasn't a word about my disappearance or about the grand jury at home. I was just about to throw them aside when I saw her come out of the elevator and head for the street. She had put her hair back up in the roll at the back of her neck, the way she had done it coming down to Colston. I waited until she had been gone a few minutes, and went out the door myself.

The afternoon papers will be out in an hour or two, I thought. They'll have something in them. I was beginning to burn with impatience, wanting to see how Buford would break the story and how well it went over with the general public.

She was sitting alone at a table in the corner. I took my tray back and sat down across from her. "There's nothing in the papers yet," I said.

She nodded. "There hasn't been time."

I knew she was right. Nobody would think anything about it until I failed to show up for work this morning. Buford, for the benefit of the others, would call the jail to see if I had come in there last night with Shevlin. Then he would call the garage and learn that the car was still out. By that time Lorraine and Hurd, and anybody else who happened to drop into the office, would be buzzing. Buford would call the boat place at the foot of the lake and learn that I hadn't come back with the boat and that the car was still parked there by the boathouse. The story would begin to spread like fire on a windy day, and the news services would probably have it by ten o'clock. I looked at my watch. It was a quarter of eleven; Buford would probably be leading a search party on the way into the swamp right now.

I was eager to get started and couldn't even taste what I was eating. "Let's go, Doris," I said. "You've got a lot of shopping to do."

She smiled. "All right. But Jack, I'm afraid you don't know much about women's clothes. Dresses and skirts have to have alterations, and we don't have time for it now. I'll just try to get something to travel in, and then buy other things when we get to Seattle. The clothes will be different there, anyway."

I hadn't thought of that, but I knew she was right. "O.K.," I said, disappointed. "But all the other things that don't need alterations—you'll get those, won't you?"

"Yes," she said, looking at me gently. "It means a lot to you, doesn't it?"

We went out into the swarming, sun-baked street where heat lay in wait and lunged at you just outside the air-conditioned doors. The first place was a luggage shop, where we bought her two matching bags and asked to have them delivered to the hotel. Then what she had said about alterations reminded me that I had better get the suit now so they could have it ready for tomorrow. She waited inside the men's store while I bought it and made arrangements to have it delivered to me at the hotel no later than two the next afternoon.

"Now, you," I said, touching her gently on the arm.

"Are you sure you want to go along?"

"Yes," I said. I began to change my mind, however, before we'd even got through shoes and handbags. I was too alone here in this jungle of women, too conspicuous, like a chained bear at a Junior League tea. It was worse than foolish; it was stupid. I'd never blend very well into this background, and too many people would remember me.

"I hate to leave you for a minute, but I'm going to have to get out of here," I said at last. We stood in a crowded aisle with the stream of women shoppers eddying and flowing around us. I gave her three hundred dollars. "I'll meet you at the hotel."

"I don't need this much," she protested.

"Don't buy cheap things. Please," I urged.

She looked up at me. "Why, Jack?"

I shook my head. "I don't know. It's something I can't explain. I just don't want you to have anything second-rate or makeshift. You've had enough of that."

I went back out into the heat and drifted with the crowds, watching with rising impatience for the afternoon papers. At the second corner a truck was unloading them at a stand and I bought one and ducked into the nearest bar. It was cool inside, and dim, and I sat down on a stool at the end of the bar, ordered a bottle of beer and opened the paper.

It was a short item, less than a third of a column, on an inside page:

OFFICER MISSING

J. B. Marshall, 27, deputy sheriff of Devers County, was reported this morning to have been missing since early yesterday in the vicinity of Stowe Lake, where he had gone to arrest a man believed to be an escaped convict. According to Wayne Buford, Devers County sheriff, Marshall left the boathouse at the south end of the lake yesterday morning in a rented boat.

I read it through twice to be sure I had missed nothing, then threw the paper aside. There wasn't much; just about what I had expected for the first break on the story. The general tone of it seemed to be that, so far, at least, they believed I had just got lost in the swamp. There'll be more in the later editions, I thought.

Impatience and restlessness had hold of me again, and I wanted to get back to her, and get on the bus and start for the Coast. I wasn't scared now, I thought; the most dangerous part of it was over. That had ended when I had got out of the swamp and down here without being seen by anyone. By anyone but Dinah, I thought, correcting myself. But she wouldn't say anything. I was sure of it now. I wondered if she were still here in town or if she had gone home. She might even be shopping right alongside Doris at this moment, I thought, and was glad again I had got out of the stores. She was sure I was meeting somebody down here, and I wondered if she would suspect anything if any of the news stories mentioned Shevlin's having been married. Probably not, I thought. Why should she?

I couldn't sit still any longer and went back out into the street. How much longer would she be? Time away from her was wasted; why didn't she hurry and get back to the hotel? Then the ridiculous illogic of this struck me; I was the one who had insisted she go shopping in the first place, and now I was impatient because she was gone. And as far as being back at the hotel was concerned, I wasn't there either. Was it time to go now? No, I thought. She wouldn't be back for an hour or more and I'd go crazy waiting.

I was passing a jeweler's and suddenly realized she didn't have a watch. That was one thing I could get for her myself. The clerk sized up my clothes and began bringing out the $37.50 and $49.95 stock. I waved them away impatiently, feeling angry again, and would have walked out and gone to another store but my eye was caught by an exquisite timepiece in yellow gold with a matching strap of golden cord, very beautiful in its simplicity, and costing $275. "Wrap it as a gift," I said, and waited, restless in the heat.

There was a later edition of the paper on the street and I bought it, but there was only a different headline on the Korean war. The story was still in its original location on the inside page, unchanged, with nothing new. No mention had been made of the grand jury at all. It'll be out later tonight, I thought, and then I'll know how they're taking it. I won't quit worrying until I know what they're going to believe. But I'm not worrying, I reminded myself. It's all right now.

I went into another bar and sat down at a table in the air-conditioned cool dimness in the rear. I ordered a bottle of beer, but when it came it had no taste and I let it die in the glass, forgotten. Taking the jeweler's box out of my pocket, I thought of looking at the watch again, but decided not to open it because it was gift-wrapped so well. She doesn't really want this, I thought. She doesn't want the clothes I insisted that she buy—at least, not so many of them—and she doesn't care whether they're expensive or not. All she wants is peace, and maybe she wants me. I hope she wants me, but maybe she never will in the way that I have to have her. She needs me because she is afraid now when she's alone, and because she is first and last a man's woman who needs a man and who could see no point in life without one, and because she likes me and maybe she loves me, but I don't think it's the obsession it has become with me.

No, I thought angrily, I've got no right to think that about her. How do I know how deeply the feels? Is she some flirtatious idiot with everything on the surface where it shows? And do you expect her to dredge up all her feelings right now when she's trying so hard to bury some of them? Things are still terribly mixed up for her, and she's scared, and what she's gone through would have driven some women out of their minds.

But, on the other hand, I thought, staring straight ahead across the dimness of the bar and seeing nothing but a still-faced girl with tortured eyes and that beautiful, dark, and mutilated hair—on the other hand, hadn't it been only the loneliness that had driven her to me in the first place? Hadn't it been just the loneliness and neglect and the sordid way she'd had to live for almost a year, seeing him come apart that way in drunkenness and suspicion? Minutely, step by step, I went back over every one of our pitifully few hours together, looking for something and not even knowing what it was. I saw her again down on her knees scouring the floor with that agonized fury as if it were herself under the harsh scrubbing brush instead of the already whitened planks. Neglect? That was part of it. What was it she had cried out once, almost in self-reproach? "I can't help the way I am, can I, Jack? Is it my fault I'm that way?" But it wasn't only that, I thought. It had to be more than that with her. She would have gone on punishing herself until she wore the floor out with the brush before she'd have surrendered to what she would have considered the cheapness of that alone. It had just been a little of this and a little of that, all adding up until it whipped her. No, I thought savagely. No, that wasn't it. I must have been more to her than just a means of escape. But I don't *know*. How could I know? How could I ever be sure?

I've got to stop this, I thought. Is this the kind of thing I'm going to go through when I'm away from her? Do I have to go on tormenting myself this way? I tried to drink the beer, but it was flat and warm by now and completely tasteless. I lighted another cigarette, forgetting I already had one burning on the tray. Suddenly, sitting still was unbearable again, and I threw fifty cents on the table and went out without waiting for my change. Sunlight blasted into the street and the glare hurt my eyes after the dimness of the bar, and heat boiled up from the sidewalk in suffocating waves. She'll be back by now, I thought. She must be back.

She wasn't. I stood outside the door and knocked again, and then a third time in an empty hot eternity of silence before I would admit to myself she wasn't there. I was cut off, alone, with nowhere to go and nothing to do but sit down in the lobby through the hell of another hour of waiting.

I heard the elevator door and turned around. She had just stepped out of it and was coming toward me down the corridor with her arms stacked high with bundles.

Chapter Twenty-one

I took them from her while she unlocked the door. We went inside and she closed it and turned to me to take them. "Let me show you, Jack. Let's open them now, darling."

"No," I said. I threw them on the dresser, but there were too many and some of them fell off onto the floor. "No. Later on. They're not important."

She looked at me wonderingly. "But I thought you wanted—"

"Yes. I did. I still do. But they can wait." I was conscious of thinking I must not make much sense to her. Or to myself, for that matter, I thought. She was still regarding me with faint surprise as I reached out and caught her, quite clumsily, and in too big a hurry and almost roughly. Her arms went up about my neck and then she gasped slightly and said, "Jack, you're hurting me."

"I'm sorry," I said. I raised my head a little and looked at her, seeing the face slightly flushed from the heat and the eyes very large and dark, almost violet now in the dimness of the room. "I couldn't help it. I can't help it. Don't you see how it is?" I went on, wildly now, and knowing I must sound like a madman to her. "I love you so much I get jumpy being away from you and I can't keep my hands off you when I'm here. God knows, I don't want to hurt you. Can't you see how it is? Don't you see?"

"Yes," she said softly. "I know. It's exactly the same with me."

"Is it that bad with you too?"

"Yes. But I don't think it's bad."

"No. Not bad. It's only bad when we're apart. It's awful then. I didn't know a man could come unstuck like this. Do you suppose I'm crazy?"

"If you are," she whispered, "I love you for it."

I raised a jittery hand and started fumbling with the pins with which she had fastened up her hair in that roll behind her neck. In my awkwardness and shaky-fingered impatience, however, I wasn't making any progress and was only messing it up. "Wait, Jack," she said gently, and quickly slipped them out. The hair tumbled down and she shook her head, freeing it. It was a dark shadow across her face and throat and I ran my fingers through it. "Is that better now?" she whispered.

"Yes," I said. "Yes. This is how I wanted it."

I put my face down against her throat and could feel the beating of her heart. The traffic sound down below us grew far away and faint, like distant surf, and I could hear nothing now except the caught, breathless, and then suddenly desperate whispering in my ear. "I love you, Jack. I love you so."

We were strangely clumsy, as if we'd never made love before, caught up in a dark and ecstatic wildness full of frenzied caress and inexpert fumbling like the very young. It had never been quite like this the other times, and when it had flown away and left us I lay quite still and wondered at it, watching the lovely face so peaceful now in repose with the eyes closed and the lashes very dark against her cheek. Like a child, I thought, or an angel, and wondered why angels never seemed to have dark hair in pictures.

In a little while she opened her eyes and we lay looking at each other for a long time without saying anything. She brought up a hand and gently ran a fingertip along my face, just touching it. I wondered if she knew or even remembered that she was completely nude, or whether it would suddenly come to her and she would be overcome with embarrassment and confusion as she had this morning. She knew, though, for in a moment she looked down at the swelling, dark-centered breasts and then back up at me with a faint wonder in her eyes.

"I guess I have no shame," she said.

"It's a ridiculous word to use," I said. "Why should you?"

"It's funny, isn't it? I keep telling myself I should, but there isn't any. Not at all. I couldn't get up this way, though. Could I?"

"No," I said. "You're trapped."

She smiled very faintly. "Unless you went to sleep."

"I don't feel sleepy in the least," I said.

"Or maybe you would be a gentleman."

"I feel even less like a gentleman than I do sleepy," I said. "I'm rotten all the way through."

"Don't you want me to put on the clothes I bought? You were very concerned about them this morning."

"I don't know," I said. I moved a little and put my face against hers, our foreheads touching, knowing it was a silly thing because I couldn't see even her eyes then, they were so near. "I think I don't know what I want. I want you here the way you are, but still I want to see you dressed up and very smart. I want to stand off and look at you and at the same time I want to be so near that there'd be no way of knowing whether there were two of us or only one. I want to talk to you, and still I want to be quiet, just watching you. I want to tell you all about it, how beautiful you are and how much I love you, and still I know there isn't any way I can really say it and that you shouldn't try to talk about it too much when it's like this, because talking takes a little bit of it away, and all the words have been worn out anyway by people who maybe only thought they felt it. I want too many different things and I want them all at once. There's a lot of it I don't understand, and maybe I never will. I can see why I want to make love to you the way we did; I can see why touching you or looking at you or being around should be exciting in that way; but there's no way to understand why I get angry just thinking about the way you had to live and the way you dressed and at your being barefoot, or why I feel the way I do about your feet and just want to sit there and hold them in my hands. Do I make any sense to you? Could anybody make any sense out of it?"

"Yes," she said softly. "It makes sense. Weren't you ever in love before, Jack?"

"I guess not. Anyway, not like this."

"But you were married."

"I know. But it wasn't anything. Even at first." It was odd, I thought now. It seemed to have been years since I'd even thought of Louise.

"Yes," she said musingly. "I think you're right. I don't think you ever have been before. I know it's a funny thing to say, but you seem to be so completely amazed by it, like a little boy."

"Now you're talking as if you were a thousand years older than I am."

"I think I probably am," she said gently.

"Have you ever been in love before?" I asked, suddenly and furiously jealous.

"You want me to tell the truth, don't you, Jack?"

"Of course," I said, not wanting her to at all.

"It was a boy who was killed on Guadalcanal in 1942. I was nineteen then, and pregnant. When his parents received the telegram I tried to kill myself with sleeping pills. They didn't work, but when I went to the abortionist, he almost did it for me."

"My God!" I said. "No."

"It had been too long. I don't know why it didn't kill me as well as the baby. Maybe it was because I didn't really care."

"But," I cried out angrily, "why, Doris? Why?"

"I don't know. It wasn't just because we weren't married. I wouldn't have minded that very much then, and wouldn't at all now. But it was the injustice of it. I hated everything. I wanted to die and I wanted to kill a baby who couldn't have been responsible for a war that did things like that. And maybe a little of it was because of my father. He was such a sweet old thing, and the disgrace would have ruined him. He'd have lost his church. Oh, I don't know. After all, I was very young, Jack. We wanted to be married in San Diego before he left, but I looked so young they wouldn't give us a license without my father's consent, and by the time I got the letter from him it was too late. He already had been shipped out."

"How did you get to San Diego in the first place?" I asked.

"I ran away and followed him. After he went overseas I came home. Daddy didn't say anything. It was after I got back that I realized I was pregnant. Of course, I was very happy about it then, married or not. But when his parents got the telegram—"

"My God," I said. "What an awful thing!"

"It was a long time ago, Jack. I mean, it's all over now."

I saw a little then of what she had meant when she had said she was older

than I was. "And it was some time after that when you met *him?*" I wondered
if either of us would ever be able to say his name.

"Yes," she said. "About a year."

We were quiet for a long time. Even though I didn't want to think about
it I kept trying to imagine what their life had been like. After a while I turned
and looked at her and asked, "Did he hack up your hair like that? Was he
drunk?"

"No," she said. "I did it myself. I tried to cut it by looking in a mirror. I made
a mess of it, but it didn't matter. It was too long, and all I wanted to do was
hack it off so it wouldn't be so hot, and so I could get it inside the cap when
I went swimming."

She certainly lived a wonderful life up there, I thought bitterly. But I'll
make it up to her now.

"Where did he get the money for all that whisky?" I asked. "He didn't make
that much from the fish he sold."

"No. He didn't buy it. I think the man who rented boats down at the store
was a bootlegger or made whisky or something. He used to give it to Roger
for repairing boats and motors and things like that. He was very handy with
tools. But do we have to talk about it, Jack?"

"No," I said. "It's all over now."

It was dark outside now. The floor lamp in the corner was turned on, and
as I sat on the side of the bed, smoking, I could see the litter of opened parcels
and the wrapping paper scattered about the floor. She had been in the bathroom for a long time, while I listened to her splashing in the tub, then she had
come out, wearing the new robe she had bought, and opened all the other
packages. Gathering up some of the things, she had gone back, promising to
put them on so I could see how they looked. As I sat there now, waiting for
her, I suddenly remembered the watch that was still in the pocket of my coat.
I'd forgotten to give it to her. When she comes out, I thought.

Thinking of the watch reminded me of the time and I looked at mine. It was
after eight. The first editions of the morning papers should be on the street
in a little while, if they weren't already. I should go down to the lobby and
get them, I thought, but it was too pleasant just sitting there waiting for her
to come out again so I could see how she looked. I'll pick them up when we
go out to dinner, I thought.

I heard the door open, and looked up and whistled softly. She was very tall
and smart-looking and cool in a white skirt and short white jacket, with a
blouse of frosty blue gathered in some kind of ruffle about her throat. The
stockings were very sheer and she had on white shoes that didn't appear to
be much more than high heels and straps.

She turned, holding out her arms. "How do I look, Jack?"

"Don't come any closer. I might try to bite you."

"Do I really look all right?"

I got up from the bed, conscious of what a crumby-looking specimen I was now beside her, with nothing on except my shorts and with the stubble of black beard beginning to show, and went over to my coat. I took out the little parcel and handed it to her.

"This is for you," I said, "because you are the most beautiful woman in the world."

She took it, looking at me wonderingly. "Go ahead," I said. "Open it. It's for you. I bought it while I was waiting for you today."

She unwrapped it and held the oblong case in her hands a moment before she snapped it open. I heard the little gasp as she looked inside. "Oh, what a lovely thing! Jack, you didn't have to do this for me."

"I told you why I did it," I said.

She looked up at me with her eyes a little wet. "Jack, I believe you *do* think I'm beautiful."

"Aren't you?" I asked quietly.

She nodded, not speaking for a moment. "Yes," she said then. "I feel beautiful, anyway."

I met her up the street and we went to dinner. It was very dim, with candles, and we had a table in a corner by ourselves. I didn't buy the papers after all, not before dinner, for I knew I wouldn't read them before we got back anyway, and the later editions would be out then. I couldn't sit down across from her and look at a paper, no matter what news I was expecting.

After a while we went back to the hotel. She went in first and I bought the papers and followed her. She had the white suit off and was changing to the robe when I got there, and we spread the papers on the bed and read them. The story was on the front page now, and growing.

"OFFICER BELIEVED VICTIM," the headlines said. They hadn't found either of the boats yet, but already the stories were full of the conjectures that I had hoped for, built on just the fact that I was still missing and that Shevlin's cabin was deserted and his boat gone. Dozens of men were searching the swamp now, and I was sure that by tomorrow morning they'd find the boats, which should clinch it. There was no mention of the grand jury investigation. It was good news, all of it. I felt better and the strain was beginning to go away. It had been a good job.

There was another thing, though, that we hadn't outrun. Just before dawn I awoke suddenly, sweating and scared, and she was screaming in her sleep. I got her calmed after a while and lay awake until daylight smoking cigarettes and thinking.

Chapter Twenty-two

When the first gray light began to filter through the drawn Venetian blinds I got up and dressed. She was sleeping all right now, quite peacefully, with a hand beneath her cheek and the dark hair swirled across the pillow. It was cooler now inside the room, and I gently pulled up the sheet without disturbing her. It was only a bad dream, I thought; she'll get over it.

In the early dawn the empty canyon of the street was almost cool; yesterday's heat was dead, and today's was waiting to be born. A street-cleaning truck went by, swishing water, and I could smell the dust being overrun and drowned the way it is in the first large drops of rain. This is the only time of day, I thought, when a city is ever beautiful.

The final editions of the morning papers were on the stands. I bought them and hurried into a coffee shop full of white tile and chrome and sat down at the counter. The story sprang out at me from the front pages, apparently getting bigger by the hour. "SWAMP SEARCHED FOR BODY," I read. "MURDER CLUE IN DISAPPEARANCE." "VIOLENCE FEARED." They had found the boats.

Wild with eagerness, I tore into the stories:

> With the discovery late yesterday afternoon of an abandoned, bloodstained boat, identified as that which J. B. Marshall, 27, deputy sheriff of Devers County, had rented for the trip into the swamp area in the upper reaches of Stowe Lake to make an arrest, hope was rapidly dwindling that the missing officer might be found alive. Wayne Buford, Devers County sheriff, revealed to newsmen at a late hour last night that evidence found in and about the boat indicated there had almost certainly been a struggle and that the young deputy may have been murdered by the man he had gone into the swamp to arrest. He cited the ominous fact that the boat had been carefully hidden and that the bloodstains found on the seat and on the upper shaft of one of the oars had been hastily scrubbed at in an effort to obliterate them.
>
> "But," the sheriff added grimly, his face haggard from the strain of the continuing 24-hour search, "the most significant and terrible of all the evidence is that missing anchor. I have been informed by the proprietor of the fishing camp that this boat was equipped, like all the others, with a fifteen-pound concrete anchor and some twelve or fifteen feet of rope. With the anchor gone and the rope cut, just recently and with a sharp knife, we have no choice but to believe...."

I sipped the coffee, hardly noticing it in my excitement. It was even better than I had hoped. And Buford was terrific. He should have gone on the stage, I thought.

"—the utter hopelessness of the search in the light of this almost in-escapable conclusion. Nobody knows just how many thousands of acres of waterway—lake and swamp and sloughs—there are up there, and it would take more than a lifetime to do a thorough job of drag-ging all of it for a weighted body lying on the bottom somewhere in the mud. However, we are not giving up. That boy was well liked by all of us, and we will not abandon the search while there is any remote possibility that he is still alive. And the man hunt for Shevlin, or Far-rell, is being pushed by every officer in the state."

The story went on with a lot more of Buford. He reconstructed the whole thing as indicated by the evidence, giving his opinion that I had arrested Shevlin and started out with him. Somewhere along the line I had grown mo-mentarily careless, Shevlin had seized the opportunity to slug me with the oar, unlock the cuffs—they had found the key where I had dropped it—and had dropped me over the side with the anchor tied to my body. Then he had gone back for his wife—for by this time it was known that he was married, though no one could remember having seen her in almost a year—and on the way out of the swamp in his boat he had hidden the rental boat and then es-caped. It was as nearly what I had planned as if I'd left him a script to read.

Full of elation, I paused to light a cigarette, and then read on, looking for some hint about the grand jury.

Young Marshall, a veteran of World War II and well known and liked throughout the county, was the only son of the late Judge Hal-stead Marshall and the last of a family quite prominent in this part of the state for over a hundred years.

I put the paper down. That last paragraph might be the answer. It carried a hint of something I had hoped for but had not dared count on too heavily. Now that I was presumably dead and nothing could be gained by investiga-tion except to raise a smell, there was a good chance they had let it die out of respect for the Judge's memory. Probably they had started, got far enough into it to see where it was going to lead, and now that I was dead they'd let it drop. I hoped so, anyway.

I paid for the coffee and went back to the hotel, walking as if a hundred-pound weight had suddenly been lifted from my shoulders and knowing that at last there was no danger. I almost ran the last few steps down the corridor to get into the room to tell her.

She was just coming out of the bathroom in her robe. I caught her excitedly and kissed her while she looked at me in wonder, and then I handed her the papers.

"Read it," I said. "We're in the clear. They went for every bit of it. No, wait." I interrupted myself. "Before you start, call room service and order your breakfast. I've already had some coffee and I'm too excited to eat anything."

"All right, Jack." She made an effort to smile, but it was a strained and piti- ful attempt, and I knew that the terror of last night was still alive there some- where below the surface. After she had made the call she started reading the news stories and I watched her face as the hope and relief grew in her eyes. When the waiter knocked on the door I went into the bathroom and hid while he set up the breakfast things. When he had gone I came out and drank a lit- tle of her coffee and watched her while she finished the papers and tried to eat. She didn't get much of it down.

"Look," I ran on, too full of plans now to be quiet, "the other things you bought will be delivered to the hotel by noon today and I'll have the suit and a change of clothes. We have luggage and can travel looking just like anybody else. So we'll check out, separately, sometime this afternoon, and catch the first bus. No, by God, we'll take the plane. We can afford it now. Why did- n't I think of it sooner? We'll take the plane to San Francisco, stay there a few days, and then go on up to Seattle by bus to see the country."

She had begun to catch my excitement now. "I think that's wonderful, Jack," she said. She called the airline and found there would be a plane at six- fifteen P.M., and made her reservation.

"You'll have to go down and pick up the ticket sometime this morning," I said. "I'll follow you and get a ticket for myself. Maybe we'd better make it pretty soon, so they won't be sold out."

She called room service and I went back into the bathroom while the waiter took away the dishes. I prowled the room restlessly while she was in the bath changing into street clothes, and when she came out I spoiled her lip- stick kissing her.

"You're just like a big bear," she said, smiling. She started to pin her hair up into that roll on the back of her neck and I took her by the arms and turned her around.

"Couldn't you leave it down now?" I asked. "After all, there hasn't been any description of you broadcast, as far as we know. As a matter of fact, no- body's seen you for a year and they don't even know what you look like. But, no, I guess not. It *would* attract attention, chopped up like that. I don't like it, though. Put up that way, I mean. Because it's so damned lovely when it's down across the side of your face."

"But after all, Jack," she smiled, "when we're alone together I always have it down. And you don't care what it looks like to other people, do you?"

"Yes, that's right. But remember that when we're out in public, the other people aren't the only ones looking at you. I am too."

"You say awfully nice things for this early in the morning."

"There is no early morning in the way I feel about you," I said, grinning. "It's always just at dusk with the moon rising."

"Sweet! Maybe, though, I could get a beauty shop appointment this morning and have it cut to even it up. It would be all right then."

"Try it," I said eagerly. "That'd be fine."

She looked up some in the telephone book and started calling. On about the third one she hit a cancellation and they said they could take her at eleven-thirty.

We went down the street to the airline office, going in separately, and she picked up her ticket while I bought one. There isn't much need for all this cloak-and-dagger stuff any more, I thought, and as soon as we're on the plane we'll call it off. It's all right now.

We went back to the hotel to wait until she had to go to the beauty shop. The rest of her packages had been delivered. I went up to my room and found that the suit and the other clothes I had bought had come, as well as the new bag. I packed, and just as I was starting out the door to meet her down in front of the hotel I remembered I hadn't shaved this morning. I'd forgotten all about it. Well, there isn't time now, I thought; I'll come back and do it while she's in the shop.

The beauty shop was only two blocks away, and we walked, going slowly along through the dense crowds and the heat. The boys were beginning to call the afternoon papers and I was just going to buy one when a sharp cry from Doris interrupted me.

"Jack! I left my watch!" She had stopped. "I took it off to bathe this morning and put it on the dresser. And when I got ready to meet you I went right over there and looked at it to see what time it was and didn't put it on. Oh, how stupid!"

"It's all right," I said. "It's in the room. Nobody'll bother it."

"But I'm worried about it. It's such a beautiful thing, and you gave it to me. And, besides, the maid will be in to clean the room."

"I know what," I said. "Give me your key and I'll run back and pick it up while I'm waiting for you."

I watched her go across the street and into the shop, and when she was inside I walked back to the hotel. The watch was still on the dresser and I picked it up and put it in my pocket. I'll run upstairs and shave, I thought, and go back to meet her. She said it'd take only about half an hour. Then I remembered the paper I hadn't bought, and was suddenly curious as to whether anything new had turned up. I went back out and bought one from the boy on the corner. He handed it to me folded and I stuck it under my arm, going up the street toward the bar I had been in yesterday. It was air-conditioned and would be more comfortable than the hotel.

The place was almost deserted, very cool and dim after the crowds and hot sunlight in the street. The barman in his white jacket was bent over a news-paper spread out on the bar, and as I went past I noted absently that it was the same one I carried under my arm, the afternoon paper with the salmon-colored outer sheet. I sat down at the end of the bar and he came over.

"Bottle of beer," I said.

He opened it and got a glass. "Quite a deal about that sheriff, wasn't it?" he asked.

I'm a celebrity now, I thought. But, anyway, a dead one. "Yeah," I said casually. "Probably never find his body, either."

He shook his head. "Not a chance, in that place. I been up there fishing a couple of times. But, say, that babe was a looker, wasn't she?"

What was he talking about? "Babe?" I asked.

"Yeah, that guy's wife. A real pipperoo."

"Wife?" I asked stupidly. What the hell, was Louise mixed up in it now? "The sheriff?"

"No," he said. "The other one. The man that killed him. His wife's picture is there on the front page."

I could feel my skin congeal inside the sweaty clothes. Somehow I got the paper out from under my arm and unfolded it, trying to keep my face still while the bar swam around me in a slow and horrible eddying of black mir-rors and mahogany and white-jacketed barmen.

I knew what it was even before I looked. For some crazy reason, the thing she had said about the watch came back to me. "I went right over there and looked at it to see what time it was and didn't put it on." I had stood right there in the cabin day before yesterday, taking a last look around, and had looked right at the picture sitting there on the mantel, beside the clock—the clock I had even noticed was stopped—*and I had never even seen it.*

"A honey, huh?" It was the barman.

Somehow I managed it. "Yeah," I said. "A honey."

I had to get out of there. But I couldn't run like that. I might get him sus-picious. Somehow I managed to dig a dollar out of my pocket and put it on the bar, to give him something to do besides just standing there looking at me. They had given it a full two columns. "SOUGHT," the caption said. "Mrs. Roger Shevlin, beautiful young wife of man sought in swamp killing." Good God Almighty, I raged, they didn't have a picture of him—only twenty thou-sand of them scattered in every law enforcement office in the South—so they had to run hers!

I gulped at the beer, almost drowning myself to get it down so I could get out of there. Fortunately I had swallowed it before my eyes had started wildly down the front-page story alongside the picture, for then I got the second jolt.

—as law enforcement officers of the adjacent county swung into the

search for the body and the escaped killers. According to Sheriff Carl
C. Raines of Blakeman County, Marshall may have been overpowered
and killed in the cabin itself or nearby, and Shevlin and his wife may
quite possibly have disposed of the body in the other direction, above
the cabin, before they fled.

I tried to put the glass down without rattling it against the wood. So now
Raines was mixed up in it, and thought she had helped to kill me, and he was
looking for them both! Buford had called the warning, and I hadn't paid any
attention. He had told me that the upper end of the lake was in Blakeman
County. I had even known it myself, but hadn't thought it was important.
But now—

Buford covering my tracks behind me was one thing, but having Raines
sniffing at the trail was something entirely different. He wasn't just going
through the motions.

Somehow I got out of the bar. Heat rolled up and hit me as I went through
the door, and I had to remember where I was to get my directions straight.
The beauty shop was up the street toward the left. But what was I going to
do? I thought of her sitting there, with that ragged hair already causing the
girls to notice her, and with everybody looking at the picture on the front
page. I've got to do something, I thought agonizingly. But what? I had to wait
for her to come out; if I went in there to get her, *that* would attract attention.
And if I got her back to the hotel, then what? Dye her hair? How did you
disguise a woman?

The heat was beginning to make me weak, and I felt sick. This was the last
intersection now, and I leaned against the lamp pole waiting for the light to
change. The beauty shop was the fourth door from the corner and I stopped
in front of it, not knowing what to do next. People going past in the hot sunlight bumped into me and I moved out toward the curb.

A sedan pulled up into the no-parking zone and stopped. Two men got out,
and as I watched in growing horror they walked into the shop. But they're
not in uniform, I thought desperately. They're not police. They couldn't be!
But there was no use trying to kid myself that they looked like the kind of men
who frequented beauty shops.

The door opened. She was coming out. I wanted to jump forward and cry
out and take her by the arm, but I stopped, rooted where I was. One of the
men was right behind her and *he* had her by the arm. I had to move to get out
of their way, for I was standing right in front of their car.

She saw me and I thought she would cry out. The terror was awful in her
eyes, but she went past me with no word and no sign of recognition. I could
swing and hit him, I thought through the black despair, but she couldn't run
in those high heels, and there's always the other one. And by now I had seen
the shoulder holsters and the guns. One of the men got in the front seat be-

hind the wheel and the other helped her in and then sat down beside her in
the back.

Nobody had said a word. The people going by on the sidewalk never knew
it. As the car pulled away from the curb her face turned toward me just for
an instant through the window and I wanted to die.

Chapter Twenty-three

Then I was back at the hotel. I had no idea how I had got there, but I was standing in her room looking around at her clothes and the two alligator bags and her robe and nightgown across the bed and feeling all the emptiness and silence of this place where she had been come crawling up over me like ants across a lidless eye. There was no escaping them, and I wanted to turn and run back out, but there was nowhere else to go and I had enough sense left to know that the emptiness was inside me and that I would take it with me when I ran.

The thing I had to do was sit down and try to think, try to see exactly what had happened. This torturing condemnation running endlessly through my mind like a singing commercial through a radio you couldn't turn off wasn't going to do anything except eventually drive me crazy, and then they'd have us both. I had done this to her, I had left the picture there where they had found it, I had been responsible for her going to the beauty shop, and I had stood there like a baby and let the police take her away to jail, but it wasn't going to help any to go on torturing myself with the knowledge.

I sat down on the bed. The maid had already been here and cleaned the room, so I was safe enough from discovery. And they're not even looking for me anyway, I thought, struggling to reorient myself. They're only looking for the people who are supposed to have killed me. Then the terrible irony of it went to work on me again and my head was in a spin. I had done such a good job of erasing myself that they had already arrested her as an accomplice in my murder.

But does she know that? I thought. Does she know that it's my disappearance she's been arrested for, or does she, in her terror, think they've found out about Shevlin? What would she do? What would she be likely to say, to cry out without knowing where she might trap herself? That was the terrible part of it. I had no way of knowing what she was going to say, and no way to get word to her to tell her what to say. I thought of those "Information, Please" experts at work on her and of all their tricks, and had to tear my mind away from it.

If she saw from the first that they had picked her up only because they were trying to find Shevlin, she would be all right. There were a thousand things she could tell them that would leave her in the clear. And all the time she would be secure in the knowledge that the crime for which she had been arrested didn't actually exist, that they couldn't actually *do* anything to her for being accessory to my death, because I wasn't dead, and that as a last resort I could always reappear to kill the charge.

But, I wondered then, suddenly, would her mind, having gone that far, go on to the next fact, the one staring me in the face right now? And that was that if I reappeared, what was I going to tell them when they asked me what it was all about and where Shevlin was? I could tell them that he had escaped from me. Sure. But what was I doing down here? Running from that grand jury investigation at home? No. *Because I didn't even know that such a thing existed.* Again, I had covered my tracks too well. And, also, if I reappeared out of limbo right here in this city where she was and to save her from the charge, it would tie the two of us together. Shevlin missing, and his lovely wife down here with me? It was a tabloid editor's dream come true, and they'd have a confession out of one of us inside a day.

I was calmer now and my mind was beginning to function, as it always seemed to do eventually when I was in a jam. It was a lot like the way I had felt that day up at the cabin on the lake. After the first shock wore off and I could see that the chips were down and I had to do something, I could think. I was conscious now of this growing clarity, this ability to see all paths at once and the dangers inherent in each one. And the first thing I could see was that I was going to have to get out of this room, and get out of it fast. I *wasn't* safe here; this was probably the most dangerous place in town for me right now. I sprang up from the bed. Why hadn't I seen it before? Someday, I thought, I'm going to realize something like that just a minute too late.

Taking the key out of my pocket, I left it on the dresser. Since she didn't have it with her and they'd know it when they searched her, it had to be here unless I wanted them to know somebody else had been here with her. As for the other things, the clothes and the bags she had bought, there was noth-ing to do but leave them. But no, I thought suddenly. I can't. I can't leave those two bags. I was with her when she bought them and helped her pick them out. The man who sold them to her could probably describe me to the police as easily as he could describe his brother. And since they were after Shevlin, they'd be backtrailing her all over town to see if anybody had seen him with her. I grabbed them up and looked out into the corridor. It was clear, and I slipped out hurriedly, closed the door, and went up the stairs to my room.

That had been close, and I'd probably caught it just in time. They would have her at the station by now. And, since they were after him and since it would be logical to assume that if she were here in town he might be too, there'd be dozens of them shaking down the hotels right this minute. The thing to do was get out of here, and the sooner the better. They'd be here any minute with her picture. Thank God, I thought, we weren't registered together and the hotel people had no reason to connect me with her. Of course, they weren't looking for me, but my description, if they had it, would be one that would stick in the mind, and I couldn't take any chances of hav-ing them begin to wonder just how dead I was.

My bag was already packed. Just for a moment, as I saw it sitting there, the agonizing hell of what-might-have-been and the despair and bitterness came rushing back and hit me. In six more hours, I thought, we would have been on the plane with all the rest of our lives before us. Then I got hold of myself. I couldn't go to pieces that way. I had to keep moving and I had to keep my head. Dragging a hand roughly across my face, I went over to the telephone and called for a boy to come after the bags. There was no use taking the cheap one I'd bought in the drugstore, I thought, and threw it inside the closet and closed the door. I had two more than I'd checked in with as it was.

We went down in the elevator, and as we came out into the lobby I looked guardedly around. There was no one at the desk who looked like a plain-clothes man. I wondered if the clerk would notice the extra bags. The boy took them on out and I settled the bill. There was a cab outside and I got in.

"Where to, chief?" the driver asked. Where? I thought. I had to go somewhere.

"Bus station." I had to get rid of those bags, no matter what I did. We crawled through snarled traffic and heat and blaring horns. The bus station was jammed and sultry, full of a loudspeaker's blasting and the roar of a departing bus. I put the three bags in lockers and stuck the keys in my pocket. All right, I thought, I've cut the trail from her to me to give myself time to think, but where do I go from here?

I pushed through the crowd to the lunch counter and ordered a cup of coffee. What had she told them? That was the question that went through my mind over and over. Everything depended on that, and there wasn't any way I could know. Suppose she had confessed? In spite of the sticky heat I felt the chill between my shoulder blades. And it was possible; I knew it. In her terror and confusion, not even knowing what she had been picked up for, with all of them firing questions at her, who knew what she might blurt out?

But suppose, I thought, trying to pick up the thread of thought I'd had before I realized I had to get out of the hotel, suppose she kept her head and hasn't said anything so far? Then we're safe enough—for the moment. The danger then would lie in the fact that eventually they might wear her down, keep hammering at her until she let something slip, or that eventually, as they kept looking for my body, they might find Shevlin's. That was a very real danger now that Raines had joined in the search, because he wasn't trying to cover anything up, as Buford was. Therefore, I had to get her out of there. But how? Obviously, the only way I could do it was by turning myself in, or coming back to life. And then they would be asking *me* the question, the big one: *Where was Shevlin?*

But wait, I thought. I was very close to it a while ago when I had to run away from the hotel. Suppose I could come back to light in some way that wouldn't indicate I had ever been down here at all or even knew her? They were still looking for me in that swamp, with some faint hope that I was still alive and only hurt and lost. Well, suppose it turned out that I was? They would release her. The charge then wouldn't be worth holding her for. That would take the pressure off her before she broke down and confessed, or let something slip.

The girl brought my coffee. "What's the matter, big boy?" Suddenly I realized she was talking to me.

"Matter?" I asked. "Why?"

She gave me a pert smile. "Well, I don't know, but you just looked so worried and kind of moving your lips like somebody talking to himself."

I've got to stop attracting attention, I thought. "Oh," I said. "It's my wife. She's having a baby."

"Oh." She started to move away. "I hope it's a boy."

"Thanks," I said. Where was I? Oh, yes. Back in the swamp. But if I came back out of there, they would probably dust off that grand jury investigation again, even providing they'd really dropped it. All right, I thought, what of it? A year, two at the most. And even a chance of a suspended sentence. We're young. We could stand it. And it would be a hell of a lot better than what we had staring us in the face right this minute.

I was working on it at top speed now. I could do it. I could get back in there, fake the scalp wound where he had slugged me with the oar, fall in the swamp a few times, wander around all night until I was dirty and bloody and haggard enough, and then start finding my way out, get picked up by some of the searchers, and have a good story ready for them. I could make it stick. But wait, I thought. I've got to get that bag back out of the locker and change clothes somewhere. I've got on the new suit, and I'd have a hell of a time explaining how I bought it while I was lost in a swamp. But that was easy. I could do it in the men's rest room. I put a dime on the counter for the coffee and started to get up, and then the other thought hit me. I sat down.

My hands were tied. I couldn't make a move until I found out what she had said to the police. God, suppose I went back into the swamp, and then, tomorrow morning, when I found my way into one of the searching parties, learned that she had confessed the whole thing! Talk about walking into a trap.... I flinched.

Her story would probably be in the papers. I had to wait for them; there was no other way. I couldn't do a single damned thing now but sweat through the whole, hot, nerve-racking eternity of this afternoon waiting for the story to hit the streets. I looked at my watch. It was twelve-thirty. It would be at least three hours, if it hit the last edition of the afternoon papers, and it might not be in them at all and I'd have to wait until around eight for the morning ones.

But in the meantime there was something else to work on. Was there any way to get word to her to tell her what I was going to try to do so she could hold on and not break down and spill everything after I had started in there?

I thought about it for just a minute. There was one slight chance.

I got up hurriedly and got some change from the cashier at the counter and went over to the bank of pay phones along the wall. I dialed. "Long distance? I want to put in a person-to-person call to a Miss Dianne Weatherford at Bigelow. I don't know the number."

"What is your number, please?"

I told her and waited. It was a slim chance. Would Dinah even be there? She was probably still here in town. And suppose she was home; would she talk to me? I remembered the way she had driven off. I could hear the terse, efficient chatter of the long-lines operators and then somewhere far off a telephone ringing. It went on, while I waited, sweating. "Hello?" It was Dinah. I deposited the coins.

"Hello, Dinah?"

"Yes. Oh, is that you, Ja—?" She caught herself in time and cut it off.

"Yeah," I said. "Look, can you get in touch with Buford? It's important, and I can't call him at the office."

"I will if he's there. He may be still down at the lake."

"Well, look," I said urgently. "Try to get hold of him. Ask him to come to your place and I'll call again exactly an hour from now. Got it?"

"All right." She paused, then went on blandly. "Oh, by the way, I see they caught that awful Shevlin woman. It was on the radio."

"Yes," I said. "I heard it."

"And isn't it funny, too, that the creature was right there in Bayou City? Where you are."

"Yes, isn't it? Remember, I'll call you an hour from now." I hung up. Wait till she sees the picture, I thought. Then she won't have any doubt of it. Well, it couldn't be helped now.

Somehow I sweated out the hour. When I called back Dinah said, "Yes, he's here now. Just a minute."

"Yes?" It was Buford, his voice as impersonal as death.

"Listen. I want you to do something for me," I said, beginning to talk fast and stumbling over myself. "They've just picked up Mrs. Shevlin. I guess you know it by now. And I suppose you're going to have to send a man down to get her. I want him to give her a message."

"Yes? What is it?" he asked coolly.

"Tell her not to worry about anything. I'm coming back."

"I thought so. That's about the way I had it figured. Well, I've got news for you. I can't do anything about your girl friend. We're not claiming her; Raines is. That place was in Blakeman County, as I told you, so now they've issued a warrant for her on suspicion of murder."

"What?" I almost shouted it.

"And another thing. Don't try to come back."

"What do you mean, don't try to come back?" The booth seemed to be shrinking, trying to choke me. "Listen, don't you understand—"

"The thing I understand is that we had an agreement and I carried out my end of it. I didn't know then that I was just financing your expedition, but I'm satisfied with it because so far it's worked. And if you come back, it won't. The minute you show up, everything'll hit the fan. I don't like to be double-crossed, so I'm telling you to stay away. Do we understand each other?"

I understood him, all right. He was warning me. He knew now what had actually happened up there in the swamp, or he was pretty sure of it, but nothing interested him except that two-bit graft investigation. She could go to the chair for all he cared, so long as he was all right. My mind grew quite cold and clear and I no longer shouted.

"I'm coming back," I said. "Don't get in my way." I hung up the receiver and walked out.

But I still couldn't go until I knew what she had told the police. It was going to be dangerous enough going in there without being able to get word to her, and having Buford trying to stop me, but it would be simple suicide if she'd confessed and I didn't know it.

I never did know afterward where I was that afternoon. It was a blur of hot streets and a million faceless people going past while time ran down and stopped like a clock no one had thought to wind. And then somewhere, later, with the sun slanting obliquely through the east-west streets and brazen on the shop windows, I heard the newsboys shouting, "Read about Mrs. Shevlin. All about Mrs. Shevlin."

I bought one and ducked inside a bar. There was another picture of her, but it was the caption I was looking for. "DENIES CHARGE." I breathed again. Thank God, I thought. She kept her head. Forgetting the beer I had ordered, I tore into the story, trying to absorb it all at once.

MARSHALL NOT DEAD—MRS. SHEVLIN

Mrs. Roger Shevlin, beautiful young wife of the man sought in the disappearance and suspected murder of J. B. Marshall, Devers County officer, denied today in a statement to police, who arrested her in a beauty shop in downtown Bayou City, that her husband had killed Marshall. According to Mrs. Shevlin, who was near collapse in the city jail following her arrest, her husband returned for her after he had overpowered the officer and escaped while the two men were on their way out of the swamp, telling her he had merely tied Marshall up with the boat's anchor rope, knowing he would eventually work free and get back to town. The boat had been hidden to prevent Marshall's finding it, to give the Shevlins more time to make good their escape.

If only they don't break her down before I can get there, I thought desperately. If she cracks.... But I didn't have time to sit and think about it. Paying for the beer, I got up and took a taxi back to the bus station, got the bag out of the locker, and changed back into the old suit in the rest room. Taking out the plane ticket and the watch so there'd be nothing in it by which they could ever connect me with Bayou City, I shoved the bag back into another locker and left it.

I can't take the bus, I thought. Somebody might see me getting off at Colston. Too many people know me there. I've got to get back into that swamp the same way I got out—without being seen. And I haven't got time to horse around with freight trains.

Thirty minutes later I was weaving through traffic in the outskirts of the city, headed toward Colston in a stolen car. It had been easy. I just walked up the street until I saw a woman park and leave the keys in the car. When she went inside a store I got in and drove off. Nothing was going to stop me any more.

Chapter Twenty-four

I stopped once and bought a flashlight in a drugstore. I'd need it, trying to get around in that swamp at night, and at dawn I could throw it in the lake. I worked it out in my mind as I drove, staying just under the speed limit in spite of the impatience riding me. I couldn't leave the car up there where I had come out of the swamp before, on the deserted country road. It would be picked up eventually, and the state troopers might begin to wonder why somebody would steal a car in Bayou City, drive it to a place like that, and leave it, forty miles from anywhere. But if I wrecked it on the main highway, on the opposite side of the bottom, it would look all right.

It was dusk when I went through Colston, and nearly nine by the time I had passed the store and the boat place on the dam at the south end of the lake. The highway swung and turned north again, along the west side of the bottom. Fifteen miles up, and only three or four miles outside of town, it swung sharply left again, away from the bottom, and here was where I crashed it by the simple method of not making the turn. I had slowed to about twenty-five, and as I went down off the roadbed and through the ditch I took out a section of fence, and then finally came to rest without much damage up against a tree. I picked up the flashlight and started out through the pines. Joy-riding kids, they'd say.

It was a still, sultry night, with no moon but a faint light from the stars. As soon as I was in the timber, however, it was black, and I could see nothing at all. I snapped on the flashlight and started up over the ridge, leaving no tracks in the dense carpet of pine needles. When I came out on top I stopped and looked at my watch. It was nine-thirty.

If I went straight out across the bottom now, I'd hit the lake about five miles below Shevlin's cabin. But I wanted to go in at least five miles above it, right into the swamp country itself. The best thing to do, then, was to go north here along the high ground for about ten miles and then swing down off the ridge.

It was fairly open up here in the pines and I made good time. At a little before one in the morning I figured I had come far enough, and turned right, going downhill. Before long the sand and pines gave way to big oaks and heavy underbrush. Inside an hour I was drenched with sweat and my clothes were badly torn. I ran into a wide marshy area where the mud and water were up to my knees, and to make matters worse, in the middle of it there was a place a quarter mile wide where a cyclone had gone through years ago. Big trees were piled like spilled matches in a nightmare confusion of tree trunks, limbs, and vines. I scrambled over, crawled under, and fought my way through the muck. Once, clambering along the trunk of a big windfall stacked crisscross above another, I slipped in my muddy shoes and fell into the tangle of big limbs below me, laying open a gash on my head and almost knocking myself out. I scrambled up, cursing and wiping blood out of my face, and then grinned sourly as it occurred to me it wouldn't be necessary now to fake any signs of violence. I'd look as if Shevlin had worked me over with a ball bat.

It was nearly four when I hit the first sizable channel of open water. I flashed the light out across it, saw that I was going to have to swim now, and stopped to light a cigarette. There wasn't any necessity for swimming it before dawn, which would be in about an hour. I sat down against a tree and went over it in my mind. This was— What day was it, anyway? Time had been alternately stretched and compressed for so long I didn't even know. Let's see, I thought, I went into the lake Wednesday morning. That night at midnight I was in Bayou City. The next afternoon, then, when the story first broke, would have been Thursday. Then today was Friday. No, I corrected myself, it's almost daylight Saturday morning. Then I've been lost in here for three nights and two days, assuming that I tell them it wasn't until very late Wednesday that I arrested Shevlin. It had taken me nearly all day to find his house, and I didn't get started out with him until nearly sunset. That would make his being able to jump me and get away a lot more plausible, anyway; it'd naturally be easier in the dark.

He'd banged me with the oar, and when I came around I was in the bottom of the boat tied up like a pig with the anchor rope. It was dark and I was down there where I couldn't see anything anyway, so I had no idea where he took me except that we went a long way. He put me ashore somewhere hours later, with my hands still tied, but not very tightly, and I'd managed to get them worked loose before daylight. The only thing, though, was that I was lost. I kept looking for the lake, and there wasn't any; there was nothing but a thousand small sloughs and the marsh and flooded areas. After a while I'd run across some tracks and started following them, thinking somebody else was up here and I might find a cabin, and then I had lost my head completely when I found I was going in circles and that they were my own. They wouldn't have any reason to doubt it; at least one man I knew of had been lost up here and never had found his way out. I shivered, thinking about it. I was taking a long chance. And not only of getting lost, either, I thought. *Suppose they broke her down while I was in here?*

I shook it off with rough impatience. It was just a chance I had to take. I lighted another cigarette, knowing that as soon as I swam the slough they'd be ruined anyway and I might as well use them up. Would I look as if I'd been lost up here for nearly seventy-two hours? Yes, there wasn't much doubt that I'd look the part. My clothes were in ruin already, ripped and sweat-soaked and bloody from the cut on my head. Of course, I had shaved on Thursday morning, but I never had got around to it on Friday and would have a forty-eight-hour growth of beard, ugly enough to convince anybody. All I had to do now was fight my way down through the swamp until I ran into some of the searchers. They would probably have a camp set up somewhere down there below and be firing guns, still hoping to guide me in. I listened now, but there was no sound except that of the frogs.

The darkness was beginning to fade now and I could see the weed-choked dark water in front of me. I stood up, threw the flashlight out into the water, and waded in. Mud sucked at my feet and I pushed forward and started swimming. It was only a few strokes to the other side, where I climbed out and began beating my way through the brush again. Inside an hour I had lost track of the number of times I had to swim. I made no effort to turn aside when open water blocked my path, for if I didn't move in a straight line I wouldn't get out of here. When the sun came up I was able to check my direction, going due south with it on my left. My progress was agonizingly slow and the cut place on my head began to throb. Vines tripped me and I fell, and at times I had to wade for hundreds of yards through water and mud up to my waist. Most of the channels I had to swim were matted with pads, and the long, twining underwater stems wound around my arms and legs and threatened to pull me under. There was no way to know what time it was any more, for my watch was long since drowned and stopped, but the sun was climbing higher. As midday approached it was harder and harder to tell direction, for the sun was almost directly overhead.

Noon came and went and I was conscious now of beginning to weaken from hunger. I'd eaten nothing since Thursday night, and the back-breaking struggle and the heat were beginning to wear me down. Suddenly I was again in the midst of the piled windrow of down timber where the tornado had left its path through the swamp, and for a while my mind was black with panic. I was lost. I was going in circles and had come back to the place I had fought my way through nearly twelve hours before. Collapsing against the trunk of an uprooted tree, I fought to get hold of myself. It couldn't be the same one. Tornadoes play leap-frog through a place like this, I told myself desperately, and this is another one. It had to be. I'd been going steadily south for hours. But how did I *know* I was going south? Part of the time the sun had been invisible down here in the timber, and for the past two hours it had been so nearly overhead it was impossible to tell direction from it.

And why didn't I hear any guns? There hadn't been a sound all morning except that of my own desperate plunging through the swamp. If I'd been going in a straight line for all that time, I should be somewhere near Shevlin's cabin and the main channel of the lake itself, and there would almost certainly be a camp set up there for the searchers. I listened now, trying to hush the sobbing sound of my breathing, and heard nothing but the infinite silence of the swamp.

I don't know where I am, I thought wildly. I'll never get out of here. And now, suddenly, I was conscious of the way time was flying past. Every minute of it they would be working on her, firing questions at her, trying to wear her down, and if she broke I'd be better off if I *did* die in here. I sprang to my feet and tried to run, crazily, the panic washing over me. Again I fell, breaking open the cut on my head. I got up, tearing ahead. Then, somehow, I was past the windfall area, and I plunged headlong into the underbrush. Vines caught me and I collapsed, struggling weakly, like a fly in a spider web, and sank to my knees and fell.

There was no knowing how long I lay there. Sanity gradually returned, and I began to be conscious of my surroundings and capable of rational thought. Mosquitoes buzzed about my face in clouds, and in the hot, humid stillness among the leaves and vines I was bathed in sweat. Thin shafts of sunlight probed through the dense foliage overhead, and as I watched them I could see they were slanting a little as the sun wheeled over into the west. I've got to keep my head, I thought. If I lose it once more I'll be done. Twenty-four hours have gone by now since they arrested her, and if I don't find my way out pretty soon she'll think I've run and deserted her and she'll break. I've got to get up and start in a straight line again, going south.

I started again, moving with the shafts of sunlight slanting across my eyes from right to left. Time ran on, like an endless belt, with no beginning and no end and nothing to mark the hours. I noticed I was beginning to fall sometimes now when nothing had tripped me, and wondered if the two blows on the head had affected me that much. No, I thought dizzily, it's only fatigue, and the weakness of hunger. Five miles through that mud and water and tangle of underbrush were the equivalent of fifty on solid ground, and there was no way of knowing how many miles I had actually walked. At times it seemed as if I were an insect trying to fight its way through a sodden sponge, pressing inward just so far and then being thrown relentlessly back. The swamp gave way before me, swallowed me up, and then closed behind, all of it looking so much alike there was no way of knowing whether I went ahead or was merely raising and lowering my dead-weary legs in some sort of slow-motion and idiotic dance in an endless dream. I began to think of her nearly all the time, forgetting for long stretches to watch the sun or the direction in which the shafts slanted through the leaves. We lay side by side on the ground in mottled shade, whispering to each other; then she was smiling at me, radiant and lovely in her new clothes, while I caught her arms to look at her. I stopped and shook my head, running a hand across my face and seeing it come away covered with dirt and blood. Stop it, I thought. Stop it! Which way was south?

And then, strangely, the forest was more open. Immense oaks towered overhead and the brush was thinning out. The ground here was dry and firm underfoot and walking was easier. I caught a glint of sunlit water off to the right, shining through the trees, and tried to run toward it, but I was too weak and fell again. When I got to my feet I staggered on toward it, the view opening up, and then I knew I had reached the lake. A hundred yards of open water stretched out past me, disappearing around a bend up to my right, and full of big weed beds along the other shore. I looked down at my feet and saw the remains of a campfire, but knew it was an old one even before I knelt frenziedly and ran my hands into the ashes. But somebody had been here! I could find them!

But where were they? Where was the sound of guns? I stared wildly around in the little open glade, so peaceful in the sunlight of late afternoon, and then, suddenly, I began to have the awful feeling that it was somehow familiar. I knew now. The campfire was my own. This was where I had camped on that first trip up here, when I had met her, and there was where the bedroll had lain and I had caught her hand and she had pulled away from me, crying, to run out toward the lake. I was back to where I had started, but now she was in jail and he was dead and I was the one who had killed him. I was conscious of the horrible sensation that I wasn't just walking in circles in space and time, but that I was actually swinging around the steep black sides of some enormous whirl-pool and sliding always toward the center.

But there is a way out, I thought agonizingly. There's always a way out. All I had to do was locate the searching parties and she would be freed when word was flashed that I had been found. But where were they? I had thought the lake would be busy with motorboats and the sound of guns being fired at intervals throughout the day and night, and here was only the same dead, lost silence I had been fighting through all day. Had they given up? Would I ever get out of here in time, before she collapsed and told them?

And then I heard it—not gunfire, but a motor starting. It was up there to the right, around the bend, sudden, staccato, and very near, so similar to the way I had heard his motor start that morning a long time ago that I was conscious again of that feeling of going around and around in some tightening and deadly spiral. Immediately after it I heard another start, and they were coming nearer. I looked up and saw them appearing around the bend, and there were not two boats, but three. The first had two white-hatted men in it, the second was being towed and was empty, and the one in the rear held two.

I've found them, I thought wildly. Shouting and waving my arms, I ran across the small open glade and down to the water's edge. They had seen me now, and I watched the boats change course a little to swing in toward the bank. I had made it, and in a little while word would be going out that I had been found alive, and she would be freed. The boats were drawing nearer. I didn't know either of the men in the front boat, but I saw suddenly that Buford was one of the two in the other one.

Instead of waving, he was swinging around in the seat with something extended in his hands. I saw the glint, then, of sunlight on steel and recognized it as a rifle, the barrel suddenly foreshortening into nothing as he brought it into line. He was directly behind the boat being towed, and even as I was throwing myself down and back in the awful realization that he was going to shoot, I saw that the second boat was carrying Shevlin.

He shot after I was on the ground and rolling. Mud exploded in my face and then I heard the crack of the rifle almost at the same time because he was so near. Before the sound had even died I was on my feet, knowing somehow that I had to get up and over the bank while he was working the bolt or I would never move from there alive. And then I was in the trees, hurtling zigzag through them while the gun cracked again. They had cut the motors and in another few seconds they would be on the bank themselves and chasing me.

I didn't know where I ran, or how far. There was just the pain in my chest and the crying sound from my open mouth as it gulped for air, and the only thing my mind could hold was the picture of that long, canvas-wrapped bundle like an old rolled-up rug lying in the bottom of the second boat. After a while I fell, unable to move, and lay there in the brush trying to still the tortured sound of my breathing enough to listen. There was no sound behind me now.

Chapter Twenty-five

I don't know how long I lay there on the ground with nothing but the numbness and the terror in my mind. We were whipped now, and this was the end. They already had her, and I was trapped. They had found him; they knew I had killed him and I was a fugitive with no plan of escape and nothing ahead but futile and senseless flight. Flight? I thought. To where? I looked down at my clothes, at the utter ruin that I had deliberately sought, and thought of the way I would look if I did get out of the swamp. Bearded, bloody, mud-caked, I wouldn't have a chance. And if Buford got to me first, he'd kill me. I knew that now. He didn't want me arrested.

Once, though I was not sure, I thought I heard an outboard motor start, far away across the bottom. One of them would go on down the lake to take the body in and get to the telephone. The other three would stay here and keep up the search until they began to pile in here with the dogs sometime late tonight. They'd call in the state police cars and swear in a bunch of special deputies to patrol the roads on both sides of the swamp, and everything moving out there would be searched. And I couldn't stay in here because in another few hours without food or rest I'd be too weak to move.

And what of her? I thought. What will it be like with her when they bring the news that he's been found? Or was that how they had found him? Had she broken already and told them? But what difference did it make now how they'd done it? It was done, and we were trapped.

We would have been in San Francisco now.... I caught myself up, almost savagely, knowing I had to keep away from that or I'd lose my mind. The sun was setting now, and I wondered if, where she was, she could see even a little reflection of it along a wall. This was what I had done to her. I was going to give her everything, and now this was what it was. I had to get up, to move, to do something to shut it out of my mind. Jumping to my feet, I started walking, aimlessly at first, and then, as some strange compulsion began to take hold of me, swinging south and then west in a large circle back toward the lake.

It was growing darker here in the timber and I began to walk faster. The direction I was going at least made a little sense. Since I was on this side of the lake and they would expect me to run east and try to get out to the railroad and catch a freight, it would be better to move west and get across the lake. Suddenly, then, I knew where I was headed. I had about one chance in a thousand of getting there, but I was going toward Dinah's. There was no use in trying to get home for some more clothes and a car; they'd be watching the house just on the chance I might try it. But maybe to Dinah's apartment.... I wanted to break into a run.

Just at dusk I came out on the bank of the lake a mile or two below where the boats had been. It was breathtakingly beautiful, like dark glass, with the wall of the trees a black silhouette against the sunset afterglow along the other shore, and as I came up I saw a big, spreading ring where a bass had risen, out among the snags. Often when I had been fishing and left the lake just at dusk like this, full of its immense and lonely quiet, I had wondered what it would be like to know that I would never see it again, and now that I was looking at it for probably the last time I was conscious of nothing except that I did not want to think about it.

I walked deliberately out into it, and as the water rose to my waist I started to swim. Halfway across I began to wonder if I would make it, exhausted as I was to the point of collapse and weighted with the shoes and clothes, but somehow I kept going. I fought my way through fifty yards of the entangling pads on the other shore and climbed gasping onto the bank. It was dark now, completely black among the trees.

I had to go straight ahead, but how? Five or six miles due west I would begin to hit the rising ground and the pines, but all the intervening distance was flat, unvarying bottom country full of sloughs and heavily timbered, with no landmarks and only glimpses of the stars. With my back against the lake shore and facing the direction in which I wanted to go, I studied the sky a moment to line up the few constellations I knew, then plunged into the darkness. I lost track of the number of times I fell and the number of sloughs I waded and swam and finally just wallowed through. I bumped into trees and entangled myself in vines, and each time I plunged to the ground it was more difficult to rise again. A dreamy lassitude would begin to flow over me like warm water and I would want to lie there in the hope that if I slept and then awoke the whole horrible dream would be gone and I would open my eyes to find that we were on the plane to San Francisco and were circling over the bay ready to land in the early dawn. Then the terror would come sweeping back and with it the bitter knowledge that if I did not get out of here before daylight I was finished, and I would force myself to rise and go staggering on. By daybreak they would have the dogs in here and I would no longer be able to hide, and of course I couldn't get across the highway and into town except very late at night, if I could at all.

It was a dream at first, and then a nightmare, and at last an eternal and monotonous black hell without fires or light where I was doomed to go on staggering forward and forever falling. After a while I began to believe I was losing my mind, because for long periods she would be moving along beside me. Once I turned and called her name aloud. The sudden sound of my voice in the silence of the forest shocked me into consciousness of what I had done, and terror took hold of me again and I thought for a moment I would cry out and run.

Time had no meaning now. It might have been an hour since I had left the lake and it might have been five. I could have covered four miles, or I could be walking in circles and be almost back there again. But then, suddenly, when I fell again I felt the dry, aromatic slickness of pine needles under my face and threw my hands about wildly, grasping at them. I had come out of the bottom and was beginning to mount the ridge.

An almost insane urgency took hold of me and I wanted to run. I had come this far, across that black maze of bottom, and suppose now that daylight should catch me before I got to Dinah's? The difficult part, the almost impossible part, lay behind, but ahead was all the danger. I had to get into town, where everybody knew me, and being seen by anyone would mean disaster. After I got up on the ridge in the fairly open pines I could make better time, and before long I began to see the winking of lights below me and knew I had reached the highway. I turned and plunged downhill.

What time was it? That was the only thing in my mind now. I still had nearly four miles to go to get into town, and then I had to get around it, skirting the back streets and alleys, and if daybreak caught me I was done for. There were very few cars on the road now and I took a chance on walking along the pavement, rather than out in the trees, to make better time. When I would see a car ahead or behind I would run into the roadside bushes and hide until it had gone past. Then I would come back out onto the road, feeling the urgency driving me, and start hurrying again, trotting and then walking and then trotting, my legs numb and without any feeling now that they were even mine. I had been walking for so long I couldn't stop. I had the insane feeling that if I fell down and went to sleep my legs would keep right on moving because I no longer knew how to turn them off.

I turned and looked behind me, toward the east, searching for the telltale fading, the beginning of the coral flush I had watched so many times from duck blinds and fishing boats. It was still as dark as ever there, but even the thought of dawn drove me forward desperately. A car topped the slight rise ahead and the sudden, searching lights were almost upon me before I could run and plunge down off the road. I've got to get there first; I've got to beat the daylight. It ran through my mind in a sort of endless chant I couldn't turn off any more than I could the walking movement of my legs. A gun, a car, these were the things I had to have. She had a whole roomful of guns and the fastest car in town.

The old familiar streets were quiet, the street lamps at the corners the only pools of light. I swung left, keeping to the outskirts and slipping along the alleys, feeling my skin crawl and prickle with sudden cold at the barking of a dog or the sound of a car somewhere on another street. I wanted to run. I was naked, skinless, a light-tortured organism fleeing toward the dark. It was less than a dozen blocks now. Ten more. Nine. I wanted to stop counting them and couldn't. At any one of them a car might swing around a corner, its lights flashing....

I cut through one more alley and I was on Georgia Street and broke into a run. The windows of her apartment were dark. Suppose she wasn't there? She must be. She had to be. She was home when I telephoned this afternoon. No, that was yesterday. It wasn't even yesterday—it was the day before, be-cause now it was almost dawn on Sunday. I ran up the walk and pressed the bell, waiting, listening for the sound of movement or of footsteps and hear-ing only the pounding of blood in my ears.

I pushed the bell again, and then I heard it. Someone was coming quietly down the stairs. The door opened a crack, there was a sharp gasp, and then she was throwing it back and reaching out for me. She led me hurriedly up the dark stairway, still holding me by the arm. There was light in the hallway, coming from the open bedroom door, and now she turned and stared at me, seeing the sodden ruin of my clothing and the blood across my face.

"Jack!" she whispered frantically. "Jack! What have they done to you?"

She had on her nightgown and robe and the coppery hair was tousled from the pillow, but I could see she hadn't been asleep. "Thank God you've come. I've been praying.... I've been praying all night! Ever since I heard. But you've been hurt!"

"No," I said. "It's nothing. I fell." I swayed and almost fell now, and leaned against the wall. The whole apartment seemed to be swinging in that big whirlpool which had caught me and I wanted to hold onto something.

Then she had hold of me again, towing me down the hall. We were in the bathroom and she was tugging at my coat and then unlacing the mud-caked shoes. "We'll leave them right here," she was saying. "Right here where he'll see them and know. I want him to know, damn him." What was she talking about? I wanted to ask her what time it was, but she was busy at the shirt and I was too numb for thought. Then I could hear the shower blasting and she was shoving me into it. I was naked, and it had never occurred to me, and probably not to her, that there was anything odd about her undressing me and pushing me into the streaming water.

"Hot," she said. "As hot as you can stand it, and then cold." The water beat down and I could feel the dirt and caked blood and sweat going away and my nerves unwinding, and then I was conscious that she had disappeared. She was back in a minute, holding a glass in her hand. "Drink this," she said. She turned her head as I stepped from under the water. I took the glass and drained it in three large swallows. It burned going down and exploded into warmth and life in my empty stomach.

I had turned off the water and was rubbing myself with a towel. She re-turned in a minute and handed me a pair of shorts around the partition of the shower stall. "When you get them on, come outside and we'll get the other things."

I slipped them on and went out and looked at my face in the mirror as at somebody I'd never seen before. It was haggard and sunken-cheeked, black with beard, and the cut place on my head was ugly, inflamed and still encrusted with clotted blood. I went into the bedroom and she was taking clothes out of a suitcase on the bed. "They're his," she said. "He keeps this bag here for trips to the city."

Then she was gone again. I couldn't keep up with her. I heard something rattling in the kitchen and then she came back for me once more, while I was putting on the shoes. She had me by the arm and was seating me at the table. While I was eating the piece of cold steak and drinking the milk she pulled up a chair and sat down, not across from me but just around the corner of the table at my left. She had her hand on my wrist and was talking, very fast.

Her voice was quiet, but still full of that tremendous urgency which seemed to have hold of her now as well as of me. "I've done nothing but think about it since I heard the news, about nine o'clock. Just think about it, and pray you'd come, that you could get here. And now you have!"

"Wait," I interrupted. What was she talking about? And through all the numbness I was conscious there was something I had to know. "How did they find him? How did they know?"

"Find him? Oh. All I heard was what was on the radio. Something about an outboard motor they couldn't find. He was supposed to be repairing it for the man down there at the store, and it wasn't there. So they got to thinking about some oil that was on the lake."

I guess it doesn't matter now, I thought. There wasn't any way I could have known the motor wasn't his. It just wasn't meant to be. That had ruined it, that and not seeing the picture of her sitting there in front of my face, but what good was there in torturing myself with it now?

Dinah was still going on, her eyes shining, touching me with her fingers. The white, gleaming kitchen and this lovely copper-haired figurine of a girl with her unstoppable torrent of speech were all mixed up now in the endless movement of the whirlpool. What was she talking about?

"I even went down and had the car serviced and filled with gasoline. We won't have to stop at all for over two hundred miles. My clothes are packed and I've got over two thousand dollars in cash in my bag, and I took the money out of your wet suit, too. We'll leave your old wet clothes right there where he'll see them, and the muddy shoes, and he'll know. Don't you see, Jack? He can't say anything, or tell anybody. He'll know you're gone and that I've gone with you and he can't do anything about it and he'll have to cover up for us, because he's afraid to have you arrested. He was going to try to kill you in that swamp if you came back. And I would have killed him, if he had. And now you're here and we can go, and he's still down there looking for you."

I began to get it, even through the numbness in my mind.

"Everybody is looking for you. They've called in the state police and all the roads around the lake are blocked, but we can get through the other way, going north. You'll be in the back, in the luggage compartment, anyway. I took out the spare tire and put in a bunch of blankets to make a bed. It's big. I measured it. I got in it myself, thinking: When I'm standing up, the top of my head is just under Jack's chin. It's plenty large enough for you. I even put in a pillow."

I had stopped eating. I stared at her. She had everything figured out, and for the first time I began to realize what a mind there was behind that lovely and reckless face.

"Nobody will ever know except Buford, and he won't talk. He can't. The rest of them will think you died in the swamp. We'll go on to southern California, with you traveling all the way in the luggage compartment and staying at night in tourist cabins. I'll cut your hair short, a crew cut, so the curl doesn't show. And you'll grow a mustache. They'll never find us. Think how it'll be, Jack! Just the two of us. I've been crazy all night, just praying to God to let you get here."

It would work. It would work perfectly. I could see it would. I could get in there in the back of the car and be out of the state before dark tonight. Buford's hands would be tied and he wouldn't even report it; there'd be no description of the car, or anything. I knew she was a little wrong about one thing, about their thinking I had died in the swamp, for the dogs would tell them I'd got out of it. But even then they'd never know where I'd gone; the trail would end at the highway, for the dogs couldn't follow me through all that oily smell and gasoline. I would just disappear into the air. Nobody had seen me get here to this place, and nobody would see me leave. It was perfect, all of it, and this girl was tremendous, this flame-haired toy with the brain of Machiavelli. I sat there looking at it for a whole minute, at the beauty of it, thinking that two hours ago I was whipped, without a chance in the world, and now escape was right here in my hand. All I had to do was get in the car with this girl and go.

Not with this girl, or any other girl, to anywhere, I thought. I knew what had brought me up out of that lake bottom, and it wasn't this.

She had both hands on my arm again, still looking at my face and talking. "It'll take me only a minute to dress, Jack. You wait here, while I change."

I looked at her. "I'm not going, Dinah."

"What?" She was staring, open-mouthed.

It didn't make any difference. She couldn't stop me. Nothing could, any more. "I'm not going with you. I want your car, and a gun. I'm going after Doris Shevlin."

Chapter Twenty-six

"Jack! Please! For the love of God, listen to me!" She had me by the arm, pulling at my sleeve. I had run into the living room and was in front of the gun case, snatching up an automatic.

"Where's the ammunition for this?" I asked. Then I saw it, and jerked out the clip to load it. "What time is it?"

"They'll kill you!" she cried out, paying no attention to my question. I shoved the gun in my pocket and grabbed her wrist to look at the watch. It was ten minutes to four. I had a little over an hour until daylight. But I still had to get the car keys from her. Would she give them to me? I thought wildly. I didn't want to have to take them away from her, but I would if I had to.

"Give me the keys, Dinah!" I said. "I've got to have that car."

She was around in front of me now, grabbing at my shirt. "Listen, Jack! Please listen to me. Oh, God, isn't there any way I can make you understand? Haven't you heard what I've been telling you? I can take you away, where they'll never find you. I want you, Jack! I want you to go with me. I'll take care of you. I'll hide you."

"Dinah! The keys." I caught her arms.

"I'll watch out for you. We'll go anywhere you say! What do you want with her? What kind of woman is she for you? Don't you know that she confessed tonight, after they got her back to Harrisville?"

Suddenly she let go my shirt and became deadly calm. "We're too wild to use our heads. We've got to stop it. I don't think you understand, and I want you to be perfectly quiet while I tell you. I love you. And I can take you out of here. You know that, don't you?"

"Yes," I said.

"And if you try to take her out of that jail in Harrisville they'll kill you. And even if you got her out, you know what would happen, don't you?"

"Yes," I said again. Somehow, in all the mad urgency of it, there was enough sense left in me to know that she was right.

"They'll have every road blocked. They've got radio cars all around that lake, and they'd be swinging out and onto every road in this end of the state in a matter of minutes. You'd be trapped. Now, will you listen to me?"

We were both silent for a minute, staring at each other. Somehow I was as calm as she was now and I understood everything she had said, and I knew that none of it made any difference at all. "Where are the keys, Dinah?"

She dropped her head and turned away from me. "They're in my purse. In the bedroom." She walked over and sat down in a big armchair, not looking at me any more or saying anything.

I ran out and across the hall to the bedroom and found the purse on a dresser. I took out the keys and the roll of wet bills that had been in my suit. Catching a glimpse of my face again in the mirror, I suddenly remembered I should have shaved, but there wasn't time for it now. I pawed hurriedly through Buford's bag, however, and found the razor and some shaving soap, and stuck them in my pocket. One of his big hats was lying on a chest, and I snatched it up and put it on. It would hide the ugly cut.

I came back across the hall and she hadn't moved. "I'm sorry about the car, Dinah," I said.

"Yes. Isn't it too bad about the car?" She turned away and put her head down on her arms.

I went down the stairs and backed the Lincoln out of the garage.

Time was a burning fuse. It was twenty-eight miles to Harrisville and I made it in twenty-five minutes by the clock on the dash. There were no patrol cars on the road, and I knew they were all back there covering the roads on both sides of the lake. Raines and all his deputies would be down there. In the wilderness of the irresistible compulsion that had hold of me now there was some part of my mind still calm and thinking about it. There shouldn't be anybody there except the jailer himself.

I stopped the car right in front of the entrance and got out. It was still dark, and the glaring pool of light from a street lamp was shiny against the leaves of the trees along the street. In one of the windows of the jail a Negro was singing, an insane dirge with something about the Lawd over and over.

I went up and knocked on the door. It opened a little and I shoved my way in. He was alone in the office, a lank, sandy-haired man of about forty-five with a lean, sour face, and tough eyes with a little yellow in them like a goat's. He was wearing wide police-type suspenders to hold up his seersucker pants, but had taken off his shirt on account of the heat.

"I want Mrs. Shevlin," I said. "Open it up." I nodded toward the steel-barred door in the back of the office.

He looked at me, and I could see he knew who I was. "Go to hell," he said.

I saw the ring of keys on his desk, next to the detective magazine he had been reading. "Open it up," I said. "What cell is she in?"

"You can go to hell," he said again. He had been sidling a little toward the desk, and suddenly he lunged for the open drawer. I hit him over the eye with the flat of the gun barrel and he doubled up on the desk. Yanking him erect, I shook him, and then threw him back against the wall. "Get smart," I said. I tossed the keys to him and he opened the door.

He was taking too much time. I shoved him in the back and he snapped out of it. Some of the prisoners had waked up by this time and they began to yell, thinking it was a lynching. We came to her cell and she had been sitting on the side of the bunk. She looked up and saw me. "Jack!" she screamed, and while he was fumbling with the lock I saw her slide to the floor. I wanted to hit him again, but by that time he had it open.

"You won't get away with this, Marshall," he said. I pushed him and he slammed into the wall and lay on the floor, moaning a little.

I knelt down beside her, wanting to gather her up and kiss her until she came around, but feeling time running past us like a millrace. I turned her over very gently. She still had on the white suit she had bought, but it was wrinkled and soiled, and didn't look cool any more. Her face was waxen white and the lashes were dark and very long, almost unreal against her cheek. I wondered if I had strength left to pick her up.

Somehow I got her up and went out and slammed the door shut. Turning the key in it, I hurried along the cell block and back out through the office. There was still no one in the street. As we went under the glaring light I looked down at her. Her head was tilted back, the face very still and white, with the long dark hair swinging free. I couldn't help it. I bent my head and kissed her on the throat.

I started to slide her into the seat, and then suddenly thought of something. What was it Dinah had said about the bed she'd made in the back? That would be perfect. There would be a lot less chance of our being spotted with just me alone up here than with both of us. I put her down temporarily in the seat while I reached for the keys to unlock the trunk. Then I noticed I was still carrying the jailer's key ring in my hand. I threw it out into the street and went around to the back, and unlocked the trunk and raised it. She went into it perfectly, curled up like a child with her head on the pillow. But suppose she wakes up there in the dark, I thought. I ran back to the front and looked in the glove compartment. There was a flashlight, as I had hoped, and I snapped it on and put it down beside her on the blankets. She'll know where she is, I thought.

I didn't want to leave her. But it's only for a little while, I thought. As soon as we're out of the worst of the danger area I'll pull off onto a side road somewhere, by a little creek, and she can get out and I'll shave myself. I put the shell down and went back and lifted the back seat up, pulled it out a little. Feeling back with my hand, I could see there was plenty of opening for air to get through, and with the shell closed the carbon monoxide from the exhaust couldn't back up on her.

I jumped into the seat, and then discovered I had left the keys in the lock of the trunk. I was getting jittery with the hurry now. There still wasn't anyone in the street and it was growing light. I ran back, snatched them out, and climbed in. It had been too easy, and I was scared.

Take it easy, I thought. Keep your head. The worst is over. They'll discover it in a little while, but the jailer didn't see the car and they'll have no description of it. I hit the starter and had just got out from under the street light when the other car pulled into the street behind us. For an instant the head-lights washed across us, glaring in the mirror, then they went out. He had stopped. Fighting the terror, I went on, picking up speed without gunning it. Just before I turned the corner I looked back. A man had gotten under the street light and was walking up the steps of the jail.

He didn't pay any attention to the car, I told myself. Sweat was greasy on my face as I swung around another corner and went up through the deserted streets in the middle of town, headed for the highway going north. When I passed the city limits I was doing sixty and gaining speed. The road dipped down in a long grade, across a valley two or three miles wide, and over the hill on the other side. Darkness was fading, with the sky growing pink over to the east, as we shot across the valley and started up the hill. They won't know which road we took, I thought. There are four of them out of town. Just before we topped the hill I looked back and the road was empty.

It was thirty miles to Woodley. That was a highway junction too, and if we got past it before they got the alarm on the air, the chances were against their having all the roads blocked. They wouldn't have enough cars. In a few min-utes I shot another look behind me and felt the terror again. Headlights had just topped a hill, far back. I hadn't passed anybody, and if a car was over-hauling us at this speed it was chasing us. It was nearly full daylight now, and I cut the headlights as we went over another rise and slowed to swing into a county road running west. At the first crossroad I turned south. About fif-teen miles down there it should bisect the highway running west from Har-risville. It did, but just as I approached I saw a patrol car go careening past, headed west. I'll be behind him, I thought desperately, and they're going to plug it somewhere up ahead. When he was out of sight I shot across the high-way, still roaring south on the secondary road.

I could feel the panic closing in. They were plugging them fast now, too fast. North was shut off, and west was being cut. About thirty miles south I'd hit the east-west highway out of Bigelow, but could I get west on that one now? They were turning me inward in a big circle, and again I had that aw-ful sensation of going around and around in a big whirlpool and sliding toward the center. I slammed around a turn and was nearly on top of a farmer in an old Ford. He was in the center of the road, and I swung down into the ditch and clawed my way back up just before I hit a culvert. The sun was up now, and I could feel it burning the side of my face. Everything looked unreal, like an impressionistic painting; all the farmhouses and barns too sharp-angled and light-struck, so they hurt the eye, and then suddenly I thought with amaze-ment that it was Sunday morning and people would be going to church and that sometime before long I was going to unwind like a broken clock spring because I couldn't remember what it was like to sleep.

The last highway going west was the one out of Bigelow. I made the turn, throwing gravel across the pavement, and then hit the brakes. A half mile up ahead a patrol car waited, sitting beside the road. I shot into reverse, swung, and was going east before he could get turned around. We were trapped now. No, I thought wildly, maybe not. It may be wide open to the east and south, because all these cars had to come from somewhere. They pulled them off the lake when they heard I was in Harrisville. If I can get through Bigelow I might get on down to Colston and shake them going east. But I had to pull away from him to get through town. It was fifteen miles and he was almost out of sight by the time I hit the city limits. I cut down side streets and missed the square, not even recognizing anything because by now it was all an endless mad race through a dream with this part just like any other and having no con-nection with the town I'd lived in all my life.

Then we were clear of town on the highway going east. The car chasing us was nowhere in sight; I slowed a little to make the turn four miles beyond, where I had wrecked the other car, then began to let it out. The pines began to blur and run together on both sides, with the highway a straight groove down the middle; the car was a projectile in a green-walled chute, gathering speed. I was too tight now, dead on my feet and lightheaded, and hypnotized by abstract speed. I couldn't think connectedly of anything; flashes of thought raced through my mind, jumbled, like small sections of a hundred mo-tion pictures pasted together and run through a projector at blazing speed. Why hadn't I heard a sound from Doris? If we could get by the lake I'd take to the country roads before we got to Colston, try to get another car. We'd be all right now if all the cars down here had been pulled out. All the ones with radios, anyway; the others didn't matter.

Then, suddenly, there was a patrol car cruising up ahead. I swung over in the groove and went around him at a hundred miles an hour. I heard the shots, and then the curve was coming up, and I had to ride it down. Ninety, sev-enty, sixty, and still too fast. It was almost right-angled to the left and poorly banked. I could feel them riding up on my tail and heard the guns again. Then we were into it and I ground the throttle, hearing rubber scream. The left wheels lifted, floating, and then were down again and we were straight, going across the dam.

There was no road block, and I breathed again. I could see a bunch of cars and men before the store and beer joint, and on the other side by the place where they rented boats, but the road was clear and they couldn't close it now. I bore down on the throttle and was gaining speed, but the car behind had ridden too far up on me on the turn. The guns were very near. The wind-shield shattered, and then I heard the tire explode. I caught it, held it for a long half second, and then lost it again, and we started over. I made it to the floor boards. It wiped the top off clean, and then we came up, the lake and sky swinging in a tremendous arc, and somehow the car was gone.

The roaring and the flight chopped off, straight-walled and clean, against the edge of vacuum. Then I was on my knees in the broken bushes while dam and lake and sky settled into place and sound returned. It was a juke box in the beer joint wailing "Falling in Love with Love" out across the water in the early morning sun, and men were running. I watched them disinterestedly, from far away, wanting only to go to sleep. Then I turned my head a little and saw the car, and I tried to scream.

It had smashed through the young willows and was lying on its side some twenty yards ahead of me, tail down along the front slope of the dam with the rear end of the trunk some four feet above the water. It was balanced precariously on its right, the open seats facing me with all the top and windshield gone, and I could even see the keys dangling from the ignition lock. And it was settling, slipping a little on the smashed greenery beneath and then hanging up, poised, precarious, to break and slip again, trunk first, toward the surface of the lake. I got somehow to my feet and began to run, holding out my arm to point, my body bursting with all the horror of the sound I couldn't make. The men had almost reached me, running past the car but up on the road above it, ignoring it because they could see no one was in it now.

I was almost there when the vanguard piled down off the road and reached me. Plunging into and through them, I took them with me, fighting, pushing, dragging them forward, still moving, trying to reach the keys and trying to form words to tell them, but making only hoarse animal sounds deep inside my throat. I saw the car slip again, and poise, hanging by a whisper to the slope just above the water where it dropped away to a depth of twenty feet against the steep face of the dam.

They thought I was crazy now, but they couldn't shoot because we were all so tangled together in a writhing mass of men. I could see the saps swinging in the sunlight, and the blows, and could even feel them faintly, like a gentle rain, painless, unreal, without effect, like something happening in a street riot I was watching in a newsreel.

It slid once more. The rear bumper was in the water now and I could see the whole front end rise a little as it balanced, teetering, ready to plunge.

And then, somehow, my voice came back and I was screaming. "The trunk! The trunk!" I could hear it, going up and up, above the blaring of the juke box and the meaty sound of fists falling and the raggedness of breathing and all the roaring in my ears. "The trunk! Get her out of the trunk!"

They must have understood, somehow grasped the fact that she was not here and they had not seen her. Some of them broke away from the heaving mass of us and lunged for the keys dangling in the lock.

They got her out just before the car slid into the water. I took five of them down there with me and got my hands on her as they lifted her, but she was already dead. Her neck was broken.

Chapter Twenty-seven

In the exact center of the moving wheel there is no movement. It is winter now, or late autumn, and one day is very much like the rest. The leaves of the trees outside the window were full of autumn color for a time, but now they are mostly gone, and I can look up the street through the naked limbs in the early morning and see the frost across the lawns. It looks very much as it did when we used to walk to school that year when she lived here, when they had the pictures of blue eagles inside the glass windows of all the stores around the square.

People come to see me and talk a while and go away. Abbie Bell comes every Sunday morning and brings me a carton of cigarettes. She recovered from the knife wounds and the case against Waites was finally thrown out of court when she didn't press the charges or testify against him. She says she feels sorry for men, and I don't know whether she means Waites, or me, or just all men together.

"You know, Jack," she said once, looking at me through the door, "it just doesn't seem possible to me that in only eleven million years, or however long they've been here, men could have got as stupid about women as they have. They must have practiced somewhere before. Imagine them trying to do anything to that poor bastard, when someday he might even get that girl back."

I never see Buford. He ran. But he'll be back.

They got Dinah's car out of the lake. She came up to see me the day it came back from the garage where they fixed it up, and said she was leaving that afternoon for California. I told her I was sorry about the car, but she just looked at me and said it didn't matter, and after a while she went away.

They brought me down here for the district court. There has been one trial, but something was wrong with it, and there'll be another. Or so the lawyer says. He is very earnest; and explained it all to me, but I guess I wasn't paying much attention. He comes in nearly every day, sometimes alone and sometimes with the other men, the doctors or psychiatrists who are working with him. They ask a lot of questions, tap me on the knees, and try to find out whether I know right from wrong, and go away after taking down a bunch of notes. They are all very earnest and seem to be trying so hard you want to help them.

Somehow, they seem to think it matters.

THE END